Leaving
Haven

Also by Kathleen McCleary

House & Home
A Simple Thing

Leaving Haven

KATHLEEN McCLEARY

wm

WILLIAM MORROW
An Imprint of HarperCollinsPublishers

This book is a work of fiction. References to real people, events, establishments, organizations, or locales are intended only to provide a sense of authenticity, and are used fictitiously. All other characters, and all incidents and dialogue, are drawn from the author's imagination and are not to be construed as real.

P.S.™ is a trademark of HarperCollins Publishers.

HarperCollins books may be purchased for educational, business, or sales promotional use. For information please e-mail the Special Markets Department at SPsales@harpercollins.com.

FIRST EDITION

Designed by Diahann Sturge

Library of Congress Cataloging-in-Publication Data has been applied for.

ISBN 978-0-06-210626-1

13 14 15 16 17 ov/RRD 10 9 8 7 6 5 4 3 2 1

To my mother, Ann McCleary,
and my agent, Ann Rittenberg.
Thanks for the encouragement, the inspiration,
and for being such brave role models. Keep blooming.

Acknowledgments

Every book is a multitude of layers, and I owe a multitude of thanks to those who helped me along the way. Thanks to my readers and friends Sarah Flanagan, Mona Johnston, Sarita Gopal, Stacy Hennessey, Laura Merrill, Lori Kositch, and Julia Loughran. Thanks to David Roop, who advised me on the many legal issues in my story, and to Michelle Rhodes and Susan Friedlander Earman. Thanks to Kendall Truitt Barrett, whose ginger scones still haunt my dreams, and who provided invaluable input on everything baking-related in the book. Her wedding cakes are the best in the world. Thanks to my agent, Ann Rittenberg, who gave me the original idea for the book, and the encouragement I needed to finish it. I feel very fortunate to work with Tessa Woodward, the most insightful editor I know, who has elevated every story I have sent her, and to the terrific folks at HarperCollins: Pam Spengler-Jaffee, Laurie Connors, Mary Sasso, Molly Birckhead, and Jennifer Hart. Thanks to the members of the Fiction Writers Co-op—what great company, and what sanity savers.

Finally, I'm lucky to have the support of an imperfect, impossible, incredibly loving family. Paul, Grace, and Emma Benninghoff have lived with deadlines, despair, elation, take-out food, repeated threats to switch careers, and much wailing and gnashing of teeth. And yet they soldier on. Thank you.

Leaving Haven

Prologue

Georgia
June 19, 2012

Georgia sat up in her hospital bed, holding her baby. She studied his little face—just visible beneath the striped blue-and-pink knit cap the nurse had pulled over his head after cleaning him off. She tried to remember how Liza had looked as a newborn, all those years ago. But this baby didn't look like Liza, maybe because there was nothing of her, Georgia, in this baby. Instead John's features bloomed on this tiny boy—the ears that stuck out just slightly, the dark hair, the full lips.

Outside the window the sun broke through the clouds and streamed into the room. Georgia noticed the shift in the light, but didn't take her eyes off the baby in her arms. She picked up one of his hands, rubbed his palm with her thumb. His fingers were long—she could see that even in such new, tiny hands—nothing at all like Georgia's own hands. The baby opened his eyes.

Georgia gazed at him. "Hi?" she said. "Who are you?"

At the sound of her voice he began to cry, loud wails that

pierced the quiet of the room. Georgia felt her breasts tingle and then the dampness on the front of her nightgown as her milk let down.

"That's great," she said to the baby. "Just great." She fumbled with the buttons on her nightgown and pulled him close, one hand cradling the back of his head. "I'm not sure I remember how to do this," Georgia warned. But he latched on right away and began to suck. Georgia looked down at him and began to cry, the tears rolling down her cheeks, dripping from her chin, splashing onto the baby's cap.

After a few minutes the baby closed his eyes, his head heavy against Georgia's breast. She lifted him and held him over her shoulder and patted his back until he burped. Then she sat up with her knees propped in front of her and laid the baby on her thighs, facing her, his head cradled by her knees and his bottom resting against her soft postpartum belly.

"So, little man," she said. "This is it, I guess."

She tried to memorize his gray eyes, the lovely weight of him in her lap, his warmth against her skin. She leaned forward and sniffed, inhaling the milky baby scent of him and something else, something that smelled almost sweet, like cinnamon.

"I love you," she whispered. "I didn't think I would, but I do."

The baby yawned, revealing pink gums and a milky tongue. Georgia picked him up and laid him down gently on his back in the bassinet next to her bed. She covered him with the silk rainbow blanket Alice had given her at the baby shower. Georgia straightened up and slipped her nightgown over her head. She opened the drawer in the nightstand and put on her bra and the flowing blue maternity top she had worn to the hospital two days ago. She pulled on the black maternity capris she'd worn that day, too. She couldn't find her comb so she ran her fingers through the tangled waves of her hair. She couldn't bear to look in the mirror right now, to see the face of a woman who would—*oh, don't think about it. Keep moving.* Her purse was in the bottom drawer, and she picked it up and rooted around until she found her nail scissors. She snipped the hospital bracelet from her wrist.

"Georgia Bing," it said, in black letters. "Baby boy Bing. June 18, 2012." She put the bracelet inside her purse.

The baby slept. Georgia slid her feet into her sandals and opened the door to her hospital room. To her right, a nurse was engrossed in the computer at the nurses' station, and to her left the hallway was empty. Georgia walked on quiet feet down the hall, opened the door to the stairwell, and walked downstairs. Her body still ached from giving birth, and her breasts, overfull with new milk, hurt with every step. She slowed her pace. At the bottom she took a deep breath and opened the door into the lobby. She smiled at the guard by the front door, hoping he wouldn't ask any questions. He nodded.

Then new mother Georgia Bing walked out into the sunlight without a single backward glance at the baby she left behind.

Part 1

I

Alice
June 19, 2012

Alice had no desire to see the baby, really. Tiny infants made her uncomfortable, with their scrunched-up faces and inexplicable cries and terrifying vulnerability. And even though she had had one of her own, she had felt nothing but relief with each passing year of her daughter's life, each step forward into some semblance of physical competence, verbal communication, rational thought. But when John called and told her Georgia had disappeared from the hospital and left the baby behind, he sounded—for the first time in all the long years she'd known him—completely confounded and lost.

When the phone rang, Alice was standing in her kitchen making meatballs, which were arrayed in neat symmetrical rows on the baking sheet in front of her. She had rinsed her hands quickly and picked up the phone, and at John's words her heart had started to race, and she could feel it now, beating a rapid tattoo against her rib cage.

"Did you call the police?" Alice said. "Never mind. Of course you called the police."

"Right. They're looking for her. The theory is postpartum depression."

Alice closed her eyes, stroked her left temple with a damp hand. "Where's the baby now?"

"Here, at home with me, which is not going too well at the moment."

Oh, Lord. Alice heard whimpering in the background. She noticed that her hands were shaking. *Georgia left the baby?* It was inconceivable. Alice sat down abruptly on one of the stools at the kitchen counter, pressed the phone more firmly against her ear, and took a deep breath. "Did you talk to Polly and Chessy? Do they have any idea where she is? Did she leave a note?"

John sighed. "Polly and Chessy haven't heard from her; I didn't talk to them, but they both talked to the police. They have no idea where she is. The nurses at the hospital were shocked; no one saw her leave. Her car is still in the parking lot. She left a note on the windshield saying she was fine and not suicidal, for what that's worth."

"She would never kill herself. Because of Liza." Alice said this with absolute certainty. Georgia had been her best friend for thirteen years, since they'd met at that Wiggle with Me class when the girls were less than a year old. Alice, twenty-two and the youngest mom in their upscale suburb, had felt so inadequate in those days—fumbling her way through breast-feeding, propping up her worn copy of *What to Expect the First Year* on the counter next to the kitchen sink so she could follow the step-by-step instructions for bathing the baby, as though she were following some kind of recipe. One day the book toppled over into the baby bath just as Alice was about to lower the baby into the tub. She had fished it out in a panic, holding a crying

Wren against her shoulder with one arm, frantically trying to separate the soaking pages so she could read what to do next. She had ended up not even giving the baby a bath, and called Duncan at work and asked him to stop by the bookstore and bring home a new copy of *What to Expect the First Year*, actually *two* copies, in case something like that ever happened again.

Then Alice met Georgia, the magical baby whisperer, who could take a screaming infant, hold the baby's face close to hers, and smile and coo in some secret language that would calm the unhappiest baby within seconds. Meeting Georgia had been the biggest relief of Alice's life. Sure, Georgia was as anxious as any first-time mother, but she also had some instinct Alice lacked. Alice was a big believer in acting the part even if you didn't feel it, and had become adept at displaying a confidence she never possessed. "Don't worry about plastics," she'd scoff when Georgia expressed fears about giving Liza a teething ring, while inside she was thinking, *I'd give my child steel wool to chew on if I thought it would get her to stop screaming.* But Georgia had an easy, natural way with babies that Alice couldn't fake. After her first lonely, terror-filled months as a new mother, Alice felt as if she'd stumbled across a clearing in the jungle when she found Georgia, a place that said, *See? You weren't as lost as you thought you were.*

"I don't know what to do," John said. Alice could hear the baby's high-pitched, hiccuping cries in the background. She thought of how much Georgia had wanted this baby, how she had looked forward to holding her son, to the intimacy of nursing, to every exhausting, delightful moment of these early days with a newborn—delightful, at least, to Georgia. Alice felt sick, deep-in-the-pit-of-her-being sick.

"I'm really worried about her," John said. "I feel so helpless—I can't even try to search for her because I've got to take care of the baby, and I haven't even *held* a baby since Liza was an infant, and that was thirteen years ago. He won't take a bottle—and he's been screaming and screaming—can you hear him?"

"Yes, I can hear him," Alice said. "I'd have to be deaf not to. But Georgia—to think she'd leave the baby—she must be, she must be so—" Alice felt her throat grow tight.

"I believe Georgia will come back in a day or two. She'll come back," he repeated, as though saying it might make it true. He cleared his throat. "She's very, very upset—she wouldn't let me in the delivery room. I didn't even see the baby until after she left. I think this is her way of making sure I understand exactly *how* upset she is."

"But you can't *know* she'll come back. She's never—" Alice's throat grew even tighter, and she paused.

"I've known her for more than twenty years, and I know she will come back. We've been part of each other ever since we met. That's like saying my *arm* will never come back, Alice, like my *spleen* will never come back. She can't not come back."

Alice absorbed this.

"Liza comes home from camp in three weeks," John said. "She's not going to leave Liza, too. You know that. Georgia will be okay, and she will come back."

Alice was silent. She didn't know if Georgia would be okay, really. Ever.

The baby continued to scream, and John raised his voice. "I brought him home three hours ago. The doctor said there was no reason not to—he's healthy, and the nurse at the hospital said he'd take the bottle when he gets hungry enough, but I'm not so sure. He won't take a bottle *from me*. Nothing I do gets him to stop crying."

Alice bit her lip. The least she could do for Georgia now, she thought, was to help her son. "You've got to hire a home nurse, John. Someone to help you with the baby until . . ." Alice let the sentence trail off. Until what? Until Georgia returned to claim her son? Until John figured out how to handle this on his own because she was never coming back?

"I'm *trying* to get a home nurse," he said, his voice petulant. "It's not like Mary Poppins, where one just appears in your living room the moment you need her." The baby's cries grew louder. "Hold on."

Alice heard fumbling, patting, more crying, a muttered curse. She sighed. True, John was in a terrible situation, but this tendency of his to get peevish—which he was just as likely to do over a fallen soufflé as over a disappearing wife—was one of the things Alice liked least about him.

"Could you come over?" he said. "Please? Just for a few hours, until I can get a home nurse? I am *desperate*."

"John, I can't."

"Alice, this is about *the baby*," John said. "It's not about anything other than taking care of this baby, who needs someone *right now*. If Georgia were here asking you for help you would drop everything and come over."

Alice thought about this. It was true. She would do anything for Georgia and her baby. But Duncan— "I can't," she said.

"Alice, I am begging you. Thirty minutes, that's all. Please: come help Georgia's baby."

Georgia's baby.

"All right," Alice said. "I'll be there in ten minutes."

WHEN JOHN OPENED the door, the house was quiet behind him, his arms empty.

"He *just* fell asleep," John said. "Finally. I brought him home from the hospital at two and it's what—five o'clock now? *Three hours* of nonstop crying."

Alice stood on the front porch, the familiar faded gray boards under her feet. She hadn't seen John in two months, since before the baby was born. John's hair was longer, curling up at the nape of his neck, and a multiday stubble covered the fine lines of his cheeks and jaw. Dark, puffy circles of fatigue bloomed under his eyes, but they were the same John eyes—rich brown, with those heavy, sensual lids. "Bedroom eyes," Georgia said. Those eyes were what had attracted Georgia to him, back when Georgia and John had first met while working at that restaurant in Albany. "He didn't say much," Georgia had told Alice, "but he'd look at me with those eyes and I'd be wet in thirty seconds."

Alice, of course, had been a little shocked that Georgia would talk about something so intimate. But that was Georgia—open, honest, direct. She was, to Alice at least, the quintessential earth mother, with her comfortable, rambling old Victorian house and the bright-colored skirts she wore (which she sewed herself) and her tendency to call everyone "darling" or "sweetie." Why, even her work—making wedding cakes—involved mothery things like warm kitchens and fresh-baked smells and tears of joy. Georgia's own mother had died when she was twelve, and Georgia had become a mother to her younger sisters and then a mother to Liza, her firstborn, and then a kind of mother to her friends and her friends' children. Alice often thought that if she died and came back around in another life, she'd want to come back as one of Georgia's children, beloved and nurtured and understood.

"Did you hear from the agency about the nurse?" Alice said. She still stood on the porch, not quite ready to cross the threshold into Georgia's house.

"They'll have someone here tomorrow morning," John said. He stepped back and held the door wide. "Come on in."

Alice hesitated.

"If the baby's settled now, I should go home," Alice said. "Wren's home and I was in the middle of making dinner . . ." Her voice trailed off. She twisted her wedding ring back and forth on her finger.

John looked at her. "Do you want to see the baby?"

Alice's heart thumped hard against her ribs. She ignored the question. "I'm more concerned about Georgia. I can't see her leaving a baby, any baby."

John ran his hand through his hair, which made the cowlick on the back of his head stand straight up. "I filed a missing persons report with the police. I gave them photos. Honestly, they believe she'll call within the next twenty-four hours— maybe not me, but one of her sisters. She'll come back. She had that postpartum depression after Liza was born. I just didn't think—"

"I didn't know her then," Alice said. By the time she had met Georgia, Liza was already six months old and Georgia was aglow with baby love. Georgia had referred to some "dark days" after Liza's birth, but had brushed them off as typical new-mother moodiness. Alice had no idea it had been anything more, that there had been any possibility of something like *this*. Alice's eyes filled, and she turned her head so John couldn't see.

"*Alice.*" John put his hand under her chin and turned her face toward his. "She'll be okay. I promise. I know Georgia."

Alice pressed her lips together firmly and shook her head, shaking his hand away from her face.

"Listen," John said. "I'm sorry I called. I knew you'd want to know about Georgia, but I shouldn't have asked you to come over. I've been up all night the last two nights, and I got a little crazy with worrying about Georgia and the baby crying and crying, and then the agency saying they didn't have a nurse—I didn't know who else to call."

Alice cleared her throat. "It's fine. I'm fine. I've got to go."

"Okay," John said. "I'll let you know as soon as I hear anything about Georgia."

Alice turned to leave.

"He's beautiful," John said. "Are you sure you don't want to see him?"

Alice felt exhausted, as though the weight of her very bones was too much for her weary muscles to hold up. Of course she was curious about the baby, but—

"Come on," John said. He stepped inside and stood back, so she could walk past him. "Just take one peek. He's asleep in the bassinet in the living room."

Alice's curiosity—or something deeper, more primal—overwhelmed her, and she did as she was told. She walked into the house, past John, and through the hallway, into Georgia's sunny, yellow-walled living room, where she had spent countless hours with Georgia, dissecting men and marriage and motherhood over countless glasses of wine, watching Liza and Wren play with blocks and Polly Pockets and their Playmobil guys. Alice stood on the Tibetan rug, with its intricate pattern of blues and reds and golds, rested her hand on the back of the blue armchair, gazed at the little porcelain statue of a laughing child in a yellow dress that sat on the cherrywood mantel. The room and its contents were as familiar to her as the sight of her own face in the mirror every morning. All at once she missed Georgia so much that the missing felt like a physical thing, a hollow ache throughout her body. Alice closed her eyes and sighed. She took a deep breath, opened her eyes, and tiptoed over to the corner of the room and the simple white bassinet where the baby lay sleeping.

He was on his back, arms thrown overhead, little hands curled into fists. Alice leaned forward to study him. He had John's full lips, no doubt, and the ears that stuck out just slightly, like John. His hair was brown, as Georgia's had been once, before she began to color it that rich auburn. His skin was ruddy. Alice tried to remember if Liza had been a ruddy baby.

The baby whimpered, and pursed his lips. Without thinking Alice put her hands to her breasts but then realized that of course she had no milk, because this was not her child.

"Does he have a name?" Alice said. John stood beside her.

"Kind of," John said. "Georgia was talking about Nicholas, or Benjamin, but we hadn't decided anything."

"She didn't name him before she left the hospital?"

"No." A guilty look stole over John's face. "But I had to fill out all this paperwork before I brought him home, and I didn't want him to come home as 'Baby boy Bing.'"

Oh, God. If John had chosen a legal name for the baby without consulting Georgia it would make everything even worse, if that were possible. "So you gave him a name," Alice said. It was a statement. She knew John.

"Haven," John said. "Haven Jonathan Bing."

"*Haven?* John, Georgia likes plain names, ordinary—"

"Georgia wasn't *there*," John said, his voice angry for the first time. "Haven Schmidt played minor league baseball with my dad; he was my dad's best friend for decades. He batted .303 one year for the Albuquerque Dukes."

Alice started to say something, but stopped. What was the point? John and Georgia would have to figure this out on their own.

The baby began to cry. Alice looked at John. He rolled his eyes. "Here we go again," he said. "He's been asleep all of twenty minutes." The crying turned into shrieks. Alice reached forward and patted the baby's head. He shrieked again and Alice pulled her hand away. She felt the same uncertainty she had felt with Wren. *What do I do now?*

She reached forward and slid a careful hand under the baby's head, for support, and another hand under his bottom, picked him up, and held him against her chest. She could feel his downy hair against her chin. He stopped screaming and nestled in against her, whimpering. She rocked back and forth for a minute or two, feeling somewhat awkward—how did other women figure out that unconscious, easy rhythm when they held babies?—until he was quiet.

"You see?" John said. "You are good with babies."

"Oh, please." Alice rolled her eyes. "Here, you take him," she said, putting a hand behind the baby's vulnerable neck again, trying to disentangle herself.

"No way," John said. "He's happy."

"John, I have to go."

Alice looked at him with pleading eyes. She pulled the baby away from her neck and cradled him in her arms for a moment, gazing down into his face. The baby looked at her for the first time, his gray eyes on hers, serious and intent. Alice was completely unprepared for the sudden rush of feeling she felt—the shock of recognition, the fierce protectiveness, the wild love.

"All right," John said. "I'll take him. Go." He held out his arms.

Alice didn't even hear him. She heard instead the whisper of the baby's yawn, the soft rustle of his clothing as he stretched one small arm above his head. She kept her eyes fixed on his tiny face.

Oh, my God, she thought, looking into the baby's eyes. *I am never going to let you go.*

2

Georgia
A Year Earlier, April 2011

The first time Georgia ever even imagined that her husband could be capable of having an affair came one May evening at the restaurant, when Amelia leaned across the table, said, "Mmmm, that looks good," speared a bite of John's chicken kebab with her fork, and popped it into her mouth. John had grinned at Nicole, his dark eyes meeting hers, and Georgia thought, *He hates it when anyone touches his food. Why is he smiling at her?* Then she thought, *Hmmm.*

For a few weeks after that she watched John more closely, trying to note whether or not he was working more hours, spending more time on the computer, paying more attention to his appearance, or exhibiting any of the other "Seven Telltale Signs Your Husband Is Cheating" that she had found online. But John seemed to work the same hours as always, read the same chef blogs, and look as sloppily handsome as usual.

"I think John may be having an affair," she said one day to Alice as they sat in Georgia's kitchen drinking tea. Or rather,

Georgia was sitting and Alice was fixing the broken drawer front that Georgia had stuck together with silver duct tape. Georgia's house, an 1890 Victorian with a 1980s kitchen, always had something in it in need of repair. And while Georgia could draw, paint, sew, hook rugs, knit, weave, bake, and even carve wood, she had little interest in or skill with home repairs.

Alice, who was at the counter bent over the faulty drawer, looked up. She had bright blue eyes and eyebrows that didn't quite match, because the left eyebrow curved up in a perfect arch while the right one was almost straight. A wrinkle furrowed the space between her brows as she focused on what Georgia was saying.

"Now why would you think that?" she said.

"I don't know," Georgia said. "There's something about that girl Amelia, his new sous chef."

"What about her?" Alice said. She put the screwdriver down on the Formica counter. "And what do you mean 'girl'? How old is she?"

Georgia scratched her nose. "I don't know. Twenty-seven? Twenty-eight? Liza and I stopped by the restaurant the other night and John took a break and had dinner with us. Then she came over to our table and tasted his chicken kebab."

Alice looked at Georgia and contemplated this. Georgia loved this about Alice, the fact that she took Georgia's concerns seriously, no matter how unrealistic or ridiculous. Alice was all the things Georgia wasn't—confident, organized, practical. From the time they'd first met all those years ago, kneeling side by side on bright blue gymnastic mats while their babies mimicked the motions of the spry young Wiggle with Me teacher, Georgia had felt reassured by Alice's steadiness, her unflappable common-sense approach to everything.

Even though Wren was Alice's first baby, she never worried about whether fluoride toothpaste was poison or plastic baby bottles caused cancer. "She'll survive," she said. She worked part-time as an economics professor, had her daughter neatly scheduled into a sport for every season, and did her grocery shopping for the entire week every Sunday. Alice's organizational skills and confidence in her own way of doing things impressed Georgia, whose house was always cluttered in spite of her best efforts and who rarely had confidence that someone, somewhere wasn't doing a better job than she was.

Alice was the one in whom Georgia confided all her secret failings and longings, like the time she'd gotten so frustrated with Liza that she'd run outside and locked herself in the car. "But you didn't drive away!" Alice had said triumphantly. "See? You *are* a good mother." Alice was the one who had rushed over when Liza had tumbled backward and hit her head on the coffee table, opening a wound that bled so much Georgia had almost fainted. Alice had pressed a dark blue dishtowel against the cut ("blood doesn't show on navy blue") and then driven them to the ER in her bloodstained white blouse while Georgia held the screaming Liza in her arms. Why, Georgia had even told Alice her most intimate secrets, like how sometimes she wished John wouldn't yell quite so loudly in her ear when they made love.

"Did she *ask* for a bite of chicken kebab first?" Alice said.

Georgia shook her head.

"That is a little strange," Alice said. "John is so weird about his food."

"Exactly," Georgia said.

"But," Alice said, "think about the setting. You were in the restaurant. John and Amelia work together, and for all you know they've spent the entire week trying to perfect that chicken kebab recipe. It would be like you tasting the mousse filling from someone else's wedding cake. A work thing."

"I guess," Georgia said. She wasn't convinced.

"Has there been anything else?"

Georgia shook her head. "Not really. There just was something about the way he looked at her."

"Did you ask him about it?"

"No. I didn't want to seem paranoid, you know?"

Alice shook her head. Of course Alice wouldn't know, Georgia thought. Duncan, Alice's husband, was as solid and reasonable and straightforward as Alice was. He worked as a lawyer for a nonprofit, mowed the lawn every Saturday, attended church every Sunday, and had never, to Georgia's knowledge, even looked at another woman since he'd married Alice. He didn't even buy the *Sports Illustrated* swimsuit issue.

In many ways, Duncan and Alice seemed like the perfect couple to Georgia. They were gentle and polite with each other, laughed a lot together, and almost never argued, even though they had a volatile twelve-year-old daughter just like Georgia did. Their life never seemed messy and chaotic the way Georgia's own life felt to her, like racing downhill on a pair of Rollerblades, always on the verge of losing control. Alice's cream-carpeted living room was perpetually fresh and clean; she had her family's schedule all written out on a big calendar, with different-colored markers for each person; she returned every phone call and e-mail *the same day*. And Duncan—he was handy and loved fixing things, so everything in their house always worked, from the alarm clocks to the garbage disposal. He never forgot a birthday or anniversary, whether it was Alice's or his aunt Jessie's. And as if that weren't enough, Duncan was also amazing in bed and did something with a feather held between his teeth that made the normally self-contained Alice lose all control, as she had told Georgia.

"You're not paranoid, Georgia," Alice said now, bending back to the kitchen drawer. "I'd think twice about what was going on if Duncan spent all day working with a twenty-something-year-old—he's only human, after all. Have you noticed anything else? Is John working more hours than usual? Is he secretive about his phone or his e-mail?"

"No," Georgia said. "I thought of all that. He's so absentminded—half the time he leaves his e-mail up on the screen staring me in the face."

"Okay, then," Alice said. "So there are no other signs anything's wrong. And every time I see you—which is pretty much all the time—you two seem to be getting along fine. You are fine, right?"

Georgia was silent. *Are we fine?* She and John had known each other for almost twenty years, and been married for seventeen. They'd met when Georgia was twenty-one, fresh out of college, working as an apprentice pastry chef at a high-end restaurant in Albany. John, seven years her senior, had been the sous chef at Truscello's, earthy, funny, with quirky devotions to things like martial arts movies and the perfect paella. Their attraction had been immediate and explosive. For the most part, her marriage was good. They shared a passion for fine food and they both loved their work. John had pushed her to turn her baking into her own business, suggested her as the dessert chef when he got catering gigs, had even encouraged her to bid on making the wedding cake for a well-known senator's nuptials—a bid she had won and that had boosted her business a thousand percent. They both adored Liza, their daughter, and even if John wasn't as involved with parenting as Georgia was, that wasn't so unusual. True, their marriage had settled into the kind of businesslike arrangement that seemed to characterize so many marriages of Georgia's generation, a constant negotiation about the division of home chores and work demands, endless rounds of if-you-take-Liza-to-soccer-I'll-do-the-grocery-shopping bargaining. But that was normal, right? If Georgia's marriage was less than fine for any reason, it was the baby thing.

"I guess so," Georgia said. Her voice was soft. "I think he's a little burned out on the infertility stuff."

Georgia and John had been trying to have another baby for more than seven years now, with nothing to show for it. Georgia's heart clenched just thinking about it. John had opened Bing's, his restaurant, the year Liza turned three, and things had been crazy after that, both of them working long hours and taking care of Liza and pouring every penny they made back into the business. It had paid off; Bing's was one of the busiest, most popular spots in northern Virginia now. Then Georgia's business had taken off, too. Once they'd decided they were ready for baby number two, Georgia had a miscarriage, and another, and another, and then didn't get pregnant again at all.

"Unexplained infertility" was the official diagnosis. They tried six rounds of Clomid, and three rounds of Femara and hCG injections, followed by eight months of acupuncture and then intrauterine insemination (twice). They tried in vitro fertilization (three times) without success, and two months ago, on her fortieth birthday, Georgia had decided—finally—to give up. It was enough to make anybody crazy. But the top drawer of her dresser still held the grainy black-and-white ultrasound images of the babies she'd miscarried, as well as a tiny blue baby sweater Chessy had given her when Georgia had announced her second pregnancy—too soon.

"That's a hard thing," Alice said, "that would strain any marriage. But I thought you'd decided to give it up."

"I did—we did." Georgia squeezed her eyes shut. Yes, she'd given up on pills and injections and inseminations and timed intercourse and ultrasounds and doctor visits and all the other things that had come to dominate her life over the last years. But she hadn't given up the hope that a miracle might still occur. That baby, *her baby*, was a tiny bud out there somewhere in the universe, and someday that bud would find her and bloom. She *knew* it. But she couldn't tell anyone that—not John, not her sisters, not Alice.

"So it's an adjustment," Alice said. "You're both getting used to the idea that you're not going to have another baby." Alice herself had never wanted another baby, but had been very supportive throughout Georgia's struggles. "Still, nothing you've said makes it sound like John is having an affair."

Alice bent back over the drawer, turned the screwdriver with a deft twist of her wrist, and smiled in satisfaction as the drawer front popped into place. "There." She looked up at Georgia and smiled. "All better now."

I hope so, Georgia thought. She smiled at Alice and said, "Thanks."

BUT A FEW weeks after that chicken kebab dinner, Georgia came home from the grocery store one Saturday and noticed a plate of oatmeal butterscotch cookies on the kitchen counter.

"Amelia dropped these off while you were out," John said, munching a cookie. His hair was tousled in the way Georgia loved. He always wore his hair cropped short, even though his ears stuck out slightly, which gave him a funny, almost little boy look at times. He was so handsome in the traditional sense—high cheekbones, straight nose, heavy-lidded brown eyes—that his less-than-perfect ears made him even more appealing, his one vulnerability.

"That was nice," Georgia said. She dropped the grocery bags she carried onto the kitchen counter. "What's the occasion?"

"No occasion."

Georgia contemplated this. John loved oatmeal cookies with butterscotch chips, but Georgia almost never made them. They were far too sweet for her taste, and even Liza turned up her pert nose at them because she wanted *chocolate*. Georgia agreed. If you were going to make a cookie involving masses of white and brown sugar, the least you could do was balance it with a good bittersweet chocolate chip.

"Is something going on between you and Amelia?" She was surprised that the words came out of her mouth—a thought, a vapor, condensing into something solid and real.

"What?! She baked a plate of cookies, Georgia," John laughed "And *Amelia*, of all people. Aside from the fact that I'm her boss, she's about twenty-six. And she has those things in your ears that make gigantic holes. What do you call them? Gauges." He shuddered. For a man who was definitely on the high-testosterone end of the gender spectrum, John was strangely squeamish about certain things—knives, piercings, blood.

"I can't even look at her ears," he said. "I make her wrap a bandanna around her head in the kitchen."

"I don't know." Georgia studied his face. "I've had an odd feeling lately."

"You have a lot of odd feelings," John said. He reached out to straighten the tissue-paper collage of a giant turtle that Liza had made four years ago, in third grade. It hung crookedly on the refrigerator. The fact that he wouldn't look at her made Georgia even more suspicious. "Go by what people *do*, not what they say," her sister Polly always said. And what John was doing was avoiding her eyes, because Georgia knew he could not lie to her face. She knew him too well.

"So is this an odd feeling I need to pay attention to?" Georgia said.

"Don't be silly, Georgie," he said. He turned to look at her and smiled that dimpled smile, those dark eyes crinkling up at the corners. It was a sexy smile, the smile of a man aware of his own power to attract, to appease, to confuse. He came over and put both arms around her, pulled her to him. "Amelia is too skinny," he murmured, brushing his lips against her neck. His hands slid down over her hips and he pressed his hips urgently against her own. "Where's Liza?"

"At Emilie's." Georgia could smell the sweet butterscotch on his breath. "They're practicing some dance routine for the talent show at school."

"Good," John said. "Then she'll be gone awhile."

He kissed her neck, above her collarbone, where he knew she liked to be kissed, and slid his hands down from her shoulders to cup her breasts with his hands. And before she knew it they were having sex right there, on the white-and-black Marmoleum of the kitchen floor. It wasn't until afterward—after they'd put their clothes back on and John had gone downstairs into his study and she'd put all the groceries away—that Georgia realized he'd never actually *denied* he was having an affair.

She took the phone into the bedroom, closed the door, sat down on the edge of the bed, and called Polly.

"I think John is having an affair," she said.

"With who?" Polly said.

"Amelia. The sous chef at the restaurant."

"Why do you think that?"

"Because he let her eat his chicken kebab right off his plate and she made him oatmeal butterscotch chip cookies today."

"All your evidence has to do with food?"

"John owns a restaurant," Georgia says. "His life is food."

"I know he owns a restaurant," Polly said, with some irritation. "I still don't see how you get from chicken kebabs and cookies to an affair."

"Because John is so *particular* about his food," Georgia said. "You know how when he cooks something he has to get it exactly right, and then do the whole fancy presentation on the plate, and then sit down with the right wine? He doesn't like people poaching from his plate once he's done all that."

"John never struck me as that anal," Polly said.

"He's not generally," Georgia said. "He's just that way about food. Which in some ways is probably what makes him such a good chef."

"Does he let *you* poach from his plate?"

"Well, yes, me or Liza. But that's it. Just me, Liza, and now Amelia. Don't you think that's suspicious?"

Polly met this last with a sigh. "Not really, Georgie. I honestly don't get the whole food thing. Everyone in my house eats off everybody else's plate all the time. I'm just happy if no one's poaching from the dog dish."

Even though Georgia was the oldest, Polly was confident and independent in a way Georgia had never been. But then Polly had left home at sixteen to attend boarding school and then had headed off to college on the West Coast, while Georgia took care of Chessy and helped their father and stayed within a two-hour drive for college so she could come home at least once a month. Polly was the organized one, the competent one, the smart one, while she, Georgia, was the caretaking one, the empathetic one, the somewhat anxious one. And Chessy, their youngest sister, was the *interesting* one, the fearless one, the talented one who everyone knew was going to do something spectacular one day.

Georgia heard the rustling of paper and an expletive on the other end of the line. "Some little rug rat dumped a half-eaten shrimp in the wastebasket in my bedroom. Can you believe it? No wonder the entire second floor smells like the beach."

"It was probably Teddy. He hates shrimp." Teddy was Polly's youngest child, and Georgia's favorite. Polly had had four kids—bam, bam, bam, bam, one right after the other, as easily as you'd sneeze after snorting pepper. Georgia envied Polly her fertility. She craved a boy like Teddy, all dimples and messy kisses.

"I *know* it was Teddy." Georgia heard more rustling and foot-steps as Polly took care of the offending shrimp. "Listen, Geor-gie. Forget the food. Is John acting weird in any other way?"

"Not really. I talked to Alice, and she thinks I have nothing to worry about."

"Are you having sex?"

Georgia's lips were still swollen from John's kisses. "Well, yes." She flushed at the memory. "We had sex on the kitchen floor about an hour ago."

"Oh, God, spare me the details. I hope you got out the Swiffer afterward. Listen, if John is having sex with you on the kitchen floor in the middle of the afternoon—after you've been married *nineteen years* or however long it is—your marriage is fine."

"Seventeen years," Georgia said. "And John always wants to have sex." It was true. He'd even wanted her when she was hugely pregnant with Liza, reveling in her round belly and blooming breasts. "I like knowing I did that to you," he would say, his hands on her swollen stomach. It was crude, but also kind of hot.

"With *you*," Polly said. She paused. "Teddy! Teddy, come here right this instant!" Georgia heard the patter of Teddy's feet down the hallway, followed by Polly's firm footsteps. "Listen, Georgie, I've got to go. But I don't think John is having an affair. When was your last hormone shot? Those things alter your brain chemistry, you know."

"I haven't done shots in two months. We decided to stop all that on my fortieth birthday. I told you."

"I know. I'm sorry. *I'm sorry.* I forgot." Polly waited a beat. "I know it's hard to give up something you've dreamed about for so long."

"It's okay." Georgia repeated what everyone said when they heard about her struggles: "I have Liza." Georgia *was* lucky; she knew it. But it didn't stop the wanting.

"You never know," Polly said. "Maybe you'll be exactly like that cliché, when people give up trying and suddenly get pregnant. Wouldn't it be incredible if you found out in a few weeks you got pregnant having sex with John on the kitchen floor today? You could name the baby Marmoleum to commemorate its conception."

"Please, Pol," Georgia said. "Don't."

"I'm sorry," Polly said. "I shouldn't have said that. It wasn't funny."

"Okay. It's just that sometimes you and your houseful of children are hard to take."

"I know. I just know how badly you want a baby, so I want it for you. I'd give you one of my eggs if I could."

"You can't," Georgia said. "Because of your thyroid. And your eggs are too old."

"Chessy would give you an egg. She's under thirty."

Georgia had thought about this. Chessy—with her petite frame and brown hair and green eyes—resembled Georgia much more than wiry blond Polly did. "A donor egg may get you the healthy baby you want," Georgia's doctor had said. Georgia had nodded, but the idea of a donor egg from a stranger seemed so, well, *strange*.

"Do you think she would? I did mention it once to John, as kind of a hypothetical. He's always said he would never adopt or use donor eggs—he has that macho streak, you know? He wants a baby that's a known quantity—no surprises. He just rolled his eyes when I said something about a donor egg from Chessy, but then he rolls his eyes whenever I mention Chessy."

"Right," Polly said. "I know."

Georgia wondered if their inability to have a baby was what was bothering John, if he was struggling to come to terms with the fact that he would never have another child, or a son. Even though he had never, with so much as a look, indicated that he was disappointed about it, she often felt she had failed him in some primal way.

"*Teddy!*" This time Polly's voice had such an air of urgency and authority that even Georgia, on the other end of the line, froze where she sat.

"Don't you dare move," Polly said. Georgia heard her footsteps creak across the hardwood floor, followed by fumbling and a curse. "Oh, my God," Polly said. "He's wearing nothing but Spiderman underpants and has covered himself, literally, in Astroglide. He must have found it in my nightstand. He's so slippery I can't pick him up to get him in the bathtub. I've got to go, Georgie. I'll talk to you later. And don't worry!"

The thought of Teddy—his plump belly and impish grin and blond cowlick—made Georgia's arms ache with longing for a little guy of her own.

Maybe, she told herself. *Maybe, I could try once more. I'll call Chessy.*

3

Alice
A Month Earlier, May 2012

Alice and Duncan lay side by side in their bed, both of them on their backs, staring at the ceiling. The bed had belonged to Duncan's Scottish grandmother, the first piece of furniture she'd purchased in the New World, made of oak with scalloped carving on the headboard. Alice had loved the bed when they were first married, not even minding that it was an old-fashioned full-size and not a queen because it meant she and Duncan had to sleep tangled together or curled around each other, always in contact, always connected. Now, though, the bed felt small, suffocating, with Alice pressed against the edge on her side and Duncan on his.

Alice knew he was awake, just as she was. This had become their new routine, their new normal. She and Duncan would sit in the living room after the last of the dinner dishes had been rinsed and put away, with Duncan in the big cream-colored chenille armchair with his feet up on the ottoman, tapping away on his laptop. Alice would sit across from him on the brown leather sofa and fold the laundry. Sometimes she graded papers, leaning over the glass-topped coffee table, or filled out forms for Wren's dance camp. Neither one of them spoke. Once in a while Wren would flit in, chatting away on her cell phone, and walk into the kitchen to grab a glass of vanilla hemp milk, her favorite snack. At some point, Alice would look at her watch, or Wren would pop in again, and good nights would be said, and Wren would disappear upstairs. Alice would stretch and say, "You coming to bed?" and Duncan would say, "No, not quite yet," and Alice would brush her teeth and change into her nightgown and lie there, on her half of the bed, until she heard Duncan come in and undress in the dark.

So on this night, a month after the Day Everything Fell Apart, Alice made up her mind to say something.

"Thank you," she said. She had decided, on that black day, that from now on every word that passed her lips would be honest. And of all the many things she could say, or had said already, the thing she most wanted Duncan to understand was her gratitude.

Such a long silence met her words that she thought perhaps he was asleep. At last she turned her head to look at his profile in the dim light—the high forehead, that strong Scottish nose, the firm jaw. He swallowed.

"For what?" he said.

"For still being here," she said.

"Honestly, I am in shock, Alice."

"I know." Alice rolled onto her side, facing him. "I found a counselor," she said. "I'm going to go, myself. And I would be happy to go with you, too, if you thought—"

"I'm not *thinking* right now," he said. He lay on his back, his eyes on the ceiling. "But I'm sure as hell *feeling*."

Alice flinched. She had never heard Duncan swear before. Not a *shit* or a *damn* or even a *hell* had once passed his lips in the fifteen years she'd known him. Duncan was one of the most courtly, well-mannered people she'd ever met, thanks to his Atlanta upbringing, an upbringing that had included dance lessons and charity balls and "yes, ma'am" and knowing that dishes are passed from left to right and that you should always hold a stemmed glass only by the stem. His gentle, genteel ways were one of the things that had drawn Alice to him from the first day they'd met, at Kramerbooks in Dupont Circle, the spring of her sophomore year. She was looking for something to read over spring break, something that had nothing to do with economics or statistics. But everything she picked up seemed either too grim (*Cold Mountain*) or too silly (Danielle Steel). She was studying the back cover of *Angela's Ashes* (more grimness!) when a voice in her ear said, "Excuse me. Have you read this?" She looked up, surprised, to see a tall, lean man next to her, with blue eyes the same color as that piece of sea glass her father had sent her once from Hawaii. His light brown hair was cropped close to his head, which made the strong angles of his cheekbones, nose, and jaw even more prominent. He held out a copy of *Midnight in the Garden of Good and Evil*. Alice, ever the introvert, shook her head.

"I'm trying to find a book for my sister's birthday," he said.

Alice thought of herself as the person someone would be least likely to approach anywhere. She didn't mean to be reserved, but something about the way she held herself seemed to keep people at bay. She knew it, and had been trying to figure it out since arriving at college, studying herself in the mirror and practicing how to relax her shoulders, ease the tiny furrow between her brows.

"I'm afraid you're asking the wrong person," she said. "I haven't read anything except economics textbooks for a year or two now."

"So you've decided to break out and read something fun like *Angela's Ashes*?"

Alice smiled. He invited her to have a cup of coffee, in the café at the back of the bookstore. The conversation flowed— Georgetown, Virginia Tech (his alma mater), economics, law (he worked for Covington & Burling), Michigan (her home state), Georgia (his), siblings (she had none; he had three younger sisters), fitness.

Alice relaxed. She liked him. They had a lot in common. They were both early risers, religious about their exercise routines, prompt, disciplined. Then he mentioned pole vaulting, which he had done in college. Alice knew sports and strength training, which she had done since she was fifteen. But pole vaulting?

"Why?" she said. She was truly curious.

He leaned forward across the little café table, his blue eyes on hers. "Because it's a thinking sport," he said. "Every time, you have to figure out which pole to use, which height to jump, which strategy to use." He sat back. "And then you fly."

He was all the things Alice had never had before in her life—competent, reliable, trustworthy—and yet he had this one exotic thing about him, this passion for a strange sport that made you feel as if you were flying.

"I'd like to see that sometime," she had said.

He had smiled at her. "You will."

Later he had told her that he had approached her because she was so pretty but also because she was so careful, picking up each book, studying the cover, reading everything on the back jacket and the inside flaps. "You seemed like a serious person, a thoughtful person," he said. "But then when we had coffee, you were charming—shy but confident, smart, and you thought pole vaulting was intriguing and not geeky. I was captivated."

Captivated. No one in the world—her faraway father, her indifferent mother—had ever found her captivating.

She looked at him now, inches from her in their too-small bed, his eyes still fixed on a point on the ceiling.

"I'm sorry," she said.

"You've said that."

"Do you want to talk about it?"

"No."

She didn't cry. She had never been a crier, and this was beyond that.

"Okay," she said. "When you want to talk—if you want to talk—I'm here." She paused. "Always. *Forever.*" She waited, held her breath.

"Okay," he said, and rolled over on his side, his back to her.

And she had to be satisfied that, for now, that was enough.

THE NEXT WEEK was the spring dance team performance at school. The dance team performed—an odd choice, in Alice's mind—to Eminem's "Love the Way You Lie," and even though they had edited the sound track and cleaned up the lyrics, Alice was uncomfortable. She worried that Duncan would be shocked that Wren was doing a dance—albeit a passion-filled, very good dance—to a song about a man who hit his wife. She wondered if Duncan was thinking about her and *her* big lie. Finally, she felt unsettled because she found herself wishing that she and Duncan could express that kind of raw, honest emotion with each other instead of the agonizing politeness that had characterized their marriage for a while, and especially this past month.

She remembered the first year they were married, when he would come home late at night from work and come upstairs to find her, taking the steps two at a time with those long legs of his, so eager to see her that he couldn't wait to take off his coat. When had he stopped doing that?

She had read an article once about a woman who lost her sense of smell. The woman was a hair colorist, and over time the chemicals she worked with had irritated the tiny nerves at the roof of her nose. First, the woman noticed that her son had a different smell when she hugged him; not bad, just different. Then she noticed that her house didn't smell the same when she made her pungent garlic tomato sauce for the spaghetti. Losing her sense of smell was gradual, the woman said—a missing scent here, a diminished fragrance there—and then it was gone. It took her a while to figure it out.

And that was exactly what had happened to Alice's marriage, a dimming, so subtle you didn't even notice it at first. Duncan had been so busy at work he didn't have time to respond to her e-mails or texts, not even with a *Got it. Thanks. Home at 8:30.* Texts and e-mails were small things, but they were moments of connection, however mundane. She and Duncan were both tired in the evening, so they didn't read to each other in bed anymore before turning out the light. He never looked at her when she changed clothes, never noticed the lacy new bra she'd bought, or the three inches she had cut off her hair. They had become roommates.

And then there had been the day last year when Duncan had come home and announced that he had quit his job at Covington & Burling ("Covetous & Boring," as he had long referred to it) and taken a job at the Mid-Atlantic Innocence Project, a nonprofit that worked to free prisoners who had been wrongly convicted. Alice had known that he found his work at Covington dull, but had no idea he had been researching jobs with nonprofits, or that he had even a remote interest in the plight of potentially innocent prisoners. It surprised her as much as if he'd told her he'd decided to quit the law for a career as a trapeze artist or a plumber, something completely out of left field. Their income dropped by more than half—a significant life change that she thought Duncan should at least have *discussed* with her first.

All of this came to her as Wren danced onstage, her strong,

wiry body moving with an intensity that startled Alice, that made her look at dancing in a way she had never imagined. All Wren's anger, her sense of injustice, emanated from her body onstage, the taut line of her neck, the fierce height of her leaps. Alice had never seen Wren like this. If only Duncan had reacted with this kind of passion to everything that had happened with Wren, or to the chain of events it had unleashed . . .

"I've never seen her dance like that," she said to him, as they waited in the lobby for Wren after the performance.

"Like what?"

"With that kind of intensity. She's thirteen, and yet she understood that character. I think what happened last fall really changed her."

"I am not a fan of that song," Duncan said.

"I figured. But Wren—" Wren had danced like someone who understood what it felt like to want to be loved and to fear disapproval and to seethe over betrayal. But Alice couldn't say that to Duncan.

"She just seemed more involved with the dance this time," Alice said.

"I guess." Duncan's eyes brushed past her, over the crowd.

Alice felt small, compressed with guilt, as she had for weeks now. She turned her attention from Duncan to the familiar faces she saw in the lobby, the parents she knew whose children had gone through preschool and kindergarten and elementary and now middle school with Wren, who showed up at all the soccer games and concerts and field days, as involved as they could possibly be. Alice wondered how many of them really knew what their middle schoolers were like.

Wren rushed up to them, flushed, breathless. "There's a party to celebrate the end of the season at Annie's house," she said. "Can I go? Her parents are home. Her mom will drive us there. I'll call you when I need a ride home."

Duncan shrugged. "Sounds okay."

"Whoa," Alice said.

"What?" Duncan and Wren both turned to look at her.

Alice didn't really have an objection, at least not a rational one. She just had the same gut-clenching protective instinct she had to everything involving Wren now.

"Well," Alice said. "Who else will be there?"

"The dance team girls, Mom. Annie, Lily, Rachel, Nicole, Ally—the usual."

"Liza? Emilie?"

"No."

Duncan raised one eyebrow at her, something she had once found endearing but now found annoying. Duncan, so essentially good-natured and decent, did not understand the Machiavellian machinations of adolescent girls. He had always viewed the world as a kind and welcoming and safe place—or at least he had until a month ago. He assumed the best of people; trusted things would work out; saw setbacks as temporary blips. For Alice, who had spent much of her life poised on a knife edge of wariness and uncertainty, Duncan's confidence in the general goodness of things had always been at once irresistible and ir-ritating.

Alice shrugged, tried to display a casual acceptance she did not feel. "Okay."

"Thanks! I'll call you." Wren turned and darted away to find her friends, her dark ponytail bouncing behind her. And as much as Alice had chafed and despaired over those early years when Wren was an infant, for a moment she wished with all her heart that she had that little girl back again, safe under her own watch.

Duncan looked at his watch. "Eight thirty," he said. "We should get home."

"Why?" Alice said. All at once she was sick of being polite, sick of pretending that there wasn't a large elephant—or two, or three—sitting in the middle of her life, squeezing the breath out of her.

Duncan looked at her in surprise. "What do you mean, 'Why?'"

"I mean why do we have to rush home? It's Saturday night. It's eight thirty. Our only child is at a party. Why don't we go out for a drink? Or go to a movie? *Do* something?"

"You're serious?"

"Yes, I'm serious."

The crowd had thinned now, and they stood alone at the side of the lobby, Duncan impeccable in his sport coat and khakis, Alice in the crisp, professional pants and silk top she'd worn that afternoon to teach. Duncan looked off into space, over Alice's head.

"Hmm," he said. "I have to think about that."

"Think about what?" The words Alice had wanted to say for the past month came bubbling up, spilling out of her. "About whether or not you're willing to be seen at a restaurant with me? About whether you can stand to spend an hour with me in which we actually have to *deal* with each other?"

"Alice." Duncan looked around, to see if anyone had overheard her. "*Shh*. This is not a conversation we should be having in public."

Alice looked up at him. She was tall, almost five-nine, but Duncan loomed over her at six-three. "Well then, where?" she said. "And when? Because honestly, I'd rather have you just kick me out and tell me you never want to see me again than go on with all this politeness. I can't stand it anymore."

Duncan looked at her, his lips compressed in a thin line. "This is not the place for this conversation, Alice," he said. He still held the program from Wren's performance in his hand, and now he rolled it up, stuffed it in his pocket, and turned toward the door. "I'm leaving." He walked down the hallway in long, angry strides, the heels of his oxfords tapping on the tile floor.

Alice watched him go. She knew that, no matter how angry he was, he would get into the car and wait for her, because he was too much of a gentleman to leave her behind in the now-deserted school, the almost-empty parking lot. He would turn on the car engine, adjust the radio, look out the window to see if he could spot her coming out the big glass doors. And what could she do? She had disappointed him enough already. Alice walked down the hall as fast as her wedge heels would allow.

They drove home in silence. Duncan pulled into the garage and they both got out. As they walked up the concrete path to the back door, Alice stumbled in her wedges. She felt her foot roll under her, a sharp stab of pain in her right ankle. She gasped.

Duncan turned. "What is it?"

"It's okay. I twisted my ankle a little. These shoes." She tried to smile. She couldn't stand to think about what she would do if she had a sprain. The one thing—*the only thing*—that had allowed her even a small measure of sanity over the last weeks was her daily workout. If she couldn't run—or do squats or do lunges or jump rope—she would lose her mind. Literally.

Alice straightened up and put her weight on the traitorous ankle, and felt shooting pain. "I can't walk on it," she said. "I'm sorry."

Duncan came back to where she stood and put an arm around her. "Here," he said. "Lean on me."

He had not touched her in more than a month. He hadn't brushed up against her at the bathroom sink or let his foot nudge hers in bed or allowed his fingers to glance against hers when he handed her a dish to dry. *Five weeks.* Alice wanted to weep at the feel of his arm across her back, his hand against her ribs as he guided her up the steps.

"Sit here." He pushed her gently onto the couch in the living room and knelt down to unbuckle her silly sandals. He pulled a pillow from the couch and put it on the coffee table in front of her, and lifted her tender ankle onto the pillow. "I'll get some ice."

She sat looking at her ankle, which was already swollen. She heard the clatter of the ice trays in the kitchen, running water, drawers opening and closing. Duncan came back in and wrapped a dishtowel around her ankle and placed a ziplock bag filled with ice cubes on top of the towel. He wrapped another towel around the bag and her ankle, to keep it all in place. "There."

He stood back and looked at it, then at her. "Are you okay?"

His kindness undid her. He should have left her hobbling outside, but of course he would never do that, because he was such a fundamentally decent man. She buried her face in her hands and cried. She had not cried during all these long weeks when he had avoided her touch, her look, her conversation. She had not cried in November when she'd found out about the cruel hoax the girls had played on Wren, and she hadn't cried when Wren had wept in her arms over the betrayal. She hadn't cried—really cried—over her mother. So many things going all wrong, and Alice had kept herself together, until now.

"No," she said, wiping her cheeks with the backs of her hands. "I'm *not* okay. I'm sorry—sorrier than you can know, because *you* would never do something like I did. I'm lonely and terrified of losing you and I can't stand not talking about it anymore. It's like I landed on the moon and I don't recognize anything, not even myself."

She took in a deep breath. "I am not a person who makes excuses," she said. "I don't have an excuse. There was nothing rational about it. But, Duncan"—she looked up at him, willing him to understand—"there were reasons it happened, reasons we need to talk about. And it has changed me, and I hope you can understand that. I'm a different person; I *know myself* in a different way now. And I can promise nothing like that will happen again."

He was silent for a long time, looking at her.

"You're not who I thought you were," he said at last.

"*I know*," she said. "And I know that must be a shock, and it must hurt. I don't—I didn't—know myself. But this has changed me."

"I hate change," he said. He picked up his laptop and left the room, leaving Alice there alone on the couch, bruised.

SHE LET HIM be. It was like soothing a wounded animal, she realized. A few years ago Wren's cat, Gremlin, the most easygoing and loving of creatures, had developed an abscess inside his ear. All at once he had become like a wild thing, slinking around the floor on his belly, terrified of every movement and sound, staring at her without recognition, out of his mind with pain. That was Duncan right now, Alice understood. And she couldn't do anything other than hold out her hands—in support, in supplication—and wait for him to come to her. He was a private and still man, Duncan, and now that she had burst through the fog of ennui and restlessness that had held her for so long, she could see that still man again, in all his sweetness.

On their second date, he had taken her to Arlington National Cemetery, of all places. It was late May, long after the peak of the cherry blossoms, and the white headstones stood bright against the vivid green of the spring grass. Alice, ever the good student, studied the map and looked for every point of interest as they walked up the long hill toward the Lee mansion.

"Joe Louis is buried here," Alice said. She had grown up in Dearborn, where her mother worked at the Eppinger factory, applying coats of white lacquer to polished brass fishing lures.

Every time her mother took her to downtown Detroit, Alice was thrilled and a little bit terrified by the eight-thousand-pound sculpture of Louis's arm that hung from bronze poles in Hart Plaza. It was so strange, that enormous arm with the clenched fist.

Duncan took her by the elbow. "I didn't bring you here to look at the graves," he said. "Look up."

"Up?" She glanced at the towering trees arcing overhead, the steel-gray sky. "At what?"

"The trees," he said. "This is the finest collection of old trees you'll find in any urban area. Some of them are more than two hundred years old; they've been here since the Lee family lived here, in the eighteen fifties."

They strolled under a giant empress tree with leaves the size of dinner plates; by the massive, two-hundred-something-year-old oak shading the Kennedy graves; and finally over to a huge American yellowwood dripping with foot-long white blossoms.

"Look at that," Duncan said, his voice full of wonder. "Yellowwoods only bloom every two to four years. That's really something to see."

Alice looked at Duncan with fresh eyes. She had immediately been drawn to the precision and order of the cemetery, the rows upon rows of matching white headstones, laid out in such perfect symmetry. And here was Duncan, looking upward, showing her something she never would have noticed. He was eager to share his knowledge, to guide her, to watch out for her—all the things she had wanted but never had. She decided right there that she wanted to marry him. She was nineteen years old.

HE DIDN'T WANT to talk, so she didn't push him. He didn't want to see a counselor, at least not yet, so she let that go, too. She waited, wondering if she should be looking for a full-time job so that she could support herself if— *Don't go there. Don't think about it.*

She tried to make things seem normal, for Wren's sake. The household ran as it always had, with Alice teaching and driving Wren to her various practices and social events and cooking dinner. Duncan came home late, often at nine or ten, and would go upstairs to chat with Wren and ask her about her day before coming downstairs to eat dinner alone at the kitchen counter, responding to anything Alice said with a polite nod. Often Alice would step outside onto the back deck after Duncan ate to feel the cool evening air against her face and breathe.

Sometimes she saw Duncan looking at her, or looking at Wren, with an odd expression on his face, but she could not tell what he was thinking.

One evening he came home from work and walked into the kitchen and said, "I have something for you."

Her heart leaped in fear as he reached into his briefcase. Was it a separation agreement? Divorce papers?

"Here." He held out a book, a blue book with a picture of a castle on the cover. She took it from him. Frommer's guide to Scotland. Back at Christmas they had talked about taking a family trip to the UK next summer, to retrace Duncan's roots.

"Maybe you can plan our trip for next summer," he said. "You know, check things out online or make a few calls."

Our trip. Next summer. Alice felt something stir inside her. It was fragile; it was whisper thin; but it glowed with a steady, white-hot light. Hope.

4

Georgia
A Year Earlier, April 2011

Over the next few days, Georgia thought about what it might be like to have a baby created from one of Chessy's eggs. Would Chessy have maternal feelings for the baby? Would Georgia love the baby as much as she loved Liza? How did one go about asking such a favor?

Georgia sat down on one of the tall stools at the counter in her kitchen, picked up a paintbrush, dipped it in blue food coloring, and began to paint the fondant peacock feathers she had made for the Bergdorf wedding cake. Getting pregnant with Liza had been so easy. Insert Tab A into Slot B and presto! Nine months later, a baby. She had taken so much for granted. She put down her paintbrush and reached for one of Amelia's oatmeal butterscotch cookies, sitting where she had left them on the counter, wrapped in plastic wrap. John had eaten so many of them that he felt somewhat sick, so now here they were, tempting Georgia.

Maybe she could ask Chessy over for dinner and bring up

the idea of being an egg donor, she thought. But then, Chessy almost never came to dinner. She did stop by once a week to pick up wedding cakes and deliver them for Georgia, something Georgia paid her far too much to do, but Chessy needed the money. She couldn't ask Chessy about something so important while they were rushing to get a cake out. She should ask her while they were doing something fun, like, like—Georgia searched her brain. For Georgia these days, "something fun" meant going to a book club meeting with a few friends and drinking wine. For Chessy, Georgia was sure, "something fun" meant going out for drinks at midnight after working on some play, and then going clubbing. *Argh.*

Georgia swallowed another bite of cookie. *I don't even like these*, she thought. *Why am I eating them?* The answer, of course, was that she was eating them because they were there, but she had to admit, petty as it was, that she was also eating them so she could feel superior about being a better baker than Amelia. As she bit into her third (or was it fourth?) cookie of the day, the phone rang.

"Hi," Alice said. "What are you doing?"

Georgia stopped eating and held the bite of cookie inside her cheek so Alice wouldn't hear her chewing. Alice was supremely disciplined and didn't eat anything with white sugar more than once a week. She never judged Georgia or chided her about her eating habits, but Georgia felt guilty anyway.

"Peacock feathers," Georgia mumbled.

"Peacock feathers?"

Georgia finished chewing and swallowed the last bit of cookie in a big gulp.

"Fondant. For a cake."

"I need to talk to you about Wren."

This was Alice's one eccentricity in Georgia's mind—the ridiculous name she had given her daughter. Wren: What kind of name was that? Georgia believed in good, plain names, like Liza. Or Ben—*if I have a boy, I'll name him Ben*, she thought, although Ben would never work with a last name like Bing. Nicholas would be good. Nicholas Bing. Maybe Nicholas Franklin Bing, after her father, Frank. Of course the reason she loved simple names was because her parents had given her and her sisters such strange names. George, Paul, and Frank—the three sons her father had wanted so much—had turned out to be Georgia, Paulina, and Francesca, names all three girls disliked. Georgia was the only one who hadn't shortened hers to a nickname, as Polly and Chessy had, because really, what nickname could you make from Georgia? Something even less attractive, like Georgie, or George. That's why she'd given Liza such a lovely, easy name—Eliza Grace. Perfect. As Nicholas Franklin would be . . .

"Georgia?"

Georgia realized she hadn't heard anything Alice had said for the last several minutes. "Yes, sorry. I got distracted by my fondant."

"I think Wren's in love," Alice said. "Has Liza said anything?"

"Wren? Really? You think she has a crush? Or an actual boyfriend?"

Georgia didn't mean to let her surprise show in her voice. Wren, two months older than Liza, had always seemed like the younger of the two. Wren was the one who played with her American Girl dolls long after Liza's dolls had been relegated to a forgotten corner of the basement, dresses dusty and ponytails askew. Wren's bed still held a menagerie of stuffed animals, gray koalas and golden puppies and orange tabby kittens, even a large plush green frog. Liza, in contrast, had redone her room this summer with Emilie's help, ripping off the wallpaper border of daisies, painting the lavender walls in bold shades of chartreuse, hot pink, turquoise, and black, of all things. The corner of Liza's room that had housed her doll collection now contained a stack of plastic drawers filled with curling irons, blow dryers, hair straighteners, and more lotions, mascaras, lip glosses, and eye shadows than Georgia had owned in her life.

"I don't know," Alice said. "Wren is on the computer *all* the time, which is not like her. And she *glows*. I've asked her a few times why she's so happy and she just says, 'No reason,' and smiles."

"Hmmm," Georgia said, picking up her fifth—or sixth?— cookie. "Do you know what she's doing on the computer? Is she on Facebook?"

"She doesn't have a Facebook account yet," Alice said. "She doesn't turn thirteen until January."

Georgia decided not to mention that Liza had had a Facebook account for three or four months now, even though she wasn't thirteen yet, either. Alice was a by-the-rules kind of person, something Georgia respected even though she herself was much less black-and-white about things.

"So what's she doing on the computer?" Georgia said.

"E-mail, I think. And she's paying more attention to what she wears, and her hair—oh, Lord, her hair. She's constantly fiddling with it and putting it up in a ponytail and taking it down and brushing it and putting it up in a bun and taking it down—it makes me crazy."

"Maybe she does have a crush," Georgia said. "Do you have any idea who it is?"

"No. I was hoping maybe Liza knew and had said something to you."

"Liza barely says anything to me these days," Georgia said.

Alice sighed. "Well, so much for my sleuthing. How are things with John?"

"Fine," Georgia said, "I think. I talked to Polly about it, too."

"Good. I didn't think you had any reason to worry."

"You know what Polly mentioned?" Georgia put down her

paintbrush, careful to rest it over a spoon so the food coloring didn't stain the counter.

"What?"

"Trying a donor egg to get pregnant."

"A donor egg?" Georgia could hear the surprise in Alice's voice. "So you're *not* done with the idea of another baby."

Georgia looked at the refrigerator, where a picture of a fat-cheeked Liza, age six months, smiled back at her. Liza had been the most perfect baby, with enormous dark eyes; tiny, perfect ears that lay close to her head; and a ready, happy smile. Just looking at the photo made Georgia want to nurse. "No," Georgia said. "I'm not done."

"Did Polly offer to donate an egg?" Alice said.

"She can't," Georgia said. "She's over thirty-five and has that thyroid thing."

"Chessy could. She looks more like you," said Alice, ever rational. "What does John think?"

"I haven't mentioned it to him yet."

Alice was silent. "Georgia, are you sure about this? You've been feeling"—Alice paused, to search for the most diplomatic word, Georgia thought—"*unsettled* in your marriage. You know I'll support you in whatever you want to do, but I want you to be sure, to be happy."

"I know." Georgia picked up the paintbrush again and twirled it between her fingers. "I think maybe John's been a little depressed about giving up on a baby. You know he always wanted Liza to have a sibling. But he never wanted me to feel like I'd let him down. So he doesn't really talk about it. But I was thinking maybe this flirtation, *if* it's even that, with Amelia is his way of making himself feel better. I noticed that thing with the chicken kebab right after I told him I wanted to stop trying for another baby."

"Men," Alice said. "I don't know why they can't just say what they feel." She paused. "So when are you going to talk to him about Chessy?"

"Tonight, I hope." Georgia didn't mention that she hadn't quite cleared it with Chessy yet. One thing at a time.

"Good luck," Alice said. "Call me tomorrow and tell me how it goes."

"I will. Thanks. And if I glean any info about Wren's lover, I'll let you know."

"Whoever he is, he better not be her lover," Alice said. But she laughed.

"All right, sweetie," Georgia said. "We'll talk tomorrow."

She clicked the phone shut and stared at the clock. Five o'clock, time for a glass of wine. She'd need it for tonight, when she planned to talk to her husband and persuade him to give her one last chance to hold a baby of her own in her arms again.

SHE AND CHESSY had talked about it once, although she doubted Chessy would remember. They'd been downtown, at the coffee shop with the brick walls and green velvet couches that Chessy loved. Chessy was so busy that the only place Georgia could ever catch up with her was at a coffee shop or the Laundromat. ("The Laundromat? Really? Can't you just bring your laundry to my house and do it here?" Georgia would beg. "How am I supposed to haul my laundry to the suburbs without a car?" Chessy would say. "Were *you* ever twenty-something?")

Sometimes the thirteen-year age gap between them seemed more like twenty years, or thirty. Georgia knew that in families like theirs—families without a mother and with a big age gap between oldest and youngest—she, as the eldest, was supposed to be a surrogate mother to her sisters, and she had tried to be. But Chessy had confounded Georgia from the moment she was born. She was a loud, fussy baby and a wriggly, irascible toddler, and instead of wanting to mother her Georgia fantasized about giving her away to some tolerant childless couple who would adopt her and move someplace far away, like the Arctic Circle.

Georgia, ever responsible, had done her best to take care of Chessy anyway in those years. She played endless imaginary games with her, games in which Chessy was the mischievous Tom Kitten and Georgia was the big rat who captured her and rolled her up in dough to make a kitten pie. For a few months Chessy demanded this game so often that Georgia started to have dreams about giant rats in chef's hats, and her shoulders ached from rolling Chessy up in Polly's big sleeping bag and unrolling her, again and again.

Georgia wasn't sure Chessy would understand *why* she wanted another baby so much. She didn't know how to explain that having Liza had made her feel normal again in a way she hadn't since their mother had died, that Liza's birth had filled at least part of that empty space. But she couldn't say that to Chessy, because Chessy had never known their mother, who had died the day after giving birth to her.

True, Georgia had had a hard month or two after Liza's birth, when the fact that her own mother wasn't there and hadn't been there for *fifteen years* cut into Georgia like a whip, opening up something fresh and raw. She had withdrawn into her grief for a while, leaving the newborn Liza to John and Polly and her father, until eventually she came out of it, drawn by her fierce love for Liza and the growing realization that even without her own mother around, she knew what to do.

Georgia knew it was difficult for Chessy—young, single, childless—to understand the yearning she felt. But that day in the coffee shop, with the disappointment of that morning's negative pregnancy test weighing like a stone inside her chest, she couldn't *not* talk about it.

"I guess Liza will be my only child," Georgia had said.

"You can try again, Georgie," Chessy said. Georgia remembered Chessy had been busy opening sugar packets and pouring them into her coffee.

"Isn't that enough sugar?" Georgia said. "I think you're up to four packets now."

And Chessy shot her that look—that you're-not-the-boss-of-me look she had so often flashed at Georgia as a toddler.

"Sorry," Georgia said. "Anyway, I don't think I *can* try again. I'm getting old, my eggs are getting old . . ."

"So use someone else's eggs." Chessy didn't even look up from stirring her coffee. "You can have Polly's eggs—hers are obviously good, right? Or mine."

It was an offhand remark, something Chessy tossed aside as casually as she tossed the empty sugar packets onto the table.

"Really?" Georgia leaned forward. "This is serious for me, Chess."

Chessy had looked up, her dark hair brushing back against her collarbone. "Well, God, of course. I don't care about my eggs—at least, not yet. And I have millions of them, right? You can have one, or ten, or however many you need."

Georgia had been warmed by Chessy's ready generosity, her guilelessness. But now Chessy was twenty-seven. And even though she was still single and not really seeing anyone and busier than ever with her Pickup Chicks (she had a pickup truck and a group of sturdy friends who moved things for people) and her acting gigs, maybe she *would* have second thoughts about donating her eggs. It was a big deal. Chessy would have to endure ten days of shots and ultrasounds and then the egg retrieval, which—Georgia knew after going through it three times herself—was somewhat uncomfortable and kind of freaky, with that giant needle sliding up into your ovaries.

The other issue, of course, was John. John and Chessy had never really taken to each other. Chessy was eleven when Georgia and John got married, an awkward almost-adolescent who had disliked John from the day she met him.

Georgia had been besotted—she and John were both living in Albany, working at Truscello's, where she made the desserts and John worked under Jimmy Amadori, the head chef. Late at night John would come home to her tiny apartment after they got off work and make pasta from scratch, carefully kneading the dough with his big hands, rolling it out delicately to just the right thickness before slicing it into slim ribbons he draped over the wooden clothes-drying rack in the living room. He'd chop up rich, ripe plum tomatoes and simmer them with garlic and onions and toss in fresh oregano and a splash of red wine. They would eat at 3:00 A.M. over the coffee table in the living room, Georgia sitting cross-legged on the floor, and John on the couch opposite her. The food was always a prelude, part of a seduction that was a foregone conclusion. John made love to her with food, and wine, drizzling it into her mouth from his, dripping it carefully into her navel, dipping his finger into the wine to trace a pale ruby-colored path down, bending his head to follow the same path with his tongue . . .

But of course Chessy couldn't be expected to understand Georgia's incredible physical attraction to John. To Chessy, John was nothing more than an interloper—the extra place mat at the Thanksgiving dinner table; the guy who rode shotgun in the car when Georgia was home, relegating Chessy to the backseat; the distraction whose ready laugh and intent gaze stole the attentions of Georgia, of Polly, of their father.

Chessy's stint as a hostess at Bing's hadn't helped much, either. John, at Georgia's urging, had hired Chessy to be hostess one summer when she was home from college. Chessy had found the computerized reservation system impossible and had taken to scribbling down reservations on napkins and the backs of receipts and business cards, leading to total confusion every

evening as people arrived for their tables. Even worse, one evening when a picky diner had complained about his tagliatelle
al ragù di piccione, saying there was too much sherry vinegar
in the ragù, Chessy, in her best theatrical voice, had informed
the customer that he wouldn't know sherry vinegar from piss.
John had fired her on the spot, and been fairly annoyed with
her ever since.

"She's nineteen," Georgia had said, in Chessy's defense.

"Right," John had said. "Old enough to know better. This is
Bing's, not some motorcycle bar."

"She was probably thinking of that expression, you know,
'full of piss and vinegar,' and it just came out."

"I don't care. It shouldn't have come out in my restaurant,"
John had said.

So now she had to figure out a way to convince John to try in
vitro once more, with a donor egg from her "screwball sister,"
as John referred to Chessy. Then she had to convince Chessy to
donate an egg, or ten or twenty. *Ay yi yi.*

IT WAS ALMOST midnight by the time Georgia finished brushing a delicate whorl of gold leaf down the center of the last of
the eighteen fondant peacock feathers. She placed the feather
down on the wax paper lining the big tray and breathed a sigh
of relief. She covered the tray with a film of plastic wrap and
slipped it into the fridge in the basement, then walked up the
stairs, thinking about John.

John had been a little quiet lately, which was odd because
he was not the type to brood. Most of the time John was
fully engaged in whatever he was doing, whether it was sauté-
ing scallops or searching the Internet for a first edition of *Ma
Gastronomie* or hitting a tennis ball—*thwack, thwack, thwack,
thwack*—against the back wall of the garage. He was in a good
mood ninety percent of the time, and when he wasn't in a good

mood he got over it faster than anyone Georgia had ever known.

But last month he had muttered something one day about how ironic it was that the *restaurant* would be the only thing he'd created that would carry on his name, if it lasted that long. She'd found a bottle of Doo Gro Stimulating Hair Growth Oil stuffed at the back of the cabinet under the bathroom sink, which was funny because John had the teeniest bald spot at the very back of his head and had never really cared about his appearance. Georgia assumed it was some kind of midlife ennui; John was forty-seven this year, the creases at the corner of his eyes deeper, his dark hair shot through with silver.

She found him in bed, the computer on his lap, watching reruns of some cooking show with a loud chef who kept repeating, "*And now* for the pièce de résistance," which was such a clichéd thing for a chef to say that Georgia couldn't believe it wasn't a joke.

"Hey," she said, coming to stand at the foot of the bed.

"Hey." He didn't look up.

Georgia reached up behind her neck to unhook the tiny clasp of her necklace. She took a deep breath. "So Polly and I were talking and she said something about donor eggs, about using a donor egg to get pregnant."

"Uh-huh," John said.

"So you'd consider it?" Georgia said.

"Hmmm."

"Buffalo!" the computer chef said. "The pièce de résistance!"

"Can you turn that down?" Georgia asked. "Really, it's incredibly annoying to listen to that when I'm trying to talk to you."

John closed the laptop and set it down on his bedside table. "Okay," he said. "Although now I'll probably never make Chef Jamie's buffalo meatballs."

"I'll live," Georgia said.

"So what were you saying?" he said. He took off his glasses and massaged the bridge of his nose with his thumb and forefinger. "God, does my head hurt."

Georgia's heart fell. Maybe now wasn't the best time to bring up Chessy's eggs.

John swung his legs over the side of the bed, stood up, and disappeared into the bathroom. She could hear him rummaging through the medicine cabinet, picking up pill bottles and shaking them.

"We have four, yes *four*, bottles of Advil here and they're all empty," he said. "That's great. Shit." Georgia heard more rattling, the sound of running water.

He came back out, palms pressed against his temples. "I took aspirin," he said. "I haven't taken aspirin since 1986. Which is probably how old that bottle of aspirin is."

He climbed into bed, lay on his back, pulled the covers up to his chin, and closed his eyes. It was the oddest position to sleep in, Georgia thought. Yet he'd slept like that, laid out like a pine board, since she'd known him.

"What did you want to talk about?" he said.

"Oh, never mind," Georgia said. "We can talk about it some other time."

"Good," he said. "I need to get some sleep." He let out a long, deep sigh.

Georgia dropped her necklace into the jewelry box on her dresser and reached up to pull an earring from one ear.

"At least I *can* sleep," John murmured. "Remember all those years when Liza didn't sleep through the night? That killed me. Thank God we're done with *that*."

Georgia paused, her hand on her earlobe. "With what?"

"Babies," John said. "Screaming, crying, pooping, sleepless babies." He yawned. "Good night."

5

Alice
Two Months Earlier, April 2012

*A*lice sat on a metal bench outside the Bender Library on a Monday afternoon, her briefcase on the concrete walkway beside her, a cup of coffee in her hand. The quad was filled with students giddy over the sunshine, the warm breeze, the impending freedom of summer. A boy in skinny jeans and a white T-shirt took off his black Converse sneakers, tied the laces together, and hurled them into a tree. Three girls in sundresses sat on the grass nearby, texting away on their phones. They looked up when they heard the *whoosh!* of the sneakers through the air, and one of the girls snapped a photo. Across the quad, a dog barked at a student who stood on a chair in front of the Mary Graydon building, wearing rainbow-striped parachute pants and no shirt.

Alice closed her eyes and turned her face toward the sun, feeling it warm her skin, the metal of the bench beside her, the concrete beneath her feet. Here she was at her beloved American University, in the middle of a spring semester in which she was teaching three of her favorite classes to some of the best students she'd ever had, with a letter from the dean in her brief-case commending a recent paper she'd published. The sun was shining after a month of rain; this week marked her fourteenth wedding anniversary; her daughter was thriving after all the upheaval in the fall—and yet Alice was so unhappy she envied the very buds on the trees for their unknowing complacency.

She kept retracing her marriage in her mind, as though if she could follow its course over the days and months and years she could discover the *one* moment that had led to this, the place where the river had encountered an obstacle and changed course. But it wasn't one moment—a shock of betrayal, a slap on the cheek, a bitter argument. None of those things had ever marred her marriage. Instead it was the accumulation of small moments—Duncan's eyes glued to the computer screen as she tried to talk to him about Wren; the empty space at the dinner table night after night because he had to work late again; his hand reaching out to turn off the light before they made love, every single time. They were little, little things, pebbles and grains of sand, carried along in the course of their marriage until they came to a still place and all those pebbles and grains grew into a pile and changed the course of things forever.

Her phone buzzed in her bag and she ignored it. The damn phone was part of the problem. It had made everything so easy, and had made it seem so innocent, at least at first. And as things progressed the phone became an addiction, as seductive to Alice as it was to the teenagers who sat across from her now, their thumbs tap-tap-tapping against the tiny screen. *I miss you,* he would write, as she was folding socks and underwear in front of the television in the evening. *You are the most adorable woman I've ever met.* Alice had never thought of herself as ador-able before. Competent, yes; smart, yes; interesting, yes; strong, of course; attractive, okay. But adorable? *I can't stop thinking about you*, he would write, as she snapped the string beans for dinner. *When can I see you again?*

The fact that she, Alice Elaine Kinnaird, was in this situation was as foreign to her as it would have been to open her eyes and see a green sun in the sky, purple grass on the quad. She had spent the past few weeks in a kind of fevered blur she had never experienced before. The routine of her days was the same; but she was not the same. She woke in the mornings and went down to the basement to work out, came upstairs and made a smoothie, zipped a Luna Bar into Wren's backpack so she would eat *something*, made coffee for herself and Duncan. Then the phone would beep and he would text her: *Are you alone? Can I call?* She edited essays and graded quizzes and prepared lesson plans and recorded grades faithfully in Blackboard, drove across the Chain Bridge three times a week to teach. *Meet me after your class. Just for half an hour.* She picked Wren up after school and drove her to ballet class, raced to the grocery store to pick up milk or toothpaste, went home and cooked healthful dinners from recipes she found in *Cooking Light*. She lay next to Duncan at night, kissed him good-bye every morning and hello every evening, as always. And yet she was a completely different woman now; she was a cheater. She felt like someone in one of those cartoons Wren used to watch, someone who looks and acts perfectly normal until he reaches up and peels off a rubbery layer of skin to reveal the monster inside.

The thing was, on some level Alice didn't feel guilty at all. She had married Duncan because she wanted someone responsible, protective, reliable—all the things she had never had in her life before. But she had been so focused on finding a safe haven that she hadn't thought about how desolate or lonely that haven might feel, hadn't thought about passion, nurturing, communication. Duncan was a good, good man, but he was also a private and reserved man. Which had suited Alice just fine, until He, her lover, had slid himself inside her body, stared into her eyes, and held the back of her neck with his hand so she could not turn her face away. He had forced her to stare into the heart of their intimacy, and it had changed her. She had spent a lifetime making do on her own, without any nurturing from her mother, with her husband's polite reserve. And she wanted, she realized now at the ripe old age of thirty-four, to love and be loved all-out, to be wanted with a greedy, reckless passion, to be held so tightly her body hurt, to be desired and babied and adored.

Her phone buzzed again. She opened her eyes and leaned forward, fished the phone out of her bag. She read the message there and felt a little thrill; followed at once by a sense of shame so thick she felt it rise in her throat. She hated the feeling of living in pieces. She looked at the phone again. Then, before she could regret it, she typed a message back and hit "send": *I can't do this anymore.* She saw his eyes as he lay on top of her, remembered the taste of his mouth, the strange roughness of his skin. *It's over.*

Alice dropped the phone into her bag, brushed a dusting of pollen from the shoulder of her blue coat, stood up, and walked across the quad, out onto the green, green grass, into the bright yellow sun.

ALICE WAS SIX the first time she spent an entire night totally alone. Rita, her mother, left at 7:30 P.M. after giving Alice her favorite dinner—macaroni and cheese with hot dogs. She showed Alice how to work the record player, and told her she could play any of the records while she was out, even Carole King and Karla Bonoff, her mother's favorites. Alice liked Carole best because she looked more solid and responsible than Karla, who was pretty and had long hair and probably went out on a lot of dates, like Rita.

"You tuck yourself in at nine," her mother said. "I'll be back at nine thirty."

Alice didn't like being home alone, but Rita always locked the door and made sure Alice knew how to dial 911. Alice spent one or two evenings a week by herself while Rita went out to dinner, usually with her boyfriend Joe, sometimes with someone else. Most of those evenings Alice watched TV and organized things: her rock collection, her markers, her shoes. She loved the feeling of satisfaction she got when everything was in its right place. She had forty-two rocks now, including a Petoskey stone from northern Michigan that her father had given her last year on her birthday. He hadn't actually given it to her, as in *handed* it to her, because he was in Canada, but he'd mailed it to her and it was her favorite rock.

On this particular evening Alice didn't mind being alone so much because it was Thursday and she could watch *The Cosby Show*. But after the show was over and after she'd arranged Rita's makeup in neat categories on her vanity—all the mascaras lined up in military precision, the lipsticks standing at attention, the blushes and powders in neat piles—she ran out of things to do. It was after nine, though, so she brushed her teeth and put on her pink flowered nightgown and climbed into bed.

She couldn't sleep. The numbers on her digital clock said 9:15 and then 9:38. She closed her eyes and listened for the sound of her mother's key in the lock, but she heard only silence. When she opened her eyes, the numbers said 10:03. At 10:30 she got up and went into her mother's room and played the whole *Tapestry* album. When it ended she went into her bedroom to look at the clock again: 11:12. She felt the first stirrings of fear deep in her belly. *What if she doesn't come home?*

She went back to her mother's room, but listening to Karla Bonoff sing "Someone to Lay Down Beside Me" made Alice sad so she put Carole King back on and lay on the floor. If a bad guy came in she figured she could scoot under the bed before he saw her. She wished (not for the first time) that she had a big brother to watch out for her, or a sister who liked to play imaginary games and organize makeup. They could hide under the bed together. When the record ended she'd sit up, flip it over, and play the other side. She dozed off, but when the music stopped the silence would wake her, and she'd flip the record again. She wondered what would happen if Rita never came home. Would her father take her to Canada? Or would she have to live in an orphanage like Annie?

She must have fallen asleep at last, because the next thing she knew she heard the sharp tap of her mother's heels across the wood floor in the living room.

"Ally?" Her mother came into the bedroom. "What are you doing in here?"

Alice sat up. She was stiff and cold from lying on the floor, and her cheek felt funny where the nubby beige rug had pressed into it. Pale morning light streamed in through the window. "You didn't come home," Alice said.

"I lost track of time, honey. I thought you'd be asleep and would never notice, and I'd be home before you woke up. I knew you were fine locked in here."

Alice's eyes filled with tears. All the worry and fear of the long, long night—combined with the utter relief that her mother was alive and here—rose up and washed over her. She hated to cry, but she couldn't help it. She was too tired to be brave.

"Oh, Alice." Her mother knelt down. "It's not a big deal," she said, "nothing to be so upset about. You were safe locked in the apartment. Okay now?"

Alice nodded. But she never forgot the night her mother

didn't come home. That was the thing about Duncan. He always came home—on time.

FRIDAY NIGHT, THEIR anniversary, marked the start of a true new year in their marriage for Alice. From the moment she had ended her affair, with that text message on Monday, the weight of her guilt began to recede. Now she could reach out and put her hand on Duncan's arm across the dinner table again, without feeling that her fingers would sear him with their dishonesty. Now she could leave her phone on the kitchen counter without panicking when she realized it wasn't in her briefcase, hidden from Duncan and Wren. It was a terrible thing she had done, but she understood herself in a different way now. It would never happen again.

But her fresh start on Friday did not go as planned. Duncan acted odd from the moment he got home from work, staring at her as though she had some spinach stuck in her teeth, asking the strangest questions.

"I have a great date planned," she said, as he walked in the door, his briefcase in hand. "You remembered we're going out tonight, right?"

She smiled at him. She was wearing jeans, a new pair of ankle boots, a pink top, and the gold hoop earrings with tiny ruby drops he had given her on their ninth anniversary.

He looked her up and down. "You look nice," he said.

"Thanks." She was so happy to be with him without the weight of her terrible secret that she felt happy and playful in a way she hadn't felt for a long time, even before her affair. She spun around in front of him. "It's a new shirt. I don't usually wear bright colors, but I loved this pink."

"Isn't pink *Georgia's* favorite color?" he said.

Alice stopped spinning. She heard his emphasis on the word *Georgia*. "I guess," she said. "Why?"

Duncan put his briefcase down on the floor and tossed his coat across one of the chairs. "How is Georgia? When was the last time you saw her?"

"Georgia?" Alice felt a clench of fear. "She's fine. I haven't seen her in a few weeks because my schedule's been crazy and she's been spending a lot of time with Chessy, but—"

"I see," Duncan said. He stared at her for a moment. "You haven't seen her in a few weeks."

"No. I've talked to her. She's okay."

He nodded. "I'm going to change," he said.

Alice poured two glasses of wine while Duncan was upstairs, and sliced a pear into neat sections, which she put on a plate with a hunk of Brie. He came back in the kitchen and looked at the glass of wine.

"I think I'll have a beer," he said.

"I'm sorry, I thought—," Alice began.

"It's fine," he said, walking over to the refrigerator. "I'm just in the mood for a beer."

Alice could not remember that Duncan had ever interrupted her before. Her heart began to beat faster, and she could feel her pulse pound in her temples.

"Is something wrong?"

Duncan turned from the refrigerator, a bottle of beer in his hand. "Wrong? Why?"

"I don't know. You seem, I don't know, a little upset or off or something."

He shook his head. "I'm not upset." He reached up and opened the cupboard and took out a large mug, made of blown glass with a heavy base, one of a set of six his best friend had given them as a wedding gift. He twisted the cap off the beer and poured it into the mug, tilting it as he poured. He sat down on a stool at the kitchen counter.

"So you really didn't have any boyfriends before me?" he said.

Alice's pulse beat everywhere now, her head, her throat, her stomach. "That's an odd question," she said. "What brought that up?"

He took a sip of his beer and shrugged.

"No, I didn't have any other boyfriends," Alice said. She put her hands on the counter, looked him in the eye. "You're the first man I ever even kissed."

"The first man you ever kissed," Duncan repeated.

He knows. He knows. He knows. Alice had a wild urge to run from the room, to run out the door, up the driveway, down the street to the bike path, and to run and run in the twilight, until she disappeared.

"Why are you asking me about Georgia and my boyfriends?"

"I'm curious."

"Do you want to go to a movie tonight?" Alice changed the subject, took a sip of her wine. "I made dinner reservations at nine at Founding Farmers for our anniversary, but we have time before that to see an early movie. Then I have a surprise."

She had booked a room (an extravagance on their budget these days) at the Hay-Adams for the night. Wren was in Montreal on a field trip with her French class, a trip Alice had agreed to with reluctance but that was, according to Wren's latest text, *awesome!!!!!*

"There's that new movie with Julia Roberts," she said. "What do you think?"

Duncan wrapped both hands around his beer glass. "You like Julia Roberts?"

Why was he acting so odd? "Well, I hated *Pretty Woman*, as you know, but I think she's beautiful and a good actress."

Duncan arched one eyebrow. "You think she's beautiful."

"Yes. Why are you repeating everything I say?"

"For clarity. I'm a lawyer."

Alice was tired of oblique conversations and half truths, her own and Duncan's.

"You need clarity on my feelings about Julia Roberts?" She put her wineglass down on the counter. "Duncan, what is going on?"

He turned his head, angled his face away from hers. "If you want to know, I was wondering if you'd ever been attracted to another woman."

This was so unexpected that Alice lost her words, opened her mouth in a round O of astonishment.

He looked at her. "We've been married a long time; our sex life has dropped off lately; you're very athletic—"

"I'm very 'athletic'? Are you kidding me? I wear pants, too. Does that make me a lesbian? What is *wrong* with you?" She paused, reconstructing their conversation of the last few minutes in her mind. "And you think I'm having an affair with *Georgia*?"

"You and Georgia are *very close*," he said.

His voice was defensive, but his shoulders slumped, and the pain of what she had done to him, even if he didn't know about it, flooded through her. She walked around the counter, and put her arms around him. "I've been distracted lately," she said, propping her chin on his shoulder. "I'm sorry. But that's *all* it is. Don't worry."

"You just always seem dissatisfied," he said. "I don't know what I'm supposed to do to make you happy."

"This," she said, burying her face in his neck, taking in the familiar scent of him, of Dove soap and starch. "This makes me happy, okay?"

"If you say so," he said. He pulled away and smiled at her, a little half smile of reassurance.

But the smile, she noticed, never reached his eyes.

6

Georgia
A Year Earlier, May 2011

Georgia meant to sit down and talk to John about donor eggs right after lunch. But then Chessy, who had stopped by to pick up a five-tier white almond wedding cake with mango mousse, called to say she had dropped the cake on the sidewalk in front of the National Museum of Women in the Arts.

"Oh, my God." For a moment, Georgia couldn't breathe. "Chessy!" she began, then stopped. "I thought you were meeting someone there who was going to help you," Georgia said. "No one could lift that cake alone."

"I *didn't* try to lift it alone," Chessy said. "I'm not a moron. And honestly, it wasn't my fault. Ez met me here, and he took one side of the board and I took the other, and after we slid it out of the truck he started walking kind of fast. I told him to slow down, but he slowed down too much and I tripped on the curb and—oh God, never mind. I'm sorry, okay? What do you want me to do now?"

"Who's Ez?" Georgia said.

"That guy I know from theater class. I told you about him. He's helping me out with Pickup Chicks. He's apprenticing to be a plumber, too, but he's really a terrific pianist. We're kind of seeing each other."

This was a lot of news for Georgia to absorb at once. But that was Chessy; her mind ricocheted from one topic to the next like a squash ball. If Chessy had been born in the 1990s, Georgia often thought, she would have been diagnosed with ADHD or ADD or ODD or some other condition characterized by a lot of letters ending in *D*, so everyone knew it was a disorder. Liza's first-grade teacher had suggested once that Liza should be "tested." John thought it was ridiculous. "I'll tell you what Liza has," he said to Georgia. "She has NFCD—Normal Fucking Child Disorder."

"Ez is a strange name," Georgia said. It was easier to think about Ez than to contemplate the enormous disaster of the smashed cake.

"It's short for Ezra," Chessy said. "Ezra Lazar Fletcher. E-L-F. Elf. All his siblings have E-L-F names, too."

"Seriously?" Georgia said. "Good God. And he *tells* people that? I'd just hope nobody noticed. Anyway, it's great he came to help you, but *what* happened?" She paused. "Are you wearing high heels?"

"I'm wearing sneakers, if you'll recall. White Converse. It figures you would try to make this all my fault."

Georgia did remember the sneakers now, which she'd noted because they looked so, well, *funky* with the dress Chessy was wearing, which was short and black and covered with little white skulls and crossbones. She wondered briefly if a child conceived from one of Chessy's eggs would grow up to have Chessy's eclectic fashion proclivities.

"I'm not trying to make this all your fault," Georgia said. "I know it was an accident. I'm sorry. But I don't know what

I'm going to do now." She pictured the cake (all those hours of work!) lying in a pile of broken crumbs and torn fondant and messy mousse filling on the pavement. The roses alone—twenty-nine perfect sugar gum roses from tiny buds to full-blown blooms, in pale shades of peach and cream, trailing up and down the sides of the cake—had taken her a day to make. Even John, who rarely noticed such things, said he thought it was one of the most beautiful cakes she'd ever made. And now she somehow had to make/find *another* cake and get it to this wedding, which was *downtown* on a Friday night, no less, with all the traffic that entailed.

The back door opened and Liza walked in, her cell phone glued to her ear. She wore a pair of jeans that were too tight and a blue tank top that didn't quite cover the straps of her red bra. She was wearing way too much eye makeup, which drove Georgia crazy. It had started last year, when Liza had become friends with that Emilie, who was a competitive cheerleader and wore so much black eyeliner and mascara that Georgia wondered why her eyes didn't stick shut every time she blinked. Once in a while Georgia wished Liza were a teeny bit more like Wren, who still liked to bake cupcakes and doodle with gel pens and read *Ella Enchanted* over and over.

"Hi, sweetie," Georgia said.

"Hi, sweetie to you, too," Chessy said. "What about the cake?"

"I was talking to Liza. Hold on."

Liza dropped her backpack on the floor, walked over to the cupboard and pulled out a bag of pretzel crisps, tucked it under her arm, and took a bottle of iced tea from the fridge, listening to whoever it was on the other end of the phone the whole time.

"*If* that is true," Liza said into the phone, "she is in so much trouble. Seriously. I'm going to kill her. She never should have said that."

"Hello," Georgia said.

"Mom, this is important," Liza said.

"I'm on the phone, too," Georgia said, "but I wanted to acknowledge your existence." She raised her eyebrows to show Liza she was making a point.

Liza rolled her eyes and said, *"Hi, Mom."*

Her face still held the faint roundness of childhood, and even though her breasts had started to bloom and her hips to round, her waist was straight, her legs slightly knock-kneed. She had inherited John's heavy-lidded eyes and strong cheekbones, but her wavy brown hair and pert nose were all Georgia. Liza often complained about her looks, about the fact that she wasn't narrow waisted, blond, graceful. Georgia wished her daughter could see her own face in unguarded moments, when all that energy and liveliness shone through her very pores. Or that she could see her body, strong and fearless, as she jumped off the high dive, chittered across the waves on water skis.

"How are you, darling?"

"I'm *fine.* I'll talk to you later."

"I may need your help, with making roses," Georgia said. "We've had—"

"Mom. I'll come down in, like, five minutes, okay? I have to finish this conversation."

Georgia remembered the days—just last year!—when Liza would come home from school, pour herself a glass of milk, get three chocolate chip cookies out of the snack drawer, sit down on a stool at the counter, and talk. She'd prattle on about her crazy world history teacher or the latest "drama" with the fifth-or sixth-grade girls, while Georgia rolled out fondant or whipped up a batch of mocha mousse filling. She and Liza both loved bad puns and Samwise Gamgee and chocolate malts and watching *What Not to Wear.*

"I've had a cake disaster," Georgia said.

"I've got a friend disaster," Liza said. "Do you understand? This is important!" She walked out, trailing the scent of gardenia perfume.

"Georgia?" Chessy said.

"Yes." Georgia stared after Liza as she walked down the hallway. Those jeans were much too tight.

"Some of the roses are still in one piece," Chessy said. "No one eats them anyway, right? So it doesn't matter if they've touched the ground."

"Of course it matters," Georgia said, her attention back on the cake. "Who knows what's been on the ground?"

She tried to think. The wedding was at six at Western Presbyterian, which meant the ceremony would be over by six thirty. *Why couldn't Chessy have dropped the cake for a nice long Catholic wedding?* The reception would begin immediately afterward at the museum. The cake had to be there when the guests arrived. Georgia looked at the blue digital numbers on the microwave in the kitchen: 3:00. She had three hours to make a substitute wedding cake garnished with dozens of sugar roses and petals and—

"The bride and groom," Georgia said into the phone. "Chess, please tell me the bride and groom on top of the cake are okay." It had taken forever to make the tiny little figures out of fondant, in part because they both had to be dressed exactly like the real couple in a photo the bride had given Georgia.

"I don't see the bride and groom," Chessy said.

"They're wearing overalls, and they're about four inches high."

"Overalls?" Chessy said.

"Yes! Didn't you notice when you picked up the cake?"

"Who wears overalls?" Chessy said. "Are they farmers?"

"*No.* I don't know. They love roses. They garden a lot. They wanted a cake with lots of roses and with themselves in their gardening clothes. And I promised I'd do it and I did it and now it's lying on the sidewalk."

"I think I found the bride," Chessy said. "She looks terrible in overalls."

"Chessy! Just salvage what you can—the bride, the groom, a rose that hasn't *actually touched the pavement*—and get back here as fast as you can."

"I thought you said that was disgusting."

"No one eats the bride and groom. They save them. We can wipe them off."

"Okay, fine. But I don't see the groom. It's the bride's day anyway, right? Maybe we can lose the groom."

"I'm hanging up now," Georgia said. She put the phone down and laid her head on the granite counter.

Georgia had decided to become a pastry chef because it was the one thing she had found that filled her with a sense of certainty and joy after her mother's death. Evy had been a very good cook, someone who knew how to balance the light, moist texture of a cream cheese coffee cake with a crunchy topping of toasted walnuts and brown sugar, and who loved eating as much as she loved baking. She was blond and blue eyed, lean and wiry like Polly, with a fine spattering of pale brown freckles across her nose. While her height was average (five-six), everything else about her was big—her laugh, her collection of vintage cookbooks (especially 1940s-era Junior League cookbooks from southern states), her sense of fun, her plans. Pink was her favorite color because, as she said, "it makes you happy just to look at it." She worked part-time as a secretary at the high school, but was home every day by three, baking. She wanted to open her own bakeshop, like the ones she had seen in Paris in her early twenties, a shop with a red awning and blue-and-white tiled floors and glass-fronted shelves filled with delicate, beautiful cakes with glazed strawberries.

At ten, Georgia loved coming home to fresh-baked ginger scones and a house that smelled sweet and warm, if warmth

had a smell. At thirteen, she thought her mother was a hope-
lessly unambitious drudge who couldn't see the world beyond
her gas range. Then an aneurysm in Evy's brain burst after
she gave birth to Chessy. She died the next day. She was forty
years old.

After that, no one in Georgia's family cooked for months,
except to warm up the succession of entrées brought by friends
and neighbors (which was why Georgia still hated lasagna).
Frank, Georgia's father, had done his best. He moved his dental
practice from downtown D.C. to an office in an old Cape Cod
house on Washington Street just three blocks from their home
in Falls Church so he didn't have to commute. He bought a
couple of cookbooks and began to make dinner most nights,
usually things like chili or short ribs or something he called
Irish pasta stew that included spaghetti, bacon, and sauerkraut.
He did the laundry, so the girls' clothes were always clean even
if their white shirts were often tinged blue from being washed
with dark jeans.

Georgia started baking by accident, when her father asked
her to make a cake for Polly's birthday in April, six months
after they had buried Evy in the tiny cemetery in the little town
in the Adirondacks near Lake Conundrum, where the family
vacationed every year. Georgia had fished out one of Evy's tat-
tered cookbooks from the shelf in the kitchen and found the
recipe for Polly's favorite cake, a three-layer butter cake with
caramel fudge icing. She followed the recipe with care, whisk-
ing dry ingredients in one bowl, milk and vanilla in another,
creaming the butter and sugar in yet another bowl, mixing it
all together in alternating batches as the recipe demanded. And
the cake was perfect! Georgia was hooked. Here was a world
you could control, full of clear rules and predictable outcomes.
She couldn't bring her mother back, but she could re-create her
Dutch Baby pancake, fluffy and golden brown, or her ginger

scones, crumbly and spicy-sweet. Of course, she hadn't anticipated days like this, days in which a perfect white cake with
mango mousse and a hint of tupelo honey would lie smashed
on the sidewalk.

Georgia heard John's footsteps on the stairs from his office.
He walked into the kitchen. "Are you all right?" he said.

Georgia straightened up. "No," she said. "Chessy just called
and there's been an accident with the cake for a wedding tonight."

John arched one eyebrow. "What kind of accident?"

"It's in pieces on the sidewalk. And the wedding is in three
hours."

"Ugh." He made a face. "Let me guess: Chessy dropped it."

"It wasn't her fault. Accidents happen."

"Right. They just happen more often to your sister than to
most people."

"That's not really the issue right now. Right now I have to
figure out how to get a cake to that wedding."

He glanced at the clock. "I'm supposed to be at the restaurant at five."

"Can't you get someone else to go early so you can help me?"

"Georgia." John's look was sympathetic. "You can't make an
entire wedding cake and decorate it in three hours."

"I know. But I can take a cake I've already made—like the
peacock cake—and redecorate it. I'll take the feathers off and
make roses and a bride and groom and I can take *that* cake to today's wedding, and bake another cake for tomorrow's wedding."

John raised his eyebrows. "Those are some impressive crisis
management skills, Mrs. Bing."

"Do you think it will work?" Georgia reached for her red
apron, which hung on a hook inside the door to the pantry.
"Their cake was white cake with mango mousse filling, and the
peacock cake is white chocolate with white chocolate mousse."

"They'll never notice," John said. "I'm a chef, and I have no idea what flavor our wedding cake was."

"It was an Earl Grey maple cake," Georgia said. "One of my best. I still have people come up to me who remember that cake."

"Can you blame me if the cake wasn't what I remember most about that day?" John flashed her an impish smile.

This was the thing about John: he could be indifferent, inattentive, lazy in a million little ways, but then he would say something utterly charming and smile that dimpled smile and make it impossible to be annoyed with him. Once, a year or two before they were married, he had called at the last minute to cancel their weekend plans to go to the Adirondacks. His friend Paul had tickets to see some unseeded hotshot tennis player named Agassi play in the U.S. Open finals in New York. Georgia had been crushed—she and John were in the heady throes of their first year together, completely besotted, and this would have been their first Weekend Away Alone Together.

"This is a once-in-a-lifetime thing," John had said. "You understand, don't you? We can go to your cabin another weekend."

Which made sense, but also made Georgia feel she was inflexible and unadventurous for being upset. "I hate being dumped at the last minute," she said.

He went to the U.S. Open anyway.

When he came back the following Monday, she didn't answer his phone calls or his persistent knocking on her apartment door. Tuesday morning she awoke and found a letter and a compact disk he had slid under her door during the night. The letter detailed the dozens of ways she was too good for him. The CD was a collection of music he had put together for her, starting out with a song from *The King and I* (who among her friends could even *name* one song from *The King and I*?) with lyrics about being a man who thinks with his heart and "stumbles and falls" but who tries and tries. The song was called "Something Wonderful." It took a peculiar mix of humility and hubris to send the song to her, she thought.

The she answered a knock on her apartment door to find a sterling silver tray, with a fresh rose in a bud vase and a plate of French toast made from homemade challah bread, with a dusting of powdered sugar, fresh raspberries, and warm maple syrup, plus coffee just the way she liked it with cream and sugar. John had emerged from around the corner with that same impish smile, those same dark eyes. Of course she'd forgiven him and they'd both been late to work that day because they couldn't stop having sex.

"Very smooth," Georgia said. "I've got to start on the roses, so they have time to dry. Could you get the peacock cake out of the fridge downstairs and take the feathers off it—gently?"

"Okay," John said. "What else?"

"I don't know yet."

John headed toward the basement stairs. Georgia tied her apron behind her waist, took a plastic-wrapped ball of sugar gum paste out of the refrigerator, and set it on the counter to warm up. She was rooting through the drawers for her rolling pin when someone knocked at the front door.

"Liza! Can you get that?" Georgia yelled.

The knocking continued.

"*Liza!*"

With a sigh of exasperation Georgia went to the front door, where she found, as expected, Chessy wearing her Converse sneakers and holding a plastic bag in one hand.

"Here's the bride and two flowers that didn't touch the ground," she said, handing the bag to Georgia. "The groom is a mess. Ez stepped on him by accident after we dropped the cake. I couldn't even scrape him off the pavement."

"Please tell me you can stay and make roses," Georgia said.

"Yes," Chessy said. "I can stay. Ez said he'll stay if you want." Chessy nodded toward her truck, parked by the curb in front of the house. Georgia could barely make out a male figure at the wheel, looking at her with his hand raised in a tentative wave.

"That's sweet, but it's okay," Georgia said. "I'd rather meet Ez another day."

Chessy shrugged. "It wasn't his fault, either, Georgia."

"I know. I'm not blaming anyone. I just don't want too many people in my kitchen right now."

Chessy looked at her. "Is Chef Boyardee going to help?"

John hated it when Chessy referred to him as "Chef Boyardee," so she did it as often as possible, even when he wasn't there to hear her.

"Yes." Georgia waved at Ez, pulled Chessy inside, and pushed her toward the kitchen. Within minutes, Georgia had set up an assembly line, in which John rolled out the gum paste in a thin layer and cut out petals, while she softened the edges of the petals with a ball tool and handed them to Chessy, who wrapped them around little cones Georgia had set up on pieces of wire wrapped in green floral tape. Chessy was supposed to attach three petals to each cone until they had thirty rosebuds, at which point Georgia would add more petals to bring the roses into bloom. But Chessy got bored and decided to make a full-blown rose while Georgia was upstairs telling Liza she needed to come down and help. Liza argued that she had too much homework, and besides, Emilie was having serious issues and had no one to talk to except Liza.

When Georgia came back into the kitchen, after resisting the urge to slap her daughter, Chessy held her rose aloft. "Look!" Her voice was triumphant. "I finished one."

It was the fattest rose Georgia had ever seen, stuffed with dozens of petals like a pom-pom for a high school float. But Chessy hadn't bothered to hang it upside down to dry, so as she waved it around the petals began to droop, first one, then another, then another.

"Oh, Jesus." Chessy looked at her rose. "Oh, no." She sat down on the black-and-white floor and began to cry.

John took one look at his sister-in-law, wiped his hands on a dishtowel, said, "I'll leave you two alone," and disappeared.

Georgia dropped to her knees and put both arms around her sister. "*Sshhh,*" she whispered. "It's okay." She pulled back and looked at Chessy, whose face was stained with tears and mascara. "Sweetie," Georgia said. "What is it? It's not like you to get upset like this. I hope this isn't about the rose—it's just a rose."

"It's not the stupid rose," Chessy said. She sniffled several times.

"And I'm *not* mad you dropped the cake," Georgia said. "Accidents happen."

"*No,*" Chessy said. "It's not the cake, either."

She raised her face to Georgia, the tears still clinging to her lashes. "I don't even know why I'm crying," she said, "because it's not something terrible, I guess." She paused and looked at Georgia with a mixture of surprise and wonder and sheer terror.

"Oh, Georgie," she said. "I'm pregnant."

7

Alice
Four Months Earlier, February 2012

The inexplicable thing about it—well, one of many inexplicable things about it—was the fact that she fell for a Bad Boy, a genre of men Alice generally disdained. She remembered once, *months* ago, talking to Georgia about Bad Boys over one of the infinite cups of coffee they'd shared in Alice's sleek teal-and-taupe kitchen. Georgia was admiring the new light fixture Duncan had installed, bemoaning the fact that John never installed light fixtures or fixed leaky faucets or power washed the deck the way Duncan did.

"But you knew John wasn't like that," Alice said. "And you married him anyway."

And Georgia had smiled in acknowledgment and said, "Right. I knew he was a Bad Boy."

Alice never really thought much about John, other than to feel bad for Georgia that John wasn't more competent and involved on the home front. John was always there in the background at birthday parties and Thanksgiving dinners and summer vacations at the lake, but he was on the periphery of her friendship with Georgia—a side dish, not the main meal. And he was not at all the type of guy—or even the type of human—who appealed to Alice. John reveled in chaos, always running twenty minutes late for everything, always talking on the phone while he drove, one hand on the wheel, the other flipping incessantly through the radio stations to find a song he liked. One time he'd been late to pick Georgia up at the airport and was so busy texting while jogging through baggage claim that he hadn't even noticed the gigantic white pillar in front of him and had run straight into it and cut his head open. He paid little attention to politics (blatantly irresponsible, in Alice's mind), rarely exercised other than playing an occasional game of doubles tennis (equally irresponsible), and devoured paperback thrillers about detectives who loved to cook. He was fetishistic about ingredients—especially mushrooms and olive oils—and enjoyed arguing about the most inane things, like whether Honus Wagner or Ozzie Smith was the greatest fielding shortstop of all time. Why, once he'd gotten so heated up during a discussion about the rules of Hearts that he'd picked up the deck of cards and hurled it into the fireplace.

"He's not *really* a Bad Boy," Georgia had said. "He's kind of devil-may-care and a little bit reckless and passionate"— Georgia blushed—"but he's also hardworking, and sweet. I don't know."

Alice had felt a twinge of envy, but dismissed it as unworthy. She would be hard put to describe Duncan as passionate about anything, even sex. Duncan was *careful* in bed. He made love to her slowly, always considerate to make sure she came before he did, then he would slip on his boxers and lie next to her, one arm thrown across her belly. Once in a while he read articles in *Men's Health* about improving your lovemaking, but if something he tried was successful—like that thing with the feather—he repeated it over and over until it drove Alice mad. "We don't need to use the feather *every* time," she had said, but he had smiled and said, "Oh, but I know what it does for you." She had finally taken the damn feather out of the drawer in the nightstand one day while he was at work and cut it into little pieces and thrown it away. When he'd reached for it the next time they were having sex and found it missing, she said that Wren must have taken it for a school project on Native Americans or something.

Sometimes Alice wondered what it would be like to have someone look at her the way John looked at Georgia, with that slow, burning sexiness, or rest a casual hand on her hip the way John did with Georgia, an inch or two lower than was really proper in public, at least to Alice's mind. Duncan didn't believe in overt displays of affection and maintained a respectful distance from Alice when anyone else was around, even Wren.

"Oh, come on," Georgia had said. "Didn't you ever go out with a Bad Boy?"

Alice shook her head. "Aside from the fact that I never really went out with anyone other than Duncan," she said, "my mother dated nothing but Bad Boys. In some ways, my mother *was* a Bad Boy. I wanted nothing to do with them." Which was true.

"You know what it is about John, though?" Georgia had said, suddenly serious. "He's not afraid of eye contact. When we met at the restaurant, you know, in Albany, he had this way of looking at me, where he would tilt his head to the side and look into my eyes while I talked. Have you ever noticed that? Most people—well, at least most men—are uncomfortable with a lot of eye contact. But John, he'll stare into your soul."

It had given Alice shivers, when Georgia had said that. But still, she was glad she herself had married a Good Boy.

ALICE REMEMBERED THE day her mother and Duncan had met for the first time, two days before her wedding. They had walked over to La Chaumière on M Street, passing dogwood trees with delicate white flowers and fading pink tulips in their last moment of glory. They sat at a table near the stone fireplace, the white stucco walls glowing gold around them. The fire crackled beside them. Rita had been alone because Arnold, her latest love interest, was fishing for trout in Minnesota.

Duncan had charmed Rita; of course he had charmed her. He asked about Michigan and he asked about Arnold. He wheedled her into talking about the days when she'd worked at the fishing lure factory, when Alice was a child. He nodded as Rita told stories about her other jobs—hostess at Vickkie's Steak House, bank teller (that lasted about two months, Alice recalled), saleswoman at Jacobsen's.

Rita had a second vodka with cranberry juice and started to tell stories about Alice, about what an organized, orderly child she had been, about her straight-A report cards and perfect attendance, about her funny little collections of rocks and sea glass and Pez dispensers. "It's like she was born an adult," Rita had said, leaning in toward Duncan with a conspiratorial smile. "I knew she'd make a great wife someday."

Rita was thirty-eight then, her blond hair thinner, her jawline loose. But she still dressed as she had during Alice's high school years, in formfitting pants and spiky heels and wild print blouses.

"Alice could cook by the time she was six," Rita went on. "She knew how to do the laundry, too. One time she even put out a fire all by herself."

Duncan had raised his eyebrows. Rita had nodded. "She was seven or eight. She was a very skinny kid. I was making doughnuts; she loved doughnuts, and I wanted her to put some meat on her bones, you know? I put the oil to heat in that big old cast-iron skillet we had—remember that, Alice? You needed two hands to lift it, it was so heavy."

Alice bit her lower lip.

"Anyway," Rita said, picking up her drink, "I stepped outside for a cigarette and ran into a friend, and we started to chat and I forgot about the doughnuts—until the fire trucks came screaming up." She shook her head. "Grease fire. Turns out little Alice came into the kitchen, saw those flames, and ran for the baking soda. Dumped the whole box onto that fire. *I* wouldn't even have known to do that. She'd heard it on TV. Then she called 911." Rita beamed at Duncan. "Like I said, I knew she'd make a great wife."

Alice saw the shock in Duncan's blue eyes, just for a second. Then he smiled and said, "My goodness! *That* must have been a surprise!" and reached over beneath the table to put his hand on Alice's knee. His touch said: *Don't be embarrassed or afraid. She is not you. I will love you and take care of you in a way she never did.*

Alice had actually dropped her eyes and looked at Duncan's hand resting there on her leg, to make sure it was real. She had reached down and squeezed his hand with her own, hard. Her squeeze said: *Thank you. Thank you for marrying me. Thank you for letting me know, finally, what it means to have a home.*

ALICE'S PHONE RANG Thursday afternoon as she was about to head out the door to teach.

"Can you meet me tonight?" he said when she answered. "For half an hour. I need to talk to you."

She felt the same excited, queasy feeling she felt now whenever she heard his voice. It was like standing too close to the edge of a precipice, and looking down, terrifying and yet exhilarating. *Yet nothing had happened.* And nothing would, she reminded herself.

"Why do we have to meet?" she said. "Can't we just talk now?"

"No."

"Why not?"

"We can't talk now because you're about to teach. Once you're done, Wren will be home. The only way we can really talk is if you leave the house later."

He knew the rhythm of her days as well as she did herself. It was amazing to think someone cared enough to pay that kind of attention. Duncan was so preoccupied with work he could barely remember that she *did* teach, let alone on what days.

"All right," she said, against her better judgment. Even as she said it, she felt the same unsettling thrill. When, in all her thirty-four years, had Alice ever done anything against her better judgment?

They met at the park, the one near Georgia's house, where the girls had played soccer from the time they were five until a year ago, when Wren quit soccer to focus on dance. Just driving into the parking lot and pulling her car up at the edge of the field made Alice feel a sudden urge to open a cooler full of juice boxes. She had told Wren she was running out to CVS to pick up a prescription; Duncan, of course, was still at work even though it was almost nine.

John came straight from the restaurant. He parked his blue Honda at the other end of the parking lot, then walked over to her car and climbed in on the passenger side.

"Hey," she said.

"Hey."

"How's Georgia?"

He leaned back against the seat, his head turned to look at her. "Better. Everything seems fine."

"And Liza?"

He sighed. "That's going to take some time to sort out, isn't it?"

Alice nodded. "For Wren, too." This is what had started it all, the conversations about how to handle the mess between Wren and Liza. Alice hadn't been able to approach Georgia about it, given how distracted Georgia was by the baby thing. So she had come to John. And that one conversation had turned into another and another. Now it was increasingly difficult to pretend that their meetings had anything to do with their troubled daughters.

John was silent. Alice sat up, her hands on the wheel, even though the car was parked, the engine off. John reached over and picked up one of her hands, held it between his own, rubbed his thumb in tender circles on her palm. She tensed, every muscle in her body on high alert, and stared at him.

"John—," she began, but he bent his mouth to hers and stole the words from her lips, the breath from her throat. His lips were full and firm and he kissed her with a kind of hunger that was as frightening as it was exciting. She ripped her mouth away from his and backed against the car door. "What are you doing?!"

He looked at her with those heavy-lidded eyes, his lashes thick and dark, and shook his head. "I think I'm in love with you," he said.

A thrill went through her at his words, a feeling of excitement in the pit of her stomach that sent a surge of electricity through her body, her heart, her mouth. She opened her mouth and almost expected sparks to fly out, like a sparkler on the Fourth of July. At the same time, she said, "No. Oh, no, no, no."

"You don't have to tell me no," John said. He sat back with a sigh and rested against the passenger-side door, so they were as far apart as possible in the confines of Alice's tiny Fiat. "All I think about, day and night, is no. I've told myself no a million times. But it doesn't change anything."

"Well, then I'll tell you no," Alice said. She sat up straighter. "I'm married. You're married. Georgia is my best friend. She's your wife and the mother of your child, *and* there is absolutely *no way* anything is going to happen between us." She felt better even as she said it, more in control.

"Oh, darlin'," John said, turning those eyes on her again, full of affection and even pity. "It already has."

AND THEN THE momentum of it all carried her forward, a glissade down an icy slope. For a few days she didn't return his texts or phone calls. She tried to keep busy, meeting with students and doing research and looking for extra opportunities to volunteer at Wren's school. She took Wren to the mall. She made love with Duncan. But none of it erased the image of John's eyes on hers, the sound of his voice saying, "Oh, darlin.'"

He texted her on the following Tuesday: *One last talk? Meet me in Old Town, by the restaurant. We can walk by the river.*

She went. And when she saw him standing there on the sidewalk, his hands stuffed in his pockets, shoulders hunched against the cold, the wind from the river ruffling his hair, she was overwhelmed with yearning. It wasn't even a yearning for John as much as a desire to be desired, to have someone want her *that much*.

He didn't say anything when she walked up, just looked at her with those eyes full of sorrow and wanting, and she hugged him and then he kissed her, and then they walked and walked, and when he led her into Hotel Monaco and pushed the button for the elevator without even stopping at the front desk she understood that this was something he had wanted and planned, and still she followed him.

And then they were in the hotel room kissing, and his tongue parted her lips and met her tongue, and she felt her body swell and flush. He ran his hands lightly over her waist and down to her hips, pulling her toward him so she could feel his hardness pressing against her stomach, and then he unbuttoned her blouse and his hands were inside her bra, his thumbs caressing her nipples as he cupped her breasts, his mouth warm against her collarbone. He slid his hand behind her back and fumbled with the hook on her bra, finally unfastened it, and slid her shirt off and her bra off. She shivered.

"God, you're beautiful," he said.

He bent his mouth to her nipple and began to trace his tongue around it in circles. His other hand caressed her other nipple, and then he pushed her breasts together and moved his tongue back and forth from one nipple to the other. The sensation shot straight down through her and she heard herself pleading *Please. Oh. Please.* Then they were on the bed and her skirt was up around her hips, and the smooth skin of his chest was pressed against her breasts and he was kissing her ears, her jaw, her neck—devouring her, really—while she moaned in a most un-Alice-like way. And even then it didn't feel like cheating, not until the moment she felt him enter her.

At that instant, her eyes widened in surprise and she thought: *Duncan and I are broken now.* And with that thought she felt tears rise in her throat and turned her face to the wall, away from him.

"Hey."

John stopped moving and held still, his weight pressing against her, his unfamiliar hardness still inside her. "Alice."

She turned her face back to him, and he saw the tears in her eyes.

"You want me to stop?"

"Yes. *No.* I don't know."

He withdrew, and lay on top of her, holding her. "I'm sorry," he said. "I thought—"

"This isn't me," she said. "I can't do it."

John rolled off her, and lay next to her on his back. "Okay," he said. "We won't do it."

She felt both relieved and oddly empty. This connection she

had shared with John over these last few months had filled a hole in her she hadn't even known was there. And now that she was aware of the hole's existence, she would be forever conscious of its presence, a great, gaping emptiness that would never leave her.

"I can't go back," she said, thinking out loud.

John rolled onto his side and propped himself up on one elbow to look at her. "Yes, you can. Just give yourself half an hour to calm down and pull yourself together."

Alice shook her head. "I don't mean I can't go home. I mean I don't know how to go back to being who I was before you and I—before we—"

"We haven't done anything, Alice, not really," John said. "Don't take yourself so seriously."

"Oh, please. We're in a hotel room together. *In bed.* Don't whitewash it."

Alice detested this kind of murky morality, the same kind of placid attitude toward right and wrong her mother had always had. "Listen, honey," her mother used to say, when Alice would point out that while it might indeed be fine to date three different men at once, she should at least let them *know* about each other, "when you get older you'll figure out things aren't so black-and-white. You've gotta learn to live with a whole lot of shades of gray." "Maybe *you* do," Alice would say, "but *I* don't."

John reached over and traced a gentle line down her chest with his finger, from just beneath her collarbone to her navel, and moved his finger in slow circles around her navel. She shivered. "Please," she said. "Don't."

"Sorry." John pulled back his hand. "God, you have a magnificent body."

"*John.*" She reached down and pulled her skirt down, and crossed her arms over her chest, covering herself.

"Hey." He reached over to brush a lock of hair from her forehead. "Alice. I wasn't looking for this, and I didn't expect it. It's a gift."

"It's not," she said. "It's a poison apple."

He smiled. "You have an answer for everything, don't you?"

"Obviously not," she said. "Or I wouldn't be here."

They were both silent. She thought of her mother, who had moved—yet again—three weeks ago. She thought of Duncan, of the way he raised one eyebrow when he was surprised or dismayed, of his long silences, of the careful, cautious way he did everything, including making love to her.

John's eyes searched her face and she reached up and put her hand against his cheek. *She could not go back.*

So she went forward. She drew her fingers down the side of his face, down his neck, ran her fingertips lightly over his collarbone, the curl of dark hair on his chest. He leaned forward, their faces almost touching, and she was breathless, panting, with fear and excitement. She wrapped her arms around him and pulled him on top of her, closed her eyes and pressed her mouth against his. She slid her hands down his back to his hips, pulled him inside her. He moved inside her slowly, finding a rhythm, then with more urgency, and the rhythm of her body met his own. Her senses were sharpened by the strangeness of it all, the way he moved inside her, the unfamiliar feel of his skin, his face. He held her face between his hands and stared into her eyes the whole time. She looked back into those dark, dark eyes—brown disappearing into black—even as she came, back arched toward the ceiling, her legs taut around his hips.

Afterward, she felt ashamed, confused, guilty—and yet, *full*. She, so careful in all things, had never imagined she would be overwhelmed by passion. What she had done was awful—the worst thing she could imagine, really. It had turned her understanding of herself inside out, as though her very skin were on backward. She realized that the weakness she had always disdained in others, despised in her mother—was hers, too, part of *her*. And with it came an unexpected sense of connection, a strange empathy with the human race.

When he called the next day, she didn't answer. She didn't answer the next ten times he called, either. The eleventh time, she flipped open her phone and said, "I can't talk to you," and hung up.

He texted her one word: *Alice*.

She thought of her mother. She thought of her straight-A record: not one B from first grade through that final semester of her master's program. She thought of Georgia. She thought of the PTA, the League of Women Voters, and the million other volunteer duties she fulfilled with such efficiency. She thought of Wren. She thought of herself twenty years from now, fifty-four and still careful and safe and responsible, faking a smile (and more) as Duncan brought out his damn feather. She thought of the way John had looked into her eyes when he made love to her, as though all the things going on between their bodies were just a small part of the union of who they were, their selves.

She picked up her cell phone, brought up John's number, typed a one-word text message to him and pushed "send" before she had time to change her mind.

YES, it said.

8

Georgia
A Year Earlier, May–June 2011

The day after Chessy announced her pregnancy, Georgia didn't get out of bed, at least not right away. She lay on her side in the half-light, gazing at the stack of books on her bedside table, which included *The Elegance of the Hedgehog* (for her book club), *Keep Calm and Carry On* (a gift from Liza last Christmas), a cookbook called *Butter Sugar Flour Eggs*, Dorie Greenspan's *Baking with Julia*, and some American Girl book on feelings she'd been meaning to read so she'd have a better understanding of what was going on with Liza these days. She hadn't opened any of them except the two cookbooks, because whenever she got in bed to read she was too tired to think about anything more demanding than pound cake.

Georgia rolled onto her back and stared at the ceiling. John, who had gotten home at 2:00 A.M., was flat on his back, face to the ceiling, deep in sleep. *Chessy is pregnant!* The thought had raced through Georgia's mind all night. Chessy couldn't be an egg donor for at least a year now, by which time Georgia would be forty-one, up against the absolute edge of her ability to bear a child. Georgia hadn't realized how hope had grown in her, unfurling like a moonflower into a sweet, white bloom. She felt the loss of that hope now. Then there was the whole idea of *Chessy* as a mother. Georgia could hardly wrap her mind around it. She was thrilled; she was jealous. The baby she had pictured in her mind for so long—a baby with John's heavy-lidded eyes and her own small nose, had morphed over these last few weeks into a baby with Chessy's wide-set eyes and John's fine, straight nose, and now had morphed again into Chessy herself as a baby, with a round face and a head covered with dark ringlets. Georgia hadn't slept all night, considering these various babies, worrying how Chessy would afford the baby, whether or not Ezra was a decent man who would be a good father, grieving the baby she had begun to believe she herself might have.

So Georgia did what she always did when she was upset. First, she rolled over onto her side and wriggled up against John, wrapping an arm around his waist and burying her face in his neck, breathing in the scent of him. John always came home smelling of garlic, something she found warm and comforting.

He shook her arm away. "I need to sleep," he murmured.

"I'm just snuggling," she said.

"It's not even daylight."

"It's after seven. I had a bad night's sleep."

"I'm sorry, but I didn't get to bed until three and I need *my* sleep. Can you at least move back over to your side?"

Georgia sighed, rolled away from her husband, and got out of bed. Then she did the second thing she did when she got upset. She went into the kitchen to bake.

She mixed up a batch of Belgian waffles, separating the eggs and whipping the whites into stiff peaks before folding them into the batter to make the waffles extra light and crispy. She sliced fresh strawberries, and warmed the maple syrup. As she worked she tried to figure out what she would do if she didn't have a second child; Liza would be gone in five short years.

She thought, when she had turned to John on her fortieth birthday and said, "I'm done," that she had *meant* it. They had been on the back porch at dusk, watching the fireflies flicker outside the screen. The very scent of the air, thick and humid and loamy, had castigated her with its fecundity, reminded her why she was ready to give up. She was tired of the constant refrain that ran through her head: *Why is Polly so fertile, and I'm not? Why can that woman in the blue coat have a baby and I can't? Why can cats and dogs reproduce and not me?* Enough.

"I want to focus on what we have," Georgia had said, "and this feels like obsessing over what we don't have."

And John had leaned forward and lifted one of her hands to his lips and said, "I love you, Georgia." And she had thought, *Maybe this is enough, the three of us.*

But the truth was, it wasn't enough. Not for her. Not yet. *Why?* Her eyes welled with tears, and she brushed them away with a floury hand. She poured a ladleful of batter onto the waffle iron and tried not to think about it.

She had eaten two waffles by the time John wandered in at nine thirty in jeans and a T-shirt, barefoot, rubbing the sleep from his eyes.

"I made waffles," Georgia said.

"I can see that," John said, looking around at the carton of eggs with the broken shells inside, the mixing bowls, the pool of spilled batter on the counter that had started to get crusty around the edges. *Here we go*, she thought.

When she baked, Georgia got so immersed in the process— the delight of mixing things, the rhythm of technique (so critical for things like biscuits and puddings and, yes, waffles)—that she was oblivious to her surroundings. Sometimes after sliding something into the oven she would straighten up and be stunned at the mess that surrounded her, the pools of melted butter on the counter, the dusting of flour on the floor, the spatters of batter on the white tile backsplash. It drove John crazy. John preferred to clean as he cooked, putting spices back into their alphabetical spots on the rack, sliding the extra chopped onion into a ziplock bag, wiping down the counters with a clean dishcloth. In every other area of his life John tolerated a high level of disarray and chaos, but his kitchen was always neat and orderly.

"How can you cook in the middle of this kind of mess?" he had said to her more than once.

"I don't see it," she said. "I'm just thinking about what I'm doing at that moment. Cooking is very meditative for me."

"Cooking in this kind of mess is like having a splinter in my skull for me," he said.

When they'd first gotten involved all those years ago in Albany, John had found her messiness charming. "I figured that any woman who could let go in the kitchen the way you did probably could let go in bed," John had told her once. "And I was right." And he had grinned that sexy grin at her and she had been delighted. But now—it was one of those things that happened after you'd been married for a long time—the traits that once seemed cute and endearing became annoying, like a soft, silky cloth rubbed against your skin over and over and over until it began to chafe and burn and drive you mad.

Georgia sighed. "I'll clean up the mess," she said. She paused. "Chessy's pregnant." She hadn't had time to tell him last night.

John looked suddenly wide awake. "*Chessy?* Who's the father?"

"This guy Ezra she's been seeing. He sounds like a good guy, but I haven't even *met* him."

"Wow," John said. "She's going to be a trip as a mother."

A mother. With those words, something about the finality of it all (and, truth be told, the unfairness of it all) hit her. Chessy was going to have a baby and Georgia wasn't and that was that. Her longing overwhelmed her.

"I want another baby," Georgia said. "I know we said we'd stop trying, but I'm not ready to give it up. I'm sorry. And my doctor said donor eggs were our best bet now that I'm over forty and I was going to ask Chessy—"

John's eyebrows shot up.

"—because Polly can't and I know you have a thing about using a 'stranger's' eggs, and now Chessy is pregnant and I'm happy for her, *I am*, but I'm also jealous. I was *meant* to have another child."

Georgia had vivid memories of her own mother, Evy, sitting at the kitchen table with her and Polly, ages six and four, constructing fairy houses out of twigs and bark and moss and pebbles and Popsicle sticks, telling them stories about how quick the fairies could fly, how sometimes you could catch them sleeping and see them curled up on leaves in the garden, or see the shimmery fairy dust they left behind. She could see Evy in her favorite pink skirt and knee-high white boots, dancing with Polly in the kitchen to that song from *The Jungle Book*, shaking her butt like Baloo the big bear. She remembered waking up one morning from a restless sleep, with a headache and sore throat, to find Evy asleep on the floor next to her bed, where she had been all night until Georgia's fever had broken.

No, one child wasn't enough. Georgia owed it to Evy to mother some more.

John sighed. "I need coffee," he said. He walked over and poured himself a full mug. Georgia waited while he rooted through the refrigerator for cream and looked for a spoon and searched for the sugar, which was out on the counter where she'd put it while mixing up the waffles and not in its proper place on the third shelf of the pantry.

"You would have had a hard time convincing me to raise a kid with Chessy's DNA," he said at last.

"That's not really the point." Georgia sat down in one of the cane-backed chairs at the kitchen table and looked up at him. "Would you try once more with a donor egg?"

John leaned back against the counter and cradled his mug in both hands. He let out his breath in a long, slow exhalation and looked at the floor. "I don't know." He raised his eyes to her face. "Eggs from a stranger feel like too much of a crapshoot."

"Our odds would be really—"

"Georgia." His voice was gentle. "I don't think so. We've done this whole fertility thing. I thought a bigger family would be fun, and I didn't want Liza to be an only child. And yeah, sure, I wanted a son. But not a son that's not really *ours*."

The baby of her dreams and daydreams vanished, poof! Gone. Georgia's arms felt empty, as though she had dropped something she had been carrying for so long it had become a part of her, another limb.

"Well," she said, her voice dry. "That's it then."

"We've got a good life."

"I know."

He came over and squeezed her shoulder, bent to kiss the top of her head.

"You'll be busy enough being a mother to Chessy's baby. She's the least maternal person I've ever met."

This was not comforting in any way, but Georgia decided not to point that out.

A knock on the front door interrupted them, followed by the sound of the door being pushed open, and Alice's voice. "Georgia?"

"In the kitchen," Georgia called out. She looked up at John. "I guess there's nothing more to say about it."

"Say about what?" Alice said. She walked in in her workout

gear—black yoga pants, a V-neck green T-shirt, a pink hoodie—and yet managed to look as fresh and polished as if she'd just come from giving a presentation on the economic crisis facing the European Union or something.

"Nothing," John said. "You want a waffle?"

Georgia could see Alice's eyes take in John's tousled hair, the day-old stubble of dark beard on his chin, the red crease on his cheek where his face had been pressed against the pillow. Georgia had never seen Duncan look even remotely disheveled, and was pretty sure Alice had never seen Duncan look disheveled, either.

"Thanks," Alice said. "I already ate."

"That doesn't mean you can't indulge in a waffle," John said. He knew Alice rarely ate anything involving white flour or sugar and loved to tease her about it. In private he told Georgia that he pitied Duncan because any woman who wouldn't let herself enjoy what was bad for her probably wasn't much fun in bed. Georgia had taken this as a compliment, since she herself had made a career out of preparing and eating food involving white flour and white sugar.

"Thanks anyway," Alice said. "But I'm not hungry. I had a big bowl of oatmeal."

"Of course you did," John said. "With heart-healthy walnuts? And antioxidant-laden blueberries? And hemp milk?"

"Yes," Alice said. "And then I did fifty push-ups. Want to arm wrestle?" Her voice was light but her biceps were rock hard. Georgia thought it was possible, maybe not likely but at least *possible*, that Alice could beat John arm wrestling.

Georgia wished John wouldn't be so prickly. He didn't get along with Chessy, he had a kind of armed neutrality with Polly, and he loved to needle Alice. Alice, though, didn't seem to care. Her mind was as quick and agile as her body, and more than once she had zinged him into silence. One time he had teased Alice, then president of the PTA, about referring to the school year as a "roller-coaster ride" in the PTA newsletter. "As an esteemed college professor I thought you'd have evolved beyond the use of clichés in your writing," John had said.

"Not me," Alice had said, arching one eyebrow at him. "You'll have to pry my clichés out of my cold, dead hands."

Now Alice turned to Georgia. "Are we still going to walk?"

"Oh, God. I forgot." Georgia sat for a minute and contemplated whether or not she really had it in her to go for a walk with Alice, who strode so fast on those long legs of hers that Georgia always felt like a dachshund scurrying along after a greyhound.

"I didn't sleep very well," Georgia said.

"A walk will make you feel better," Alice said.

Georgia thought of the second waffle she had just eaten. "Okay."

Half an hour later they were on the path that ran on top of the rocky cliffs above the Great Falls of the Potomac. After the first five minutes Georgia felt breathless and wished they could walk just a little bit slower, but she was happy to be out, with the warm May sun slicing through the trees overhead, the fringe trees in bloom sprouting up from crevices in the rocks, the endless rushing of the falls murmuring in the background.

"So what's up?" Alice said, turning her head to look at Georgia as they walked. "It's not like you to spend a twenty-minute car ride gazing out the window in silence."

"Chessy is pregnant," Georgia said.

Alice came to a dead halt. "Seriously?"

Georgia nodded, happy for the rest, however brief.

"Oh, Georgia."

Alice's face was so full of sympathy that Georgia started walking again, because she didn't want to cry.

"And she's going to keep the baby?"

Georgia nodded. "Ez—the father is this guy Ezra she's been seeing—wants to marry her. Chessy says she's not ready to get married, but they're going to move in together next month and start saving as much money as they can. Chessy thinks she'll still be able to do her Pickup Chicks business once the baby arrives."

Alice smiled a knowing smile. "Right. Because it's so easy to haul furniture and drive all over town with a newborn."

"I'll help her as much as I can."

"Won't it break your heart?"

"Yes."

"You could still use a donor egg."

"Except my husband doesn't want to."

"Did you ask him?"

Georgia ducked to avoid a branch and stopped and turned to hold the branch back so it wouldn't slap Alice. "I asked him," she said. "And the answer was no."

Alice stood still on the path. All at once Georgia knew she was going to cry and turned and headed off down the path at a pace that would have matched Alice's stride for stride.

"Georgia, wait!"

Tears rose in her throat and Georgia kept walking. She heard footsteps behind her, felt Alice's arm grasp her elbow.

"Hey." Alice pulled her to a halt, looked into her eyes. "You are the best friend I've ever had, and the best mother I've ever known. But even you have to be aware that wanting this baby is starting to seem"—Alice looked around her, at the sun-dappled forest, the dun-colored rocks—"like kind of an obsession. Are you really not ready to give this up?"

Georgia wished she could help Alice—or Polly or John or Chessy—understand. But it wasn't an explaining kind of thing. She shook her head. Georgia could feel the longing emanate from her skin. Sometimes she felt her sorrow and desire on her face as visible as if the words *I want a baby* were tattooed across her forehead.

"I'll give you my eggs," Alice said. It came out of her all at once, like a breath she had been holding in and holding in and had to release.

"What?"

"I'll give you my eggs."

Alice never ever said anything unless she meant it, as Georgia well knew. Alice also never said anything—anything important—without thinking it through first. For Alice to offer this meant Alice had been thinking about it and had talked it over with Duncan and had researched it online and with her own doctor and had likely even discussed it with Wren's pediatrician, to assess how such a thing might affect Wren. The words "I'll give you my eggs" from Alice's lips were as real and true as the bright blue sky above them, the granite beneath their feet.

"I don't know what to say," Georgia said. She sat down on one of the boulders at the side of the path.

Alice stood opposite her. "I mean it."

"I know you do."

"We look enough alike."

This was true. She and Alice both had brown hair (although Alice's was lighter than Georgia's) and faces that were similar in shape (oval, not too round, and not square like John's), and light eyes, although Alice's were a definite blue and Georgia's were green. And Georgia would have killed for Alice's long, thick eyelashes. More than once, people had assumed she and Alice were sisters because of their dark hair and blue-green eyes, even though Alice was a good six or seven inches taller.

"I know you need to think about it, and to talk to John." Alice's voice was calm. "I've already talked to Duncan, and my doctor. And I—we—want to do this for you."

Alice pushed herself away from the tree she had been lean-ing against. "So, that's that. I've offered, and the offer stands, for however long you want to think about it." She smiled at Georgia. "Now let's walk. If you have time, we can do the five-mile loop instead of the three-mile."

Georgia stood up. She opened her mouth to say something, to say thank you at the very least, even though that seemed inadequate. But before she could summon the words, Alice reached out and grabbed Georgia's wrist with one hand.

"Hush," Alice said, looking into Georgia's eyes. "I know. I want to. You're the closest thing to a sister I've ever had, or ever will have."

And she let go of Georgia's arm and set off down the path, beneath the tender pink leaves of the white oaks and the yellow blooms of the tulip poplars. Georgia watched her, just for a second, and then scrambled to catch up.

9

Alice
Six Months Earlier, January 2012

I'm going to teach you how to make an omelet," John said.

"I can cook," Alice said.

John smiled and shook his head. "Not like I can, honey."

She looked at him and tried to suppress a smile. John was one of the most annoying men she had ever met, and yet—she understood better now why Georgia had married him. He was cocky almost to the point of arrogance, opinionated, messy—but he also was whip-smart, intense, and, when something really engaged him, surprisingly focused. When she had come to him about Wren's crisis in November he had listened, his eyes on hers, nodding, asking questions. He'd been defensive, of course—what parent wouldn't be?—but he had understood, really *understood* on a gut level, in a way Duncan had not. She had decided during that first conversation that the best way to deal with the whole thing would be for her to handle it with

John, since Georgia was in no condition to handle anything and Duncan just did not get it.

So in the last six weeks Alice and John had spent hours together, talking and texting and e-mailing and meeting in odd places like the Great Wall Supermarket, where no one spoke English, and Alice looked at the live turtles and fish and snakes on display and walked the aisles with John as he searched for things she'd never heard of, like *kai-lan* and *galangal*. Sometimes they met in Alice's car, parked on the street in some unfamiliar neighborhood, with Alice leaning back against the driver's-side door and John, who hated the cold weather, hunched up in the passenger seat trying to stay warm.

The talk centered on only their daughters at first. What Liza had done to Wren was flat-out cruel. The feelings it aroused in Alice were something visceral that scared her with their intensity. She responded to this fear by forcing herself to focus on details, to gather evidence, to make a case of hard facts. She printed out all the e-mails that had been sent to Wren and organized them by date. She took notes during every phone call with Emilie's mother and kept those in another folder, also organized by date. She even took notes during her early conversations with John.

"God, you are one organized woman," John said, when she showed him her folders.

Alice was embarrassed. It was true; she was not haphazard and fun like Georgia.

"I know," she said. "It's a little compulsive, but I want to make sure I'm accurate. I don't want my need to protect Wren to keep me from thinking clearly, so—"

"Hey," John said. "Being organized is not a bad thing. God, Georgia drives me crazy sometimes. Do you know what it's like to live with someone who can't remember where she filed the title for the car or her birth certificate, and who loses her credit cards two or three times a year?"

As the weeks progressed, their conversations centered less on Liza and Wren, and more on themselves. They were both perfectionists—John about his cooking, Alice about almost everything. They were both only children, something they talked about a lot, because John had hated being an only child, as she had, and had never wanted Liza to be an only. Alice even told him a little bit about her mother, something she rarely discussed with anyone. But John was a good person to talk to, someone who didn't take things as seriously as she did, worrying them over and over in her mind until they were chafed and worn.

She teased him about watching martial arts movies (something that annoyed Georgia no end) and he surprised her by telling her about getting beat up as a kid, watching Bruce Lee movies, and becoming fascinated with wing chun, a kind of self-defense. "It's all about being relaxed but focused," he said, "so you can use an opponent's own energy against him." Alice, who had spent a lifetime trying to learn to relax, told him about the joy she found in strength training, how she'd taught herself to do pull-ups by standing on a stepladder, gripping the bar, and lowering herself down slowly, until she built up enough strength to pull herself up. It required so much concentration that it drove everything else from her mind, for that moment at least.

They talked about the kids, about Liza's recklessness, Wren's naïveté. They talked about how funny it was that they had known each other for a dozen years but never really known each other. The only things they *didn't* talk about, other than in passing, were their spouses, something Alice hadn't even noticed until the last week or so.

Now, though, here she was alone with John in his restaurant

at ten o'clock on a Tuesday morning, ostensibly to discuss what to do about Emilie and Liza, and realizing, with a growing clarity, that she had been lying to herself for quite a while.

"This is called a Poor Man's Omelet," John said. "I can make it while we talk."

He stood at the stove in the restaurant's small kitchen, with a black sauté pan on the burner in front of him. Alice stood at the side of the stove, trying not to lean against anything because she didn't want to get a grease stain on her new pants, which she had bought because she was now teaching an evening economics seminar for journalists and wanted to look even more professional than she usually did. So she had spent quite a lot of money on the pants, which were in a color called Nocturnal Sea and felt worth it to Alice because they made her somewhat athletic butt look much more curvaceous, although she chided herself for even having that thought.

"Two cups of cubed French bread," John said, turning around to the cutting board that lay behind him, on the kitchen island. He picked up the cutting board and slid the bread cubes into the pan, where they began to sizzle in the hot olive oil. "Day-old bread is actually even better for this than fresh bread. It makes better croutons."

Alice had no desire to learn how to make an omelet—she was quite adept at scrambled eggs, thank you very much, since she had made them throughout her childhood for dinner at least three times a week while her mother was out on dates or with her bowling league or playing bridge. Alice didn't really like eggs now. She hated bridge, too.

"So, back to Emilie," Alice said. "I called her mom, as we discussed, and explained that Emilie was the ringleader behind this bullying of Wren, and that if it happens again I'm going to the principal."

John nodded, and reached over to grab a spatula from the

metal canister on the counter next to the stove. His hand brushed against her arm.

"And you know what she said?"

John slid the spatula under the bread cubes and flipped them over with an expert twist of his wrist, and lifted his eyes to her face. "What?"

"She said, '*My* daughter? I still haven't seen any real evidence that there's a problem.'" Alice waited a beat to let this information sink in. "And this is *after* I forwarded her all those e-mails. She said anyone could have written those from Emilie's computer. Seriously."

Duncan had reacted to this anecdote with a placating remark about people wanting to believe the best of their own kids. But what Alice wanted was outrage.

"That's taking mother love a little far," John said. "She doesn't want to believe her Precious is a conniving bitch."

Which was exactly what Alice had been thinking but was too polite to say.

"Now," John said, "add a couple cloves of minced garlic and tomato." He picked up another, smaller cutting board and scraped the garlic into the pan with the blade of a knife. It sizzled and sent up a rich aroma, and he added a handful of chopped tomatoes. "Smell that?"

"Yes," Alice said. "I love garlic. So I've been thinking about what I want to say to Dr. Lawson, the principal. If I tell her the whole story, it drags Liza in, and some of the other girls as well as Emilie."

"I know. And you know I've talked to Liza. But that's the price she's going to have to pay for being part of this in the first place."

"But if I go to the principal, Georgia will have to know this is more than the little blip she thinks it is."

John sighed. "Right. And Georgia will be very upset, which is the one thing that can't happen right now."

He reached for the large bottle of olive oil on a shelf above the stove and drizzled it over the croutons and garlic, then reached for a bowl on the counter. He poured several well-beaten eggs from the bowl into the pan and began to shake the pan as the eggs sizzled. Within what seemed like seconds he had slid a spatula around the edges, placed an inverted plate over the pan, flipped the whole thing over, and slid the omelet back into the pan, with the cooked side now up.

"Neat trick," she said.

"That's what all the women say," John said, and looked at her and grinned.

And there was something about that grin, and the look in his eyes, that made Alice realize that she did not really need to be standing in the kitchen of Bing's alone with John. She understood that these meetings with John, which had started out of a real need to do something about the situation with Liza and Wren, had become something more, and that she should not be here, dressed in too-expensive pants that made her butt look good.

"I have to go," she said.

"What do you mean? I made you an omelet!"

"I hate eggs," Alice said. "I should have told you."

He looked at her with eyes that knew.

"Okay," he said. "Till next time."

There won't be a next time, Alice thought.

ALICE HAD MEANT it, after that day at the restaurant. She would not meet with John alone again. But then Wren came home from school a week later and said, "They're still doing it."

"Doing what?"

Wren put her backpack down on the stool at the counter, unzipped it, and reached inside. She pulled out a folded piece of paper and handed it to Alice. "I found this in my locker."

Alice, who had been in the middle of reading a conference paper on equilibrium dynamics in economic growth models, closed her laptop. She opened the piece of paper. "Hey, babe," it read. "Looking good today. Love the shoes. Your boy, Al."

"That's it," Alice said, standing up. Her throat felt tight, the muscles of her neck and jaw taut. She realized that both her hands were clenched into fists and uncurled her fingers. "Enough. This ends now. Do you know who it was?"

"Mom, I don't want you to tell the principal. Everyone will hate me."

"*Wren.*" Alice walked over to her daughter, held her sweet, troubled face between her hands. "If you don't stand up to bullies, it *never* ends. It's not right. You don't deserve this."

"I know," Wren said, turning her head away from Alice so that Alice dropped her hands. "But you don't understand what it's like to be in seventh grade."

Which was true, in a way. Alice in seventh grade had not been pretty or outgoing, like Wren, or good at dance or sports or English. She had liked math, which was the only thing about seventh grade that felt easy and natural. She wore no-name jeans and sweaters that looked like the popular Forenza sweaters but weren't, because she had to buy her own clothes at places within walking distance of the apartment and not at stores like Benetton and The Limited that were all the way out at the mall. Most of the girls talked to each other in ways Alice didn't really understand, a kind of code she hadn't been given. Her only friend was a boy named Selden Howard, a math genius with a sarcastic sense of humor and a passionate devotion to Bob Dylan.

And of course Alice had no idea, none, about how to *mother* a girl in seventh grade. Wren's adolescence had flummoxed her in a way she had never felt flummoxed before, because she had no road map for parenting a child Wren's age, and the guidebooks, as Alice thought of all the parenting manuals, were much less specific once a child left toddlerhood. Alice's memories of her own mother during those years included awakening and walking into the kitchen to make herself a piece of toast to find her English teacher (her *married* English teacher) drinking coffee at the kitchen table after spending the night with her mother. Since Wren had started seventh grade, Alice had done what she had always done since becoming a parent: (1) read how-to books and (2) studied other mothers, especially, irony of ironies, Georgia.

"If it seems like I don't understand, then explain it to me," Alice said. She needed to *get* this. "Because I cannot understand why, after all you've been through, you would not want me to talk to the principal so these girls are held accountable. Once they're done with you they'll move on to someone else. Is that what you want?"

"No!" Wren said. She walked over to the refrigerator, pulled open the door, and stood there staring at its contents.

"Be reasonable," Alice said. She sat down on the stool next to Wren's backpack, noting even as she did the cheerful pink and purple and green polka dots that covered it, the little charms Wren had clipped to it, the ballet slipper sticking out of one pocket. She thought of Wren's eagerness back in September when she'd picked out this new backpack for school, and she thought of how this year was unfolding now. It made Alice want to slap Emilie across her smug, overly made-up face.

Wren emerged from the refrigerator. "Can we move?" she said.

"What?"

"We could move this summer. You can teach anywhere, and Dad works so much we never see him anyway. We could move someplace not *too* far, like"—Wren closed her eyes and scrunched up her face in thought—"like Annapolis! Then we could see Dad every weekend. And have a boat."

The three of them had spent a day in Annapolis once when Wren was ten, sailing on a sightseeing boat around the bay, eating blue crabs at a restaurant on the water, walking up and down the long pier.

"We are not moving to Annapolis," Alice said.

"Then how about you homeschool me?"

"Wren! Running away isn't the answer."

Wren came over and picked up her backpack, slung it over one shoulder.

"Maybe not for you," she said. "But it sounds good to me." And with that, she disappeared into the hallway and up the stairs to her bedroom, leaving Alice in the kitchen, wishing for a road map, the kind that showed you which direction to go when you felt totally lost.

ALICE WAITED UNTIL after dinner to tell Duncan. She sat at the kitchen island, her elbows on the granite countertop, twirling the stem of her wineglass between her fingers.

"They're doing it again," she said.

"Who?" Duncan said. "Doing what?" He stood across from her at the kitchen sink, wearing his evening (and weekend) uniform of Levi's jeans and a button-down shirt in tattersall plaid (this one in blue), open at the neck to reveal the white undershirt beneath. He turned on the faucet and began to rinse the dinner dishes and load the dishwasher.

"Those girls. They stuck a note in Wren's locker today. They're bullying her again."

"A note?" Duncan said. He picked up the sponge and began to wash a wineglass.

"Yes. Teasing her about 'Al.' "

"That's unfortunate," he said. "But I'm hoping she can develop a thicker skin." He looked up from the sink. "Did you notice the lightbulb in the den was burned out again? I think there's something wrong with that fixture."

That was Duncan, moving from life crisis to lightbulbs in the blink of an eye.

"*Screw* the light fixture," Alice said, with more heat than she intended. "Our daughter is being harassed."

"My goodness," Duncan said, looking at her in surprise, his brows raised, his eyes open wide.

Alice was hit with a completely irrational urge to slap him. "Surely you have something to say about this nastiness with Wren," she said, "other than 'my goodness.' You say 'my goodness' when someone tells you they can do a backflip off the diving board, or that their grandfather was a world-class wrestler, not when someone tells you your daughter is being bullied."

"Well, I wasn't sure if one note in her locker constituted bullying," Duncan said. He resumed his careful rinsing and stacking of the dishes.

Wren appeared in the doorway, her dark hair pulled back into a ponytail, her blue eyes—so like Duncan's!—rimmed with red because she'd been crying. She was fine boned and petite, a throwback to Duncan's mother, Clara. The sight of her face, pinched with sadness, stabbed at Alice's heart.

"Why do you think they're so mean?" Wren said.

"I don't know," Alice said. The intricate dance of female friendships still confounded Alice, who had never really grown close to another woman until she befriended Georgia.

Duncan turned off the water and cleared his throat. "You have to ignore them," he said. "This too shall pass."

"It hasn't passed yet," Wren said.

"Do you want some ice cream?" Duncan said. "I was just going to have a bowl of mint chocolate chip."

"I don't like mint."

"We have mocha, too."

Wren nodded and sat down at the counter. Alice reached over and rubbed her back in slow circles, feeling the fine bones of Wren's shoulders beneath her hand.

"I'm going to take care of this," Alice said. "Once and for all."

"Don't call the school," Wren said.

Alice looked at Duncan, an entreaty. He shrugged. Nothing ruffled the steady, placid way he viewed the world. Alice wanted outrage; she wanted fierceness. She wanted Duncan to howl a battle cry and charge forth to defend their daughter, to do what she herself would do.

But that was not Duncan. Alice left the two of them to their ice cream and slipped out onto the back deck, into the cold January air, the clear black night. She looked behind her to make sure the door and windows were firmly closed, pulled her cell phone out of her pocket, and called John.

He answered on the first ring. "Where are you?"

"Home. Outside."

"What's up?"

"They're doing it again. Someone slid a note in her locker today, signed 'Your boy, Al.' I just want to kill someone."

"The little fuckers."

Alice felt a vicarious satisfaction. "John, one of the little"—Alice couldn't bring herself to say the word—"*terrorists* is your daughter."

"*Was* my daughter," John said. "We have had several talks, as you know. If Liza wrote that note or even witnessed the writing of that note it will be the last thing she remembers."

Alice was silent. "I thought it would stop," she said, "after you talked to Liza."

"It will stop," he said. "After I talk to her tomorrow."

Alice heard the clank of pots and pans, a babble of voices.

"I'm at work and I've got to get the dinners out," John said. "Meet me at the park Thursday and I'll update you."

And Alice, who just a week ago had sworn to herself there wouldn't be a next time, heard herself say, "Okay. Thursday is good. At two?"

"Two," John said.

It was that easy.

10

Georgia
Eight Months Earlier, October 2011

$\mathcal{G}$eorgia lay on her back on the table, her eyes on the white acoustic tiles of the ceiling. Alice stood next to her, by Georgia's head, one hand resting lightly on Georgia's shoulder.

Georgia could not count the times she had done this, lain on an examination table exactly like this one, with the white paper crinkling beneath her every time she moved, steeling herself for another disappointment. The last time she had been pregnant (four years ago, after the first in vitro attempt), she'd had a positive pregnancy test and then come in at six weeks, just like now, for an ultrasound, only to be told the embryo didn't have a heartbeat. The same thing had happened right before her second miscarriage—the positive pregnancy test, the early ultrasound, the lifeless, floating orb on the screen. Those incidents—and the others, because there had been others—ran together in her mind now, a slide show of sympathetic glances from technicians, silent rooms, her own tears.

But now, Dr. Gopal moved the wand and pointed at the

screen. "There. See that? It's the heartbeat. And just one. Per-fect. Twins are always riskier, and at your age I'd rather mini-mize the risks."

Georgia stared at the screen in shock. And there it was, un-deniable: A rapid, steady blink, a tiny heart, beating in a strong, mesmerizing rhythm. An embryo. A baby. *Alive*.

The tears ran from Georgia's eyes down the sides of her face into her ears. "There's never been a heartbeat before," she said.

Alice squeezed Georgia's shoulder. "It's great, Georgia. It's real!"

Georgia turned her head and looked up at Alice as the doctor continued to measure the small blur on the screen. "You know, there's no way I can begin to—"

"Georgia, don't." Alice shook her head. "We agreed: You're grateful. I know it. Duncan knows it. We're happy for you. Now, it's about you and your family and your baby."

Georgia believed this, at last. She and John had been to counseling (something John hated but had been willing to do), and Alice and Duncan had gone for counseling. It had all been very civilized, and they had discussed every possible aspect of the whole situation from every possible angle until even Geor-gia was sick of it all. Of course, she still wondered about things, like what if the baby not only looked like Alice but *acted* like Alice as the years went by? Alice had little quirks, as every-one did, like the way she tilted her head to one side, right ear toward right shoulder, whenever she was thinking about some-thing. Or the way she reached up and twirled her hair with one finger, winding it around and around. And what about Wren, and Liza? They would both have an equal genetic connection to the new baby, even though it would be Liza's little brother or sister. It was strange territory, a moonscape. What would they tell the girls? And when? There were other weird things, too, things Georgia hadn't even thought about but that John had asked about: *Do you think you'll feel a sense of obligation to Alice, like you'll have to do any and every favor she might ever ask?*

"Alice never asks for favors," Georgia had said, which was true. Alice was the most self-sufficient person she had ever known. "There are definite pros and cons to using a friend," the counselor had said. "It's my job to be sure you consider them all."

Well, she had considered them all and then some. Of course, at times Georgia wished she had an anonymous egg donor, someone with great genes who would forever be a shadowy person in the background. But then she wouldn't have a baby at all, because John had flat-out refused to deal with an unknown donor.

Alice was a known quantity—known and loved. And with the sight of that tiny heart beating, beating, beating there on the screen and deep inside her own body, Georgia knew she had done the right thing.

"Your baby is about the size of a raisin right now," Dr. Gopal said. "Right on target for six and a half weeks."

Your baby. Georgia hugged the words close to her, cuddled them in her mind. The doctor finished, and Georgia sat up.

"We've got to celebrate," Alice said. "What do you want to do?"

"I want to go to Kendall's and eat ginger scones," Georgia said. "Slathered in butter. I've been craving ginger all week."

"All right," Alice said. "I'll even eat white flour and sugar with you in honor of the occasion." She smiled. "But not ginger; I hate ginger, which just goes to show you that this baby is definitely all *yours*."

"I know," Georgia said. And she did.

SHE WAITED ANOTHER week to tell her sisters. They headed north on a brilliant early November day, to the cabin in the Adirondacks where they had gone every summer since Georgia was born, and even before. Their mother had spent every summer vacation with her family in the little three-bedroom log cabin on Lake Conundrum since 1950. Now she was buried in the cemetery two or three miles down the road from the cabin, with a fine view of Hoffman Mountain to the west, and the ponds and forests of the Pharoah Lake Wilderness Area to the east. "But she's so far away," Polly, then eleven, had said, after the funeral. "But we'll visit her every summer," Frank had told her. "Your mom came here every summer when she was a little girl, and you will, too."

Polly insisted on driving, and Chessy said that riding in the backseat made her feel like throwing up, so of course Georgia said she'd sit in back, even though she hated being in the back because she could never quite hear anything unless she leaned so far forward that the seat belt practically cut her in two. At first the three of them—especially Polly—had been almost giddy with the freedom of escaping for this long weekend without kids, spouses, significant others, or even pets. Chessy had balked at this last stipulation, because she usually brought her dog, Charles, everywhere with her, but the sisters had stood firm: No distractions. No taking care of anything or anyone but ourselves for four whole days.

Polly had been talking all the way through Maryland in an attempt to convince Chessy to move in with her for a while after the baby came, and Chessy was equally adamant that she was going to handle the baby on her own, no matter what.

"I'm not questioning your ability to be a good mother," Polly said. Her eyes were on the traffic in front of her. "But a baby is hard work, not to mention *expensive*." She emphasized this last word, because it was the one weak point in Chessy's case, her ability to afford this baby. She and Ez were not going to get married, at least not yet. Ez was working as an apprentice plumber, but had several years to go before he could qualify as a master plumber, and Chessy wanted him to continue with his acting because she thought he was so gifted.

"I know babies are expensive," Chessy said, shifting in her seat. She was eight months along now, her belly a round curve over the line of her seat belt. "But we've got it all figured out."

"But what about the insur—," Polly began.

"I said, *we've got it covered*," Chessy said. "I am twenty-seven, you know, not fourteen."

"Okay, okay," Polly said. "But we're here to help you, you know that."

Chessy rolled her eyes. "Yes, I know that. And thank you." She looked at Polly. "I could remind you, though, that you are my sister, not my mother."

"Fine," Polly said. They drove along in silence for a while. Polly looked in the rearview mirror and caught Georgia's eyes. "You're uncharacteristically quiet," she said.

"I'm trying not to throw up," Georgia said. "I hate the back-seat."

"At least you're not pregnant," Chessy said.

"Chessy!" Polly's voice was a reprimand. "Really. Have a little sensitivity, can't you?"

"Georgie's over it," Chessy said. "Aren't you? You gave up on the baby thing on your fortieth birthday, right?"

"That doesn't mean she doesn't still want one," Polly said. "And she's been unbelievably supportive about *your* baby. You could try thinking about someone other than yourself once in a while and not rub her nose in it."

"I'm not rubbing her nose in it!" Chessy said. "I just said she probably doesn't feel like throwing up as much as a pregnant person feels like throwing up. Jesus, Polly. Take a pill."

"Listen to yourself," Polly said. "You *sound* like you're four-teen, not twenty-seven."

"It's because you insist on acting like my mother and treating me like I'm an adolescent," Chessy said. "I didn't mean to hurt Georgie's feelings, she knows that." Chessy twisted in her seat to look at Georgia. "Are you upset? I'm sorry if you are."

Georgia shook her head.

"You see? She's fine."

"She's not fine," Polly said. "Or she'd actually *say* something. She's always quiet when she's upset."

"I'm fine," Georgia said.

In truth, she was happy to listen to Polly and Chessy bicker without having to say anything, to watch the rolling hills pass by the windows, to think.

"So why are you so quiet?" Polly said.

"I'm not," Georgia said. "I just don't have anything insightful to say about Chessy feeling like she wants to throw up."

"You did hurt her feelings," Polly said to Chessy.

"She's not that hypersensitive. Give it a break, Polly." Chessy turned again to look at Georgia. "Honestly, is this hard for you? I'm sorry if I've been—"

"Oh, shush," Georgia said. "It's fine." She took a deep breath. "I'm pregnant."

A stunned silence met her words.

"Are you serious?" Polly said.

"Of course she's serious," Chessy said. "Why would she make that up?"

"I can speak for myself," Georgia said. "Although it's hard to get a word in with you two sometimes."

"That's because Polly never stops nagging," Chessy said.

Polly snorted.

"It's still early," Georgia said. "Eight weeks. But the doctor thinks everything looks good, really good."

"Wow," Polly said. Her eyes sought Georgia's in the rearview mirror again.

Georgia's eyes met Polly's and she smiled. "I know. But don't worry. I think this time it's going to work."

Polly's eyes filled with tears. "The baby has a heartbeat," Georgia said. "My doctor is confident everything is fine. *Don't* worry, Pol."

"Really?" Polly said. "Wow." She shook her head in disbelief. "Just think, after almost thirteen years suddenly I'm going to be an aunt to *two* babies in the same year. My kids are going to be so excited. And Teddy! He'll have *two* new cousins to play with." Polly turned her head quickly to look at Chessy. "So, Chess, your baby and Georgia's will be just a few months apart. It's perfect."

Chessy greeted this with silence.

"Chessy?" Georgia said. "Are you okay?"

"Yes," Chessy said, staring straight ahead out the windshield. "I'm fine. I'm happy for you, I am. I know how long you've wanted this. It's just—" She bit her lip.

"It's just what?"

"You're stealing my baby thunder," Chessy said. "You and Polly do *everything* first, and there hasn't been a baby in our family since Teddy three years ago, and *my* baby was going to be the youngest grandchild, and now it won't even be that."

"I'm not stealing your baby thunder," Georgia said. "This is your first baby. Everyone is excited about that. You'll have your baby half a year before mine is born. Come on, Chess."

"I know." Chessy sighed. "It will be good in some ways." She turned in her seat to look at Georgia. "I can't believe it," she said. "I noticed you were putting on a little weight, but I just thought you were getting fat." She paused. "Hey! I can give you my maternity clothes once I have the baby. Yours are all a million years old, right?"

Polly looked sideways at Chessy's outfit, which consisted of a pair of black maternity leggings, a long lace tunic, and, inexplicably, a fake-fur vest in a strange shade of orange. "Great idea, Chess!" she said, her voice bright.

Georgia smiled. "I'd love that."

"It's incredible you were able to get pregnant this time," Polly said. "What happened? You just got pregnant?"

"No, we did IVF again."

"And it worked this time!" Polly's voice was elated. "And you didn't even have to use a donor egg. That is so great."

"Mmmm," Georgia said. She was still unsure how to handle all this egg donor business, how much to tell, how much to conceal. She and John and Alice and Duncan had agreed they wouldn't discuss it with Wren and Liza until later, after the baby was born. Beyond that, they had decided not to tell anyone outside their immediate families.

Georgia looked out the window again. They were crossing the wide swath of the Susquehanna River now, bordered on both sides by the brown-gold trees of late autumn. The next time she crossed this river headed north would be next summer, with her new baby strapped in the backseat. She still could not believe it.

"Can I just say now I don't want to hear any more from either of you about your giving birth stories?" Chessy said. "God, I could recite them in my sleep."

"That's Polly," Georgia said. "She has four of them. I only have my one measly story."

"None of them are that interesting, no offense," Chessy said.

Georgia and Polly exchanged glances in the rearview mirror. "They get a lot more interesting once you've been through it yourself," Polly said.

Chessy started to say something but Georgia's cell phone rang, and she saw it was Liza. "Hush, will you?" Georgia said, as she flipped the phone open.

"Hi, honey. How are you?"

"I'm fine," Liza said. "How's your trip?"

"Well, fine. We've only been gone three hours."

"I know. I just wanted to say hi. I miss you."

Georgia was silent for a moment. This was not at all like Liza. Well, it was like Liza-at-ten or Liza-at-eleven, but not at all like Liza-at-almost-thirteen.

"Is everything okay?" Georgia said.

"Yes," Liza said. "I'm going to Emilie's after school, then Emilie's mom is dropping me at the restaurant and I'm going to help Dad."

"Why are you calling me from school?" Georgia said, looking at her watch. "Aren't you supposed to be in class?"

"It's my lunch break. I was thinking about you, and about the lake. I wish I was going with you."

"I do, too, sweetheart."

"Remember when Wren and I took the floats down the creek and they popped and we had to walk all that way to the bridge?"

"That was crazy," Georgia said. For years, Alice and Duncan and Wren had spent a week in the Adirondacks every summer with Georgia and John and Liza. The girls played on the small sandy beach at the end of the bay, digging elaborate palaces with moats and rivers, finding sticks and pebbles for tiny stockade fences and stone pillars. When they were older they went for long canoe rides, just the two of them, or practiced doing dances and cheers in the meadow next to the cabin, Wren showing Liza the steps over and over, and applauding when she finally got them down.

"I just wish I was there, with you."

Something in Liza's voice caught Georgia's attention, and she sat up straighter. "Sweetie, what's going on? Is everything okay?"

Georgia heard noise at the other end of the line, other voices.

"Nothing," Liza said. "I was just thinking about how fun the lake was. Have fun, Mom. I've got to go." And Liza hung up before Georgia could say another word.

THE NEXT MORNING Georgia awoke to the bright September sun streaming in through a gap in the flowered curtains. The bed across from hers was empty; Polly must have either driven to town to get groceries, or gone for a run. She lay in bed for a few minutes listening to see if she could hear Chessy moving around downstairs, or Polly returning from wherever she was, but the cabin was quiet. Red-winged blackbirds chittered in the marshes by the lake. The cool air in the room nipped at her face and she burrowed deeper under the blankets. She'd forgotten how cold it could be in the Adirondacks in the fall.

She lay there in kind of a dreamy half sleep, feeling, as she always did here, as though the lines of time were blurred, as though she could be six or sixteen or thirty-six, here in this room with the yellow pine walls and the ancient oak dresser and the flowered curtains, dark green with bright yellow daisies. Nothing about this room had changed in forty years; neither had the lake outside the windows, or the forest beside the cabin, or the undulating mountains beyond that. Georgia loved the continuity of it all.

The only time it had seemed jarring was in that awful first year after her mother died, when coming here had been at once the most reassuring and the most horrifying thing of all. Everything was exactly the same, as always. *Here you are*, the cabin and the mountains and the lake seemed to say. *Let us take you in*. But the idea that all this just went on—the wind ruffling the curtains, the water lapping at the shore, the leaves of the birches rustling in the breeze—when her mother was dust, a memory, was almost too much to bear. She had glared at the curtains in bitter resentment that summer, thrown stones into that awful placid lake, spat at the silent forest. She had hated all of it for being there, so calm and unchanging.

Georgia rolled over. She wished, for the first time in a long time, that her mother were here. Maybe it was something about being pregnant again. She remembered those terrifying first months after Liza was born when she'd been racked with terror that something would happen to her, Georgia, so she wouldn't be around for Liza. She'd developed mastitis in the first week after Liza's birth and been convinced the golf-ball-sized lump in her breast was a sudden, malignant tumor in spite of the doctor's reassurances. For the next few years she had agonized over every freckle, every cyst, every headache, sure she was about to be struck down and severed from her daughter. The miscarriages and infertility—symptoms of lupus or leukemia or ovarian cancer—had fueled her hypochondria even further. Finally one night she had awakened John, worried about a throbbing headache that Advil wouldn't cure. "It could be an aneurysm," she had said, "like my mother." And John had turned agonized eyes to her and said, "I know. And what do you want me to do? Every time you worry, I wonder, 'Could she be right? What should I do?' But if I say, 'Let's go to the ER,' you tell me I need to be more reassuring. And if I tell you not to worry because it's probably nothing, you tell me I don't take you seriously enough. Georgia, this has got to stop."

She knew he was right, but she couldn't still the fear. Growing up without a mother had completely changed her life, as it had changed Polly's and Chessy's. She had asked Polly once if she felt the same fear about dying prematurely and leaving her children behind. Polly had said, "Of course I think about it. How could you not? But I figure it's pretty unlikely. So I don't worry about it." But then, that was the difference between Georgia and Polly.

Georgia closed her eyes and felt a sudden wave of nausea.

She opened her eyes, looked around the room, and leaped out of bed just in time to vomit into the plastic wastebasket next to the dresser. She waited, kneeling there on the floor, to be sure she was done, and stood up, wiping her mouth with the back of her hand. *This is good*, she said to herself. Nausea meant raging pregnancy hormones, which meant her little embryo was thriving. It was reassuring.

"Georgia?" Polly's voice called up the stairs. "You okay?"

"I'm fine," Georgia said. "Just pregnant."

"Need any help?"

"No. I'll be right down."

Georgia went into the bathroom to empty the wastebasket and rinse out her mouth. She sat down to pee, still half-asleep. It wasn't until she stood up and turned around to flush that she saw the blood.

11

Alice
Eight Months Earlier, November 2011

*W*ren's voice on the phone sounded odd, desperate. "Can you pick me up right now?" she said. "I feel sick."

"Now?" Alice looked at her watch. "It's one fifteen."

"I know. I feel sick. I need to come home."

Alice sighed. She had two lesson plans to prepare for tomorrow's classes, as well as a quiz to write up, and she had to take Gremlin to the vet at three forty-five. "Are you in the clinic? Let me talk to the nurse."

"I'm not in the clinic. I'm really sick so I'm in the bathroom and I need you to come to school and get me now."

"What do you mean? Are you throwing up?"

"No. Yes. Yes. Come now."

"Wren, I can't come to school and just drive away with you. You have to go to the clinic and get sent home, or I have to come check you out. You know the rules."

"Mom"—Wren started to cry—"I have to come home before

the bell at three. There's no way I can take the bus. Please, come get me now."

Her voice was so insistent, so pleading, that Alice heard herself say, "All right. I'm coming right now. I'll go to the office and talk to Ms. Henderson."

"Thank you. Text me when you get here and I'll meet you in the lobby."

"Are you skipping class?"

But Wren had hung up.

THE STORY CAME out all at once, so confusing that Alice didn't understand half of it, so Wren had to take some deep breaths and drink some vanilla hemp milk and then tell it again. They sat at the glass-and-chrome kitchen table, in the fine cherry-wood chairs Alice had chosen so carefully. Alice leaned forward, her eyes glued on Wren. Wren sat on the edge of her chair, her words tumbling over themselves like water over stones.

For two or three months now, Wren said, she'd been exchanging e-mails with a boy at school, a boy who signed his e-mails "Alonzo All-Star Superman Briggs" or, as their correspondence progressed, "Al." He'd e-mailed Wren initially in September, mentioning that he liked her cheerleading routine at the football game, and asking if she'd write him back. She had been flattered and of course had written him back, a friendly note of thanks, curious as to his identity.

"I don't want to tell you who I am," he wrote back. "I'm kind of shy around girls and it's easier writing to you than talking to you."

She wrote him again. They started to e-mail back and forth every day, then several times a day. He told her more and more about himself. His parents were divorced, he was an only child, and he loved basketball, football, baseball, and soccer, in that order. He hated the same teachers she did, liked the same books she did, and had even been to the Adirondacks and knew Lake Conundrum, where she vacationed with the Bings. She told him about her secret desire to go to the School of Performing Arts in New York, about how she felt like she didn't really fit in with the "popular" girls like Liza and Emilie, but didn't know where she did fit. He said he understood.

Alice tried hard to follow the story through Wren's hiccups and tears. Wren logged on to the computer and showed her bits of the correspondence. Alice was still incredulous that her daughter, who was not stupid, would pour her heart out to some unknown correspondent online.

"But, Wren," Alice said. "How could you get so involved with someone you didn't know?" She felt a sudden clutch of fear. "How do you even know he was really a student at your school? Did you tell him where we live? Did he try to meet you in person?" She was completely unprepared for what came next.

"No, he didn't try to meet me in person," Wren said, "because he wasn't real." She lifted one elbow and wiped her nose on her shoulder. "It was someone else pretending to be Al. Al was totally made up." She looked at her mother, her eyes full of embarrassment and confusion. "It was Emilie and Liza."

"What?!"

"And today they told everyone at school." Wren started to cry again. "And they made jokes about it."

Alice felt her rage rise in her like a live thing. Her head pounded.

"Wren." Alice leaned forward and locked her eyes on Wren's. "This was an unbelievably mean thing to do, and Liza and Emilie will have to be punished for it. It was cruel, it was wrong, and it may even be illegal."

Wren's eyes filled. "I feel so bad," she said. "I really liked Al. And he liked me."

Alice stood up, walked around the table, and knelt on the

floor in front of her daughter. She hugged her, hard. "I know you did. And I'm sorry."

"Mom, you can't tell anyone," Wren said. "If you do anything it will make it worse."

"Worse?" Alice sat back on her heels. She still could not believe it. She wanted to smash something.

"Wren, this is bullying. I have to talk to Georgia, at the least, and I have to talk to the school."

"Please, *no*. I can pretend I don't care, that it's not a big deal."

"It *is* a big deal. It's a huge deal. We can't just ignore it."

"*Please*. I only called you to come get me today so I wouldn't have to ride the bus. Don't tell. They'll hate me forever."

"*Wren*."

"Mom, please."

Alice stood up. "Listen, I'll talk to your dad when he gets home from work. We'll figure out how to handle this, and we'll talk to you about it, okay? I won't make any phone calls—yet." She put a hand under Wren's small, pointed chin and lifted Wren's face toward hers. "This is jealousy. You are a wonderful, trusting, talented, beautiful girl. I know this hurts, but don't let it crush you."

Wren looked at her with those big dark eyes. "Will you make me hot chocolate?"

"Of course. Good idea."

She gave Wren one more hug, and let her go.

"You promise you won't call anyone?" Wren said over her shoulder as she walked out of the kitchen.

But Alice pretended to be busy with the cocoa and didn't answer.

ALICE HAD BEEN stunned to find herself pregnant after her honeymoon, two months before she graduated from Georgetown. They had planned to wait at least five years to have a baby, to give Alice time to get her master's. Alice loved school—she'd spent the last four summers taking courses, hence her graduation in just three years—and couldn't wait to start graduate school. And she needed time to adjust to the idea of having a baby—something Duncan had made clear he wanted from their third date. She had no confidence she'd be a good mother—look at the role model she'd had.

"This is a terrible time for us to have a baby," she had said to him. "I'm supposed to start graduate school in the fall." She was so terrified that she even suggested, once, that maybe they should consider giving the baby up for adoption, wait to have a family until she was finished with school, more ready and capable than she was now. Alice had wanted to be a teacher her whole life; she wanted to get her graduate degree. She had seen what being an unwilling parent had done to her own mother and didn't want to be that mother to her own child.

"Oh, Alice," Duncan had said. "You'll be a great mom. You're the most competent person I know. You'll be able to handle school and the baby. I'll help. It will work out."

But then, Duncan was almost thirty, settled into a good career at Covington, ready for a family. And so Alice found herself on an unexpected train, hurtling toward motherhood. She spent her last trimester working on her master's, poring over texts and writing papers on micro- and macroeconomic theory, econometrics, economic history. At night, charts and numbers danced through her dreams, mingled with dreams about babies falling downstairs.

None of her friends were even married yet, let alone pregnant. They liked to go out drinking or dancing or prowling for guys after work, all things Alice couldn't do now. Duncan worked long hours. Alice spent a lot of time alone, trying to come up with ideas for her thesis and ignoring her burgeoning belly. The first time she felt the baby kick was in summer school, in Professor B.'s quantitative economics class. The kick startled her so much she almost fell out of her chair. *Oh, my God, it's alive!* she wanted to shout, like someone in a bad horror movie. But this wasn't a horror movie; it was Alice's life.

When Wren was born, after ten hours of a textbook-perfect labor and delivery, Alice's first thought was that she was so *small.* She weighed barely six pounds, less than a sack of grapefruit. Her skin was so pale Alice could trace the fine, threadlike veins in her eyelids, see the quick throb of her heartbeat at her temples. She looked so vulnerable and yet so exquisite in her tiny perfection. Alice felt a rush of love and terror like nothing she had experienced before or would ever experience again.

"She looks like a little bird," Duncan said.

The baby opened her mouth and began to cry.

"'A shrill clamor rises like jingling from tiny, high-pitched bells,'" he quoted.

"What?" Alice said.

"From a poem. 'Baby Wrens' Voices' is the name of it."

"She's a wren," Alice said.

Duncan smiled. "That would be a good name for her."

Alice thought he was mad. *Wren* was not a name for a child. Alice wanted to give her daughter a reasonable, human being name, a name like Emily or Beth.

Duncan continued the poem: "'Who'd have guessed such a small house contained so many voices? The sound they make is the pure sound of life's hunger.'"

Alice looked at the baby in her arms—who really did look like a wren and who was certainly screaming with the "pure sound of life's hunger"—and was filled with love for Duncan, who held things like this poem in his mind, and with love for this tiny, precious baby, the most unusual and special creature ever born, who should have an unusual, special name.

"Okay," she had said. "Let's name her Wren."

She bent to the infant in her arms. "Hello, you," she said, trying to get over the fear she felt. "I'm your mother."

THE FIRST THING Alice did after taking Wren's cocoa upstairs was walk down to the basement, pull on her red boxing gloves, and punch the heavy bag hanging in the corner as hard as she could. She hit the bag with a succession of eight or ten hard punches, then turned slightly and gave it a couple of solid roundhouse kicks for good measure. She stood there for a minute, panting, and realized that she had not even begun to expend her anger. She took off the gloves and walked in circles around the big room in the basement for a few minutes until her heart stopped racing, then walked over to the pull-up bar, reached up, and did five quick chin-ups. She walked in more circles.

She did not want to be this angry; she couldn't think clearly, and she hated not thinking clearly. She should call Duncan; she should call Georgia; she should call the school guidance counselor, and the principal. But she couldn't, because she was so angry that she was liable to lose her temper and start yelling or—even worse, burst into tears.

Liza. That was the thing that made this betrayal so deep. Liza and Wren had known each other for all of their twelve years. They'd napped together in each other's cribs while Georgia and Alice drank tea; played and hugged and bickered and made up together; and spent every birthday and Christmas Eve and July Fourth together. Sure, they'd always been different, almost like the sisters in the fairy tale "Snow White and Rose Red," because Wren was so quiet and pale and Liza so rambunctious and rosy. But they had seemed such perfect complements to each other. Wren was the graceful, natural athlete who patiently taught Liza dance steps and cheers, applauding when, after hours and hours, Liza would master something that Wren could do in her sleep. Liza was the fearless adventurer who encouraged Wren to jump off the high dive at the pool, and taught her how to drive the little outboard motorboat at the lake, demonstrating for her how easy it all was, why there was nothing to be afraid of.

And Liza was so creative! One time Alice and Georgia had taken the girls out to lunch for Wren's sixth birthday. The waiter brought over pages for the girls to color, a picture of a boy with a pail gathering blueberries. Wren had colored her page with great care, choosing dark blue for the berries, green for the leaves, light blue for the boy's overalls, yellow for the sun. Liza, in turn, drew strawberries and watermelons on the blueberry bushes, colored them in with furious scribbles of red and bright pink, colored the boy's overalls purple, and drew bright orange stripes on them. She drew pale lavender clouds in the sky, colored in a sunrise with yellows and pinks, filled every square inch of the page with color so there was not one dot of white space left. Her picture was crazy, but beautiful. Alice, who would never have colored outside the lines herself, had been awestruck.

Every year on Wren's birthday Liza made something for her—a wooden box covered with pebbles Liza had found at the lake, tie-dyed soccer socks, a wallet made of multicolored duct tape. Alice had always thought that Liza loved and admired Wren. Sure, they'd started to go their separate ways a little in seventh grade, but Alice had thought that was just because Liza was entering adolescence sooner. Why, Alice had even felt a little sorry for Liza over this past year because she'd grown so tall—long and lanky like John but without even John's minimal athleticism, so that she was always tripping over her own feet. And she was hopeless at sports but persisted in playing them anyway because all the popular kids played sports. Georgia often bemoaned the fact that Liza did so little with her artistic talent. But now Liza had used her creativity—albeit of a different sort—to perpetrate this awful prank on Wren.

Alice was on her fifth set of chin-ups when she decided that the thing to do was go to Georgia's house and talk to her. She had spent enough of her energy on the heavy bag and the pull-up bar; she could stay composed. She glanced at her watch. She had just enough time to go to Georgia's, have a calm talk with her about Liza, and get home to take Gremlin to the vet. She walked upstairs, grabbed her purse and car keys, and yelled up to Wren.

"Wren! I'm going to run to the grocery store and I'll be back in half an hour."

No response.

"Wren! Are you all right?"

Alice walked upstairs, peered into Wren's room, and saw her asleep on her bed. Her eyelashes were still crusted with salty tears, and she had one arm around Beary, the stuffed gray panda she'd had since she was a baby. She looked so young and vulnerable. Alice wrote Wren a quick note, put it on the bed beside her, pressed her lips together in a thin line, and headed downstairs and out the door to Georgia's.

ALICE STOOD ON Georgia's familiar front porch, feeling her heart pound in her chest in a most unfamiliar way. Her hands were shaking, so she held one wrist tightly with her other hand. She heard footsteps from inside and took a deep breath. John opened the door.

"Well," he said. "Hello, Alice."

Damn, she thought. John was not the person she wanted to talk to. "Is Georgia here?" she said.

His smile faded. "Georgia's in the Adirondacks," he said. "With her sisters."

"Oh, right. I forgot. I'm sorry. Never mind. I'll talk to her when she gets home. She gets back Monday, right?"

"Maybe," John said. "She's in the hospital. I thought she might have called you."

"What?" Alice's stomach lurched.

"She's going to be fine. She had a little bleeding, which is not unusual. Everything looks great on the ultrasound. She needs to be on bed rest for a few days, maybe limited bed rest once she gets home. But she's fine."

"Oh, God." Alice's mind whirled. *Poor Georgia.* But Wren! Alice couldn't talk to Georgia about Liza and the bullying now, with this uncertainty. But how could she *not* talk to Georgia about it, not *do* something? Alice, for the first time in her life, had absolutely no idea what to do. "What happened? Is she—"

"Don't worry," John said. "Polly said the doctor there is great. Everything is going to be okay."

Alice bit her lip.

"Listen. They ran a bunch of tests; nothing is wrong. Georgia is worried, of course, but that's Georgia. If she gets a splinter she's convinced some drug-resistant staph infection isn't far behind."

Alice didn't smile. Her throat felt tight. "This is not hypochondria, John."

"I know. I know. But there's no need to go running off to the Wailing Wall yet."

"I'm not the Wailing Wall type," Alice said, her voice dry, and John laughed.

"That's the understatement of the year," he said.

Alice stood there on the uneven boards of the porch, trying to decide what to do. "Is Liza here?"

"Liza? No, she's at a friend's." He looked at her, and must have seen something in her face, or caught the tension in her voice. "What does Liza have to do with this?"

Alice couldn't contain it. "She's been bullying Wren," she said. "For months. She's been involved in a vicious, hurtful prank, and someone needs to rein her in." She looked at him. "It's *Wren*," she said. "Do you understand?"

"Liza?" John said.

"Yes, Liza," Alice said. She spat the name.

"You better come in," John said. He took her elbow and guided her inside. He sat her down at the old pine farm table in the kitchen.

"You want coffee?"

"Sure." When she was nervous, as she was now, she had a habit of wrapping her left thumb and forefinger around her right wrist in a tight circle and then rolling her wrist back and forth within that circle as though trying to break free of handcuffs. She had tried for years to stop doing it. Holding something between her hands, like a mug, helped.

John poured a cup of coffee for her, brought it over, and sat down opposite her. "Tell me," he said.

Alice, her voice tight, told him what Wren had told her just an hour or two ago, although it seemed like days or months now. There was before Wren had been hurt and there was after, and they were two different worlds.

"Shit!" John said, after she'd told him everything. "God, that's terrible."

He looked so pained that Alice warmed to him, a little.

"How's Wren?" he said.

"Crushed," Alice said. "Hurt. Betrayed."

John shook his head. "I am so sorry." He put his elbows on the table and rested his head in his hands. He sat back and shook his head again.

Alice was silent, letting it all sink in. It was odd to be sitting at this table with John. She had spent countless hours here, drinking tea or coffee or wine with Georgia, chattering away while Georgia mixed up cake batter or rolled out fondant. She couldn't remember ever once, in the last twelve years, sitting here with John.

"You're sure it was Liza?" he said. "Wren is sure?"

Alice nodded.

"But *how* do you know? Girls say things—," he began.

"Oh, please. Wren would not lie about this. Why would she make this up? And I saw the e-mails. I don't have *proof* that Liza wrote them, although I'm sure we could find that proof on a computer in this house."

John was silent for a long time. At last he said, "God, this is a mess. I can't tell Georgia; this would upset her beyond belief and she can't be upset right now."

"You can't do *nothing*," Alice said.

"I know that," John said. He looked at her for a long time, then looked down at the table. He began to play with the edge of the blue place mat there, curling the edge up and unrolling it, over and over again.

"I was bullied when I was thirteen," he said. "I don't like to think about it, and I don't like to talk about it. I was skinny and my ears stuck out and I was not very athletic and I loved to cook. Believe me, none of those qualities make you popular among adolescent boys. It got worse and worse. I used to hide in the bathroom during lunch. One day they tackled me in the boys' room, stripped me, took all my clothes, and left me there buck-naked. They also left a girl's dress. So my choice was to walk out into the hallway naked, or in a dress. I chose the dress, of course. I tried to outwait them—I waited forever after the bell rang for everyone to go back to class after lunch—but they had kids lined up and down the hallway." He sighed. "I changed schools. My father wanted me to be an engineer, and I told him the math teachers were terrible and he switched me to a science magnet school in our district. I hated science, but it was better than my old school."

Alice looked at John and saw him not as the easygoing, insouciant, reckless man she had always pictured him to be, but instead as the boy he must have been at twelve or fourteen—tall and thin, with arms and legs too long for his body, those ears that stuck out, uncomfortable in his own skin, terrified and trying not to be.

"So you know," Alice said simply.

"Yeah," John said. "But I can't believe that Liza would do this. Why?"

"I don't know. I've been asking myself the same question."

"I'm not even sure how to handle this," John said. "This is the kind of thing Georgia would handle. She'd know what to do."

"*I* don't know what to do," Alice said, "other than to make sure Wren isn't bullied anymore. Duncan doesn't even know about all this yet."

"I can't tell Georgia," John said. "She's supposed to be resting and not worrying."

"Agreed," Alice said. "So you have to talk to Liza."

John sighed. "Yes, I have to talk to Liza."

Alice pushed back her chair and stood up. "Honestly, *I'd* talk to her but I'm so angry I can't be around her, at least for a little while. I'm sorry."

"Don't be sorry. Look, I'll call you." He stood up and pulled his phone out of his pocket. "What's your cell number?" He looked up at her and smiled. "Funny to think you and Georgia talk every day and I don't even know your phone number."

"Right," Alice said. "And I don't know yours."

"Give me your phone," John said. "I'll put mine in your contact list." He took the phone she handed to him and started to punch in his number.

"Wait," Alice said. "Sometimes Wren picks up my phone. I don't want her to know you're texting me or calling me, because she's going to think I've told you about Liza. She really, really didn't want me to talk to you and Georgia, at least not yet."

John shrugged. "I'll change my name." He finished typing and handed it back to her. "There. I'm Jane. What's your number?"

She told him.

"Okay. You're Alec on my phone, for the same reason. That way if Liza picks it up and sees a text from you she won't wonder why we're in touch."

"Very James Bondish of you," Alice said. She put the phone in her pocket.

John smiled and raised one eyebrow at her. "What's life without a little intrigue?" he said. His smile faded.

"Alice, I'm sorry," he said. "I am."

His eyes were so dark brown the pupils almost disappeared, making his eyes look black, bottomless. She remembered Georgia's voice saying, *"Most people—well, at least most men—are uncomfortable with a lot of eye contact. But John, he'll stare into your soul."* Alice shivered.

"Thank you," she said. Then she turned and walked out the door, and went home to her husband and child.

12

Georgia
Seven Months Earlier, December 2011

She is amazing," Polly said. "Honestly, I wouldn't have expected it."

"It kills me I can't be there," Georgia said.

She was sitting propped against the old oak headboard of her bed at home, wearing yoga pants and one of Liza's hoodies, with the phone pressed against her ear. After her bleeding episode in the Adirondacks, she had been ordered on "limited bed rest" for the duration of her first trimester, which was ending in one more agonizing week. Everything was fine; the bleeding had stopped almost as soon as it had begun. Still, better safe than sorry, Dr. Gopal said. So Georgia had spent the last six weeks in bed, getting up only to go to the bathroom, brush her teeth, and fix herself lunch. She had moved through every stage of emotion—fear, anxiety, depression, anger, boredom—and now the boredom, the *crushing* boredom, was blooming into furious frustration because Chessy was in labor and Georgia wasn't there.

"Ez is a champ," Polly said. "He's in with her now. She's re-fused all meds—she hasn't even had Tylenol, for God's sake—and she's doing this focused breathing that I always thought was bullshit, to tell you the truth. But then, I signed up for an epidural the minute the anesthesiologist said hello."

"God, I want to be there," Georgia said. Georgia herself had eschewed all pain medication when she'd given birth to Liza. Of course John—the man who hated blood and needles and couldn't even look at ear piercings too closely—thought she was crazy. "It's some macho female thing," he had said. "I don't really get it. But it's your body. Your choice." And he had stood by her head and told her to keep breathing and tried not to look too shocked when she'd let out those otherworldly screams there at the very end. She would have been able to help Chessy so much!

"I want to talk to her," Georgia said. "Can I talk to her?"

Georgia heard footsteps, a door opening, someone panting, a curse. Polly's voice returned. "Georgie? I'm sorry. Things are getting kind of intense right now. I'll call you as soon as I can. I'm sorry you can't be here, too. Focus on *your* baby; that's your job right now. Love you."

Georgia threw her phone down on the bed. She looked at the clock; six more hours until Liza got home from school; almost twelve hours until John would return. She tried to imagine Chessy in labor. She thought about Ez, who was so shy he had spent almost forty-five minutes repairing a clogged drain in her kitchen one night when she'd had him over for dinner, because it meant he didn't have to spend as much time trying to talk at the dinner table. She tried to imagine Ez coaching Chessy through her labor. She thought about her own labor, about John's face when he had first seen Liza. He had been so excited (or so disgusted, because the baby was coated in blood and that white stuff) that he hadn't been able to figure out her gender.

"Go ahead, Dad, tell Mama the sex," the doctor had said, holding the baby up in John's face. And John had just stared, his mouth a round O of surprise. "I don't know!" he said. They had all had a good laugh about that later. She wondered what it would be like when she gave birth to this baby.

She stared at a crack in the plaster ceiling—a crack she now knew intimately, like the lines on her own face—and tried to think about something else, like cakes. Over the past weeks she had distracted herself, or tried to, by designing different cakes in her head, things she'd never tried before, like a cake in the shape of Briggs Stadium, her father's favorite ballpark, or an Eiffel Tower cake with fireworks shooting out of the top. She was sick of cakes.

She reached across the bed for her phone and called Alice, who had been oddly out of touch these last few weeks. She and Alice usually talked on the phone at least once a day, and got together several times a week to walk or have coffee or a glass of wine. Georgia would have expected Alice to drop by even more often now that she was confined, to cheer her up in her usual efficient, no-nonsense Alice way. But instead Alice had been absent, too busy to even chat on the phone.

Maybe Alice felt weird about the egg donation, Georgia thought, now that the pregnancy was a reality. Or maybe she felt guilty about the fact that Georgia was on bed rest, felt like she'd contributed a faulty egg. Or maybe she felt strange about her genetic connection to the baby now. It was hard to know *what* went on inside Alice's well-coiffed head.

Georgia herself felt better and better about all of it. Georgia wanted a baby that looked just a *little* like her, and given the fact that she and Alice had the same color hair and similar eyes, this baby would. Even more important, Alice's eggs were a known entity, no risk that ten years hence the baby would turn out to be a psychopath or suffer some horrible genetic illness because

of a history that hadn't come out in the egg donor question-
naire. And now that her breasts were tender and her abdomen
bloated and her body *felt* so pregnant, she realized that it was
just like being pregnant with Liza. This baby would know the
steady beat of her heart, her sudden flushes of anxiety. And she
would know if the baby was energetic or calm, liked tomatoes
or bluegrass music (which Liza had responded to in utero). Already she felt that the whole process of carrying this baby created a bond as real and strong and true as John's connection to
the baby, or Alice's. This baby was Georgia's, her beloved, her
own. She could feel it in her bones.

Alice's phone rang and rang, and Georgia hung up without leaving a message. She picked up the laptop computer,
which lay beside her on the bed, and flipped it open. Liza had
borrowed the computer last night to work on a homework
project, and Georgia was pleased that John, who had been
more thoughtful than usual throughout her time in bed, had
brought it back down from Liza's room this morning so Georgia wouldn't walk up the stairs. Over the past weeks she had
streamed every episode of every television show that had ever
caught her attention, and a few that hadn't. What else was
there to do?

Liza's Facebook page was open on the screen. Georgia saw a
series of messages, a back-and-forth between Liza and Emilie.

Wren is causing big problems, Emilie had written. *She's telling
everyone you're a bitch. Today she told everyone at lunch you're
just jealous. She says you* wish *a guy would want to actually have
conversations with you, and that's why you did it.*

I hate Wren, Liza had written back. *She wants everyone to
hate me.*

From Emilie: *She was crying in English today. She told Ms.
O'Connell that you were really mean.*

From Liza: *She is going to get me in so much trouble.*

Georgia stared at the screen in shock for a minute, and read the messages again. Wren! How dare she! What a terrible way to treat Liza, especially after all their years of friendship. Georgia could feel her heart pump faster, the anger fill her veins. Why, they were like sisters. *Sisters.* Shit. Georgia sat up in bed. She and John and Alice and Duncan had spent two whole counseling sessions discussing what and when to tell their daughters about the egg donation. They had finally decided to wait until after the baby was born, in case something went wrong during the pregnancy. And while Georgia had anticipated that Liza and Wren might not stay as close as they had been as kids, she had never imagined that they might actually hate each other one day. What now?

Georgia picked up her phone. This time, she didn't call Alice, since Alice never answered. Instead, she texted Alice, three words: *Liza and Wren?*

Her phone buzzed seconds later.

"Georgia?"

"Yes! You are so hard to reach these days."

"I'm sorry. Work has been crazy—finals are next week. What's this about Liza and Wren?"

"I don't know. Why don't you tell me?"

Alice paused. "Did Liza say something to you?"

"About what?"

"I don't know. About Wren? Why do you think there's something going on between Liza and Wren?"

Georgia drew in a deep breath. "Because I just read a bunch of messages on Facebook about Liza and Wren. Liza left her Facebook account open on the computer. And it seems pretty clear from what I read that Wren is bullying Liza."

"What?"

Alice's voice was so shocked, so outraged, that Georgia felt a little better. Alice *should* be shocked and outraged that Wren, of all people, would be cruel to Liza.

"I've got the messages right in front of me."

"Wren is bullying Liza." Alice said this as a statement, but her voice sounded confused, as though she were trying to convince herself that such a thing might be possible.

"Well, yes." Georgia read Emilie's message out loud to Alice.

Alice responded with a long silence. "I'm sure there is more to it," she said at last.

"More to *what?*" Georgia said, feeling outraged herself. "Wren is telling other girls Liza is a 'bitch.' And she's telling *teachers* bad things about Liza. What more do you need to know?"

"I'll talk to Wren," Alice said. "You shouldn't worry about this right now."

Georgia felt the same fierce rush of maternal love she had felt when she had held Liza for the first time. "I'm on limited bed rest, Alice, which doesn't make me of limited mental capacity."

The words sounded harsh, harsher than she intended, but there they were, slicing through the easy rapport of all the years of their friendship. But friendship was one thing; her daughter was another.

"Of course not. I didn't mean it that way."

Georgia sighed. "I'm sorry. But the idea of these girls attacking Liza, or spreading rumors about her—kids can be so mean, and now with the Internet and cell phones it's even worse. It makes me feel like killing someone."

"I understand," Alice said. "*Believe me,* I understand. Listen, Georgia, I wasn't trying to insult you. And I know it must be agonizing to be stuck in bed. But let me talk to Wren and see what's going on. Just give me a little time before you talk to Liza."

"Why?" Georgia said. "What difference does it make if I talk to Liza?"

"You don't need all this drama." Alice sounded flustered.

"Well, I've got it, don't I? I can't give up on mothering just because I'm pregnant." After the words left her mouth Georgia realized how ridiculous they sounded.

Alice exhaled, a long, slow breath. "I know," she said. "I'm sorry."

Georgia's anger diminished, a little. She felt sorry for Alice. It would be a shock to find out your child was a bully, a kind of commentary on your own parenting. And Wren wasn't a bad kid. To tell the truth, Georgia wouldn't have imagined that Wren—still so immersed in her ballet slippers and Gail Carson Levine books and American Girl decorating tips—could get caught up so quickly in this adolescent Mean Girl bullshit.

"It's not you, Alice," Georgia said, trying to make her voice warm and generous. "Kids do strange things. Even though Wren is involved in this bullying, I'm sure it won't last. And I'm sure you'll handle it the right way and she'll learn something from it."

But she was talking to the air. Alice had hung up.

LIZA WANDERED INTO Georgia's room after school, an apple in one hand and her cell phone in the other.

"Hey, Doodle. How was school?"

Liza sat down in the armchair across from the bed, threw her legs over the arm of the chair, and rolled her eyes. "Please do not call me 'Doodle.' Fine."

"What's going on?"

"With what?" Liza took a bite of her apple.

"With school?"

"Nothing. It's middle school. It sucks."

"Don't say 'sucks,'" Georgia said. "How's Wren? I haven't seen her in a while."

"Wren?" Liza put her apple down and swung her legs around, so she was sitting upright. "What do you mean? Why?"

Georgia looked at her daughter. "You left your Facebook open on the computer, honey. I saw some messages there between you and Emilie, and I'm worried. I know Alice is my best friend, but if Wren is bullying you, you can talk to me about it."

Liza blushed a furious red, and looked down at the floor, then up at Georgia. "I can't believe you read my Facebook!"

"It was up on the screen, Liza."

"It's private."

"Sweetheart—"

"Wren is not bullying me. Stuff is always going on with the girls this year." Liza slid down in the armchair until her chin was almost resting on her chest.

"I read what Emilie wrote, about the things Wren has been saying about you. That's not okay."

Liza sat up again and faced Georgia. "*Mom.* Were you ever in middle school? People say mean stuff about each other all the time. You can't worry about it."

"Of course I worry about it."

Liza sighed. "Well, don't. Dad says you're not supposed to worry about anything right now, because of the baby."

Lord. John and Alice, between the two of them, were so overprotective that Georgia was starting to feel sorry she had told either one of them she was even pregnant.

"I can handle it. Do you want to tell me what's going on with Wren?"

"Nothing." Liza fiddled with the edge of her sleeve. "Everyone loves Wren. She's tiny and pretty and nice and good at everything. She dances and she's a cheerleader and she's good at every sport. Everyone loves her."

Georgia looked at her daughter, with her too-long legs and arms, her too-tight jeans, her beautiful face covered in too much foundation. "People love you, too, Liza."

Liza shrugged. "Not like they love Wren." She put her apple

down on Georgia's dresser. "I have a ton of homework. Do you need anything before I go upstairs?"

Georgia wished she could pull Liza into bed with her and cuddle her the way she used to when Liza was two, or six, or even ten, her arms wrapped around her, her chest pressed against Liza's rib cage. When Liza was tiny, a bright-eyed toddler of one or two, Georgia used to spoon her and whisper nonsense into her ear: "I love you more than applesauce. I love you more than cupcakes."

"Honey—"

"Don't worry, Mom. Everything's fine." And she was out the door and up the stairs before Georgia could even remind her to take her apple core from the dresser and throw it away.

ALICE STOPPED BY at midday the next day, with a batch of carrot-ginger soup, a salad with apples and walnuts, and a crusty baguette from the expensive little grocer Georgia loved. Georgia felt some trepidation when she heard Alice's voice in the front hall, her cheery "Georgia? Lunch!" and the sure tap of her heels on the hardwood floor.

Georgia had hoped when she heard the knock on the front door that it would be Chessy, who had given birth to a daughter at 5:55 P.M. the day before and had promised to come by with the baby as soon as she left the hospital. "Tell me everything," Georgia said, when Chessy had called with the news. "I'm not telling you anything," Chessy said. "I'm not one of those women who goes on and on about my dilation and effacement and every push. Forget it. It was *intense*, that's the only word for it." And Georgia had had to be satisfied with that, at least until she saw Chessy and the baby in person.

Alice heated up the soup and brought a tray in to Georgia, with a linen napkin and a bud vase with a late-blooming camellia she had plucked off the tree by her back door.

"You're babying me," Georgia said. "I am allowed to get up to make lunch."

"So enjoy being babied," Alice said. "You'll have your hands full soon enough."

Georgia scootched up against the headboard, and Alice put the tray on her lap. Alice sat down on the end of the bed, by Georgia's feet.

"I talked to Liza," Georgia said.

Alice stiffened.

"And of course she told me there's nothing to worry about, but I can't help but worry. And I talked to John about it, or tried to, but he was so odd. He said he'd take care of it, which surprised me, because he usually wants nothing to do with this kind of 'drama,' as he calls it. Did you talk to Wren?"

Alice nodded. "I'm sure there's a lot we don't know. I hope it will blow over."

Georgia thought this was a ridiculous response from responsible, thorough, efficient Alice. "Blow over? But—"

"Georgia!"

Alice stood up at the sound of the front door opening, and Polly's voice.

"Are you decent? The gang's all here, and I mean *all*."

Chessy came in first, wearing a flowing rust-colored top with a batik print and black leggings, with the baby in her arms. Polly was behind her, holding on to Teddy with one hand. Ez, who looked as though he hadn't slept in four days (and likely had not), hung back in the doorway, probably hoping another male might show up to mitigate the overwhelming estrogenic effect of Chessy, Polly, Georgia, and Alice all reveling over a new baby, and a female baby at that. Ez shot Teddy a quick look of solidarity, but Teddy was already on the floor trying to slide under the bed. Ez looked like he wished he could do the same.

Alice scooped up the lunch tray and took it over to the

dresser, and Chessy sat down on the edge of the bed, leaning forward so Georgia could see the baby's face inside the bundle of blankets.

"She's so big!" Georgia said. She noted the baby's hair, a soft brown, and her eyes, a pale gray. Maybe her baby would look like this one, plump and brown haired and light eyed. Ez had dark hair and dark eyes, like John.

"Eight pounds, twelve ounces," Polly said.

"She's fat," Chessy said, "so she certainly doesn't take after Polly."

"Does she have a name?" Georgia held her breath. She had hoped Ez would be willing to give up on the E-L-F naming tradition in the Fletcher family.

"Lily. Lily Blue Francesca Fletcher," Chessy said.

"Lily Blue?"

"Yes. I love the name Lily and she was conceived during a blue moon. Lily Blue." Chessy's voice dared her to argue.

Ez, still holding up the door frame, blushed at the mention of conception. Chessy shot him a look. "After the last thirty-six hours, Ez, you can't be embarrassed because I say the word *conceived*. I mean, you just saw—"

Ez raised a hand. "Yeah, I know what I saw."

Georgia took the baby from Chessy's arms and held her, bent forward to sniff the top of the baby's head. "Oh, Chessy. She is so beautiful."

Georgia held the baby for the entire half hour they all stayed. Alice tried to leave, but Polly waved her back, saying, "Oh, come on. You're family, too." Alice did come over to admire the baby, who was fast asleep in Georgia's arms, but professed no desire to hold her. Georgia asked for details about the birth, at which point Ez turned pale and Chessy said, "Forget it. I vowed never to be a 'birth story' person and I have no intention of going back on that vow." Then Polly said she had to pick up

Gracie, her five-year-old, from kindergarten, and Chessy said she had to go, too, because she had completely ignored Pickup Chicks while she was in the hospital and at least had to check her e-mail.

There was a lengthy search for Polly's keys, which were found in the basement after Teddy confessed to dropping them down the laundry chute. Chessy and Ez had to change the baby's diaper, which involved pulling way too many supplies out of an overstuffed diaper bag and way too much discussion about the best way to hold the baby's legs and wipe her bottom and fasten the sticky tape on the front of the diaper, until Polly finally said, "You could have negotiated peace in the Middle East in the amount of time it's taken you to change one diaper. Can we get going, please?"

Georgia felt buoyed by all of it, light with hope after the fear and boredom of the last few weeks. Here she was, pregnant with the baby she had so longed for, surrounded by her sisters and this beautiful, healthy baby of Chessy's and by Alice, her dearest friend. Her business was booming and she loved her work, and John was happy with Bing's, which was booming, too. Sure, Liza was a bit of a worry, but what adolescent wasn't? She had everything she had ever wanted, and more.

She flashed a smile as Polly bent to kiss her, as Ez held up the baby's tiny arm in a little wave good-bye. Even Chessy said, "I can't remember when I've seen you look so happy, Georgie," and made some wry joke about labor and childbirth wiping the smile off her face. Everyone laughed—everyone, that is, except Alice, who had looked solemn throughout the entire visit.

But then, Georgia thought, *if my child was a bully I'd probably feel kind of blue, too.*

13

Alice
Ten Months Earlier, August 2011

I'm sorry," the postal clerk said, "but the machine won't accept your debit card. Do you have another card?"

Alice stared at her, confused. She was paying for a roll of stamps, forty-four dollars, and could not believe their checking account was so depleted. She had paid the bills just two days ago, and Duncan's paycheck should have gone into the account this morning.

"Today is Friday, right?" Alice said.

The clerk nodded. "Do you have another card you want to use?"

In a daze, Alice handed over her credit card, rolling through numbers in her brain. Once she was back out in the car, she logged on to their checking account and there it was, in red letters: "Balance, -$115.43."

She called Duncan. "I'm sorry, Alice," he said, "but I can't discuss this right now. I've got to be in court at two."

"Of course you do," she said. For a minute she felt badly

about being snippy with Duncan, who was never snippy, but then she thought: *Why shouldn't I be upset? Why do I have to figure all this stuff out?*

She had always felt proud of her egalitarian marriage and her egalitarian husband, the man who cleaned up the kitchen every night after dinner, who reorganized the pantry and tossed out any can or carton past its due date, who ironed his own shirts. When some of the other women in her book group or fitness class complained about their husbands, Alice was notably silent. She didn't have anything to complain about. Duncan noticed when she was tired; he noticed when things needed to be done; he pitched in and helped all the time. She was lucky.

But things had been less egalitarian since he had started this job with the Innocence Project. Little chores that had been his domain had fallen to her, like booking the rental house for their summer trip to the Outer Banks, or collecting all the recycling on Tuesday nights, or untangling all the doctors' bills and insurance claims. It hadn't seemed like much at first, but over the past four months the list of things Alice had taken on so Duncan could save the world had become a little overwhelming, and the resentment she felt was beginning to seep into all the corners of their life.

Their finances had taken a hit, too. Alice wasn't afraid of living on a tight budget—she had spent most of her life doing without—but she did feel that Duncan should at least have talked it over with her before making this huge change. She said as much after dinner that night, once Wren had gone up to bed and she and Duncan were in the living room in their usual spots, Duncan in the armchair with his feet up on the ottoman, his computer on his lap, Alice on the leather sofa, folding laundry.

"You know our checking account is overdrawn," she said. She stood up so she could fold one of the big flat sheets from their bed, careful that it didn't brush against the crystal vase on the coffee table.

"Right. I'll figure it out," he said.

She put the folded sheet on the bottom of the empty laundry basket. "I didn't realize things were that tight."

"It's just juggling," he said. "Sometimes I mail a bill and it gets there faster than I thought, before our paychecks go in. I'll take care of it."

Alice felt an edge of irritation. "Maybe I should handle the bills," she said. "Because you're so busy these days."

"This is the first time we've been overdrawn," Duncan said. "It won't happen again."

"It never happened when you were at Covington," Alice said.

Duncan looked up from his laptop. "And what's your point?"

Alice pushed the laundry basket away. "We are living paycheck to paycheck now, and we haven't done that for *years*. To be honest, I'm still surprised that you made this job change without discussing it with me first."

"You knew I hated my job at Covington."

"Yes. But a lot of lawyers hate their jobs. It's not that I expected you to stay there forever if you were unhappy, but why didn't you talk to me about it?"

"I did. I told you about that case I worked on, with that woman from Dynergy. She should never have been convicted."

Alice nodded. "Right."

"It just wasn't fair." Duncan shook his head. "And I hate that."

"I know," Alice said. "But it's quite a leap from working on *one case* that ended badly to quitting your job as partner to work for a nonprofit. And I admire the work you do—I do. I believe in it. But why didn't you talk to me before you jumped?"

"Because I thought you knew how I felt."

"How could I know how you felt if you didn't talk to me?"

"Because you're my wife."

Duncan said this with a certain stubbornness, the same way you would say "Because the sky is blue" or "Because the earth is round" or something else that was so obvious it shouldn't require explanation.

Alice raised her eyebrows. "And—?"

"And you knew I wasn't the kind of person who would be happy forever representing investment companies in insider trading investigations. I made a leap to doing something that really matters to me."

"I understand that." Alice didn't know how to make her point without sounding selfish, as though she didn't care that some poor sod spent nineteen years in jail for a crime he didn't commit. "Of course I want you to have work you love, but you made a leap from a job that paid a lot of money to a job that pays a lot less money and that requires you to work more hours. I'm not saying that's wrong, but it's affected our life quite a bit."

His pale blue eyes caught hers. "Our mortgage is small because we bought the house in 1998, and we're both fairly thrifty—or 'Scottish,' as my mother would say. I didn't think it would be a problem."

"You still should have talked to me," she said. To Alice, this whole issue revealed the downside of his desire to protect her, to guide her, to watch over her. She had loved his protectiveness at nineteen; now that she was in her thirties she didn't want to be protected quite so much.

"I don't question your decisions," he said. "What made you decide you wanted to donate an egg to Georgia? That came out of the blue, in my opinion."

"I talked that over with you," she said, throwing the unfolded pillowcases back in the basket. "We talked about it for weeks."

He shrugged.

Alice couldn't really explain—not even to herself—why she wanted to donate her eggs to Georgia. But the minute Georgia had mentioned the idea of donor eggs, back in April, Alice's first thought had been *Mine. Georgia could have my eggs.* The idea had lurked in her mind even before that, on days when she and Georgia would run across a mom with a young baby in Starbucks or at the mall, and Georgia's features would shift, her smile would dim, and sorrow and longing would color her whole being. *I would give you a baby.* She was six years younger than Georgia, healthy, fit, in her prime childbearing years. But she was an uncomfortable mother; Georgia was a natural.

Part of it was her own yearning for the kind of mother she had never had, as well as her yearning for the kind of mother she would never quite be. Part of it was her longing for a sister, for someone who would be her friend and confidante and adversary and yet linked to her forever through a fierce, shared love. Part of it was her yearning to do something worthwhile, something more meaningful than teaching bored eighteen-year-olds the fine points of Keynesian theory. She had explained all that to Duncan, and to the counselor at the fertility center. Duncan had been fully on board.

"Do you *not* want me to donate my eggs?" she said to him now. "Because I've been on birth control pills and Lupron injections and FSH injections and am about to burst with eggs. If you've changed your mind, now is the time to tell me, not next week."

"I haven't changed my mind," he said. He turned his eyes back to the computer in his lap. Alice watched him for a moment, trying to read his face as he read. The longer she looked at him the more unfamiliar he seemed, like saying a word over and over and over in your mind until it loses all meaning and begins to sound like nonsense.

"Duncan?" She heard the uncertainty in her own voice.

He looked up, and flashed a smile at her and became himself again, pale blue eyes crinkled up at the corners, the smile breaking the stern planes of his face into something friendly, familiar. "What?"

"Nothing," she said. "You'll figure it out about the check-book?"

And he nodded and went back to his computer.

ALICE'S MOTHER SAT across from her in the booth, her fingers drumming against the wooden table. Alice's mother was every-thing Alice was not: petite, blond, absentminded, fond of gold jewelry and bright prints. She wore that kind of blouse now, something silky with a draped neckline, hot pink with black zebra stripes.

"You should have another one, Ally," her mother said. She was passing through D.C. on her way to Florida with Oliver, her latest boyfriend, whose name Alice could only remember because it began with O like *Ohio*, which was where her mother lived now. "I *loved* being in a big family. I would have had a mil-lion more kids if your father had stuck around."

"I'm sure you would have," Alice said, choosing to ignore the dig at her father. She decided not to point out that none of Rita's "love interests," as Rita called them, had stuck around for more than a year or two, which made her father's *three* years with Rita seem like a veritable lifetime of commitment.

Rita could not have picked a worse time to blow through town. Alice was on day nine of her fertility drugs. She had gained almost nine pounds, and her breasts were sore, her ab-domen bloated, and she was so cranky she wanted to stab her mother with a fork when Rita greeted her at the restaurant with, "Ally! You look so much better with some meat on your bones! Don't tell me you've started actually eating dessert!"

This was the way Rita had always talked to her, as though Alice were some kind of robot, a superdisciplined superhuman who didn't know how to let go and have fun like normal people. Alice had tried to point out to her more than once that normal people often had normal childhoods; childhoods in which the adult *acted* like an adult so the child didn't have to. But what was the point? Rita was Rita and she had her own view of the world, and nothing Alice said or did was going to change that now.

"Duncan and I are happy with one," Alice said, wishing the waitress would hurry up with their sandwiches so Rita might get distracted and change the subject. She wondered if Rita, who was so completely clueless about almost anything regarding Alice, had somehow sensed that Alice's body was as ripe and fertile as it could be at this moment. The ultrasound she had had this morning had shown six perfect eggs, and the egg retrieval was scheduled for tomorrow.

"I'm sure you're happy with one," Rita said. "But I bet Duncan wants more."

This was the other thing about her mother: she adored Duncan and was convinced that Alice did not love him/understand him/attend to him as well as she, Rita, would have had *she* been his wife. The fact that Rita had never been a successful partner to anyone other than her cat, Tallulahbelle, for more than thirty-six months was lost on her. Rita thought Alice had made "the catch of the century" when she married Duncan, the lawyer with the impeccable manners and big salary, who had blue eyes and a firm jaw to boot.

"Duncan doesn't want more kids," Alice said.

"Of course he does. That's why he married someone young, like you."

Alice wished, as she had wished her whole life, that her mother would express some interest in Alice herself—her teaching, her research, her work with the PTA, her fitness pursuits, the latest book she'd read, her political views, anything. But her mother tended toward two topics—men and motherhood—and she didn't consider Alice to be particularly informed or competent on either one.

"Actually," Alice said, casting a grateful eye upon the waitress as she placed their sandwiches in front of them, "Duncan married me because he thinks I'm smart, and intriguing, and reliable, and capable, and *sexy as hell*." Duncan had never actually *said* he found Alice "sexy as hell," but Alice threw that in because she knew her mother thought she was too reserved and far from sexy.

Rita looked at her and raised one eyebrow. "Well, I hope that's true," she said. "If that's how he feels after ten or however many years of marriage, good for you."

In fact, Alice wasn't sure Duncan still felt that way at all, but her mother was the last person she could talk to about that. Since he'd started this new job, he'd been even more distracted, more tired. When he came home from work he would brush his lips across her cheek and then disappear into the living room and his laptop. He was tired, and not the "touchy-feely" type anyway, as he said. Alice didn't consider herself "touchy-feely," either, but she did wonder what it might be like to be with someone who came booming into the house after work, calling out her name, or who would come up behind her and wrap both arms around her and nuzzle her neck, the way Cliff Huxtable did to Claire. Their sex life had dwindled to a lazy once a month, a perfunctory conjunction with Alice on top, a quick roll over, Duncan on top, and then a kiss good night.

Rita eyed Alice's sandwich, the "Power Veggie" on seven-grain toast. "All that healthy eating," she said. "You think that really makes a difference?"

Alice paused, one hand holding the sandwich, halfway to her mouth. "Yes," she said. "I do." She had been extra careful with everything she put into her body over the last three months to be sure her eggs were as perfect as they could be for Georgia, without a trace of pesticides or pharmaceuticals or alcohol.

Rita shook her head. "We're all gonna die anyway," she said, picking up the Reuben she had ordered, dripping with melted cheese and Thousand Island dressing. "Might as well have fun."

"I can have fun without eating junk," Alice said, and then wished she could retract her words because they sounded so self-righteous and prissy, all the things her mother accused her of being.

"Well, I believe in having fun," Rita said. She put her sandwich back down on the plate. "And speaking of fun, Ally, listen. I came through town today on purpose, kind of, to see you. Ollie has a great job opportunity in Chile, and I think we're going to go."

"In Chile? What does he do?"

"He's a mechanic, he works on big trucks. There's lots of opportunity down there and it seems like an adventure."

"An adventure?" To her surprise, Alice felt a sudden panic, the same panic she had felt at six or nine or ten when Rita would head out the door for the evening. *Don't go!* She pressed her lips together to keep the words inside her mouth.

Rita picked up her sandwich and took a big bite. She nodded.

"But for how long? Where will you live? What about Wren?" Rita was a haphazard grandmother at best, but Wren adored her nonetheless.

"A couple of years, maybe two or three," Rita said, when she finished chewing. She picked up her napkin and wiped her mouth. "You can fly down and visit with Wren. It'll be a great adventure for you. We'll be in Santiago, I think. Ollie has the details."

Alice pressed her knees together under the table so her legs wouldn't shake. It was absurd, this reaction of hers.

"But you're fifty-two." *What a stupid thing to say.*

Rita arched one eyebrow at her, the same thing Duncan did to express surprise, dismay, puzzlement. "And what does that have to do with anything?"

"I don't know." Alice felt herself flush and turned her face toward the window, away from her mother. "What if you get sick and you're in Chile? Or what if I get sick or Duncan dies or something?"

The panic Alice felt was as unexpected as her mother's news, an icy ball of fear that started in her belly and rose into her chest and throat. It was crazy, because Alice and Rita had never been close, not even when Alice was little. Rita had been an indifferent mother at best; a dangerously negligent mother at worst. But she was, still, Alice's mother, the only mother she would ever have, and Alice could not imagine a world without her. She thought suddenly of her grandfather, her mother's father, who had visited once when she was a little girl. She had had a bad earache, and he had leaned forward to blow a warm breath of cigar smoke into her ear. It had soothed the pain right away. She longed for that kind of comfort now.

"I'm not eighty," Rita said. "And I'm going to Chile, not Antarctica. And you and Duncan both look pretty healthy to me."

"I don't want you to go—" Alice wanted to say "Mom," but she had never called Rita anything other than "Rita" her whole life. "Okay?" There, she had said it.

Rita smiled at her and reached across the table to pat her hand. "You're a funny girl, Ally. You always were. You'll be fine if I go—you're a married woman with an almost-grown-up girl of your own and a good job. It won't matter much to you if I'm in Ohio or Argentina."

"But—"

"You should eat this Reuben," Rita said. "You look good with a few extra pounds." She proffered her sandwich to Alice. "I've got to go soon."

"You can't just tell me something like this and leave," Alice said.

Rita sighed. "I'll come back in three weeks, on our way back home. We can talk more then."

"I don't want to talk more then," Alice said. She felt about six years old again, frightened her mother might never come back. "I want to talk now."

Rita's eyes met Alice's, blue on blue. She picked up the uneaten half of her sandwich, stuffed with corned beef (and all its concomitant nitrates) and processed cheese and pale orange dressing, and held it out to Alice.

Alice took the sandwich from her mother and bit into it. It tasted so good she almost wept.

14

Georgia
Two Months Earlier, April 2012

Georgia had never felt so strange. Not physically—physically she felt wonderful, even though she was more than seven months pregnant now, the sight of her own toes a distant memory under her giant, burgeoning belly. She had gained just seventeen pounds so far, and her ankles and fingers hadn't swelled as they had with Liza, so she could still wear her wedding ring and her favorite shoes. Her hair brushed against her collarbone, glossier than ever, more auburn than ever even though she hadn't had it colored since she got pregnant, and her eyes were clear and bright. She walked every day, often with Chessy and Lily Blue since Alice was so busy now, and her legs were toned and firm, her skin tanned by the spring sun. She glowed.

But inside she felt a strange unease. Every day she woke with the sense that she had forgotten something important, something critical like turning off the gas burner or where she had hidden her mother's diamond ring. But she'd jump up to find the stove cold, her mother's ring where it always was, in a little bag nestled among her lingerie in the top drawer of her dresser. She felt uneasy about Liza, although Liza insisted she was fine, and about John, who had been jumpy and distant for weeks now, turning away from her in bed, averting his eyes when she changed.

"I thought you liked me pregnant," she said to him one night, turning on her side in bed to face him. "Remember with Liza? We had so much sex I thought the baby would come a month early."

"It's not you," John said, lying on his back, eyes closed. "I'm thirteen years older than I was then and I don't have the sex drive I used to. And I work a lot and we have a teenager. Don't worry."

But there it was, that unease. It was like walking into a spiderweb and feeling as though thin, gossamery threads were clinging to you everywhere, even once you'd brushed them away. Something was still there, light as a whisper and unseen.

And Alice was strange, too. Georgia made jokes to herself sometimes about feeling as though *she* were the one who had stepped through the looking glass, into a world in which everything looked normal on the surface, but wasn't, really.

"Pregnancy jitters," Polly scoffed, when Georgia tried to explain how she felt. "It's hormones."

Georgia didn't think so. But because she had no other explanation, she had no choice but to agree.

GEORGIA COULD NOT for the life of her find her phone. She called it from the kitchen phone and it rang and rang, but wherever it was, it was ringing out of earshot. She needed to text Liza, who was at school, to remind her that she was picking her up early today for a three o'clock dental appointment. Maybe she could use John's phone. Georgia tiptoed into the bedroom, where John lay napping, and picked up his phone from his bedside table. He'd worked until one this morning, gotten up at seven for a tennis match, gone back to bed at nine, and was now in a deep, heavy sleep. Georgia tiptoed back out. She stood in the kitchen and started to type out a text to Liza when another text came in, from some guy named Alec.

Enough, it read. Georgia ignored it and continued to tap out her message to Liza. Another text arrived from Alec. *I'm sorry*.

Dear God, Alec, whoever he was, was a pain in the ass. Every time a text came in, Georgia lost track of what she was typing to Liza and had to start all over. The phone beeped again.

You excite me more than any man I've ever known, but I can't do this, Georgia read. *It's over*.

She froze, shook her head to clear it, and looked at the phone again. She must have misread the message. But when she read it a second time, it said exactly the same thing: *You excite me more than any man I've ever known, but I can't do this.*

Alec found John exciting? Georgia felt all the blood drain from her head, then her heart. She grabbed the counter, and even that wasn't enough to calm the dizziness so she sat down abruptly on the floor. Her mind raced so fast she could almost feel it, like little pinballs ricocheting around her brain. John had been acting strangely for months, even before she got pregnant. She remembered that time almost a year ago when she'd called Polly, worrying that John might be having an affair. She remembered talking to Alice about it, and Alice's confidence that John would never cheat. She remembered the odd feeling she'd had about Amelia, although Amelia was so *young*. And even though Alice and Polly had reassured her over and over that she had nothing to worry about, she hadn't been able to still the persistent small voice inside her that said, *Something is wrong*. John had been *absent* from her in some fundamental way for a long time. But she had never, in her wildest dreams, imagined he might be *gay*.

The baby kicked inside her, a thump against her rib cage, and reflexively she put a hand against her belly. She was too stunned to cry. Her mind raced through scene after scene with John—John on their wedding night, using his teeth to peel off her panties; John using a pastry brush to paint whorls of melted chocolate on her breasts and then bending his head to lick it off; why, John had had sex with her right here on this kitchen floor just a year ago. And he was *gay*? Georgia simply could not believe it. But there it was, the evidence, in black and white on the touch screen of John's phone, some man named Alec writing, *You excite me more than any man I've ever known*.

Georgia drew in a deep breath. Maybe there was another explanation. Maybe Alec was apprenticing in John's kitchen at Bing's and was amazed by John's culinary skills. Or maybe he was a new player in John's Tuesday night tennis clinic, and was blown away by John's backhand. But would any heterosexual man ever write to another heterosexual man, "*You excite me*"? No, Georgia thought. Absolutely not.

The doorbell rang. Georgia remained where she was on the floor. She was just so, so *surprised*. Everything she thought she knew, about John, about herself, was dissolving, shifting, like some alien being in a movie.

The doorbell rang again, and someone started knocking. The knocking continued, stopped, and a minute later Georgia heard someone knocking on the glass of the kitchen window and looked up to see Duncan, of all people, peering in at her.

"Are you all right?" he said, his voice loud so she could hear him through the glass.

She nodded.

"I need to talk to you," he said.

This in itself was so bizarre—Duncan arriving at her house at ten on a weekday morning, apparently alone, without Alice— that Georgia was motivated to roll over onto her hands and knees and push herself up into a standing position. She leaned on the counter for a moment to make sure she wasn't still dizzy, but her head seemed fine so she walked around into the hallway and opened the front door.

"Are you okay?" Duncan asked again. "I'm sorry to disturb you. When I saw you sitting on the floor I was worried."

"I'm fine," Georgia said. "But are *you* okay?"

Georgia had never seen Duncan look anything other than serene and unruffled, even in the face of crises large and small. Somehow he always emanated a sense of mild good humor and well-being. Once, the four of them had been out to dinner downtown and as they were walking from the car Duncan had stepped in dog poop on the sidewalk in his good shoes. "My goodness," he'd said, "can you believe that?" He had carefully scraped it off with a piece of folded cardboard. John would have let loose with a stream of choice epithets, kicked the wall, and sulked for thirty minutes if the same thing had happened to him.

But now Duncan looked flustered, with his hair standing up as though he'd run his hands through it repeatedly, a white toothpaste stain on his collar, his polo shirt untucked and hanging out over his khakis.

"Yes, thank you, I'm fine," Duncan said. He stepped into the front hall. He cleared his throat and said, "Well, actually I'm not fine. Can I talk to you?"

"Now?"

Duncan's forehead creased into a worried line. "Is this a bad time? I'm sorry, Georgia, I should have called you first."

Georgia was still trying to imagine John with another man and failing miserably. But she nodded at Duncan and led him into the kitchen, where they both sat down at the old pine farm table.

"I wouldn't have bothered you but this is important. It's about Alice."

Duncan looked so worried, so unstrung, that Georgia forgot John for a minute.

"What is it? Is she hurt?"

"*No*, no. It's—" Duncan paused, and his face twisted. Georgia could see the pain and confusion in his eyes as he tried to wrap his mind as well as his mouth around the words he needed to say.

"I don't know any way to say this, other than to say it straight out," he said. He looked down at the table, then up at Georgia. "Alice is gay."

Georgia stared at him.

"I'm still kind of in shock," Duncan said. "And I wanted to talk to you—you're her best friend. Honestly, I even wondered if maybe you and she"—Duncan's face reddened—"if you two had—I don't know. I don't know how to say this."

Georgia chose to ignore the very bizarre idea that she—almost eight months pregnant—might be having an affair with Alice. "Alice is *gay*?" Georgia said. "How do you know?"

Duncan looked at her. "So you didn't know, either? It's come as a complete surprise to me. I mean, I can't believe it. All these years I've known her, we've been together, we've—" Duncan blushed again. "I don't know what to think." He sat back in his chair and let out a long breath. "That makes me feel a little better, to know that I'm not the only one who had no idea."

"How do you know?" Georgia repeated. She knew she must be dreaming, and if her semiconscious brain could push harder, she'd wake up.

"I found these text messages on her phone," Duncan said.

Something buzzed in Georgia's head. She squeezed her eyes shut tight.

"I know, it stunned me, too," Duncan said. "Last week she fell asleep early one night, and I was out reading in the living room when her phone started beeping. One text message after another kept coming in. Wren was on that field trip last week, the one to Montreal with the French class, and I got worried— she's been through a lot lately—" He stopped and caught Georgia's eye. "I'm sorry. You know. Anyway, so I picked up Alice's phone, and there it was."

"There what was?"

"The message. From someone named Jane."

"What did it say?"

Duncan's blush spread from his collarbone to the roots of his hair, and diffused itself across his face until even his ears were red. He looked at the ceiling. "It said, and I quote, and please excuse the language, Georgia: '*I miss your sweet pussy and can't get enough. I have to see you again.*'"

He brought his eyes down to look at her again. "Jane. Some woman named Jane wrote that to my wife."

Georgia heard the buzz of a fly trapped between the window and the screen behind her. She felt her heart beating in her chest, *thump, thump, thump,* each beat more forceful than ever with all the extra blood whooshing through her veins at this stage of her pregnancy. She looked down at the table and noted the white stain in the wood, made long ago by a wet glass.

"This was last week?" she said at last.

"Yes," Duncan said. "I didn't tell Alice about it, although I did kind of hint to her that I wondered if she might be gay." He blushed. "I'm afraid I even suggested she might be involved with you."

"With *me*?" This was moving from the bizarre to the ridiculous at the speed of light.

"I haven't talked to Alice about it; I haven't talked to anyone about it. But it's been difficult for me. You're her best friend.

I thought she might have talked to you, or you might know—I don't know."

Alec. Jane. Alec. Jane. The idea that John and Alice were both gay *and* had been carrying on affairs *and* hiding their sexual orientations for years—it was too incredible to be believed. And too coincidental. Jane. Alec. Jane. Alec. John. Alice. John. Alice.

Georgia went completely still. She felt her heartbeat in her temples, a throbbing pulse at the side of her head.

"I'm like some terrible cliché," Duncan said. "My whole life—what I thought was my life—has been a lie."

Georgia took a deep breath. "Duncan," she said, "your life has not been a lie. Alice isn't gay."

"What do you mean? The text—"

"*Shh.*" Georgia sat back in her chair. "The text isn't from Jane, it's from John. Your wife is having an affair with my husband."

Duncan looked at her, confused. "John?"

"John is 'Jane.' Alice is 'Alec.' Don't you see?"

"No," Duncan said. "That can't be true."

"It is true." Georgia knew it. She knew it the way she knew she would take a bullet for her child, the way she knew gravity was real. Some things were just irrefutable.

All at once Georgia was exhausted. She closed her eyes. The baby inside her kicked, wriggled, kicked again. She put a hand to her belly. *Hello, you. I'm here.* Her eyes flew open.

This baby she carried, her heart's desire, was the biological child of her husband and his mistress.

Part 2

15

Georgia
June 18, 2012

Georgia refused to let John in the delivery room, which was awkward at first because the nurse kept insisting he should come in. Finally, panting in pain and exasperation, Georgia said, "I don't want him in here because he's having an affair with my best friend, okay?" She didn't go on to say that this baby who was about to be born was the genetic child of her husband and said best friend, because it was too much for Georgia herself to get her mind around, let alone try to explain to a complete stranger. But after the nurse said, "Seriously?" and Georgia nodded and began to brace herself as another contraction rose deep within her, the nurse went to the door and said something to John and whoever else was out there, and Georgia didn't see John again. The nurse, whose name was Lakesha, must have told all the other nurses because everyone was extra nice to Georgia after that, and one nurse even came in and told Georgia the whole story of her own lying, cheating, no-good husband, who had slept with her daughter's teacher for a year.

"And she didn't even get an A," the nurse said with indignation, as though a top grade for her daughter might have eased the sting of her husband's infidelity.

"Maybe if your ex was better in bed Olivia would have gotten the A," one of the other nurses said, and they all laughed.

At that point, though, Georgia didn't give a shit about the nurse's ex-husband or his mistress or the nurse herself or even John, because she couldn't think about anything but the towering pain that was ripping through her now at such short intervals that she couldn't tell where one contraction ended and the next began. At some point Polly came in and took her hand and told Georgia to squeeze it, but Georgia didn't want to touch anyone or anything or *be touched* by anyone or anything. Chessy arrived shortly after that and came over and said, "I thought I could help, but honestly it's making my vagina hurt just to look at you. I'm still sore, you know."

"Chessy, this is not about you," Polly said.

"I *know* that," Chessy said, "but you could still have a little sympathy. I gave birth six months ago to a kid with a head the size of a bowling ball. The memory is pretty fresh."

"I'm sure," Polly said, "but maybe you could get over it for just five minutes and support Georgia."

"I *am* supporting Georgia," Chessy said. "I'm here, aren't I? Even though blood and hospitals freak me out. Just because you have a wide pelvis and babies with small heads doesn't mean you have to be so unempathetic, Polly. Really."

"Me, unempathetic?" Polly said. "Oh, that's rich. Just listen to—"

"Shut up!" Georgia yelled. *"I want drugs."*

Polly called the nurse, who paged the doctor, and the doctor came in and checked her and said, "You're too far along. It's too late."

"You don't know what you're talking about!" Georgia yelled

at her. The doctor smiled in what seemed to Georgia to be a very patronizing way. "It's not too late!" Georgia said. "You're wrong. Give me the epidural now!"

The doctor shook her head and smiled again and Georgia thought she had never hated anyone in the world as much as she hated the doctor and her smile at that moment, but then she remembered John and Alice and decided she hated them more. Just the thought of Alice and her long, lean, workout-honed body made Georgia feel like throwing up, especially as she looked down at her gigantic belly and swollen toes, which were all she could see of her feet. "I'm going to throw up," she said, and the doctor stopped smiling and got a basin and held it for her while she vomited. She wiped her mouth with the back of her hand and tried to smile at the doctor to show she was sorry for screaming at her, but her smile must have come across as some kind of horrible grimace, because Chessy said, "Jesus Christ, Georgie, stop making that face or you're going to give me nightmares for the rest of my life!"

"It won't be long now," the doctor said. "Another ten or fifteen minutes and you'll be ready to push."

Georgia grabbed a fistful of sheet in each hand as the next contraction took hold, riding the wave of pain and waiting for it to peak. In some dark, unthinking part of her she was grateful for the pain, relieved to have something *physical* to wrestle with, to hate, to release.

Georgia had spent most of the last six weeks crying. Things had unraveled very quickly on that Black Tuesday when she discovered the text messages and Duncan arrived at her door. The shock of figuring out the affair had made Georgia sick, literally sick, and she had begun to retch, there at the kitchen table. Duncan—ever the gentleman, even in extremis—grabbed a wastebasket and held her hair as she threw up. The commotion had awakened John, who walked into the kitchen in his T-shirt and boxers, still groggy with sleep, to find Duncan Kinnaird soothing his pregnant wife. At the sight of John, Duncan stood up and threw what Georgia believed must have been the first punch of his life, which caught John on the cheek just under his left eye, opening a cut that bled like crazy. Duncan was so stunned by the success of his punch that much of his anger had dissipated, and he stood there watching the blood pour down John's cheek and saying, "Wow. Oh, wow," over and over. Georgia had finally stopped vomiting and turned around and said to John, "You need to leave. Now."

Duncan wouldn't leave Georgia until he was sure she was okay. He asked her where the kettle was and filled it while she rummaged through the drawers for a navy blue dishtowel (blood doesn't show on navy blue!), which she threw at John, who was in the bedroom trying to put his pants on with one hand while holding a bag of frozen peas to his cheek with the other hand. "Don't bleed on the bed," Georgia said. "Or the rug. Take as much as you can pack because you won't be living here again."

Every time John tried to say something, every time he said, "Georgia—," she held up her hand and said, "Don't. Don't say my name. You don't deserve to say my name." For some reason, she couldn't stand to hear him say it. She needed her name to be solid, real, consistent, because everything else about her self and her life felt unrecognizable now.

Duncan made her a cup of tea and sat at the kitchen table while she called Polly, told her about John and Alice, and asked her to pick Liza up after school and take her overnight while Georgia figured out how to explain to Liza that her father was moving out six weeks before her mother gave birth. John came into the kitchen, the bag of peas now wrapped in the blue dish-towel, his eye swollen almost shut. Duncan looked at once horrified and gratified by what his fist had done to John's face.

"Georgia—," John said once more, at which Georgia winced and Duncan stood up and said, "I think you better leave now," and John had left.

"I'll wait until your sister comes," Duncan said, but Georgia shook her head.

"You have your own life to deal with," she said.

"I don't want to see Alice," he said. "Not yet."

"Do you want me to call her?"

"God, Georgia, no. Of course not."

Georgia felt a strange calm. "I want to talk to her, if it's all right with you."

"If it will help you, okay." Duncan had put his arms around her then in an awkward gesture of comfort, an uneasy hug that was somehow redolent of their spouses' embraces. Georgia pulled away and cleared her throat.

"Thank you," Georgia said. "I'm sorry."

As soon as he left she called Alice. "I know," Georgia said, when Alice picked up the phone.

"What?" Alice said.

"Everything."

Alice didn't speak for a long, long moment. "You mean about Liza and Wren?"

Liza and Wren? "No," Georgia said. "I mean about 'Alec' and 'Jane.'"

"Oh, God."

"Duncan knows, too. And I'm just wondering why, *why*—" Georgia stopped. What did it matter? What did any of it matter? Alice and John had betrayed her, her marriage was over, and that was the reality of Georgia's life now. "Forget it, Alice," she said. "I don't know why I called." And she hung up.

On some level, Alice's betrayal hurt even more than John's. It made no sense, she knew, to feel that way, but there it was. Alice was her friend, her confidante, the person she would have turned to in this crisis for love and empathy and the kind of sensible, objective counsel her sisters couldn't provide because they were so angry. And in some ways Alice's betrayal surprised Georgia more than John's. For years Georgia had devoured the daily advice columns in the *Washington Post*, which had to do with infidelity of some sort four or five times a week. She remembered the year before when she had called Polly because she had some vague sense John was interested in Amelia. These things happened sometimes in long-term marriages. But they didn't happen in long-term *friendships*.

Alice was her rock, her true north, steady and unwavering. Things were clear-cut with Alice; there was right and there was wrong and you did what was right and didn't make excuses. Alice's betrayal was the greatest mystery Georgia had ever encountered in her life.

After that Polly and Chessy arrived, the cavalry charging in, and the next day Georgia had to sit down and talk to Liza. And as much as Georgia hated John, she loved Liza more, and she was not going to poison her against her father. Georgia explained that sometimes people went a little crazy, especially when they were middle-aged, like John.

"Being in your late forties is kind of like puberty," Georgia said. "People can do strange things. Dad has been feeling restless and he needs some time apart so he can think more clearly and then settle down with us again." Of course hell would freeze over and the skies would rain red drops before she would ever let John move back in, but Georgia thought it best to take things one step at a time.

She explained how much they both loved Liza. She reassured Liza that *it was not her fault*, not even one-tenth of one percent her fault. She didn't say that John was such an incomparable asshole that his visage should grace the marquee of the Asshole Hall of Fame. She didn't mention Alice, and she didn't say anything about the baby, because of course Liza had no idea that her soon-to-be sibling had been conceived via a donor egg.

Liza had been upset; of course she'd been upset. But Polly and Chessy came by and talked to her; over the next few weeks her friends rallied around her. And to tell the truth, it was something to be so central to the drama that everyone in their small town was talking about, about Georgia and John Bing's sudden separation, with that poor Georgia seven and a half months pregnant. Liza was the center of a lot of attention.

It was messy; it was distracting. Georgia was grateful for Liza's distraction because it meant she failed to notice the most basic things, like the fact that Alice never came around, even though she was Georgia's best friend and this was the biggest crisis of Georgia's life. But given the unpleasantness between Wren and Liza earlier in the year, maybe that didn't seem so strange.

Georgia had had just one brief conversation with John in the last six weeks, a phone call that lasted long enough for her to let him know that she would not say anything negative about him to Liza; that he should find a new—and permanent—place to live; and that she had already hired a very good lawyer.

"I'm sorry," he said.

"Oh, well, that changes everything," Georgia said, her voice thick with rage.

"What about the baby?" he said.

Georgia didn't know. She didn't know what to do with the fact that this baby she knew and loved already with all her heart was the baby of her husband and his mistress. She was so conflicted she couldn't talk about it, not even to Chessy and Polly.

"I just want to get through the birth," she said. "I can only cope with this one little piece at a time."

But now the baby was here. Georgia wanted to yowl with the pain, and did. She hated John, she missed John, she wanted

John. She felt the same way about Alice. She loved the baby; she hated the baby; she didn't want to see the baby; she couldn't wait to hold the baby. More than anything, she wanted her mother, who had been dead now for more than twenty years, or her father, who had been dead for four.

At last, with a long, guttural scream that was so animal-like Georgia did not even recognize it as her own, she pushed the baby out of her body and into the harsh, glaring world.

16

Alice
June 18–19, 2012

*A*lice heard about her son at the grocery store. It was one of the strangest moments of her life, standing in the checkout line at Harris Teeter, fumbling in her purse for her frequent buyer card, and hearing a woman two people behind her say, "Do you know Georgia Bing? She had her baby. A little boy."

Alice had been in meetings all day, and stopped at the store on the way home to pick up something for dinner. At the mention of Georgia's name, she looked up to see someone she recognized vaguely from PTA meetings, Sophie, with a last name Alice couldn't remember, whose son was in the same grade as Wren and Liza. She was talking on her phone, one hand resting on the handle of her grocery cart.

"Right," Sophie Something said. "They're separated. It's sad. We're setting up a dinner brigade. I'll e-mail you the sign-up."

Poor Georgia, Alice thought, thinking of the succession of lasagnas likely to descend on Georgia's doorstep. And then she felt a flush spread through her body, an electric tingle that started at the top of her head and radiated down her arms and legs. A baby that was half Alice was out in the world now, a boy, a son—hers, but not hers at all.

All along, Alice had believed that Georgia's baby was Georgia's baby. "It's like donating blood or a kidney," Duncan had said. And in some ways, to Alice it seemed even less real than that. Why, when you gave blood you could sit there and watch it flow out of your vein and into the plastic tubing and on into the bag, red and rich and real. Alice had never seen the eggs she'd given to Georgia; never seen the embryo one had become. And Georgia's burgeoning belly had felt like it had nothing to do with her, Alice, at all. It was Georgia who threw up every day for three months, Georgia who gained all those pregnancy pounds, Georgia whose ankles swelled, whose back ached, whose skin grew dappled with faint, silvery stretch marks. It was not Alice.

But now now the baby was here and Alice couldn't help but wonder about him. Did he have her long hands and feet, her oval face, her fine, straight hair? Was he solemn and watchful, the way Wren had been? Did he look like John?

Alice paid for her groceries in a trance. She was shocked when she pulled into her driveway and turned off the engine to realize that she was home; she hadn't even been aware she was driving the car. She sat there for a moment, with the windows open, the warm June sun streaming in through the windshield, listening to a squirrel rustling in the hydrangea bushes along the side of the driveway. Georgia, John, Duncan, Wren, the baby—so many people pushing themselves into her thoughts, and yet the person she couldn't stop thinking about was her mother.

Rita would love to know she had another grandchild—of sorts. But of course Alice hadn't told her about the egg donation. Rita had left for Chile in February, almost four months ago. And now that she was gone, Alice missed her more than she could have imagined. Maybe she could have visited her in Ohio, talked to her about this whole sorry mess. At the very least, Rita would not have judged her. She had made far too many mistakes of her own to look harshly on the mistakes of others—something Alice had not understood or appreciated until now.

Alice was as lonely as she had ever been in her life, and she had been a lonely child. She had lost her only real girlfriend in losing Georgia; she had lost John, who had been her closest friend throughout the bullying ordeal; and she might still have lost Duncan. She had earned every one of her losses through her own choices, and she knew it. Even Rita—Alice had spent her life judging Rita for her many lapses, keeping her at arm's length, feeling superior. And now Rita was gone, too, at least for the foreseeable future. But Alice had a daughter to care for, a job to execute, a household to manage, a marriage to salvage. All that was left for her was to pick up the pieces and go forward.

Alice wiped the tears from her cheeks with the palms of both hands. She cried all the time now—she, who until this year could have counted on both hands the number of times she had cried. With Duncan and Wren she was as possessed as she had always been, at least most of the time. (She *had* cried in front of Duncan that night last month when she had sprained her ankle.) But when she was alone—in the car, in the shower, in her tiny, windowless office at AU—she wept and wept. Now that she had started crying, at the ripe of old age of thirty-four, her supply of tears seemed bottomless. Alice sighed and opened the car door, got out, lifted the bags from the trunk, and carried them into the house.

When Duncan walked in the door after work, she waited for him to put his briefcase down by the back door and riffle through the stack of mail on the counter before saying anything. At last, when he put the mail down and looked over at her, she said, "Georgia had her baby. A boy."

"Really." His voice was a statement, not a question. Then, "Is she all right?"

"I think so. I found out only because I overheard someone at Harris Teeter talking about it." She didn't want him to think she'd been in touch with John. She wondered if John had seen his son yet. She had had no contact with John or Georgia after that one brief, awful phone call from Georgia, on the Day Everything Fell Apart. She didn't know anything about either one of them, other than what she heard in passing at PTA meetings or track meets or from Wren. She knew only that Georgia had not told anyone in town about Alice's affair with John, and she knew it because people in town still smiled at her and spoke to her and called to ask if she could help out with field day or the bake sale.

"Well," Duncan said. "They have a lot to figure out."

Alice nodded. This was yet another thing she had lost, in her mind: the right to talk about Georgia or John to Duncan.

"What if she doesn't want to keep the baby?" Duncan said.

The air in the room was still in the sultry heat of the June afternoon; Alice hadn't turned on the air-conditioning for the summer yet, hoping for a few more days of open windows and fresh air. She had thought of this. It was hard to imagine any woman wanting to raise such a baby, a baby who would be a constant reminder of the greatest betrayal and heartache of your life.

On the other hand, the woman at the heart of this drama was *Georgia*, the most natural, loving mother Alice had ever known, the woman who could pick up a red-faced, screaming baby and stare and coo as though she were gazing at something exquisite and beautiful. Why, once she and Georgia had been out walking and had run across a woman wheeling a sleeping infant in a stroller. Georgia had stopped and asked if she could peek at the baby, and the woman—a pretty enough woman, with blond hair and blue eyes—had pulled down the blankets from around the baby's head to reveal the ugliest baby Alice had ever seen. The baby had a sloping forehead, and so much hair not only on her head but also around her temples and at the base of her neck that it looked like fur. Her eyebrows were thick and furry, too, and she had squinty little eyes and a flat nose. Alice had been wide-eyed with surprise, speechless, but Georgia had squealed and said, "Oooh, she's gorgeous. Look at that perfect little rosebud mouth. I could just eat her up." And it was true, the baby's one redeeming feature had been her mouth, something Alice hadn't even noticed in her shock at the baby's overall beastliness.

Alice felt a small trickle of sweat at her temple, and wiped it away with one hand. "I don't know what will happen if Georgia doesn't want to keep the baby," she said.

"You might want to think about that," Duncan said.

"What do you mean?"

"You signed that egg donation agreement. The agreement said that you did not intend to parent any children born as a result of the egg donation, and that you did not want physical or legal custody."

"I don't," Alice said. "*I* don't want the baby. It's not *my* baby; it's Georgia's. I've never felt like it was my baby."

Duncan's blue eyes held hers, and he didn't look away. He hadn't looked at her like that in a long time. "How would you feel if John and Georgia decided to put the baby up for adoption?"

Alice felt her gut clench, her heart thump hard against her ribs. "I don't know," she said. "They wouldn't do that."

"Wouldn't they?"

Now Alice's whole body grew hot. She felt sweat dampen her armpits, the small of her back, felt a flush across her chest.

"Why are you asking me all this?"

Duncan sat down on one of the leather bar chairs at the kitchen counter and looked at her again.

"Alice, this is the reality of your—our—situation right now. You might as well think about all the possibilities so you're not surprised when they become realities."

"They would never put the baby up for adoption."

Duncan's glance was at once bitter and sympathetic. He pushed his chair back from the counter and stood up. "You never know what people will do," he said. "Even the people you know best will surprise you; isn't that true?"

Alice could only nod.

THE NEXT DAY she was making meatballs when the phone rang. She had deleted "Jane" from her contact list long ago, so she didn't recognize John's number when it appeared on the screen. At the sound of his voice her heart began to race and she felt the now-familiar ache in her throat that meant she was about to cry. She missed him, and it was terrible to miss him.

He told her Georgia had disappeared, had left the hospital and the baby less than forty-eight hours after giving birth. Alice heard the baby screaming in the background. And then he asked her to come over.

"John, I can't."

"Alice, this is about *the baby*," John said. "It's not about anything other than taking care of this baby, who needs someone *right now*. If Georgia were here asking you for help you would drop everything and come over."

"I can't," she said.

"Alice, I am begging you. Thirty minutes, that's all. Please: come help Georgia's baby."

Georgia's baby.

"All right," Alice said. "I'll be there in ten minutes."

ALICE CAME BACK from John's house still in shock over the sense of *familiarity* she had had when she held the baby, a moment of déjà vu. It was as though the baby were a beloved and long-lost friend, someone she had been waiting and hoping to see again, and now here he was at last, exactly where he was supposed to be and should have been all along. She had never, in her wildest imaginings about what might happen once the baby was born, thought she would feel such a *bond* with him.

She debated whether or not to talk about it at their counseling appointment that evening. Duncan had finally agreed to see a marital counselor, and they had met with Dr. Jenkins three times now. Alice had approached the first appointment in terror. After all, she was Alice the Evil Adulteress and Duncan was Duncan the Good, the Wronged Husband. Dr. Jenkins had asked Duncan about his hurt, listened to him, understood him, even drawn out of him the somewhat astonishing—to Alice— information that he had not only punched John in the face but had punched a hole in the wall of his closet, too.

But Dr. Jenkins had surprised Alice by asking her what *she* was mad about.

"I'm not," Alice had said. "I'm sad. I'm guilty. I feel terrible about what I've done."

Dr. Julia Jenkins looked at her with a face full of empathy. She was more than six feet tall, with blond hair cut into a short, shaggy bob, chiseled cheeks, a wide, generous smile, and warm brown eyes. She was in her late sixties, Alice guessed, but dressed in boot-cut jeans and wedge sandals and a long, slim-fitting black tunic. She emanated calm, compassion, understanding. Alice wanted Dr. Jenkins to be her mother. Actually, she wanted to *be* Dr. Jenkins, so she could radiate that kind of peace, too.

Alice wanted to be a good therapy patient, just as she had always wanted to be a good student, a good daughter, a good citizen, a good teacher, a good mother, a good wife. But she wasn't mad.

"Okay," Dr. Jenkins had said. "Just think about it."

And over the next few days, Alice thought about it. Of course she was mad, but how could she say she was angry that Duncan was so patient and responsible and kind? How could she say she was furious that he was working so many hours for so little pay when he was doing something so meaningful, so selfless? How could she say she was mad that he protected her, took care of her, guided her? She couldn't.

"You know, Alice," Dr. Jenkins had said when Alice came to see her alone. "Good people have affairs, too."

"Good people like Duncan don't," Alice had said.

She took full responsibility for her affair; it was a choice she had made with her body and heart but also with her mind. She knew what she was risking, but some part of her had never believed the risk was real. She had not allowed herself to imagine that they would be caught. But she also knew that her affair had bloomed because she had felt something vital was missing from her life, because John was rain on thirsty earth.

Something about the way John had looked at her, locking his eyes on hers while they made love, had made her feel *seen* for the first time in a long time. It was as though the Alice she always presented to the world—careful, competent, controlled—had been stripped bare and thrust onto a stage, terrified and vulnerable, and John had said, "*That one.* That's the Alice I want." She had never imagined that anyone would want that Alice, certainly not Duncan, who kept his eyes closed when they made love, who admired nothing more than competence and calm, who didn't feel a need to discuss things with her, even things as important as his career. John's attention had made her realize that another Alice existed, and that she had been locked up too long and had to get out.

Now here was yet another Alice, one she hardly knew, one who had fallen in love at first sight with a three-day-old infant that was hers but not hers. Was she supposed to lock that Alice away, too?

Alice had made a list of all the reasons she should not even think about keeping the baby, from the legal issues to the complicated question of how to explain it all to Wren, but no matter how many cons she wrote down on the left-hand side of her paper, she kept coming back to one thing: *I am his mother, and I love him.* The feeling was as clear and pure and direct as the rays of early morning sun streaming through the kitchen window onto the bamboo floor. And Georgia didn't even want him; that was the thing.

Alice waited until they were in the counselor's office to talk about it.

"I'd like to talk about the baby," Alice said. "About the possibility of keeping the baby." She said it straight out, without preamble, because it was such an outrageous thing to say that to try to soften it with explanations or excuses would be insulting, she thought. Better to lay it out there, raw and whole. She had no right to ask Duncan to consider it, and she knew it. His loyalty already was more than she deserved, and she knew that, too.

"What?" Duncan sat next to her on the soft beige chenille couch. Dr. Jenkins sat across from them in some kind of ergonomically correct white leather armchair. A painting of white clouds in a bright blue sky hung on the wall behind her. Alice had stared at the painting every session, studying the clouds. They were probably there to get people's minds off the all-too-earthly problems they brought to Dr. Jenkins, Alice thought, all the mud-bound grief and infidelities and terrors.

"Have you *seen* the baby?" Duncan said.

"I saw him this afternoon. John called in a panic and asked me to come over. He brought the baby home from the hospital and couldn't get him to stop crying."

"And you went." Duncan said it as a statement, not an accusation, but Alice flinched nonetheless.

"Yes, I went. I tried to call you first, Duncan, to let you know, to make sure you would be okay with it, but I couldn't reach you. And I swear to you I went for Georgia, *not John*, because Georgia wouldn't want her baby to be crying and crying and inconsolable. I thought it was the least I could—one thing I could—," she faltered.

"You did promise Duncan you wouldn't have any contact with John," Dr. Jenkins said.

"I know," Alice said. "I'm sorry. And I didn't mean to—I didn't recognize his number when he called, and when I heard the baby—" Her damn tears rose again and she pressed her lips together, cleared her throat. "I went for Georgia, as one little thing I could do to make it up to Georgia, even though she would never know about it."

"I understand you wanted to do something for Georgia," Dr. Jenkins said. "But you need to understand that Duncan may have a hard time if you don't make his need to be able to trust you your top priority."

Alice nodded. "You're right." She looked at her husband. "I'm sorry." Dear God, had she ever said any words more often in her life? *I'm sorry. I'm sorry. I'm sorry.*

"He's a beautiful, beautiful boy," she said. "And it's just—I don't know what's wrong with Georgia, but I don't know that she'll ever want him, given—given everything." Alice looked down at the floor, her face burning with shame. But the thought of the baby and his wide-open innocence calmed her. She looked up at Duncan. "And John can't raise him alone, and

I don't think he'd want to raise him on his own. And we could do a good job with him; I know we could. But it's a lot to ask, and I have no right to ask." She waited.

Duncan looked at Dr. Jenkins.

"Tell her the truth," Dr. Jenkins said. "She's told you what she wants; you can tell her what you want."

Duncan turned his face sideways, toward the wall, where another cloud painting hung. He turned back to face Alice.

"I think," he said, his blue eyes on hers, "it's time you got a lawyer."

Hope flickered in her chest. "To figure out if we have a right to the baby?"

"No," Duncan said. "To figure out the divorce."

17

Georgia
June 19–20, 2012

As soon as Georgia slipped out the front door of the hospital, she pulled a black baseball cap from her purse and put it on, as well as her sunglasses. She walked into the parking lot to find her station wagon, still parked where she'd left it when she'd driven herself to the hospital the day before yesterday, so furious with John that she wouldn't get in the car with him, even in the midst of a contraction. She slipped a note under the windshield on the driver's side. Then she walked across the lot to the metro station, and sat down on a bench to wait for the next train.

She was not a planner. Polly was a planner; Alice was a planner. For the last ten years, Alice had started planning in May for their annual summer trip to Georgia's cabin—outlining all the dinner menus, buying up suntan lotion and bug spray and Band-Aids on sale, making cookies and casseroles and freezing them. It was all Georgia could do to remember to pack a bathing suit. And inevitably, at some point during the vacation,

Georgia would get frantic because she had forgotten something critical—like Bananagrams, which the girls played over and over on vacation—only to have Alice say, "Don't worry. I brought it."

But something about her anger had sharpened Georgia's focus, and turned her into a very good planner indeed. From the second she had figured out the affair, she thought about how she would leave the baby, *Alice's* baby.

She knew where she would go. She knew she wanted to be alone, for a few days at least. She knew she didn't want anyone to think she was crazy or suicidal, hence the carefully worded note she left on the windshield of her car. She had planned every step with precision.

Two weeks ago, she had driven down to Union Station, parked, and waited on a bench inside, watching the ticket line. When she saw a young woman with a toddler at the end of the line, Georgia had approached her.

"Do you mind getting a ticket for me?" Georgia had asked. "Standing in line these days, you know—" She had gestured toward her enormous belly.

"Sure," the woman said.

"I'm going to upstate New York," Georgia said, "to visit my mom after the baby comes. Could you buy a one-way ticket for this date?" And she had handed her a piece of paper with info about the train and some cash. No one would remember the woman with the toddler buying a ticket. Georgia was too likely to stick in someone's memory, with her gigantic pregnant belly, her face blotchy and swollen from crying for days on end.

She had picked the date—June 19—out of the air. Her baby was due June 18, but might come early, she thought. And she could always change the date of her ticket. But, miracle of miracles, her labor had started the evening of June 17, and the baby had been born after midnight. So her ticket for today, June 19, was right on the money.

It would be a long day and night of travel. The metro she waited for now would take her to Union Station, where she would catch an Amtrak train to New York. In New York she would take another train, along the Hudson to Albany and then north to Westport. From there, she would take a mountain taxi to the cabin on Lake Condundrum, where she could stay undisturbed for a few days, and think about what she wanted to do next. She was paying for everything in cash.

She had researched the law so she would know what it meant to leave the baby behind. Because she had left him at the hospital, warm and well fed and in his bassinet, where a nurse would find him as soon as he cried, Virginia's safe haven laws would protect her, and she couldn't be prosecuted for abuse or neglect or cruelty. But it also meant the state could "terminate her parental rights," a phrase that pierced her very soul with its finality.

She thought of the baby, up there on the third floor of the hospital in his bassinet, his belly full of her milk, his face relaxed in sleep. Tears stung her eyes. *The baby*. She loved him; she didn't want to, but there it was. She had imagined over these long last six weeks that the minute he was released from her body she would feel released from the grief and white-hot anger that had plagued her since she found out about the affair. The baby was John and Alice's baby, not her baby. She could not, *would not*, love him. But when the nurse had lifted him into her arms after all those hours of labor, he had opened his eyes at the sound of her voice, squinting in the strong light of the delivery room. And she had gazed back into his eyes and felt, to her astonishment, the same kind of fierce, pure love for him that she had felt for Liza.

She didn't want to love him. She thought of John and Alice and their skinny bodies intertwined on a bed of fine linens in some posh hotel. She had no idea where or how they had consummated their affair, but imagined it had been someplace like the Hay-Adams, all white and cream and gold, with custom Italian bed linens and plush down duvets and a fireplace. The idea that they were doing *that* while she was sitting at home with her swollen ankles up on the coffee table, rubbing cocoa butter into the stretch marks on her belly and gestating *their* biological child—no. She did *not* love this baby.

The lights on the metro platform flashed; the train was arriving. Georgia stood up. She stepped onto the train and the doors closed behind her. Being on the train was just like being pregnant, she thought. After a certain point, you were absolutely committed, and there was nothing you could do but finish the ride.

At Union Station she purchased a few things—toiletries, a lightweight cardigan, a scarf. She bought a card, so she could write to Liza, and a book, something to take her mind off her life. She boarded the train, wrapped herself in her new cardigan, put on her sunglasses, and went to sleep. She slept as the train headed north through Baltimore and Wilmington and Philadelphia. Just outside of Philly, the pain in her breasts woke her up and she went into the bathroom and tried to express some milk, but it was so impossible—leaning over the tiny sink, trying to brace herself with her legs as the train swayed from side to side and lurched around curves—that she gave up and resigned herself to being in pain until Albany. She had to switch trains in New York, so she wandered into a deli in Penn Station and bought tea and a turkey sandwich, but the sandwich turned her stomach so she left it untouched and just drank the tea.

She watched the broad waters of the Hudson River out the window of the train as it moved north to Albany, watched the landscape roll through farmland and low-slung hills and the soft peaks of the Catskills. She was heading north, her favorite direction. She used to say that every time they got in the car to drive to the Adirondacks in July: "I love going north. It's my favorite direction." John thought it was a silly thing to say, and they had the same back-and-forth every year, with John saying things like "What? So if you have to drive south or east it ruins your day? What if you lived at the North Pole? Would you just stand still?" It was a conversation they had for Liza's benefit, because it always made her laugh and because it had become tradition.

Georgia sighed as she thought of Liza, whose well-being was the most difficult, painful part of this entire ordeal. Right now Liza was at camp, where she would be until mid-July, when Georgia was scheduled to pick her up and bring her to the cabin. At that point Georgia would have to tell her *something*.

The timing of Liza's camp had been the one bit of good luck Georgia had had over the last few months. Every summer for the last four years, Liza had left for a month at camp the day after school got out, which this year fell on June 15. They had registered her for camp a year ago, long before Georgia knew she was pregnant. Liza loved Camp Pokomac (shorthand for Pok-O-MacCready), a haven of High Peaks sunsets and crisp Adirondack nights nestled on the edge of a clear, cold lake. They'd discovered it one rainy day during their vacation at the cabin, when they'd driven north to explore antique shops and eat pie at a local diner. Liza had gone to Pokomac for two weeks the summer she turned ten, and had loved rock climbing and tromping through the woods to find salamanders and bonding with the other girls. She'd been back every year since, and this would be her final year as a camper; next year she would be a counselor-in-training.

Liza had offered to give it up as soon as Georgia had told her there would be a new baby, but Georgia had wanted her to go. After all the stress and drama of middle school, she needed to go be a kid for a month, Georgia said. Georgia also did not put much stock in the idea that entire families should be present to watch the miracle of birth; it was bad enough to have your husband present, witness to some of the most undignified moments a human could experience. So Liza was off at Pokomac now for three more weeks, climbing mountains and paddling kayaks and smelling like campfire smoke, which meant that Georgia had three more weeks to figure out what she was going to tell Liza about relinquishing the baby.

She couldn't say, "I can't handle being a single parent," because now she was a single parent to Liza. She couldn't say, "The baby really belongs to Alice and your father," because Liza didn't know about the egg donation—or the affair, for that matter. She would have to tell Liza *some* version of the truth, because there was no other way to explain—to Liza or anyone else—why she would abandon the baby she had wanted for more than ten years.

"You don't have to see the whole staircase, just take the first step," her father used to say, quoting someone she couldn't remember. Georgia decided to adopt that as her life's philosophy, starting today. She took a long slug from the bottle of water she had bought in D.C. and pressed her hands against her aching breasts. Soon the train would pull into Albany and she would get on the next train, and then, sometime around midnight, she would finally be at the cabin, where nothing ever changed.

IN FACT IT was almost 1:00 A.M. by the time the mountain taxi turned onto the long dirt drive that wound through the woods to the cabin. Georgia had realized about forty miles before that Glenn Dobbs, who checked on the cabin throughout the winter and "opened" it for them each summer, might not have gotten around to opening it yet, which meant that she would arrive to a cabin full of dust and dead insects and mouse droppings and no running water. She had tried to still that thought, but now it pushed back. *What will I do?* Finally she saw the dark outline of the cabin's peaked roof against the blue-black sky, the sharp silhouette of the pines. She paid the driver in cash, and asked him to stay long enough with the headlights on so she could see her way along the path to the front door. Tree frogs trilled out their crazy songs from the trees at the edge of the lake, cutting through the stillness of the night. The key was on the ledge in the rock of the chimney, as usual, and as she turned it in the old metal lock she said a little prayer.

She stepped inside and flicked on the light. The pine walls glowed yellow. The oak coffee table was wiped clean of dust, the floors swept, the pillows on the old blue gingham couch fluffed and ready. She saw the wood box next to the fireplace filled with split wood and strips of birch bark and twigs for kindling. She could have wept with relief. She walked into the kitchen and turned on the faucet and the blessed water came out. *Thank you, Glenn.*

She went back to the front stoop to bring in the few things she'd bought in Albany—a toothbrush and some toothpaste, toilet paper, sanitary supplies, a bottle of water, an apple. She ate the apple standing on the screened porch, listening to the lake lap at the dock. She thought about the summer she *had* planned, before all this, about being here with Liza and Polly and Chessy and their kids and the new baby, her baby boy. Every time she thought of him the tears welled up and her arms ached. She would not think of him for five full minutes, she decided, and glanced at her watch: 1:25. She opened the screen door and tossed the apple core out into the night for the raccoons or the deer or whatever found it first.

She peered up at the stars, so clear and vivid here, and spotted the arcing handle of the Big Dipper, the long tail of Draco, the dragon. When she and Polly were little their father used to take them out at night in an old, flat-bottomed wooden row-boat, the oars creaking in the rusty oarlocks, until they were in the middle of the bay. They'd lie down on piles of beach towels and blankets and stare up at the stars while their father pointed out the constellations. He always brought with him a map of the night sky that he had ripped out of *National Geographic*, studying it with a flashlight and then peering upward over the rims of his eyeglasses. Draco was her favorite. Polly liked Cygnus, the swan, which was just like Polly, who loved everything girlie and sweet. Their father, like Georgia, preferred Draco.

It was funny to think now how much her father had wanted a son, because he'd been such a wonderful father to all three of his girls, as attentive and loving and protective as could be. She had wondered sometimes if he was lonely, living in that house full of estrogen, with his three daughters and two female cats. He had haunted her thoughts these last few months, once she'd found out the baby she was carrying was a boy. Frank would have loved having grandsons, would have taken them fishing, would have showed them how to shoot baskets, hammer nails, repair plumbing. Frank was the kind of man who was good at everything. But he'd died six months before Teddy was born. For a moment she was glad Frank was gone, so he didn't have to bear witness to her humiliation with John, her abandonment of this baby who bore no blood relationship to herself or her father, but who would have delighted him anyway.

She glanced at her watch. *Shit:* 1:27. She couldn't even go two minutes without thinking about the baby. Her eyes filled with tears again.

"What am I going to do?" She said it out loud to the night sky.

But the sky had no answers. She let the screen door fall closed with a bang.

Then she went inside, took two of the Xanax she had stashed

in her purse, pulled on a T-shirt of her father's she found in a dresser drawer, and went to bed. She slept then, slept as soundly as she ever had in her life, as if all these last few weeks had never happened.

Indeed, she slept as soundly as her newborn son, who lay in a bassinet five hundred miles away.

18

Alice
June 20–21, 2012

Alice hated beaches, especially big beaches with board-walks, like Rehoboth. She could not understand why—when it was hot and sticky and the weight of even a cotton T-shirt felt like heavy armor—anyone would want to join throngs of other hot, sticky people, bumping against each other, breathing in the scents of sweat and suntan lotion and hot dogs. And even if you carved out your own little space, sat under an umbrella at the edge of the sand, far from the water, you still had to deal with the masses of people walking by in their too-small shorts or swimsuits, rolls of flesh jiggling with each step. Just the thought of it made Alice's skin crawl. She had said as much to Wren, weeks ago.

"I can't go to Rehoboth," she had said.

"Mom," Wren had said. "It's *fun*. Please. I promised Nicole."

Alice had looked at her daughter, the pale blue eyes, the thick fringe of dark eyelashes that gave her a look of wide-eyed innocence. Wren shared Duncan's Scottish features—high cheekbones, straight nose, those sea-glass-blue eyes. But some-times Wren would flash a smile, or turn her head to the side, her profile silhouetted against the window, and Alice would have a moment of déjà vu and see herself in her daughter, her own cautious smile, her own long, slender neck. But it was just a moment. Wren was Duncan's daughter, through and through.

But Wren was also herself, as evidenced by her desire to go to the beach, a place both Alice and Duncan detested.

"How about if I take you to Smith Mountain Lake? Or Deep Creek Lake?" Alice said. *Anyplace that doesn't involve skee ball and bumper cars.*

"Because the whole point is to go someplace where there's a boardwalk," Wren said.

Long ago, back in the fall when the bullying first began, Alice had promised Wren a vacation, something to look forward to, to mark the end of middle school. "I want to go to the beach," Wren had said, and Alice had agreed. *Of course. Anything to make this child happy, this child who has been mistreated so.*

The bullying issue with Wren had been resolved, as so many of these things were, in a way that really was no resolution at all. John had talked to Liza. Alice had talked to the school guidance counselor and the principal. She had called Emilie's mom. The guidance counselor had talked to Wren and Liza and Emilie, separately and together. The girls had apologized; Wren had forgiven them. Since then the girls had maintained a wary truce—Wren and Liza polite, Wren and Emilie distant. Alice had been vigilant, and John had been surprisingly watch-ful, too, monitoring Liza's texts and phone calls, reading the computer over her shoulder. There had been blips—like the note from "Al" in Wren's locker—but then the girls had moved on to the next drama, the next machination.

But Alice knew what girls could be like; she had often enough been the target of their susurrations in the hallways in middle school when she walked by in her baggy sweaters, her no-name jeans. When she would turn to look one of them in the eye there would be only a sweet smile, a *"Love* your sweater, Alice," and giggles as she walked away. And she had witnessed often enough Rita's stealthy, almost indifferent cruelty, her casual lies to her many boyfriends, to Alice herself.

No, females were tricky, not to be trusted. The only woman Alice had ever loved and trusted was Georgia, whom she missed now with all her heart.

"What did your father say?" Alice had asked.

"Dad said he'll do whatever you want," Wren said. She brought her laptop over to where Alice sat at the kitchen counter. "See? Look at this place I found! You and Dad can read books or something while Nicole and I hang out on the boardwalk."

Alice peered at the screen. She saw a sunny kitchen, a living room with a big window facing the beach, an outdoor shower. Better to be there with Duncan, perhaps, than here, where their very bed was a reminder of Alice's treachery.

"Okay," Alice said. "We'll try the beach."

So Alice took her sensitive daughter and her failing marriage and her longing for a baby she couldn't have to a place she couldn't stand. Welcome to Rehoboth.

DUNCAN CAME ALONG reluctantly. "You could take the girls on your own," he said. "I've got a lot of work."

"It might be good for us to get away," Alice said. "It's only three days." She told the truth: "It will be lonely for me without you. The girls will be off on their own on the beach and the boardwalk." *I don't want to practice being single, not yet.*

He shrugged. "All right."

Duncan had barely spoken to her since they had returned from their visit to Dr. Jenkins, since he had put that harsh word out in the space between them. *Divorce*. Dr. Jenkins had tried to get them to talk about it, in the ten minutes before their session ended, but Alice had said, "I can't." Of course she had thought about it and feared it and, yes, brought the possibility of it into being, from the moment John had pressed his lips against hers there in the front seat of her car. But it had been a ghost, an image, a vapor on the horizon. Now it had taken shape, a clear outline, solid and dense and black.

"I don't think the baby is the issue," Dr. Jenkins had said. "Whether or not you decide you want to adopt the baby isn't the issue. *Your relationship* is the issue. Everything else flows from that."

They had driven home in silence; they had avoided each other in the time since. But now here they were, together for seventy-two hours, day and night.

Of course they couldn't afford the lovely rental Wren had found online, with the living room overlooking the beach. Instead they had a tiny two-bedroom apartment over a garage, two blocks from the ocean. But it had a sunroom all along one side with big windows and comfortable armchairs, a turquoise rug on the floor. It was clean. Nor could they afford an expensive weekend rental, so Duncan agreed to take a few days off and they rented the place from Wednesday to Friday.

The first day unfolded pleasantly enough. Wren and Nicole woke by ten and they all walked to the beach, which wasn't too crowded yet. They rented boogie boards and tried to ride the waves, like the other boarders they saw. Wren got the hang of it first—timing the wave just right, pushing down slightly on the nose of her board so the wave would lift her up, skimming across the surface of the water. Duncan, too, figured it out quickly and soon was doing tricks, shooting across the front of a wave, rolling the board and popping back up to finish riding the wave. Alice forgot sometimes that he had been an athlete, someone who had known exactly how fast to sprint to plant the pole for maximum lift, how to take off, how to arch his body just so over an unforgiving bar.

He still was in fine shape, something else she hadn't thought about in a long time. For years he had awakened early every morning and gotten dressed in the dark, headed outside to run, and then come home to lift weights in the basement. She looked at him now and wished she could pull him to her, press herself against his lean chest, his solid shoulders, not for sex—although she felt herself thinking about that, too—as much as for the reassurance of the steadiness of him, the consistency of him.

They had not had sex since last November, more than six months ago. Duncan's new job, the changes in Alice's body from the pills and injections she had to take to donate her eggs, the bullying—one thing after another had crowded into their life together, each one more urgent than the last, demanding every ounce of attention, time, and love they each had to offer. They had nothing left for each other. She had said something about it once, months before she began her affair with John, when Duncan had come home late yet again from his new job, tired, distracted, interested in nothing more than gulping down a warmed-over bowl of leftover beef stew and falling into bed.

"We never have sex anymore," she had said. "I miss it."

Duncan's face had flushed, even his neck turned red. At first she thought he was angry, but his voice was soft, apologetic, and she realized he was embarrassed. "I'm tired, Alice," he said. "I'm sorry. But I'll try to make time for it."

She didn't know how to respond. Was this what happened after a decade of marriage, that sex became a chore to cross off the weekly to-do list? She thought back to the early days of their marriage when Duncan would come home from work, ducking his head as he came inside the front door of their tiny apartment in Georgetown, and grin from ear to ear at the sight of her there, reading some textbook at their unsteady kitchen table, as though he couldn't believe his good fortune that she was still there and hadn't disappeared during the day, a phantom he had conjured in his mind.

She would say, "I'm almost done with this chapter; give me fifteen minutes," and he would nod but stand behind her, his hands resting on the back of her chair, the tops of his fingers barely brushing her shoulder blades. She would feel her body grow warm, feel her nipples swell and harden, feel the dampness between her legs. She would read a sentence over and over, trying to focus, aware of nothing but Duncan behind her. Sometimes he would bend forward and brush his lips lightly against the back of her neck or her shoulder, then stand up again, waiting. She would turn the page of her book with a careful concentration, as though she were hardly aware of his presence. Still he stood there, his breath deep and quiet, his body warm.

She always broke first, pushing the book across the table, twisting in her chair to look up at him, reaching up to pull his face down to hers, his lips against her own. They would shed their clothes as they moved toward the bedroom, where Duncan would push her down onto the bed and admire her for a moment in the light that spilled in from the kitchen and the streetlamps outside. Then he would lean forward and cup his warm hand around one of her breasts, put his mouth to her other breast, caress her with his hands and tongue before lowering himself on top of her. She had never felt so adored—at least, not until John.

She flushed now thinking about John, but with guilt, not desire. She closed her eyes and lay back on her towel in the sand, under the blazing June sun. She wished the sun could scorch John's touch from her skin, his memory from her brain.

"You're going to get burned."

She put a hand over her forehead to shade her eyes and looked up at Duncan, who stood next to her, dripping.

"I have sunscreen on. SPF five thousand, I think."

He didn't smile. She sat up.

"I'm going to take the girls to play some games on the board-walk," he said. "Get them out of the sun."

"Okay." She stood and gathered up her book, the spray bottles of sunscreen, the bottles of water, her hat.

"You don't need to come," Duncan said. "You hate the board-walk."

Alice looked at him in surprise. "I'll come."

He shook his head. "Stay. You can read, or go for a walk on the beach. Take a break."

He wore a blue Washington Nationals baseball cap and his sunglasses, and Alice couldn't read his eyes. *Does he really think I deserve a break?* she thought. *Or does he just not want to be with me?* She had no idea. She stood there, uncertain, but before she could figure it out, her husband turned, yelled out to the girls, and headed off down the beach away from her, until the three of them—Duncan and Wren and her friend—were lost in the crowd, and Alice was alone.

THAT NIGHT ALICE and Duncan sat in the sunroom of their little rental apartment, drinking margaritas, watching the sky turn pink above the treetops, above the ocean two blocks away. Wren and Nicole were in their room watching a movie on the laptop. Alice took a long swig of her drink and worked up all her courage. It was easier here in the fading light, with the changing sky beyond the windows, something to watch.

"So do you really want a divorce?" she said. Her words hung in the humid air, still and heavy.

A long silence. "Do you?" he said.

It hadn't occurred to her that the choice could be hers. "No," she said.

The sky outside the windows darkened to deep indigo, lightening to lavender and pink just above the horizon, where the sun had disappeared. She heard people laughing on the street outside, the sound of the waves in the distance, the slam of a car door. She couldn't see Duncan's face in the half dark. She looked out the window at the silhouette of the trees black against the sky.

"I've never done anything out of passion in my whole life," Alice said. "I've been mature and responsible since I was four. And the bullying with Wren—it made me so angry; I didn't know what to do with all that *feeling*. And you seemed so calm about it."

"It bothered me," Duncan said, from the shadows of his chair. "Of course it bothered me."

"But you didn't show it."

"You think *I've* never done anything out of passion in my whole life, except punch John Bing in the face," Duncan said. "But when *I* needed something more, something to make me feel more alive—because, believe me, you're not the only person who feels that way—I found a new job. I looked for that in my career, not in another person."

Duncan's voice was even, but Alice felt his words as a slap.

"But that was part of it," Alice said. "You changed jobs like that, without even talking to me about it—it made me feel like I wasn't even part of your life." She shifted in her chair to face him, leaned forward. "And the money—you know how that scares me, having to always worry about having enough to pay the bills, living on noodles like I had to when I was young. You could have talked to me about it first. I wouldn't have stopped you, or discouraged you, but we could have planned for it, been partners."

"You're right," Duncan said. "I should have talked it over with you. But I'm forty-two and I'd been working at Covington for sixteen years and it felt like being trapped in an elevator I didn't want to be on."

A light went on in the living room behind them, the girls making popcorn in the kitchen. Alice started to stand up, but Duncan said, "Sit down. They can't hear us."

"Anyway," he said, "when David called me about the job with the Innocence Project I was already feeling restless; you knew that. I met him for lunch and I said yes on the spot." He paused. "It was impulsive; it wasn't like me." He looked at her and raised his eyebrows.

She nodded. How many times in the last month had she apologized for her affair, how many times had she said, *I'm sorry; it was impulsive; it wasn't like me?*

"This job has changed things for me," Duncan said. "I love what I do, and it matters." His voice grew soft. "You know I've been working since last September on this Dan Boyle case. The guy has been in jail for *nineteen years*. And it's stunning, how his case has been bungled. It's like I have a moral obligation to set it right. What I do now isn't about money; it's about someone's *life*."

"I know," she said. "It was just so sudden."

"We've been married fourteen years," he said. "I guess I thought you knew how desperate I was to get out of Covington; I thought you understood." He cleared his throat. "I should have talked to you. Honestly, I panicked. I started to feel like my entire life was set: associate, then partner, then senior partner at Covington, the same cases and coworkers and Christmas parties for the next thirty years. You've always been so supportive, I didn't think . . ." His voice trailed off.

Duncan had messed up; he was trying to say that now. Steady, reliable, consistent, predictable Duncan had felt trapped, had wanted more, had acted on impulse. He was imperfect, too.

"I felt trapped, too," she said, "but not by you. By me—by how I'd lived my whole life. I don't know; I can't explain it even to myself."

He sighed.

"Do you really want a divorce?" she said, very low.

"I don't know," he said. "It's too soon."

The door from the living room opened, spilling light into the darkened sunroom where they sat. The girls tumbled in, laughing about the movie. Alice got up to finish cleaning up the kitchen, and Duncan moved into the living room, to read on the sofa by the lamp.

Later that night in bed, Alice reached out for him in the dark. She ran her hand along his cheek and leaned forward and kissed him, a tentative touch of her lips against his. He kissed her back. She inched closer and wrapped her arms around him, nuzzled his jaw with her nose. She felt the muscles in his shoulders grow tense under her hands, felt his back stiffen.

"I can't, Alice," he said, breaking away, rolling back toward his side of the bed. "I'm sorry. I'm not there yet."

Guilt washed over her. She rolled onto her side, her back to him. She held herself very still. She heard a rustle of sheets, felt Duncan press himself against her back, wrap his arm around her, spoon her.

"Let's just sleep," he said.

She pushed her body against his, relaxed into his embrace. And for that moment, it was enough.

19

Georgia
June 20—22, 2012

*G*eorgia awoke to the sweet song of a white-throated sparrow. She felt the warmth and brightness of the morning even before she opened her eyes. She was on her back—it felt so good to sleep on her back again after all those months of being so huge!—and she shifted and rolled over onto her side.

"Oh, my God," she said aloud. Her milk had come in. Her breasts, which were a respectable C-cup when she wasn't pregnant and had ballooned to the size of cantaloupes over the last month, now looked like watermelons ready to burst. As she looked down, she felt a familiar tingle and her milk let down, soaking through her T-shirt and dripping onto the sheets and the mattress.

Of course, she began to cry. She got out of bed, pulled her T-shirt off, and slipped on a plaid flannel bathrobe of her father's that she found hanging on a hook by the bedroom door. Since his death four years ago, she and her sisters had left the cabin as it was, full of Frank's clothes and fishing gear and baseball caps.

None of them were ready to be orphans, and at the cabin—that timeless place—they could still pretend Frank was just out fishing, or in town getting the newspapers, chatting up the checkout girl at the Grand Union. They had scattered his ashes across the lake one night, out in a rowboat under a sky full of stars.

Georgia walked into the kitchen, leaned over, and expressed as much milk as she could into the sink, crying the whole time. As she did it she realized that expressing the milk just meant that her body would produce *more* milk, that she'd be trapped here forever, producing milk and pouring it down the drain. She had forgotten how difficult and messy these first few days were. The sheer volume of milk stunned her. But if she didn't express it her breasts would hurt so much she couldn't stand it, at least not now.

She slipped into the bathroom and took a long, hot shower, silently blessing Polly for convincing them to install the new hot-water heater last summer, washing the salt from her face, the tangles from her hair, and the aches from her body. She pulled on those same damn maternity capris and maternity bra and her father's sweatshirt, and walked out to the shed where her father's truck was parked. Glenn had clearly taken care of the truck when he'd opened the cabin, because it was clean and shiny and started the minute she turned the key in the ignition. She drove into town, where she bought a few groceries and a large cup of coffee, since she could have caffeine again. She bought a bottle of wine, too. She kept her sunglasses on and her father's fishing cap, the red one he used to wear all summer long to keep the sun off his head, and didn't see anyone she knew.

By the time she drove back up the driveway to the cabin, she felt calmer. She stepped out of the car. The sun warmed her skin, and a light breeze lifted her hair and blew a few wild strands across her face. The sharp, reassuring smell of balsam permeated the air, and she could hear the buzzing of insects in the trees. She picked up the bag of groceries and walked past the front steps and around to the side of the screened porch, so she could put the wine into the porch fridge on her way to the kitchen. As she walked she saw a large bird skim across the surface of the lake and squinted to get a better view—a heron, coming in to fish among the shallows at the edge of the bay. She stood for a moment watching the bird and marveling at the length of its giant wingspan, remembering last July when she had been here with Alice and Duncan and John and the girls, aglow with love for Alice and the incredible, selfless gift she was offering to Georgia.

They had both started on the pill that week, to synchronize their cycles. Georgia knew how much Alice hated to take medication, to put anything artificial into her body, and yet Alice had made light of it all, joking about her swollen breasts, her bloated abdomen, her mood swings. "It's not me, it's the hormones," she would say with a laugh, an excuse for any lapse in good humor, memory, attention. But at the same time, she had eschewed all alcohol, even a glass of wine; insisted on driving all the way to Ticonderoga for groceries because she could get organic milk there; and started meditating for ten minutes a day—something she absolutely hated to do—because she wanted to reduce the stress hormones in her blood, all so she could produce the best possible eggs for Georgia. Georgia felt a tenderness toward Alice that she had only ever felt for Liza and, years before, for motherless baby Chessy.

That had been their best vacation together, last summer. Duncan and John had always been uneasy comrades; Wren and Liza were growing apart as they entered adolescence; but Georgia and Alice, the glue that held it all together, were closer and happier than ever, and their gaiety and ease with each other washed over all of them.

They would head out in the big boat every day, all six of

them, and zoom to the middle of the lake, where the girls would leap overboard and climb onto the big yellow inner tube John tossed out for them. They would zip around the lake with the girls on the tube behind them, skimming over the surface of the water, screaming for John to do "the whip"—cut the boat hard so the tube shot out sideways. It made Alice nervous to watch—more than once Georgia caught her giving John a look of fear and almost contempt, as though she thought he was not to be trusted with Wren's safety—but then she would relax and flash that brilliant smile at Georgia.

Duncan was an adept water-skier, carving graceful turns on the slalom ski, sending giant rooster tails of water arcing overhead. Alice didn't water-ski—she didn't like speed unless she generated it herself with her own two legs, she said—but she was an expert swimmer, and would stand on the back of the boat, execute a perfect dive into the water, and glide down the lake in a crawl that looked almost effortless. She always dove out of the boat right before they headed home for lunch, and would swim back to their bay and their dock and arrive on the porch almost at the same time they did, because they had to fuss with tying up the boat and finding sunglasses and sunscreen and cell phones and hanging up wet towels and filling a bucket for everyone to dip their mucky feet in before walking in the door.

They spent the afternoons reading on the porch or napping in the hammock, admonishing the girls to use enough sunscreen, playing an occasional lazy game of cards. At dusk the four adults would head out in the boat again, with a cooler of beer and lemonade (since neither Georgia nor Alice was drinking alcohol), a loaf of crusty French bread, tangy Cheddar cheese, and sweet red grapes. John would cut the engine as they entered the narrows at the end of the lake, where the loons yodeled their beautiful, eerie cries to each other, and sharp-eyed eagles perched in the tall white pines, looking for trout. They didn't talk, really, during those cocktail hours, just listened to the boat brush against the lily pads as it drifted with the current, watched for elusive beaver, whose sleek brown heads could sometimes be spotted moving quietly across the water, breathed in the clear air. Once in a while John would brush a lazy finger up and down her arm, or wink at her and smile. Georgia felt as content as she ever had in her life.

They always saw herons there, walking on long legs in the marshes, like the one she saw now. Georgia could not believe that she had been that person, so happy and full and confident in the absolute rightness of her life, just last summer. It was a lifetime ago. Georgia's tears rose again, and she picked up her groceries and headed back into the cabin, into her new life, the one without a husband, without a best friend, and most definitely without a baby.

GEORGIA SPENT THE next two days reading, crying, expressing milk into the sink and the shower, and eating. She read two bad mystery novels her father had left on the bookshelf, books with wisecracking detectives who could all cook incredible meals and make love like porn stars and who had had emotionally traumatic childhoods. She ate an entire box of Freihofer's chocolate chip cookies, chewing mindlessly as she lay on the couch, turning the pages in whatever bad book she was reading. She ate an apple for dinner and drank two glasses of wine before climbing into bed and crying herself to sleep. When she awoke Friday morning she decided she had to do something normal and active, so she dug the canoe paddles out of the storage closet, walked down to the dock, blessed Glenn yet again for having the canoe in the water and ready to go, and paddled across the bay, looking for loons.

She was gone more than an hour. It was almost 10:00 A.M. when she returned, with the sun high over the mountains, the firs casting short shadows across the grass. She didn't see the figure on the porch, not at first. But then she opened the screen door and saw Chessy standing there, holding Lily Blue.

Georgia jumped.

"I'm glad you're still alive," Chessy said. Her voice was tart.

Georgia stepped onto the porch.

"I'm sorry," she said.

Lily began to wriggle in Chessy's arms. Chessy shifted the baby to her other shoulder and patted her back.

Georgia put the canoe paddle in the corner, leaning against the wall, and dropped her life jacket on the floor next to it. "How did you know where I was?"

Chessy gave her a withering look. "Oh, please. Duh."

"Does John know?"

"I don't think so. I know he's no rocket scientist but you'd think even *he* could figure it out."

"It was a dumb thing to do, I know, to run away like that. I just didn't—" Georgia's eyes filled.

"Oh, God, Georgia, it's not *that* big a deal," Chessy said. "Don't get so melodramatic. I should tell you now that if you're going to cry every five minutes I'm not going to be able to stand it. It's bad enough the babies cry all the time; I don't need it from the grown-ups in my life, too."

"I'm sorry," Georgia said. She wiped her nose on the shoulder of her sweatshirt. "I can't believe you came all the way up here to find me."

"Polly drove," Chessy said.

"Polly's here?"

"Yes. She dumped her kids with her sister-in-law. She's in

town getting groceries. You've got nothing to eat here except apples and Freihofer's."

"I know. I haven't felt like cooking."

"You could microwave a cup of ramen noodles. Really."

"Fine." Georgia unzipped her sweatshirt. "Are you here to lecture me? Because I'm really not in the mood."

"No, I'm not here to lecture you."

Lily Blue wriggled in Chessy's arms, and Georgia was overcome with guilt.

"I'm sorry, Chess. It was really good of you guys to come. And you had to bring Lily, too, on that long car ride. It must have been a nightmare."

"Lily?" Chessy said. "Lily's asleep in the living room, in the Portacrib."

Chessy turned, so Georgia could see the bundle in her arms, which of course was a bundle much too small to be Lily, which indeed was so small that it could only be a very, very young baby, a newborn baby. Georgia flushed.

"It's *your* baby, you idiot," Chessy said. "Who John named Haven after some baseball player, but I bet you can have it changed legally. At least it's better than Jeremiah, which was another name John mentioned. Then people would have sung that stupid bullfrog song to him his entire life."

The baby turned his head and made a little snuffling noise, and at that Georgia's milk let down, soaking through her bra and her T-shirt.

Chessy arched her eyebrows. "I guess this means you're glad to see us," she said. "Here." She handed the baby to Georgia.

Georgia held her breath and took the baby in her arms. Her body curved around him, a parenthesis. He nestled into her, rooted at her collarbone, and began to cry.

"He's hungry," Chessy said. "We've been giving him bottles but he's not too happy about it. None of us are very happy right now. That's a long freaking car ride with two babies. Polly is used to driving with screaming kids. But I'm not, at least not yet. Can you feed him?"

Georgia sat down in the nearest rocking chair. She could breathe again, now.

"Hello, you," she said.

The baby squinted at her, then opened his mouth and began to cry. She pulled him to her and cradled him, pulled up her shirt and pulled down the front of her bra, and put the baby's head to her breast. He whimpered and she guided her nipple into his mouth and he latched on and began sucking, his fist opening and closing against her breast. It felt so natural, to have this baby in her arms. She knew him, after all those months and months of carrying him. He was as familiar to her as she was to him. She felt the tightness in her shoulders relax, the knot in her stomach begin to unfurl.

"Polly had this theory that if we left at two A.M. the babies would sleep for the first five or six hours. But no one told the babies that." Chessy sat down in a chair across from Georgia and laid her head down on the table. "I hope you appreciate this."

"I do." Georgia sat back, still stunned. "I can't believe John let you take the baby."

"Hmmm," Chessy said.

"What do you mean, 'hmmm'?"

Chessy sat up. "Well, that's the thing, Georgie."

"What's the thing?"

Chessy looked up at the wooden beams on the ceiling. "John called after you left the hospital to see if we knew where you were. It was very confusing. Because we didn't know where you were, of course, but we didn't want John to know that. And the hospital needed your room. So John checked out with the baby and went home."

"Yes?"

Chessy picked up the saltshaker from the table and played with it, turning it over and over in her hand.

"Well, John was freaking out. He couldn't handle the baby by himself; he claims he doesn't even know how to make a bottle of formula. He asked Polly if she or I would take care of the baby for a day or two."

Georgia nodded. "Okay."

"So yesterday we *finally* got Polly's kids all squared away." Chessy rolled her eyes at the trouble caused by Polly's prolific breeding. "And then we brought him here."

Georgia felt a sudden sense of panic. "You mean, you didn't tell John you were bringing him here? Did John expect him back?"

"That's not exactly clear."

"What do you mean, 'That's not exactly clear'?"

"John said, 'Could you take him *for now*,'" Chessy said. "But he didn't actually define how long 'for now' is." She looked at Georgia's stricken face. "And he didn't say, 'You have to keep him in Virginia.'"

"Because it never occurred to him you'd take the baby any-place else!" Georgia looked down at the infant in her arms, at his perfect little face, then up at her sister.

"Chessy, if John decides he wants the baby back, he could come after you—us—for kidnapping. And you crossed state lines! Jesus." Georgia tried to remember what she knew about kidnapping from watching *Law & Order*. "Oh, my God," Georgia said. "It's a federal crime. We could be prosecuted for a federal crime for having the baby here."

"I guess it's time," Chessy said, "to make a plan."

20

Alice
June 22–23, 2012

They were home from the beach on Friday by dusk, with the fading daylight causing the old bricks of their house to glow orange, the trees with their new June leaves hanging still in the humidity. They dropped Wren's friend off at her house, and pulled into their own driveway in a silent postvacation dejection, a combination of too much sun and not enough sleep and the prospect of a return to the routine of everyday life. Nothing had changed at the beach, really. The possibility of divorce still buzzed in Alice's brain, a rattlesnake ready to strike. Duncan had not said he wanted a divorce; nor had he said he wanted to stay married. They hadn't talked at all about the baby, who haunted Alice's waking thoughts, whose absence in her life left her with the strange feeling that she was missing something vital, like a kidney.

She felt a little frantic about Georgia. She couldn't call John or Polly or Chessy to find out anything, and if she called one of their mutual friends, like Jen or Stacy or Karly, the entire town would be talking about why Alice Kinnaird and Georgia Bing were no longer on speaking terms, and they'd note that Georgia's husband had moved out last month, and *that* equation would add up in the blink of an eye. Then Liza and Wren, who had reached a tentative truce, would be the focus of so much gossip and scrutiny and divisiveness that they'd all have to move to Mongolia.

Alice admired Georgia's discretion. Georgia was intense and emotional and loved to gossip, and the fact that she had clearly not told a soul about the affair surprised Alice. But it was the only way to handle it without hurting Liza even more. Georgia was, at all times, the best possible mother.

Alice finished unpacking and picked up her little red Moleskine notebook, the one she carried everywhere so she could jot down things she needed to remember, items to pick up at the grocery store, calls to make, birthday cards to get. She had made a list while they were at the beach of all the things she needed to do to get her life in order. She was done with teaching for the summer, and now she could tackle the list item by item. She scanned the list:

To Do

1. Do one thing to improve my marriage every day.
2. Meditate for 10 minutes a day. [This one was not of Alice's choosing but had been suggested—no, demanded—by Dr. Jenkins, who felt that Alice needed to relax. And Alice, who had tried meditation a few times and hated it beyond words, had agreed to give it ten minutes a day for two weeks.]
3. See the baby again.
4. Do one thing to help Georgia every day. Do it in secret.
5. Research legal options regarding the baby.

On the next page she had written a list of questions, things she needed to figure out—although not while she was meditating because that was when you were supposed to be thinking about *nothing*, which was a ridiculous mandate and, frankly, a waste of ten good minutes.

Do I want to be married to Duncan? Do I want the baby? Do I want the baby even if adopting him leads Duncan to divorce me?

Alice read her list of questions, then drew a big X across the page. She was a doer, not a thinker, and was not at all comfortable with all this figuring things out and talking things over—and over and over and over. This had been one of the biggest surprises about therapy for her, the discovery that Duncan actually *wanted* to talk about his feelings and their relationship. She had thought they were alike in their happy reserve, content to live side by side without delving into who said or did what and what it meant and why and how they might have said or done it differently and whether or not it triggered something their mother or father had said or done or *hadn't* said or done. It was enough to drive anyone mad.

She loved Duncan; that she knew. And it wasn't something she knew after endless discussion and analysis; it was intuitive, like picking up a crying baby, or reaching out your cold hands toward a warm fire. She had loved him even when he walked through the kitchen door that day in April, his hair disheveled, his shirt untucked, cradling the bloody, swollen knuckles of his right hand in his left palm. Her phone was still in her hand, Georgia's voice still in her ear: *I know. Everything. Duncan knows, too.*

She had had a wild impulse to run, so she wouldn't have to face what she always had known was a possibility but had seemed until that moment a mirage, something remote and unreal. But this was real: Georgia knew, Duncan knew, and Duncan was standing in the kitchen, looking not annoyed (since he was not prone to strong displays of emotion) or even angry, but *confused*.

She had stood perfectly still when he walked in, her body taut as though poised to flee, her eyes wide, her heart beating so rapidly and so hard she felt the pulse of it in her fingers, her head, her ears.

"Georgia called you?" he had said.

She had nodded, her tongue thick in her throat.

And he had looked at her and said, "Well, of all the things I imagined in my life, I never expected this."

She stood mute.

"He's so *messy*," Duncan said. "You always said you thought he was a slob." He looked bewildered, as though the fact that Alice had cheated with someone as sloppy as John was even more astonishing than the fact that she had cheated at all.

"I'm sorry," Alice said. She felt light-headed.

"I just don't understand," he said. He looked down at the tile floor, as though he might find an explanation written there.

"I don't, either," she said. "I know that's no excuse, but I never expected anything like this to happen, either. It surprised me, too." She paused, took a deep breath. "And I am so, so sorry."

He raised his head to look her in the face. "*I'm* sorry, Alice. I must have let you down, or this wouldn't have happened. I didn't realize . . ." His voice trailed off.

She looked at him, the hurt and guilt—*as though he had anything to feel guilty about!*—as plain on his face as the bright blue "war paint" Wren had drawn across her cheeks and forehead for Spirit Week at school.

"Oh, no," Alice said. "No, no. It wasn't you."

She looked at his hand. Had he fallen? Had the shock of her betrayal sucked the air from his lungs, buckled his legs beneath him?

"Are you all right?"

"What?"

"Your hand."

He looked down, at the blood on his knuckles, the bright red stain where his hand had grazed against the front of his white shirt.

"Yes." He looked up at her. "I punched John. In the face."

Alice winced. Duncan Kinnaird, the most gentle, gentlemanly man she had ever known, had punched someone in the face, because of her. And not only that, but now he stood here in the kitchen of their home, not blaming her or accusing her, but trying to figure out what *he* might have done to drive her away. It pierced her.

"I didn't even think about it. Georgia was sick—I was helping her, and he walked in and I just punched him." He looked at his hand again. "It's not my blood; it's John's."

A strange calm filled Alice, something cool and still. She stood erect, one hand on the counter, one hand at her side, in a room she knew was her kitchen, in a house she knew was her home, but seemed now like another country, a place she had never visited before. She bent to one of the drawers next to her and took out a clean dishtowel, taking care to choose dark blue, not white. She walked over to the sink and turned on the water, let it run until it was good and cold, and held the dishtowel under the faucet until it was soaked. She twisted it in both hands to wring it out, walked over to Duncan and took his battered hand in her own, held the cold, damp cloth against his knuckles, and curled her fingers underneath his palm. He flinched at her touch.

"I'm sorry," she said. "I'm sorry. I am so sorry."

She knew without even thinking about it that her infatuation with John was over. Something about the intensity of John's desire for her, the fullness of his attention, had made her feel wanted in a way she had longed for all her life. But it wasn't sustainable. She wasn't even sure she wanted that kind of attention and connection in her everyday life—it was too much.

One time when she had visited John in the restaurant he had made a little treat for her, bacon-wrapped figs stuffed with blue cheese. She had put the fig in her mouth and bit down, tasting something at once juicy and crisp, sweet and rich and salty— she knew right away it was the single best thing she had ever tasted in her life. Her eyes had widened with pleasure and John had laughed—yet you couldn't live on that, meal after meal, day after day.

So she had held Duncan's bruised hand that day in her kitchen and thought: *I'm done with John; I don't want that every day*. She didn't need meditation or a notebook of questions to figure that out.

Alice looked at her to-do list again. She drew a big X through that, too. Then she picked up her green pen, and started a new list, on a new page:

To Do

1. Stay married.

Then Alice wrote one more sentence: *Everything else flows from that*.

"When do we get to meet the baby?" Wren said. She was practicing headstands against the wall in the living room while Alice folded laundry. Alice couldn't see her face, just her ribs outlined through the thin fabric of her maroon tank top, her slim hips and legs up against the wall.

"What?"

Wren tilted her feet away from the wall, tumbled over, and sat up. "The baby," she said, her face red from the inversion. "Georgia's baby."

Alice's heart hammered in her chest. "The baby?"

"Yes! Liza's little brother. She wrote me from camp. She won't see him till Visiting Day at the camp next week."

"Liza is writing you?"

"Mom"—Wren, who was not prone to exasperation, rolled her eyes—"would you stop repeating everything I say? Yes, Liza wrote me. She doesn't have a cell phone or computer at camp so she writes letters. I wrote her back; she loves getting mail there. We always write when she's at camp."

Alice put down the towel she had been folding. "That was before," she said. "I didn't know you and Liza were writing each other. I thought things with you two were different now."

Wren made an *arrghh* sound, deep in her throat. She sat with both legs stretched out straight in front of her and leaned forward, until her forehead touched her knees. "I cannot believe how you hold grudges," she said.

"I do not hold grudges."

"Yes, you do. You've been mad at Liza since the 'Al' thing, and that was over *months* ago. You don't even hang out with Georgia anymore. If *I'm* over it, you should be over it."

Alice tensed at the mention of Georgia's name. "The 'Al' thing was pretty awful. What Liza did was terrible."

"Mommy . . ." Wren sat up and looked at her. She called her this to tease—or annoy—her sometimes, because Alice was not the type of woman anyone would call "Mommy."

"What?"

"You don't know everything about what happened with Liza. A lot of it was Emilie; some of it was me, because I was hanging out with Nicole all the time." Now Wren stretched her legs out to the side in a wide V and leaned forward, touching her forehead to the carpet in a dancer's stretch.

"Wren!" Alice leaned over from the couch to touch her daughter's ankle.

Wren sat up and looked at her mother, arched one arm overhead, and leaned to the side in another stretch. "What?"

"None of that bullying was you. You did nothing to deserve that."

"I know. But I'm just saying, there was a lot of stuff going on then with all the girls and we're over it now. You should be, too."

Alice looked at her and thought, *I will never understand females.* She wished she could call Georgia, tell her everything, get Georgia—who had grown up with sisters—to interpret for her the strange thoughts and feelings of her own gender.

Wren sat up again, and tucked a stray tendril of dark hair behind one ear. "And Liza is having a really hard time because her parents split up, like, totally suddenly. Liza's not even sure if she and the new baby will stay with their dad on weekends, or what's going on. It's hard."

Alice closed her eyes. She had broken the first rule of being the decent person she had always wanted to be, the considerate person who was nothing like Rita: *First, do no harm.*

"I'm sure it's very hard," Alice said.

"That's why I want to be there for her." Wren lay flat on her back on the floor, put her palms on either side of her head, and pushed herself up into a bridge. Alice had never been that flexible in her entire life.

"I can't believe you can trust her after what happened. How can you just pick up your friendship?"

"Because Liza and I have been friends forever. The 'Al' thing started out as a joke, and then Emilie started getting into it. Liza tried to stop her."

"But she *didn't* stop her. And she didn't come to you about it."

"Right. She made a mistake. I kind of ditched her this year for Nicole, so her feelings were hurt, and she was mad."

"None of that justifies Liza's behavior." Alice found Wren's upside-down face as disconcerting as her words.

"Mom"—Wren lowered herself onto her back and sat up—"I forgave Liza. You should be able to, too."

Alice was silent.

"And I want to be there at the lake when Liza gets out of camp. It's going to be really weird because this is the first time in Liza's entire life that John won't be at the lake."

"But, we're not going to the lake this year, Wren. We talked about that."

In May, after everything fell apart and it was clear the Kinnaird and Bing families would never vacation together again, Alice had explained to Wren that they were going to skip their annual summer trip to Lake Conundrum, which always fell in mid-July, and do something else. Alice had suggested a trip to the Grand Canyon, or Yosemite, someplace western and dry and different from the Adirondacks.

"But *why*?" Wren had asked. "We always go to the lake."

Alice had given some vague reply about the demands of a newborn and the Bings' need to spend time together as a family, but canny Wren had questioned everything she said. Finally Alice had said, "We can't take *every* summer vacation with the Bings. Sometimes we need to focus on our own family," which was true enough.

But now Wren seemed to have forgotten those earlier conversations. "That was before. Liza needs me."

Alice shook her head.

"Mom. You and Dad don't have to go. But Liza said I can come, and she said Georgia *wants me to come*."

"When did Georgia say that?" Alice's mind whirled.

"I don't know. Before Liza went to camp."

Before the baby was born. Before Georgia disappeared.

"Dad said it's fine. He said maybe you guys would drive me up there and drop me off and then go spend a weekend in Lake Placid or something."

"He did?"

"Mom!" Wren rolled over and stood up and faced her mother. "You're acting like someone who is totally stupid or something. Everything I say, you either repeat or you say, 'What?' 'He did?' 'She did?' What is your problem?"

"I don't know," Alice said. "I didn't get enough sleep last night."

"Well, talk to Dad," Wren said. "Or call Georgia. Because I really want to go to the lake."

Over my dead body, Alice thought.

"CAN YOU EXPLAIN why you want the baby?" Dr. Jenkins said.

Alice sat alone on the soft beige couch in Dr. Jenkins's cream-colored office on Saturday morning. She understood that everything in Dr. Jenkins's office was calculatedly neutral, a room that was supposed to make you feel like you were encased in soft cotton wool, so you felt safe enough to sink back in the cushions and talk about your dark, vivid secrets, your rage and frustration and failure and desire. Duncan had had his own solo visit with Dr. Jenkins last week; now it was Alice's turn.

"Georgia doesn't seem to want him," Alice said. "And John never wanted a second baby as much as Georgia did, and he can't raise this baby alone—I don't think he wants to. So nobody wants him, the baby."

Dr. Jenkins nodded. Alice wished she could feel better about this whole therapy thing, which Duncan had taken to with such surprising devotion.

"Alice"—Dr. Jenkins's voice was gentle—"Georgia and John

could put him up for adoption. He would be very much wanted by whoever was lucky enough to adopt him."

Alice shook her head. "But what if he decides to search for his biological parents someday? Would he find Georgia, because her name is on the birth certificate? Would he find out she ran away and left him in the hospital? How do you think that would make him feel? He'd never even know about *me*."

"I'm sure your information would be available in records somewhere. You are the biological parent."

"I know. But if he finds out that his mother went to all the trouble of getting pregnant with a donor egg, then took one look at him and ran away—can you imagine?" Alice paused.

"Yes, I can imagine," Dr. Jenkins said. "And believe me, people find out stuff like that about their parents and survive. So you're telling me you want to keep the baby, at the risk of losing your marriage, so the baby doesn't feel unwanted at some point?"

Alice stared at the clouds over Dr. Jenkins's head.

"Well, when you put it that way it sounds ridiculous," she said.

"I'm not trying to make you feel ridiculous." Dr. Jenkins leaned forward in her chair, elbows on her knees. "I want you to listen to your own voice, to figure out what you really want. It's clear to me you want this baby; I think you need to figure out how much you love Duncan and how important it is to you to keep your marriage intact."

Alice sighed.

"Did you want a second child before this?"

"No."

"But when you saw this baby, you felt a bond with him."

"Yes." Alice remembered the shock of recognition she had felt when Haven had opened his gray eyes and looked at her, the surge of love.

"Because of John?"

Alice shook her head. "No. I mean, I cared about John, I was infatuated with John, but I don't have any romantic notions about wanting the baby because he's the 'product of our love' or anything like that."

Dr. Jenkins sat back in her chair. "I think you need to sit with this, Alice, to really let yourself understand whatever it is that is drawing you to this baby."

Alice looked at the clock. "Okay," she said, hoping that "sit with this" didn't mean more meditation. "I've got to go," she said. "I know we still have a few more minutes, but I need to pick up Wren from dance practice."

Dr. Jenkins nodded. "I understand."

Alice stood up, said a polite "Thank you," and walked outside to her car, the car in which John had first leaned over and kissed her, first said, "Oh, darlin'." But her body didn't spark at the thought of him. She didn't want the baby because of John. Alice climbed into the car and sat there, thinking.

For most of Wren's life, Alice felt as though there had been some kind of crazy mistake putting her in charge of such a perfect, amazing, vulnerable creature. She, Alice, was not the kind of person who could really be a good mother to anyone. She had no role model for mothering, no natural instinct like Georgia, not even an affinity for the company of other women who could pass on their wisdom. Raising Wren had felt like bowling in the dark.

But now—Alice had done this terrible thing, but she knew herself in a different way now. It was as though, in failing herself and Duncan and Georgia, she had gained the compassion that completed her as a full human being.

She wanted the baby, she realized, because for the first time in her life she believed she could be a good mother.

21

Georgia
June 23, 2012

"I t doesn't surprise me so much that Chessy would do something like this," Georgia said, as Polly set the table on the porch for dinner. "But I'm stunned *you* went along with it."

Polly rolled her eyes. "I forgot the salad dressing," she said, and disappeared back into the kitchen.

"You still have a lot of questions to answer," Georgia called after her.

The wind had died down and now, at dusk, the lake was absolutely still, reflecting back the vivid green and gold of the trees along the shore, the clear blue and pink of the evening sky. Georgia leaned back in her chair and stared at the lake, at the same view she had known since she was four, the same view her mother had loved. She could see Chessy's dark head in the water, swimming just off the rocky point at the tip of their bay. As she watched, Chessy rolled over onto her back and floated for a moment, her face golden in the late sun.

Polly returned with a bottle of salad dressing and a basket of bread, cut into neat slices.

"Do you need any help?" Georgia said.

Polly shook her head. "You're a new mother. New mothers get waited on—at least for a few days. Don't get too used to it."

"Please," Georgia said. "I'm not the get-waited-on type."

"Eat something," Polly said. "You haven't had a decent meal in three days. You can't make major life decisions on an empty stomach." She put the bread down, and turned to head back to the kitchen.

Georgia reached out and caught her wrist. "Polly."

Polly stopped, and turned. "What?"

"What do *you* think I should do?"

Polly shook her head and made a little clucking sound with her tongue, something their mother used to do. Of the three of them, Polly was the most like Evy, blond, with that slight smattering of freckles across her nose, and the same way of making that clucking sound when she disapproved of something, the same habit of sitting in a chair with both legs tucked up underneath her, the same loud laugh.

"Georgia, I can't tell you what to do, not with this. You love this baby or you don't; it's not something you can talk yourself into. Do I believe you could do a good job of raising him, even on your own? Of course. You're a great mother, and you've got me and Chessy living nearby, and Liza's old enough to help. But you're the only one who can figure out whether or not you can see him as himself, and not as a constant reminder of John and Alice."

"I know. And I don't know."

"I don't think you can figure it out sitting up here alone. That's why we came, and that's why we brought Haven with us. So you can know." Polly paused. "To me," she said, "it's like adoption. Once you bring a baby home and take care of it, it's yours. You love the baby, the baby loves you—the genetics don't matter. At least, that's how I feel."

"Said the woman with four biological children," Georgia said.

"Which is why I think I'd love an adopted child just as much as a biological one," Polly said. "Look at how different my kids are, from each other and from Steve and me. Teddy and all that fearlessness—he didn't get that from us. But I can't imagine loving him less if he were half Martian and half Eskimo and had *nothing* of me in him, because he's *Teddy*. He's great."

A timer buzzed.

"That's the pasta," Polly said. "Dinner will be ready in ten minutes."

Georgia heard a whimper as Polly headed back into the kitchen. The babies were both asleep in the living room, the room behind where Georgia sat now. She got up and tiptoed in to peek at them. Lily was in the portable crib, on her back with one arm flung overhead. She looked more and more like Ez now that her gray eyes had darkened to brown, her plump little body had started to lengthen. Haven—Georgia was still getting used to that name, but it was better than referring to him as "the baby" all the time—was in his car seat, his head lolling to one side, dimpled fists resting on his thighs. They were so perfect, the two of them.

Georgia watched them for a few minutes, the soft rise and fall of Haven's chest, the flutter of Lily's eyelids. She heard the sizzle of sausages as Polly dropped them into the iron skillet to cook for dinner, the slam of the screen door as Chessy returned from her swim. The late-afternoon sun slanting through the windows lit up the yellow pine paneling on the walls and floor so the entire room glowed gold. The air was warm and balsam-scented. Georgia felt herself dissolve into everything around her—babies, cabin, forest, water, sky. She was *happy*, she realized, at least at that moment. It was so surprising, so unexpected, that she felt disoriented, like a nocturnal creature emerging from a cave into bright sun.

Chessy's voice behind her startled her out of her reverie. "Are they still asleep?"

Georgia nodded.

"Figures," Chessy said. She tilted her head to the side and hopped on one foot, trying to shake water out of her ear. "I spend ten hours in a car with them and they scream the whole time, and you spend ten minutes with them in the cabin—a place you can actually *escape from* if the crying drives you insane—and they do nothing but sleep."

"If you keep hopping around like that you'll wake them up," Georgia said.

Georgia shooed Chessy toward the porch, and followed her out. Chessy wore a black halter one-piece suit that hugged and covered her in all the right places. Men always looked at Chessy for a few moments too long, even men who knew better, like that English teacher Georgia had threatened to slap at Chessy's high school graduation. Georgia had had that kind of body once, too, although now, five days after giving birth at age forty-one, she doubted she would ever have that kind of body again.

Chessy saw the table set for dinner on the porch. She leaned across to pick up a piece of bread and stuffed it in her mouth. She was still dripping wet, her hair wrapped up in a Little Mermaid beach towel.

"I'm glad Lily is going to have a cousin close to her in age," Chessy said, still chewing her mouthful of bread. "They'll be buds."

Georgia's euphoria faded. Was Haven really Lily's cousin, when they shared no blood connection? She sat down in one of the rickety wooden straight chairs at the table.

"I don't know if he's her cousin," Georgia said. "They're not really related, are they?"

"They are if you keep the baby," Chessy said, her voice matter-of-fact. She sat down across the table from Georgia. "Which I think you should do, even though you haven't asked me. And I didn't even *like* babies until I had Lily, but now I'm crazy about her and I think I would be even if I found out tomorrow she'd been switched at birth and wasn't related to me at all."

"Finally, something you and Polly agree on," Georgia said.

Chessy shrugged, and reached for another piece of bread. "What Alice did *sucked*," Chessy said. "And don't even get me started on Chef Boyardee. But the baby had nothing to do with that."

Polly came in bearing a bowl of spaghetti with sausage and broccoli and sweet cherry tomatoes. Georgia realized how long it had been since she had eaten a real meal. Since right after the baby was born. Three days? Four?

"Haven is your baby," Polly said. She put the bowl down, pulled out a chair, and sat down. "I can't tell you what to do, but I can tell you that emotionally, spiritually, intellectually, even legally—I believe he's your child."

"I don't know if he's mine legally, since I abandoned him in the hospital," Georgia said. "And you *took* him—that can't be legal."

Polly piled a large helping of pasta onto a plate and passed it to Georgia. "Georgia, you're jumping to all kinds of wild conclusions about exactly what is going on here. John *asked* us to take the baby. We brought the baby *to his mother*. It's not like we climbed through a window and kidnapped him."

"John didn't ask you to bring the baby up here," Georgia said. "And he certainly didn't ask you to bring the baby to *me*."

"Eat your pasta," Polly said. "You don't have to figure this out in the next five minutes. There's cheese here." She passed a little blue bowl filled with grated Parmesan.

"We have to call John and let him know the baby is here,"

Georgia said. "He may have called the police. There may be an Anna Alert or whatever it is out on the baby."

"Amber Alert," Polly said. "And no, there isn't."

"Someone should put out an Alice Alert," Chessy said. "I still can't believe that your best friend—"

"I don't want to talk about Alice," Georgia interrupted. She turned to Polly. "Have you had any contact with John since you picked up the baby?"

"Yes," Polly said. "Of course. Because I'm the only one here who doesn't have new mother brain." She reached for the bottle of wine on the table and refilled her glass. "I'm also the only one here who isn't nursing, so I guess I'm the only one who can drink. Cheers." She raised her glass toward her sisters and took a sip.

"Anyway, Chessy and I went over to your house yesterday. John looked like hell. He said he hadn't slept since the baby was born, and that his chef had called in sick at the restaurant and he didn't know what to do. He asked if we'd take the baby for a day or two, just until he got a nurse. So we packed a bag of stuff for the baby and then we left. But we did send him a text later."

"A text? Saying what?"

"I think it began, 'Dear unspeakable prick,'" Chessy said.

Polly shot her sister a look. "Would you back off, for a few minutes at least?"

She turned to Georgia. "The note said we were taking Haven for a few days to give John a break, and that we had been in touch with you and you were fine but understandably depressed."

"And—?"

"And that's it," Polly said. She speared a piece of sausage with her fork. "I don't believe in overexplaining."

"So John has no idea you brought the baby up here?"

Polly popped the sausage in her mouth and shook her head.

"Has he called you since he got the note?"

"He texted Chessy. She's never been his favorite, as you know—no offense, Chess—but I think he's deeply scared of me right now."

Georgia turned to Chessy. "What did his text say?"

"'Thanks for babysitting,'" Chessy said.

"'*Thanks for babysitting*'? That's it?" Georgia stared at her sister, incredulous. "Wow." She put down her fork and stared through the screen at the lake, unseeing. "Maybe *he* doesn't want the baby. And if I don't take him and John doesn't take him, then what will happen to him?"

Nobody spoke for several minutes. A cry from the other room broke the silence. Georgia pushed her chair back from the table.

"I'll get him," she said. She walked into the living room, where the baby lay crying in his car seat. She scooped him up and cradled him against her chest, his face against her collarbone. *Haven*. It was a silly name, but it was growing on her. "*Shhhh*," she murmured, her lips against his head. She began to sway in the easy, unconscious rhythm of motherhood. "Hush, little peanut," she whispered. The baby squirmed.

She walked back out to the porch, and Chessy grinned at her. "See? He *is* your baby. You knew it was him crying, and not Lily."

"He's a newborn. They have a different cry. It doesn't take some maternal homing instinct to figure that out."

Chessy shrugged. "Fine. I'm just saying."

Georgia sat down and cradled the baby with her left arm, so she could pick up her fork and eat with her right hand. But he began to cry. Georgia didn't want to nurse him again— nursing was one more step on the slippery slope of growing too attached—but her breasts were so full and so sore that she told herself she was doing it for *herself*, and unbuttoned her shirt. He latched on right away.

"Stop looking at me like that," Georgia said to her sisters, who both wore smug expressions. She looked down at the baby. What if John didn't want him? What then?

The baby stopped nursing and wriggled, cried again. Georgia put down her fork.

"Here," Polly said. "I'll take him. You need to eat."

Polly reached over, picked him up, and sat him in her lap, facing the table. She wrapped one arm around him, under his armpits; her other hand patted his small back. "He's a good burper," Polly said. "And he hasn't spit up yet, unlike my kids, who did nothing *but* spit up."

"Maybe he's inherited John's cast-iron digestive system," Georgia said.

She leaned forward over her plate to take a bite of spaghetti, her eyes on the baby. "Hello, you little man," she said.

He opened his eyes wide and looked at her. His eyes were a pale gray. His eyebrows, light brown, didn't quite match, with the left eyebrow arching up while the right one was almost straight. A tiny wrinkle formed above his nose as he stared at her in concentration. Georgia felt a sudden shock.

Oh, my God, she thought. All at once she saw Alice's face, looking up from fixing the broken drawer front in Georgia's kitchen, her blue eyes open wide, her brown eyebrows that didn't quite match, the little furrow between her brows as she focused on their conversation.

She put down her fork and stared at him for a moment. This child was not hers. And what she felt, when she gazed into those familiar eyes, was not love.

Georgia thought she might be sick.

GEORGIA WALKED DOWN to the dock and watched the light fade over the trees across the lake, watched the sky darken from pale blue to indigo to almost black.

In the eight weeks since John had moved out, Georgia had raged, mourned, exulted, despaired. Her anger had almost consumed her at first; fury not just at what John had done to her and to their marriage, but at what he'd done to Liza, to the unborn baby, to their *family*. Over and over again she imagined John stroking Alice's lean thighs, John pressing his lips against Alice's, John's eyes gazing into Alice's eyes as he moved inside her. It was sickening. The rage she felt shook her body, twisted her gut, made her dizzy.

She had seen him exactly twice since the day she had discovered his infidelity: once at a meeting with the lawyers to draw up the legal terms of their separation, and once when he had stopped by to pick up Liza for an overnight. He had called her many times, but she never answered the phone. If she picked up by mistake, she hung up as soon as he said, "Georgia?" He texted her; he e-mailed her; he even wrote her a letter that arrived one day in the mailbox, addressed in John's looping, almost unreadable scrawl. She had found his handwriting charming once because it was bold and messy and unrestrained, like John. Now she found it hateful, more proof of his reckless nature, and she ripped the letter into pieces and threw it in the garbage without reading it.

"I made a mistake, Georgia," he said to her the day he came to pick up Liza. Liza was already in the car. "A big mistake. But it was *one* mistake, and I—" She had held up her hand to silence him. "Don't," she said. "I don't want to hear it, and I don't care."

But she did care; of course she cared. When she wasn't angry she grieved, a grief so raw and ugly it made her feel like some kind of animal. She cried in great, gulping sobs until her eyes were swollen; one day she cried so much she burst a blood vessel in her eye. She knew John had loved her, really loved her, when he had married her and for a long time after that; it was possible he loved her still.

She remembered odd, small things, like the note he had written with her Christmas gift the year Liza was born, or the dinner he had made to surprise her for their anniversary one year—Javanese roasted salmon with crispy fried leeks, a salad with pears and walnuts, a dessert of warm chocolate soufflé cake with honey-vanilla ice cream. He had fussed so, wanting to include every one of her favorite flavors in the meal. Another time, when Georgia was taking a woodworking class, he gave her a lightweight hammer with a smooth wooden handle that was the perfect size for her small hands. Her hands were blistered from the too-big hammer she had been using, and she thought the little hammer was the most romantic, thoughtful gift she had ever received. She still had that hammer, only now when she looked at it she wanted to pick it up and smash something.

On top of all the anger and the mourning, she missed him; that was the damnedest thing. She hated him, she couldn't stand the sight of him, and yet she missed their life together, his whistle from his office in the basement, his chef's clogs left in inconvenient places all over the house, the way he would come into the kitchen when she was working on a cake, swipe a finger through the icing in the bowl, then dab it on her nose and kiss it off. John had taken up a lot of space in the house and her life, with the trail of tennis balls and chef's jackets and books he left littered everywhere, his booming laugh, and the way he'd greet Liza—even now, even teenage Liza—with "Hey, Doo," the nickname he had bestowed on her as a newborn when he called her Liza Doolittle (because she lay there in her crib and did so little) and then just Doo.

In many ways, John had been a good husband and partner. But then he had focused all that tenderness and affection and attention on someone else. And *that*, to Georgia, felt like a greater betrayal than the sex.

When she had looked at the baby tonight across the dinner table, she had looked into Alice's eyes, seen Alice's face, and realized with complete clarity that this child was not hers. The baby she had wanted was part and parcel of the family she had wanted, the family she hadn't had, because her own mother had died. Before Liza was born she had thought that becoming a mother would fill the emptiness she had felt ever since Evy's death, but it hadn't. Then she thought another child—a sibling for Liza—would make things complete. But that wasn't it, either. The emptiness was something inside her. Georgia had spent her entire life defining herself through her caretaking. As a teenager and young woman she took care of her father and Polly and Chessy; as an adult she took care of John and Liza, too. She mothered her nieces and nephews, her friends and her friends' children; she mothered the brides whose cakes she baked. She was a caretaker, a nurturer; it was who she was and what she did.

But now here she was, smashed up against the limits of her own maternal nature. From the moment she had gazed into the baby's eyes tonight, every ounce of maternal feeling she had for him had died. She did not love this baby; she did not want to mother this baby. In fact, she couldn't stand the sight of him.

For the first time in her life, the *only* person she wanted to nurture was her own howling, wounded self.

22

Alice
June 24, 2012

The one thing Alice had learned since her affair was that
no matter how well you thought you knew someone (whether
another person or yourself), you could still be surprised, *very*
surprised.

The first surprise came Sunday afternoon, when Duncan
drove her home after church, parked next to the curb, walked
her to the front door, and said, "I have something I have to do.
I'll be back in a few hours."

"Okay," Alice said. She didn't ask where he was going; his
manner seemed to say *Don't ask any questions.* He did come
inside and change out of his suit, as he usually did after church
on Sundays, but instead of putting on his Levi's and a polo
shirt, he put on a pair of clean, pressed khakis and a button-
down shirt, and picked up his briefcase. Alice wondered why, if
he was going to work, he didn't just *say* he was going to work,
but there it was.

"Is everything all right?" she said.

He nodded. He stood for a minute in the kitchen and looked at her, and he looked so sad—all his features sliding downward, as though whatever joy and hope lived in him was melting— that it pierced her. She started toward him, arms outstretched, but when she drew near he flinched and said, "I've got to go. I'll see you later." He turned and walked out the door.

Alice stared after him and wished, not for the first time, that Duncan had even one good friend she could talk to, someone to guide her through the darkness of his spirits in this post-apocalyptic phase of their lives. But she and Duncan were both loners and had always been loners. As a child Duncan had been preternaturally smart. Numbers and even abstract mathematical concepts organized themselves quickly and neatly in his brain; he had never scored less than one hundred percent on any math test (including the SAT, GRE, and LSAT) in his life. He was shy and reserved like his father; polite and soft-spoken like his mother, a socialite who drank too much, a fact that Duncan and his father and his siblings went to great pains to ignore or, when it couldn't be ignored, to hide. When Alice first met Duncan that day in the bookstore she had felt a flash of recognition—the same solitariness, the same wary look, the same set of the shoulders, tensed and pulled upward as though in anticipation of a blow, that she saw in herself.

It had been wonderful, finding someone like her, someone else who knew the feeling that all those laughing people in bars and cafés were in on some secret you had never been told. But she and Duncan were *too* much alike. At nineteen, she had been thrilled to find someone cautious and careful and responsible and reserved—the opposite of everything she had known in life with her mother. Now, at thirty-four, she wondered who she might have become if she had spent some time on her own, been forced to seek out friends, support herself financially, participate in the world without Duncan as her safety net. Maybe if they had had a wider circle of friends, those shared hardships and joys and jokes would have been like the plaster that filled in the little cracks that characterized every marriage, preventing it from crumbling.

Alice put down her coffee cup. For a long time she had believed that their friendship with the Bings was all they needed. She and Georgia were best friends; Wren and Liza were best friends; and John and Duncan got along well enough, and if they weren't truly close, well, that's because they were men. But the Bings had always had other close relationships, too, with Georgia's sisters and their families, friends from John's restaurant, brides or mothers of brides Georgia had gotten to know over the years.

Alice and Duncan didn't have a village the way Georgia and John did. They just had each other. And Alice had no idea what would happen now that each other wasn't enough.

THE NEXT SURPRISE came an hour later, when she called the restaurant to talk to John.

She wanted to find out two things: if Georgia was all right, and whether or not Georgia wanted to keep the baby. She had discussed this with Duncan after they came home from the beach, because she wanted to be totally transparent with him.

"I want to call while you're here, so you can listen to our conversation and know there is nothing going on," she had said.

The corners of Duncan's mouth had tensed, just for a moment. "You can call John," he said. "I don't need to listen in."

"But—"

Duncan shook his head. "It's fine."

And Alice had said what she said at least ten times a day: "Okay. I'm sorry."

"Mr. Bing is out of town," the voice on the other end of the phone said now. "He won't be back for several days."

"Out of town?" Alice stood in her front yard, in her running shorts and T-shirt, with a squirrel chirruping at her from the upper reaches of the old cherry tree. "Do you know where?"

"No," said the voice, a woman who had identified herself as Mickey when Alice called. "Would you like to make a reservation?"

"No," Alice said. "I'm a friend, a family friend. I need to speak to Mr. Bing. Do you know how he can be reached?"

"I'm sorry," Mickey said, her voice polite and upbeat. "I don't have that information. Are you sure you don't want to make a reservation? We serve brunch all day today."

"*No*," Alice said. "Thank you."

She hung up and stared at the street, unseeing. Had John gone to retrieve Georgia, wherever she was? Had he brought the baby with him? She tried to imagine John racing off with the baby to persuade Georgia to come back. But her imagination failed her. She couldn't get further than picturing John trying to strap a screaming baby into a car seat, fumbling with buckles and straps and tiny flailing arms, and then swearing a blue streak before deciding to just stay home.

Alice tucked her phone into the pocket of her shorts and started to jog down the street at her usual quick pace, her mind so busy she didn't see the lush June gardens clamoring against the walkways in front of the houses she passed, the carpet of pale pink petals from late-blooming cherry trees beneath her feet.

She turned the corner and ran down Columbia Street, under a green cathedral arch of white oaks and elms and maple trees. Maybe she wasn't meant to have the baby. Certainly if John could talk Georgia into a reconciliation, maybe the next logical step was for Georgia and John to raise the baby. If that were the case, of course, she, Alice, would get out of the way and out of their lives and accept that the baby was forever lost to her. But if Georgia and John got back together but Georgia didn't want the baby, or if Georgia and John divorced and neither of them wanted the baby, why then . . .

Alice slowed her pace as she turned onto the pebbled path that led through the park. She had thought, back in those heady first few weeks of her affair with John, that she might really love him. John was lively and unpredictable and outgoing—all the things Duncan was not. He appealed to her even as she didn't understand him. For instance, why in the name of God would John lose his temper over something as silly as the rules of a card game, something she had witnessed one summer at the lake when they'd all been playing Hearts? Or how could he go weeks on end without working out? But then she didn't really understand Duncan, either, with his long silences and inscrutable looks and mild manner. The punch he had thrown at John was the first completely unpredictable, emotional thing she had ever known him to do.

"I'll tell you the secret to men," she remembered Rita saying one day, sitting at the kitchen table in the little apartment they shared when Alice was eleven or twelve. "They want to be liked." She had blown out a long stream of smoke. "That's it. That's all they want."

Alice had looked up from the macaroni she was eating and nodded. Well, of course. Everyone wanted to be liked, didn't they?

"Most women don't really like men. At least, they *act* like they don't, always criticizing what they do or what they say." Rita had flicked the ash from the end of her cigarette into the pink-and-gold ashtray.

"I like men," Alice had said. She thought of her father, whom she couldn't really remember but who sent her presents from all the faraway places he worked. She thought of her grandfather, who had blown that warm, sweet cigar smoke into her sore ear.

Rita had given Alice a skeptical look. "You weren't very friendly to Eddie."

Alice had hated Eddie, Rita's last boyfriend, who had talked to her in a baby voice as if she were about four. She narrowed her eyes. "He was dumb."

"You see? That's exactly what I'm talking about," Rita had said. "That attitude that women get, that they know a bunch of things men don't. Women are scary to men. They have monthly cycles and they're emotional. They talk a lot and they laugh at inside jokes. They look fragile but they're not, really. They're very confusing. So if men know you *like* them, they relax and they're happy." Rita had paused. "Remember that, kiddo," she said, pointing her cigarette at Alice. "That's all you need to know."

Alice jogged past the swings where she and Georgia had spent countless hours pushing the girls back and forth, back and forth. As far as she was concerned, men were just as confusing as women, no matter what Rita thought.

For the last part of her run, Alice sprinted in intervals—one minute of sprinting, one minute of running. Arms pumping, knees high, heart racing—she loved pushing her body to its limits, feeling every bit of herself pulse with life. She rounded the corner to her own house, the house with neat black shutters on red brick, window boxes spilling over with variegated ivy, blue lobelia, red geraniums. She slowed to a walk, then paused and leaned forward, hands on knees, to catch her breath and allow her heart to slow down.

If she was able to keep the baby she could get one of those running strollers and run with him. And Wren, who loved babies, would be a wonderful babysitter. Alice felt warm thinking about Wren as a big sister, about Wren moving forward in her life with the comfort of a sibling. If Haven was hers, then

Wren would never know the odd loneliness Alice had always experienced, would never have to say, "I'm an only child."

"Haven Kinnaird." Alice said it aloud. "Haven Duncan Kinnaird."

The name felt good in her mouth. It sounded just right.

WHEN ALICE WALKED in the front door she caught sight of the stack of mail on the hall table that had piled up while they were at the beach: catalogs, bills, and flyers for GREAT DEALS on everything from oil changes to Tahitian vacations. A colorful photo caught her eye and she pulled a postcard from the pile.

"*¡Saludos de Valparaíso!*" it read on the front. The photo showed a small city on a bay, with craggy, snowcapped mountains in the distance. Alice studied it. She had never been outside of the United States, except the one time she and Duncan had gone to Quebec for a long weekend when she was pregnant with Wren. She flipped the card over.

> *Dear Ally,*
>
> *Well, here I am in Valparaiso for my honeymoon. My first time in Chile and my first wedding and I'm 52. Who would have thought? It is winter here but not too cold; much better than Ohio in January but not as good as Ohio in June! Ha! We got married in Santiago and go back there on Sunday. Tell Wren I saw ten pelicans and they are the biggest birds I ever saw. Wish you girls and Duncan could visit us here—you should come! Finally your mom is a married woman.*

She hadn't signed it—Rita struggled with the same thing Alice did in figuring out her nomenclature; she was unwilling to be "Mom" but not quite hip enough to be truly comfortable with being called "Rita" by her only daughter. Alice read it through twice. So her mother, who had refused to marry Alice's father, was now married to a man named Oliver whom Alice had never met. Not only that, but her mother hadn't even told Alice she was *thinking* about getting married, let alone asked her if she might want to come to the wedding, or be a part of the wedding.

Rita had moved to Chile in early February; Alice's affair with John had started two weeks later. Alice thought now that if her mother had just stayed put in Ohio, indifferent but still present, the affair might never have happened. But her mother's move to South America had left her with a sense of free-falling, as though the rickety rope bridge to which she'd clung all her life had suddenly given way. She had not realized how much she needed or wanted or, yes, loved her mother, how much she hoped that even after all these years her mother might one day be the loving, attentive, reliable mother she had always longed for.

And now, now here was this postcard reminding her yet again how little she mattered. *Screw you*, Alice thought, surprised at her own rage. *I don't need you, either.* She ripped the postcard in half and dropped the pieces on the floor.

"Mom?" Wren appeared at her elbow, barefoot, wearing boxer shorts and a tank top.

"Yes. Hey." Alice felt flustered, and bent to pick up the pieces of postcard. "You missed a good sermon at church this morning."

"I like sleep better," Wren said. She paused until Alice was upright again. "So you're cool with this whole Lake Placid thing?"

"The Lake Placid thing?" Alice turned to look at her daughter.

"Yeah, with me and Dad. You know, this week."

"This week?" Alice couldn't mask the shock in her voice. She saw the puzzled look on Wren's face and tried to make her voice sound neutral, casual. "Right," she said.

Wren yawned. "It's kind of a pain since we just got back from the beach so I won't have any time to see my friends, but I really want to see Liza."

Alice drew in a deep breath. "Remind me of the plan."

Wren gave her a strange look. Since when did Alice, master organizer, not remember what was going on with the family?

"Dad and I are leaving for Lake Placid tomorrow. Visiting Day at Liza's camp is Tuesday." Wren looked at her as if to say, *You remember all this now?*

Alice wondered for a moment if she might have dementia. The lyrics of a song her mother's boyfriend Steve used to play on the record player, back when Alice was six or seven, echoed in her head, a song about finding yourself in a place both familiar and strange. *You may ask yourself, well, how did I get here?*

The front door opened and Duncan walked in, his skin damp with the midday June heat, the hair at his temples dark with sweat.

"Oh, good," Wren said. "You're here. Mom's confused about our Lake Placid trip. You explain. I need to eat."

Wren flitted off toward the kitchen. She often moved through the house in dance steps, a pas de bourreé from the living room to the kitchen, a series of jetés into the dining room. She did that now, a little cabriole down the hallway.

Alice turned to Duncan. "Lake Placid?"

He put his briefcase down on the floor with a sigh. "Can we talk in the bedroom or the office, someplace with a door?"

He didn't want Wren to hear whatever he was about to say. Alice nodded. She put one hand on the table, bent to untie her running shoes, slid them off. She stood up and walked down the hall to their bedroom, trying to still the rising sense of panic in her chest. Duncan followed her and closed the door behind them. He sat down on the edge of the bed, their bed.

"Alice, I want to get over this, but I can't—at least not yet. And I don't know if I can ever."

Hope was a warm thing, and now Alice felt cold.

Alice sat down across from him, on the ottoman of the cream-colored armchair where Duncan often sat to read at night.

"I spent the morning consulting with a colleague of mine who's an expert in family law." Duncan looked at her. "I don't wish you ill—I really don't. You seem to want this baby very much. You did relinquish your parental rights in the contract you signed when you agreed to be an egg donor." He rubbed his forehead with one hand. "The courts won't like the fact that you changed your mind—it makes you seem a little flaky. If, on top of that, you're separated or divorced, that's another strike against giving you custody, you see?"

Alice sat very still, her back erect, the the ottomn warm under her thighs.

"And you have to think about John and Georgia. I have no idea whether or not they're trying to salvage their marriage, but do you think you can support this baby without any child support from John?"

Alice couldn't even shake her head or nod. She sat, frozen.

"Well, I assume he'd offer child support," Duncan said, "but if I were Georgia I'd be fairly unhappy if my husband were paying child support to you for this baby."

He cleared his throat. "Then there's the whole issue of Wren and Liza. That's not a legal issue so much as a moral one. How will you explain to Wren that Liza's baby brother is now *her* baby brother instead? And how do you think it will affect Liza?" He sighed. "There is a lot to think about here, and a lot at stake. I can go into it with you in more detail later if you want."

Alice's lips were dry, and her throat felt parched. She licked her lips so she could speak.

"What does this have to do with Lake Placid?"

"Wren, for whatever reason, is eager to see Liza. She's been upset about not going to Lake Con for the first time ever. There's a masters vaulting camp in Placid this week. I talked to Georgia before the baby was born about taking Wren up to visit Liza for a day at camp, and she thought it was a good idea. So I made reservations at a hotel in Placid for four nights. We'll drive up tomorrow, Wren will see Liza on Tuesday, and we'll drive back on Friday."

He stood up. "I don't know where Georgia is or how she's doing, but I'm assuming she would want me to go ahead and bring Wren up to see Liza, as we had planned." He looked at Alice, who still sat on the ottoman, mouth agape.

"And I think you need some time alone to figure things out." He shrugged. "For that matter, so do I. I can't raise John Bing's son, Alice. So if that's what you want, we need to talk about the next step."

He walked to the bedroom door and paused, one hand on the wrought iron doorknob.

"Good luck," he said.

23

Georgia
June 24, 2012

So Ez and I are getting married," Chessy said the next morning. She sat between Georgia and Polly on a towel on the little town beach, with Lily sitting between her legs, halfway on the sand. Lily held a pink plastic trowel in one hand, and was banging it with enthusiasm against an overturned blue bucket.

Georgia and Polly both turned to look at Chessy.

"*Married?*" Georgia said. "When did you decide that?"

"Last month," Chessy said. "He's been asking me forever but I wanted to be sure he wasn't marrying me because of the baby." She smiled. "I'm pretty convinced he likes me. The baby is just gravy." She bent forward and squeezed one of Lily's fat thighs with one hand. "You're gravy, aren't you?"

"That's great!" Polly said. "I like Ez." She nodded in approval.

Georgia agreed. Ez would be a good partner to Chessy. For one thing, he adored her. More than once Georgia had caught him watching Chessy as she sat at the dinner table telling some story, her face animated, her voice loud and lively, one hand reaching up to flip her dark hair back behind her shoulder. He looked, at those moments, amazed, as though he couldn't believe this vivacious, intelligent, beautiful woman was with *him*. But he was stubborn, too, and where Georgia and Polly and their father had spoiled Chessy—the motherless infant—Ez would not. Back in March they had all been together for dinner one night at Georgia's, and Chessy had bemoaned the fact that she and Ez couldn't go to some all-day concert in May, featuring six of her favorite bands.

"I'll babysit for you," Georgia had said. "I could take Lily for the day."

Chessy had squealed with delight and jumped up from the table to hug Georgia, but Ez had sat stony-faced and silent.

"That's very generous," he said at last. "But we can't accept. You've already had complications with your pregnancy, and you'll be almost at your due date then. It's too much."

"She'll be fine," Chessy had said. "John will help. Liza can help."

Ez shook his head. "Lily is our responsibility. We'll go to WMZQ Fest next year."

Georgia had been impressed—John would never have thought about the fact that babysitting for twelve hours at that stage of her pregnancy might be hard. Another time, during her fifth or sixth week of bed rest, out of her mind with boredom and frustration, she had broken down in tears as Ez and Chessy were leaving after stopping by with Lily.

"This is like some form of torture," she had sobbed. "I just lie here and worry I'll never have a healthy baby like Lily."

Chessy had murmured some platitudes, but the next day Ez had shown up with his electronic keyboard. He set up the keyboard in a corner of her bedroom and played for more than an hour—Rachmaninoff and Chopin and something by Franz Liszt that was so lovely Georgia completely forgot her achy pregnant body and her terrors and felt the tense muscles in her shoulders relax, the stiffness in her neck start to loosen. She had loved Ez ever since.

"It's wonderful you're getting married," Georgia said. She put one arm around Chessy and hugged her, hard. She tried not to think of her own marriage, of all the hope and confidence and exuberance she had offered up at the altar. She remembered her wedding night, lying in bed with John wrapped around her, thinking, *How could anyone get divorced after the power of those vows?* She had been so young and naïve. She hadn't pictured the years of infertility, the squabbles over cleaning up the kitchen or whose turn it was to get up with the baby, the creeping boredom, the irritation that could slide so easily into anger or, even worse, contempt. She had never imagined lies, betrayal, adultery.

"When's the wedding?" Polly sat up and reached forward as Lily grabbed a fistful of sand and brought it to her mouth. "Oh, no, you don't." Polly pried open Lily's small fist and brushed the sand away. "Here." She handed Lily another plastic trowel before she could begin to squawk her outrage.

"Tuesday," Chessy said.

"Tuesday when?" Polly looked up at her.

"Tuesday. June twenty-sixth Tuesday."

"What?" Georgia and Polly said it in unison.

"That's the day after tomorrow," Polly said.

"I know," Chessy said. "But it makes sense to do it now, since we're all here. I always thought that if I ever got married I'd want to get married here, in the meadow next to the cabin. And then have a picnic."

"That's crazy," Polly said.

"Oh, don't look like at me like that. This is not a big affair like your wedding; it's casual, just the immediate family. Ez is coming up tomorrow. Ez's friend Harris is coming down from

Burlington, so he'll have someone here. I thought Liza could take a day off camp and be my bridesmaid. Her camp is, like, an hour from here, right?"

Georgia stared at her, speechless. Chessy turned to face Polly. "And if you want Teddy and Jane and Sara and Grace in the wedding, too, that would be great. If they could get here by then."

"*I* didn't plan to be here by then," Polly said. "I thought the plan was we were driving up here to get Georgia and bring her home. No one said anything about a wedding."

"Well, when are we all going to be together up here again?" Chessy said. She picked up Lily, who had started to cry, brushed the sand off her bottom, and sat her in her lap, then fished in the bag behind her for a bottle.

Georgia hadn't thought beyond lunch, which was about all the future planning she could handle these days. "Chess, I just gave birth five days ago. I'm not exactly in wedding shape."

"It's not *your* wedding," Chessy said. "Don't worry; it's casual. Ez is wearing khakis and a white shirt but no tie; I have that white dress I got in Mexico, remember? I bought a couple dresses for you and Polly, too. Or you can wear whatever you have."

"I'm not worried about what I'm going to *wear*," Georgia said. She felt hot and cross all of a sudden. "I'm worried about my *life*. We have this baby here"—she gestured toward Haven, still asleep in his car seat under the mosquito netting—"who you stole from John and who belongs to I don't know who. For all I know, I'm wanted for kidnapping now. I'm in the middle of divorcing my husband, who has been sleeping with my best friend, who, by the way, is the biological mother of this baby. I'm trying to figure out how I'm going to explain to my thirteen-year-old daughter that the little brother she was so excited about isn't genetically related to me and is not going to live with us, not to mention the fact that said little brother is actually the little brother of her sometimes best friend. On top of all that, I have to get back to running my business so I actually have an income to live on once I'm single."

A long silence met her words, a silence broken only by the sound of Lily slurping at her bottle, the soft rustle of the breeze through the leaves of the trees at the shoreline, the lapping of the small waves against the sand.

"God," Chessy said. "When you recite it all at once like that it makes it sound like you should have your own reality show. Okay, I understand your life sucks right now and you have some things to figure out. But that doesn't mean you can't relax for a day and enjoy my wedding. You don't even have to make the cake; we'll get a Carvel ice cream cake."

"What about Ez's family?" Polly said. "He has parents, right? And his little E-L-F siblings."

"His parents are in the Foreign Service; they left for Kenya two weeks after Lily was born," Chessy said. "His little sister, Lizzie—Elizabeth—went with them. His brother, Eben, is a fishing guide in Alaska, and they're not that close, anyway."

Polly closed her eyes and turned her face up toward the sun. "I'm in. I'd love to leave my kids with my sister-in-law for a few more days and stay here. A wedding is a great excuse."

Georgia stared at Polly, the sensible one. "Are you crazy? What about the baby?"

Polly opened her eyes. "What about him? He's happy enough here."

"That is not what I meant, and you know it."

Polly slid her bottom forward until she was flat on her back on the towel, knees bent, her feet buried in the warm sand. "I, for one, am thrilled to be having a vacation. And you, Georgie, need more time to figure out what you want. I know you said last night after dinner that Haven's face reminded you of Alice and you didn't want to keep him, but I think you need to take more time. What's a few extra days?"

"Ez will be here after lunch tomorrow," Chessy said. "When his friend Harris gets here, he can have Dad's old room, and you and Polly can share her room upstairs, and Ez and Lily and I can have the other room."

"It's bad luck for Ez to see you before the wedding," said Georgia, who was well versed in every possible bridal superstition in almost every culture.

Chessy shot her an exasperated look. "Right. And the fairies will come tonight and sprinkle fairy dust on our eyelids while we sleep. I'll take my chances."

Haven began to cry, a low wail that soon rose to a series of shrieks. Polly sat up and looked at Georgia expectantly.

"Don't look at me," Georgia said. But his cry went straight through her.

Polly stood up and went over to the baby, squatted down next to him, and pulled back the mosquito netting. "Hey there, peanut," she said. "Don't worry. Somebody loves you." She shot a pointed look over her shoulder at Georgia. "I'm not sure *who*, but somebody loves you." She scooped him up and held him against her shoulder, patted his tiny back.

Georgia felt a familiar tingle in her breasts and looked down. Two large wet spots stained the front of her T-shirt.

"I don't want him, Polly," Georgia said. "You can't keep trying to make me love him." She scrambled to her feet, picked up her towel and shook it out, and wrapped it around her torso to hide the milk stains on her shirt. "Chessy has formula with her; it's in the diaper bag." She slipped her feet into her sandals and headed toward the steps at the back of the beach that led up to the road.

"I'm walking home," she called over her shoulder. "I'll see you there."

And she left her sisters on the beach, babies in their arms.

POLLY'S PHONE RANG after dinner that night as they were cleaning up the kitchen, or rather as Georgia was cleaning up and Polly and Chessy were soothing the babies. Polly sat with Haven in a rocker on the porch just outside the tiny kitchen, giving him a bottle and talking through the doorway to Georgia. Chessy, who had finished feeding Lily, was now waltzing her daughter around the porch on her shoulder.

"Will you get that?" Polly said as her cell phone rang.

"I'll get it," Chessy said. She waltzed over to the table at the other end of the porch and scooped up the phone with one hand, holding Lily all the while.

"Hello?"

Chessy's face changed. "Right," she said. "He's with us."

Georgia came out from the kitchen, holding a dishtowel in her hand. "Who's on the phone?" she said.

Whoever it was continued to talk and Chessy rolled her eyes, the phone pressed against her ear. "What do you mean, 'Where are we?' Where do you think we are?"

Polly sat the baby up and held him against her shoulder. "It's John," she said to Georgia, as though Georgia couldn't tell by the expression on Chessy's face, the way one side of her mouth had lifted in a sneer.

"Georgia's fine," Chessy said. "No thanks to you, of course." A long pause. "That's stalking." Chessy said. "You're stalking us. I think that's illegal." She held the phone away from her ear and smiled as John's voice rose. Georgia couldn't make out what he was saying.

"You *asked* us to take him," Chessy said into the phone. "Don't get so hysterical. There's no 'kidnapping' involved. You *asked* us." She paused. "Uh-huh. What difference does it make? You said, 'Can you take him *for now?*' It all depends on your definition of 'for now,' doesn't it? Really."

She listened again. "Oh yeah? Well, we do, too." She slammed the phone down on the table.

"Hey," Polly said. "That's my phone. Be careful."

Chessy sighed. "Well, that didn't go well."

"What do you mean?" Georgia said. "What did he say?"

"He wants the baby back," Chessy said. "He says the baby is his responsibility, and since he fucked up his other responsibilities he doesn't want to fuck this up, too."

"John said *that?*"

"Not in exactly those words. But it's what he meant."

"What did he *say?*"

Chessy sighed again. "Well, he's smarter than I thought. He's figured out we're up here. So he's on the way. He's already past Baltimore." She glanced at the time, displayed in glowing numbers on the phone.

"Which means, if he doesn't stop a lot, he'll be here before breakfast."

24

Alice
June 25, 2012

$\mathcal{A}$lice had never considered herself much of an actress. She had been too shy to get involved in theater in high school or college, and wasn't even very good at telling little white lies of the "I love that dress" or "The soufflé was delicious" variety. When Wren was little, she had delighted in playing imaginary games in which she was a feisty Dalmatian and Alice was the evil Cruella de Vil. But Alice always felt so self-conscious play-acting, even with her six-year-old daughter, that she would stumble over her lines and say something like *"Give me those puppies!"* in what she thought was a mean voice only to have Wren roll her eyes and say, "No, Mom, you're supposed to be *evil*."

But on Monday morning, Alice put on a great performance. She awoke early and made fresh coffee and filled a thermos for Duncan to take on the road. She made breakfast sandwiches for Wren and Duncan—scrambled egg whites on whole-wheat toast, with a little cheddar cheese for flavor. She made sure they had sunscreen and bug spray and hats and swimsuits and beach towels, as well as aloe vera gel in case they got too much sun anyway. She put an extra fleece in Wren's duffel bag because Adirondack nights could be cold, even in late June. Binoculars, flashlight, two decks of cards, matches, first-aid kit—finally Duncan turned to her and said, "I think we've got it all. We're only going to be gone four days."

"Yeah, really, Mom," Wren said. Wren sat half upright on a stool, with her upper body sprawled across the kitchen counter. She wore her pajama bottoms and a T-shirt and flip-flops, and planned to curl up in the car and go back to sleep as soon as they drove off.

Alice felt her smile stretch across her face like plastic wrap, too tight and artificial. "Okay."

Wren slid from the stool, picked up her pillow and put it under one arm, then came over to Alice and leaned into her, the top of her head nestled under Alice's chin. "Bye. See you Friday."

Alice kissed the top of her head. "Bye. Have a great time, chicken. Say hello to the Adirondacks for me."

"Okay." Wren opened the door and walked down to Duncan's car, packed and ready to go at the curb.

Duncan picked up the bag Alice had packed with the thermos and sandwiches and protein bars and cut-up apples. He didn't look sad, as he had yesterday, Alice noted. He looked almost relieved. Alice swallowed hard.

"I didn't really thank you yesterday," she said. "For doing all that research. I haven't been thinking very clearly. I appreciate it."

He nodded.

Don't go! Alice put her hands over her mouth; the words were so loud in her heart she thought they had made their way to her lips.

"What's wrong?" Duncan said.

Alice dropped her hands to her sides and cleared her throat. "Nothing."

He put his hand on the doorknob, and she couldn't help it. "Please come back," she said.

He looked at her. "Of course I'm coming back. We'll be back on Friday."

"I don't mean just that. You know what I mean."

He sighed. "I can't make any promises, Alice."

She closed her eyes as he opened the door, listened to his steps on the brick walkway, the gentle squeak of the storm door as it closed behind him. She didn't open her eyes until she heard the car door slam, the engine start. Then she waved through the glass, as her husband and daughter drove away.

ALICE CLEANED UP the kitchen, made the beds, threw in a load of laundry, did three sets of push-ups, and it was still only 7:15 A.M. The day stretched before her, long and empty. She sat down at her desk in the corner of the kitchen, opened her laptop, and checked her e-mail. She went through the news she liked to read online, looked up the weather in Lake Placid (78 degrees and sunny) and in Santiago, Chile (58 and rainy). She tried to do some research for the paper she was writing, but she couldn't focus and kept reading and rereading sentences about employment-to-population ratios and wage elasticities and co-efficients in female labor supply equations until none of the words made sense. Finally she closed her laptop in disgust.

She threw the laundry in the dryer and did four sets of chin-ups. She vacuumed. She wished, for the first time ever, that she knew something about gardening, because digging up a bed of soil or carrying rocks or laying flagstone would distract her mind and tax her body in a way she craved right now. And then, because she felt jumpy and scared and not at all like her usual self, she did something her usual self would never do: she sat down on the front stoop and called her mother.

"ALICE? IS EVERYTHING all right?"

"Yes." Now that she had her mother on the phone, Alice wasn't sure what exactly she wanted to say. "I got your postcard," she said.

Rita's voice relaxed. "Great! Can you believe we got married?"

Alice paused. "No. Yes. I mean, I don't know. I was kind of surprised you didn't mention it to me before you left, or at least before you actually got married."

Rita laughed. "Oh, honey, we didn't decide to do it until we got here. And I knew you were busy with teaching and your family and I didn't want you to feel like you had to come all the way down here to see me get married. I'll send you a picture. Olly has one of those fancy phones and he took pictures."

Alice bit her lip. She held her own "fancy" phone pressed against her ear, as though she could press herself right into her mother's voice, her mother's womb, and then come out differently and do it all over again, relive her life to this point.

"Duncan left," she said.

"What?"

"Duncan left. I had an affair and everyone found out and now we may split up."

"You're kidding me."

"No," Alice said. "I'm not kidding."

"Duncan had an affair? He never seemed the type—and believe me, I know the type."

"No, *I* had the affair. Me. *I* cheated on Duncan."

"What?"

"I cheated on Duncan."

A long silence met her words. "Well, honey, you could knock

me over right now," Rita said at last. "I would have sworn *you* weren't the type."

"I'm *not*," Alice said. "Does there have to be a type? I don't even know how or why it happened, really. It just happened, and it was a huge mistake."

Alice heard her mother exhale and could picture her, small chin tilted up, blowing out a stream of cigarette smoke.

"Welcome to the club," Rita said. "I always thought it was too hard to be as perfect as you tried to be."

"I didn't try to be perfect," Alice said. She already regretted confiding in her mother. "I just tried to be normal."

"I'm not criticizing you." Rita blew out another stream of smoke, there in Chile, five thousand miles away. "Where did Duncan go?"

"To the Adirondacks," Alice said. She watched a fat robin peck in the dirt beneath the crepe myrtle at the end of the walkway.

"For good?"

"No, for the week. With Wren. He's coming back on Friday."

"So he hasn't actually left you for good."

"I don't know." She thought about telling her mother everything—about the egg donation, about Liza and Wren, about John, about Georgia's disappearance and the new baby— but it was too much. "We're in counseling, but Duncan doesn't know if he can get over it."

"Huh." Rita paused to absorb all this. "Who's the guy?"

"The guy?"

"The guy you cheated with."

Oh, why not? Rita had likely done the same, or worse. Alice sighed. "John Bing. My best friend Georgia's husband."

A stunned silence, then Rita started to laugh. "Now that is *big*," she said. "I've gotta give it to you. When you fall off the straight and narrow, you don't just take a little step off the path. You *leap*. Wow."

Alice ignored her mother's laughter, and her words. "I don't want to lose Duncan."

"Why not?"

"What do you mean, 'Why not?' He's my husband." Alice's irritation with her mother grew. Would she never learn to stop expecting Rita to be a normal, sympathetic, nurturing mom?

"I like Duncan," Rita said. "You know I like him. He's a wonderful guy. But if you stepped out on him, clearly something's missing."

"Nothing's missing," Alice said. "There were a lot of unusual circumstances."

"There always are," Rita said.

Alice stood up, the phone against her ear, and brushed the dust from the back of her shorts.

"Why can't you just be a *mother* for once?" Alice said. "It was bad enough I had to be the adult my whole childhood; can't I get even one ounce of empathy from you now? It's not like I've demanded all your time and attention throughout my life." She couldn't stop herself. "You didn't even invite me to your wedding!"

Alice heard rustling, a low voice, more rustling. "Hang on. Olly just came in." Alice waited, a wire pulled taut.

Finally Rita came back on the phone. "Ally? Sorry about that." She sighed. "Listen, I'm sorry you're having a hard time. I really am. I didn't mean to make you feel worse. But would you really have taken the time and spent the money to fly all the way down here for my wedding? Half the time I don't think you like me all that much, and I figured you'd disapprove anyway, since you don't know Olly and since I never married your father."

"I don't not—," Alice began.

"Oh, hush," Rita said. "Let me finish. Look, I wasn't the best mother in the world and I'm sure you have plenty to be mad about. But it's not like I woke up every morning and thought, 'How can I screw this kid over today?' I was working full-time at the Eppinger factory, which wasn't exactly fun and games, and then when I came home I wanted to blow off a little steam, have a drink, go dancing. I was seventeen when you were born. Your dad left before you were two, and I was on my own. You were in college by the time I was the age you are now."

Alice didn't care. She was six years old again, and scared. "You didn't take care of me!" she said. "You never paid attention! It's a miracle I didn't get kidnapped or abused or burned or something."

"Maybe," Rita said. "Look, what do you want me to do about it now? I messed up. I did the best I could. I'm sorry. I *am* sorry. Maybe now that you've screwed up a little you'll understand that's what happens; that's how people are."

"That's not how *all* people are," Alice said.

"Really?" Rita said. "'Cause I'm seventeen years older than you and I still haven't met the person who's never made a mistake."

Alice didn't know what she wanted from her mother. Remorse? Insight? Forgiveness? Whatever it was, she wasn't going to get it, at least not right now. "I have to go," Alice said.

"Ally—"

"Congratulations," Alice said. And she clicked the phone off.

FOR THEIR THIRD date, Duncan took Alice kayaking on the C&O Canal. She counted their initial meeting at Kramerbooks as their first date, because he had asked her to have coffee; then he had taken her on that walk through Arlington National Cemetery. He met her at the boathouse in Georgetown at 6:00 A.M., under pink skies that cast a rosy tinge on the early morning river and made the bridges glow. She was there before he was, watching the water, when he appeared at her elbow and handed her a cup.

"Cream, no sugar," he said.

And that small thing—the fact that he had noticed and remembered how she took her coffee—pierced her. No one had ever attended to her likes and dislikes before. Alice had hated ketchup her entire life, and yet once a month Rita would decide to cook a real dinner and make a meat loaf drowned in ketchup. But Duncan noticed and remembered and even respected her preferences.

She remembered a few other things from that date—the bluebells carpeting the woods along the shore, the field chickweed blooming white in the meadows, three turkey vultures circling overhead—but what stood out for her, the thing she never forgot, was that cup of coffee. *Cream, no sugar.*

Duncan studied her and learned her because he felt she was worth learning. And that's who Duncan was, a man who noticed things and paid attention and took the time to study and learn things he loved, like the law and trees and that poem about baby wrens. And now, Duncan was gone.

On a sudden impulse, Alice went into Wren's bedroom and pulled out the photo album she had made for her sixth birthday. Georgia, the artistic one, had gone through a scrapbooking phase, and had persuaded Alice to spend far too much money on special scissors and punches and paper and stickers and an album with archival paper, whatever that meant. They had both made special albums for the girls' birthdays that year, a kind of *This Is Your Life* recapitulation of key moments, year by year.

The album Georgia had made for Liza had been beautiful, with delightful hand-drawn borders on every page and clever cutouts of panda bears and flowers and lollipops. Alice's album for Wren was much more straightforward, photos in neat rows, with lots of white space and captions in Alice's careful print.

She turned the first page, to the photo of Duncan holding newborn Wren in the hospital. Duncan stood sideways, his face turned toward the camera, with both arms wrapped around the baby, who was curled against his chest with her head on his shoulder. Her eyes were open and alert, and one tiny fist gripped the neckline of his polo shirt. She was so small in Duncan's long arms, against his strong chest. Alice remembered looking at the photo several days after Wren's birth and feeling her own chest constrict with her love for the two of them, her *family*, the first real family she had ever had.

She sat on the edge of Wren's bed and pushed aside the pile of leggings and T-shirts and dirty clothes Wren had left there. She set the album in her lap and studied the photo—the way Duncan's hand curled protectively around the baby's small thigh; the way his head was tilted just slightly toward hers; the dimples in Wren's small fist as she clutched his shirt. She thought about the other baby, the one she had held just a few days ago, who had opened his eyes and looked at her with her own eyes, her own expression. But that moment had lost its power. She heard Duncan's voice say, *How will you explain to Wren that Liza's baby brother is now* her *baby brother instead?* She heard him say, *I can't raise John Bing's son, Alice.* John Bing's son.

Alice looked down at the album again. *Her* child, *her* family, was right here in this photo, lived right here in this house. She was, indeed, an imperfect woman and imperfect wife and imperfect mother, but it was all she had to offer. And that was enough.

Alice closed the album, put it down on the bed, and stood up. Then she jogged down the stairs to her own bedroom, pulled her black suitcase from under the bed, and began to pack.

25

Georgia
June 25, 2012

John still hadn't arrived by the time the sky grew pale above the mountains on the eastern shore the next morning, by the time the loon screamed its own wakefulness across the lake. Georgia awoke at six and stood on the porch gazing at the water, listening for the sound of tires on the gravel drive. An early morning mist hung above the surface of the lake, caressed the rocks along the shore, curled through the trees. She could hear the sweet whistle of a white-throated sparrow in the woods and, beyond that, stillness. The baby had slept in Polly's room last night; Georgia had expressed enough of her abundant milk to fill several of the bottles Chessy had brought, then she had put in her earplugs, latched the hook on her bedroom door, and slept.

She heard the creak of footsteps on the stairs and turned to see Chessy, carrying a bright-eyed Lily on one hip.

"How can you be standing on the porch?" Chessy said. "It's freezing." She wore blue flannel pajama bottoms and an oversized red sweatshirt proclaiming I LOVE NAPS.

"I keep expecting to hear John's car."

"Maybe he got lost," Chessy said. "Here." She handed Lily to Georgia, and bent to put on their father's black rain boots, which sat under the table on the porch.

"Are you going somewhere?" Georgia said.

"Yes. I'm going to the kitchen to make coffee and my feet are freezing. I didn't bring slippers."

Georgia followed her into the kitchen and sat down, the baby in her lap. She picked up a set of tin measuring spoons from the counter and handed them to Lily.

"Maybe John was in an accident," Chessy said, rooting through the cupboard.

"You don't have to sound so hopeful about it," Georgia said.

Lily banged the spoons against the table. A baby's cry came from upstairs, then the creaking of the floorboards as Polly got out of bed. The crying rose to wails. Polly's voice was a murmur, a river of comfort, and Georgia felt a pang of guilt that Polly was the one up there soothing Haven.

"Did he sleep through the night?" Georgia asked Chessy. The uninsulated walls in the cabin, built as a summer escape in the 1930s, were paper-thin.

"Are you crazy?" Their father's boots were too big for Chessy and she walked around the kitchen in shuffling steps. "He's what—six days old? What do you think?"

He's not my baby, Georgia said to herself. *He's not my baby.*

"Every two hours," Polly said, coming through the doorway with the baby on her shoulder. She walked over to the fridge, took out one of the bottles of Georgia's milk, and handed it to Chessy. "Here, will you warm this up?" She looked at Georgia.

"I breast-fed all four of mine. This bottle business is a pain in the neck."

Georgia shrugged and bent to kiss the top of Lily's head. She looked up. "John's not here yet."

Polly shifted the baby to her other shoulder. "Knowing John, he stopped for dinner, had a few beers, and pulled into a Motel 6. I bet he's sitting at the counter in some diner on the Northway right now, giving the cook pointers on how to scramble eggs."

Chessy smiled. "Right." She switched the coffeemaker on and took out the jar of baby oatmeal she had warmed in the microwave. She sat down at the table next to Georgia and reached for Lily. "So," she said, "let's plan my wedding."

"I have maternity leggings I can wear," Georgia said. "In black."

"I brought a dress for you," Chessy said. She looked at Polly. "And one for you."

"If they have puffy sleeves or giant bows on the butt forget it," Polly said. "I'm too old to be Little Bo Peep. And nothing matching. I'm too old for sister dresses, too."

"Very funny." Chessy slipped a spoonful of oatmeal into Lily's mouth. "I think that bottle is warm now."

Polly picked up the bottle from where it sat in a simmering pan of water on the stove, then handed the bottle and the baby to Georgia. "I did the night shift," she said.

Haven nestled against Georgia. She picked up the bottle and held it to his lips. He pushed it away with his tongue.

"Why don't you just nurse him?" Chessy said.

"Because I don't plan to *keep* nursing him." But of course the baby wriggled and turned his face toward her breast and rooted with his small mouth against her, and her milk let down. With a sigh, she put the bottle down on the table, and unbuttoned her shirt. He latched on and looked up at her, his gray eyes studying her face. *Don't memorize me, little man,* Georgia thought. *Don't get accustomed to my face.*

Chessy glanced at the clock. "Ez should be here by two," she said. Lily banged a pudgy fist against the top of the table and Chessy spooned another bite of oatmeal into her mouth. "I have a list somewhere of everything that needs to get done."

"*Where* are you getting married?" said Polly. She poured herself a generous cup of coffee. "And who's performing the ceremony?"

"Well, we were going to get married in the meadow," Chessy said, tilting her head toward the window. "But it turns out Ez is allergic to hawkweed so we've decided to get married on the town beach. Reverend Finster is performing the ceremony."

"Reverend Finster?" Polly arched an eyebrow at Chessy.

"Yes, don't look at me like that. He's a *real* minister, from that Community Church in town. We've had several phone conversations with him."

"What denomination is he?"

"I don't know. Some kind of Protestant. Ez and I are meeting him at four today." She looked up at Polly. "Will you take Lily then? Just for an hour."

"Oh, my God. I finally have a few days of blessed freedom from my kids and now you two want to do nothing but saddle me with yours." Polly rolled her eyes, but she nodded. "All right. Fine." She drew her eyebrows together in a mock serious face and stared at Lily. "Promise me you'll be good, you little demon child, you."

"She's not a demon child," Chessy said.

"Haven is the only demon child here," Georgia said.

Polly and Chessy turned to her. "He's a *baby*," Chessy said. "An *innocent* baby."

"It was a joke," Georgia said. "But I'm not going to—" She

stopped as she heard a noise outside: the hum of a car engine and the sound of tires on the gravel road.

"Oh, God," she said. "John's here."

GEORGIA UNLATCHED THE baby's mouth from her breast and buttoned her shirt. "What if he's got the police with him or something?" Georgia felt wild, unmoored, as though she might fly apart in little pieces and go floating up to the ceiling.

"I just heard *one* car," Chessy said. "He's not bringing the police. You watch too many crime dramas on TV."

The baby, separated abruptly from his breakfast, began to cry. The tires outside came to a stop and a car door slammed.

"He's got balls, I will give him that," Chessy said. "Coming up here knowing all three of us were here." She stood up, propped Lily on one hip, and stepped out onto the porch, Polly close behind her.

"Well, well, well," Chessy's voice said. "If it isn't Chef Boyardee."

Georgia cradled Haven against her shoulder, then stood up and followed Chessy.

John stood outside on the wooden stoop. He cleared his throat. "I want to talk to Georgia," he said. His eyes caught sight of her face. "Georgia, please. Can we talk?"

He was pale, even for John, who spent his life in a kitchen. A dark stubble of three or four days' growth stood out against the whiteness of his skin. His hair was unkempt, as though he had run his hands through it over and over. He wore jeans and a black T-shirt and held his arms crossed over his chest with a hand in each armpit, probably to keep them warm. The mist still clung to the lake and hung over the swamp grass by the shore, and the air was chilly and damp. Georgia almost— *almost*—felt sorry for him.

"I don't want the baby," she said. She stepped out from behind Chessy. "It was Polly and Chessy's idea to bring him here; not mine. I had nothing to do with it."

"Can I come in?"

John didn't wait for an answer. He opened the screen door, which squeaked in protest, then banged shut behind him. Georgia expected him to stand right there next to the door, ready for a quick escape, but he walked over to where she stood. His glance flickered to the baby, and back to Georgia's face.

"Here," she said. She peeled the baby off her shoulder, wrapped her hands around Haven's little chest, her hands under his armpits, and held him out toward John.

John looked at her. "What?"

"Take him. I don't want him. He's yours. You and Alice are welcome to him."

John didn't move. "Listen. I drove almost all night to get here, except for a one-hour nap in the car in the parking lot of some Stewart's on the Northway. I'm in no condition to drive back to D.C., with or without the baby. I came to talk to you."

Georgia took a step forward. "Take him," she said.

John reached out and took the baby, holding him as Georgia had, with both hands under the baby's armpits. "Georgia, come on. What am I going to do with him right now? Where am I going to go?"

Georgia leveled a look at her husband. "Get a room," she said. "You have some recent experience with that, don't you?"

John sucked in the air sharply between his teeth, as though he'd been punched.

"Okay," he said. "I'm sorry."

The baby, his little bowed legs dangling in midair, began to cry. John's eyes never left Georgia's face. "I came here to apologize, and because I want to talk to you about our family, about us, about the future. I'd rather talk to you alone"—he shot a look at Chessy—"but if you want me to get on my knees here, in front of your sisters, and beg you to forgive me, I'll do it."

"I don't want to talk to you," Georgia said. The hurt she felt was deep and true, and John on his knees on the worn painted floorboards wasn't going to change that.

"Georgia, please. I fucked up—God, did I fuck up!—and I am so, so sorry."

"Hey," Chessy said. "Watch your mouth. There are children here." She put a hand over one of Lily's ears.

The baby cried harder, and John cradled him against his shoulder. He rubbed the baby's back and murmured something to him in a low voice. Georgia remembered how he had held Liza like that, walked through the house with her at night, murmuring recipes and cooking wisdom in a soothing voice. *Always use a stainless steel pan to brown butter; you can see the butter change color better. Once you've browned the butter, stir in the balsamic vinegar, salt, and pepper.* "Why recipes?" Georgia had asked him once. "Why don't you sing to her?" John had looked at her in genuine surprise. "Recipes are what I love," he had said.

John caught Georgia looking at him and returned her gaze, staring at her in that way he always had, like he saw something pure and strong inside her, the sculpture beneath the stone. Before this, it had always made her feel seen and known in a way she hadn't felt with anybody else, as though her flaws, both real and imagined, had vanished and she was her most beautiful self.

"Stop looking at me like that," she said.

"We are a family," John said. "And I don't mean the kids. I mean you and me. *You* are my family. We're, we're—*mated.*"

Georgia felt her tears rise. "Not anymore," she said.

Polly took a step forward. "I think you should go," Polly said.

John looked at Polly in shock. "I don't want to go. I drove all night to get here."

"Take the baby and go," Georgia said.

"Georgia, please. I don't even have diapers or formula or that thing for him to sleep in, that cot thing. And I'm not here for him, I'm here for you."

"The bassinet," Polly said.

"Whatever it's called," John said. He looked at Georgia. "You're my family," he said, his voice stubborn. "We're mated."

"That's a stupid thing to say," Georgia said. "I don't even know what it means."

Haven's cries grew louder and he began to wail, in that high-pitched newborn scream of distress. It was too much for Georgia. She walked over and took Haven from John, patted the baby's small back, and rubbed her cheek against the top of his soft head.

"All right," she said. "I'll finish feeding him before you go, and Polly will get his things together for you."

Georgia knew that Polly and Chessy wanted her to keep the baby, believed that she was *meant* to keep the baby. But *she* didn't feel that, and she hoped her eyes said as much now. Polly held her gaze, sighed, then nodded and went back inside, returning to hand the bottle to Georgia before disappearing upstairs. Georgia could hear her folding up the Portacrib, zipping up bags as she packed the baby's things. Chessy stayed on the porch, swaying to and fro with Lily, glaring at John.

"It's fine, Chess," Georgia said to her. "You can leave us alone."

Chessy wrinkled her nose at John, then shuffled back inside in her big boots.

Georgia sat down in one of the old green wooden rockers and tried to give Haven the bottle, but he turned his face away and cried. "He won't take a bottle from me," she said, "but he took it from Polly and he'll probably take it from you. I've got five or six bottles of breast milk you can have, and once that's gone he should take four ounces of formula every four hours." She unbuttoned her shirt again and pulled the baby to her.

"I'm not going to remember what to do," John said. "I don't want to make a mistake."

Georgia grabbed the Little Mermaid beach towel Chessy had hung on the back of the rocker and draped it over her shoulder, to keep the baby warm and because she didn't want John to watch him nursing and get any warm-and-fuzzy, let's-be-a-family ideas.

"You can ask *Alice* what to do," Georgia said. "She's very well organized." Her words came out as short and tight as if they'd been snipped off with scissors.

"Georgia, I am not asking Alice about anything. I have seen Alice exactly *once* in the last six weeks, and that was only because I was in a complete panic about how to handle this baby on my own. That is *over*." John paused and looked at her. "Can I sit down? Is it okay if I sit down?"

Georgia nodded and he sat down in a rocker next to her. She thought about telling him that he should sit in one of the uncomfortable, straight-back wooden chairs, but then she dismissed the thought as petty and remained silent.

They rocked in silence for a few minutes; the baby, full of warm milk, nodded off to sleep in Georgia's arms. She reached one hand under the towel to button up her shirt.

"You should take him now, when he's full and sleepy," Georgia said.

"I don't want to take him," John said, "without you. I mean, I love him, I want him, but I came here for *you*."

Georgia had nothing to say to her husband, really. She wanted only to rock, back and forth, back and forth, and to stare at the lake and not think.

"I don't want him," Georgia said. "I thought I did, but I don't. He looks like Alice. I'm afraid that every time I look at him, I'll think about"—she saw again the image of Alice's long, lean legs wrapped around John's hips, John thrusting into Alice, John shaking his head back and forth the way he did when—"about you and Alice. And when I think about you and Alice . . ."

Georgia's throat was so tight it was hard to get the words out. "When I think about you and Alice, I feel hurt and rage. The baby deserves better than that. He should have a mother who can look at him and feel nothing but love. I can't do that."

John was silent for so long that Georgia finally stole a look at him, to see if he had heard her. He sat rocking next to her, his feet flat on the worn, gray-painted floorboards, his hands on his thighs, staring at the lake. Tears filled his eyes.

Georgia's heart was a stone, and stones did not melt.

"Chessy said you wanted the baby back," she said. Her voice was even now. "I was worried you were going to call the police and have Chessy and Polly—and me—arrested for kidnapping. They thought if I spent time with the baby I'd change my mind, that I'd want to keep him. But they were wrong."

John continued to rock. "The only call I made to the police," he said at last, "was when you disappeared. Because I was worried about you."

"I wish you'd been worried about me a little sooner," she said. "Like before you screwed around with my best friend."

"I was lonely," he said. "I know that's not an excuse, but it's an explanation."

"It's a cliché," Georgia said.

"There's nothing I can say that isn't," John said. "Is there? But I miss you; I miss Liza; I miss our family. I love you. I want you back. Having you gone makes me feel, I don't know, unconnected from everything, from my entire life."

"I'm sure," Georgia said.

"Oh, come on, Georgia, *talk* to me. You've refused to see a marital counselor, you wouldn't let me be there for the birth of the baby, you won't answer my letters or phone calls—you're pissed, and you have every right to be pissed. But we had sixteen years of a pretty good marriage before this. Doesn't that count for anything?"

"Seventeen years," Georgia said. "And evidently it didn't count to you."

"Bullshit." John stopped rocking. "I love you. I have loved you from the day you walked into Truscello's. But this didn't happen in a vacuum."

"Don't you dare make this my fault."

"I'm *not*. God, if you would listen for *one minute*, maybe we could actually have a conversation. I was scared, okay? You are a great mother, the best. You've done an amazing job with Liza. But sometimes—" John looked around the porch, as though the words he wanted might be hanging from the rusty hook on the wall, scrawled across the checkered oilcloth on the table "Sometimes, you're *too good* a mother."

Georgia sat up straighter in the rocker. "What's that supposed to mean?"

"It means that from the minute Liza was born, I was a second-class citizen in my own house. I didn't know how to deal with an infant but you knew everything, because you'd taken care of Chessy. Every time she cried, every time she had a fever or stubbed her toe—I love her, she's my daughter, but you did *everything* for her, and your attention always went to her first."

"Of course. She was a baby."

"She hasn't been a baby for ten years."

"So you felt compelled to have an affair with my best friend?"

"*No*. Maybe. I don't know. All I know is that I've been irrelevant for a long time now. Even once Liza wasn't a baby, then it was all about trying to have *another* baby. I've spent more time jerking off into a jar over the last ten years than I have making love to my wife. You know what *real* loneliness is? It's living in a house with someone who's so preoccupied with what they *want* that they pay no attention to what they *have*."

"John—"

He shifted in his chair, so he was facing her. "We spent almost ten years focused on trying to have another baby. And I love you and I knew that's what you wanted to make you happy, so I went along with it—even with using donor eggs from Alice, which, to tell you the truth, made me pretty uncomfortable. Then you were on bed rest, and terrified about losing the baby. Alice came to me about what was going on with Liza and Wren because she didn't want to worry you. *Finally*, a parenting thing I knew something about! I was *needed*. So I spent more time with Alice than I should have."

"And then you had to fuck her." Georgia used the harsh, ugly word because the pain inside her felt so harsh and ugly.

"No," John said.

Georgia braced herself, her shoulders tense, awaiting his anger.

"And it makes me sadder than I can tell you that I crossed that line," he said.

Georgia bent forward, curling over the baby in her arms. She and John had shared a bed every night for more than eighteen years. Often at night when she climbed into bed, John would reach over for her cold hands, press them between both of his own, then raise her hands to his lips and blow his warm breath on her fingers until they were warm. "Give me the fingers that can out-chill sorbet," he would say, "the hands that put granita and gelato to shame," and she would offer her hands to him, pressed together as though in prayer. She had missed the warmth of John's hands at night, missed that familiar ritual. She understood loneliness, too.

"I've spent the past eight weeks sleeping on a couch in my office in the restaurant," he said, as if he had read her mind, "and even if I were sleeping in a penthouse it wouldn't change anything. I hate it. I miss you."

She wouldn't look at him now, so he talked to the top of her head. "I'm not proud of what happened; I feel shitty about the whole thing, about myself. I never thought I was the kind of guy who would cheat. But I did. I can't change that."

He was so close to her she could smell his skin, the familiar scent of garlic.

"You know, Georgia, I'm as comfortable with you as I am with my own shadow. You fit me. I can't get from anyone else what you have given me, and you know that applies vice versa. We're *mated*."

We're soul mates, that's what he means, Georgia thought, even if he couldn't articulate it. She buried her face in the top of the baby's head. She had always felt that way about John, too, until the discovery of his affair with Alice made her wonder what she lacked, made her feel fat and uninteresting and disorganized and awful.

The chittering birds and the breeze in the forest filled the silence between them. At last John said, "You know, there's this Japanese word, umami, that describes a fifth taste. It's not salty, sweet, sour, or bitter. It's a, a"—he searched for the word—"a *sensation* that makes your mouth water, something so delicious you can't explain it as one thing. It's full and rich and coats your tongue and it has an aroma, too. It's what you taste in a perfectly dressed Caesar salad—that tang of Parmesan cheese and anchovies and Worcestershire. It's the mating of the things together that makes it work, elevates it to something beyond."

Screw John and his stupid TV chef shows. Georgia wouldn't look at him.

"That's our marriage, our family," he said. "I want you back.

We're *mated;* we're something different together, something better."

Georgia leaned in deeper toward the baby in her arms, curled herself around him. She thought of herself curled into a ball at night, alone in their big bed. She thought about John rolling out gum paste and cutting out rose petals to help her with the cake. She thought about John murmuring recipes to infant Liza, trying to soothe this baby she held now. She thought about the hammer he had given her, about his unwavering belief that she was so amazing she could do anything—bake a cake for a senator, carve a dovetail joint, have a baby, even when she had failed at it again and again.

Georgia looked up. "I don't want to raise a baby who is going to keep Alice Kinnaird in my life."

"Alice doesn't want to be involved with the baby."

"How do you know that?"

"You think Duncan would agree to raise him after all this? You think she'd want to raise him alone?" John paused. "If you really don't want him, then we have to consider putting him up for adoption. Because I don't think *I* can raise him alone."

The baby in her arms shifted in his sleep. Instinctively, Georgia tightened her hold. At that moment Polly appeared in the doorway, with the diaper bag in one hand and a duffel bag in the other.

"There are enough diapers and wipes here for a few days," Polly said. "His bottom is a little red, but just use that A&D ointment on him when you change him. His clothes are in the duffel bag. There are some receiving blankets in there, too, if he needs to be swaddled, and a couple of clean pacifiers."

John looked as though she had just given him the code to launch the nuclear missiles that would blow up the world, and now expected him to go do it. Chessy walked onto the porch behind Polly, carrying Haven's car seat and the bundled-up Portacrib. She brushed past John, pushed open the screen door with her foot, and placed the baby gear on the ground next to John's car. Polly followed her and put the baby's bags down next to the car, too.

John looked at Georgia with the gaze she remembered from all those years ago, with those eyes so dark brown they were almost black, with that intensity that made you feel like you were the only person in the room, the only person in the universe.

"What do you want me to do?" he said.

26

Alice
June 26, 2012

*A*lice didn't sleep well because the one-room cabin she had rented for the night smelled so musty she couldn't stand it. At one point, tossing and turning at 2:00 A.M., she considered going out to find a twenty-four-hour store so she could purchase a sponge and a bottle of Pine-Sol, but the idea of driving through the blackness of an Adirondack night with no idea where she was going kept her in bed. She wore her running leggings and a long-sleeved T-shirt so her skin had as little contact as possible with the sheets, which were also of dubious cleanliness. The thought of bedbugs crossed her mind, too, but she decided that in the big picture of her life right now, bedbugs were a minor concern.

She had crossed the Blue Line into the Adirondack Park around nine, shortly after dark. She had no idea where Duncan and Wren were staying in Lake Placid, and she didn't think she could drive an additional two hours on black and unfamiliar roads. When she hit Opal Lake she recognized the exit for Lake Con, where she had spent so many summers with the Bings, and remembered Dun Roamin', the motel just off the exit.

Every "room" at the motel was an individual cabin, with its own tiny porch and parking space. Alice's cabin had knotty pine flooring and walls and even a knotty pine ceiling, and the whole place made Alice feel claustrophobic for the first time in her life, as though she were in some kind of knotty pine coffin. The cabin was barely big enough to contain a double bed, a pine dresser, and a straight-back wooden chair.

After several more hours of wakefulness, listening to some small creature rustle inside the wall behind the knotty pine paneling near her head, she threw back the covers and got up and brushed her teeth. A hot shower seemed like her best hope for the day, but when she pulled back the shower curtain she found something vaguely green coating the tiles, and decided to skip the shower. She splashed cold water on her face, and brushed her hair back into a ponytail. She changed into a clean sports bra, T-shirt, and hoodie and pulled on a fresh pair of running tights. When she stepped outside she was surprised at the cold nip of the air, surprised, too, by the sharp, sweet scent of balsam, by the quiet. She threw her suitcase into the backseat of her car and drove into town to see if she could find a diner or a service station open this early.

Alice had always liked the little town of Opal. Several old homes with mansard roofs and dormers and turrets lined the main street on the way into town, and the town itself was a mix of the practical, like the Grand Union and the Town Store (which sold everything from camping gear to original works of art), and the fanciful, like the Internet café that also sold antiques. The commercial area of town stretched for two or three blocks, ending at a small park at the far end with a fountain that changed colors at night, something that had delighted Wren and Liza when they were little. Beyond the park was a bandstand overlooking the long expanse of Opal Lake.

Alice realized that in the ten-plus years they had vacationed with the Bings here, they had never once gone out to breakfast. She drove slowly down the main stretch, looking for signs of life, and noticed lights on in a little restaurant with a blue-and-white awning and several cars and trucks parked out front. She pulled over and parked across the street in front of the twenty-four-hour Laundromat, which was empty. A dog barked from somewhere by the park. She zipped up her hoodie and walked over to the door of the restaurant, where she read:

BREAKFAST ALL DAY.
BEST HOME FRIES IN THE NORTH COUNTRY.
OPEN 5:00 A.M. TO 10:00 P.M.

With a sigh of relief Alice pulled open the door, and walked into warmth and the smell of coffee and fried potatoes. She always felt self-conscious being alone in a restaurant, and looked around for a place to sit. Two police officers in uniform sat at the counter drinking coffee; an elderly couple at a table by the window picked at their sausage patties. She walked over and sat down at an empty table in the back.

The waitress had just filled her cup with steaming black coffee when the door opened again. A man came in sideways, pushing the door open with one elbow because he had both hands wrapped around the handle of a car seat, with a bundled-up baby inside. Alice's eyes went immediately to the baby, a very tiny baby, fast asleep. The baby wore a little strawberry cap and was wrapped in a silk rainbow blanket exactly like the one she had given Georgia at the baby shower back in January, back in another life, when she was an honest wife and Georgia was her best friend and John—

Alice looked up, at the man carrying the baby. He turned, and the door closed behind him. He didn't see her at first, but she saw him. And of course there was no place for her to go, no place to hide. His eyes searched the restaurant for a table, glazed over her, came back, opened wide. And then John Bing came over and sat down across from her, and set their baby in his car seat on a chair next to them both.

NEITHER OF THEM spoke for a minute. Alice was too stunned to speak, and John—John looked so exhausted that he seemed beyond words, beyond surprise. Alice pushed her coffee cup across the table toward him.

"Here," she said. "I'll get another."

He wrapped grateful hands around the mug and took a sip.

"Have you found Georgia?"

"Found her and lost her," he said.

"What is that supposed to mean?"

"She's here, at the cabin at the lake. That's where she came when she left the hospital. Her sisters figured it out and took the baby and brought him up here, and then I drove up after them yesterday or the day before or today—whatever day it is." He looked at her. "Sorry. I haven't had much sleep."

"Georgia's here?" Alice's eyes flew to the door of the restaurant, as if a wronged Georgia might walk in at any moment, crying, *How could you? How could you? How could you?*

"Yes. And she told me yesterday she doesn't want anything to do with the baby, or our marriage. She and her sisters practically threw the baby at me with all his stuff. I hadn't slept in so long I didn't think I could drive back to D.C., so I rented one of those claustrophobic little cabins at that place down the road,

Finished Wanderin' or Stop Ramblin' or whatever it's called. I tried to nap all day, but the baby wouldn't sleep for more than twenty minutes at a stretch. I was up most of the night with him, too."

"Dun Roamin'," Alice said. She had driven right up the driveway to her own little cabin after checking in. Of course she had paid no attention to the other cars parked in front of the other little cabins, not that she could have seen them in the dark.

"Yeah." John rubbed a hand across his eyes. "At least it had a microwave, so I could heat the bottles." He glanced over at the sleeping baby. "This is the longest he's slept since yesterday afternoon."

John propped one elbow on the table, rested his chin in his hand, and looked at Alice. "I should be stunned to see you here, I suppose," he said. "But I'm beyond being surprised by anything."

"I'm here for Duncan," she said.

The waitress came over and put down another coffee cup and filled it. "Cute baby," she said. "He looks like you, Mom."

Alice glanced at her in terror.

"It's supposed to be a compliment," the waitress said. "You folks know what you want?"

"I'll have oatmeal," Alice said. "With fresh fruit, if you have it." She reached for the cream and poured a splash in her coffee.

"I'll have two eggs over easy. Tell the chef to flip them as soon as the whites are set on the bottom. I'd also like bacon extra crisp, and home fries, also crisp," John said. He turned to Alice. "Are you telling me Duncan is here, too?"

"Duncan and Wren. They're spending the week in Lake Placid. Today is Visiting Day at Liza's camp and they worked it all out with Georgia that they'd come up and take Liza for the day. I guess I thought you knew."

"Shit." John rubbed his forehead. "I forgot about Visiting Day."

"It's okay. Georgia didn't. She arranged it all with Duncan. Then Duncan and Wren are spending a few more days in Lake Placid. Wren was really disappointed about not coming to Lake Con this year." She wrapped both hands around her coffee mug and stared down into it.

"Yeah, *that* would have been a fun family vacation." John looked at Alice. "Georgia is not going to forgive me. And she says she doesn't want the baby. I don't know what I'm going to do."

Alice closed her eyes. "I'm sorry," she said. She opened her eyes again to look at him. "What do you want?"

He sighed. "Alice—"

"Oh, God, don't." She leaned forward toward him. "Don't say something about how much I meant to you and how you're sorry but Georgia is the love of your life. I don't know what happened. You were like an earthquake in my life. And I care about you and in some strange way I'm grateful to you, but I don't want to waltz off into the sunset with you. Duncan is my touchstone."

John nodded. "I think Georgia is my touchstone, too."

An uncomfortable silence fell. John looked and felt almost like a stranger to Alice, like the quirky, somewhat unreliable, intense, disorganized man he had always been. How she ever could have seen him as anything else, as anyone other than Georgia's husband, was a mystery to her now.

John looked down at the gold-flecked Formica tabletop, and cleared his throat. "I do want to say I'm sorry, Alice. I started something I never should have started, and I'm sorry for the effect it's had on you and your family and your life. I knew it was wrong, and I did it anyway, and I'm sorry."

"I did it, too," Alice said. She thought of what Rita had said, *Maybe now that you've screwed up a little you'll understand that's what happens; that's how people are.* She did understand; she didn't blame John. It was her own choice, her own failing. "It's not you, John," she said. "It's forgiving myself that's hard."

The baby stirred in his car seat, opened his mouth, and yawned. Alice looked at Haven, but didn't feel the yearning for him she had felt before. The yearnings she felt now were for her *family*, for Duncan and Wren and herself together, the three of them, the way they had been before.

"What are you going to do about the baby?" she said.

"I don't know. I can't raise him by myself. I work fifty or sixty hours a week, and don't get off most nights until midnight or later. I've spent the past eight weeks sleeping on a couch in my office at the restaurant, and taking showers at the gym. How is that going to work with being a single parent?"

The waitress appeared with two dishes in hand, and placed Alice's oatmeal in front of her, sprinkled with small, bright red strawberries. She put John's breakfast down. "Chef says if he gets those home fries any crisper they'll be home cinders," she said.

"They look fine," John said.

And because the waitress was standing there, blocking her view of the door, Alice didn't see them come in. She only heard Wren's voice.

"Mom? Mom! What are you doing here?"

THE WAITRESS TURNED and Alice saw them then, Wren dancing toward her across the restaurant, Duncan still holding the door open, staring at Alice and John with a look of complete shock. Alice stood up. She wanted to yell, "It's not what you think!" across the restaurant to him, but she couldn't make a scene, especially not in front of her daughter, who had no idea about any of this.

"The baby! Oh, my God, it's the new baby! Has Liza seen him yet?" Wren came over and bent over the car seat to inspect the sleeping Haven.

"He's cute," she said, straightening up. She slid into an empty chair on the other side of Alice. "Hey, John. I can't believe I got to meet the baby before Liza did! Don't tell her that, okay? I don't want her to feel bad. So, Mom, what are you doing here?"

"What are *you* doing here? I thought you were in Lake Placid."

"We had a flat tire." Duncan stood a few feet away from their table, as though he didn't trust himself to come any closer. Alice was still standing, one hand on the back of her chair.

"Yes!" Wren said. "And Dad changed it, but then I was starving so we stopped for dinner at that place in Chestertown—remember, that place with the great chocolate malts? And then it was crazy dark and we were worried about finding our way to Lake Placid, and then Georgia called Dad and asked him about coming to the wedding today. So we stopped for the night at that place with the cute cabins, Dun Roamin.' "

Oh, my God, thought Alice. *Next I'll find out that Georgia and Chessy and Polly and my mother and her new husband all spent the night there, too. And what wedding is she talking about?* But she had to act normal, be normal, for Wren. She sat down.

"I can't believe it," Alice said. "*I* spent the night there! After you left yesterday I missed you, and I realized I should have come. So I threw some stuff in the car and came after you. I really, really wanted to be with you." She spoke to Wren, but her eyes never left Duncan's face.

"Really." Duncan's voice was clipped and tight.

John looked wide-awake now, his hands wrapped so tightly around the coffee mug that his knuckles were white. He shot Alice a look of utter helplessness and regret, a look that said, *I'm sorry. I'm sorry. I'm sorry.* He looked up at Duncan. "I came up to see Georgia," he said. "I was pretty surprised to run into Alice here."

"I'm sure," Duncan said.

Haven squirmed, yawned, and began to cry.

John sighed. "Hey, Wren. You want my breakfast? I have to feed the baby." He pushed his plate toward Wren. "Best home fries in the North Country, or so I'm told."

"No, thanks," Wren said. "I hate runny eggs. Do they have waffles here? I'd love some waffles."

Duncan still stood, unyielding. Alice turned to Wren. "Will you do me a huge favor? Run to my car—it's just down the street in front of the Laundromat—and bring me my heavy sweatshirt, will you? The blue one. This hoodie is too thin. I'll order waffles for you."

John unbuckled the baby from his seat and lifted him to his shoulder, then bent to retrieve a bottle from the diaper bag at his feet.

"I want to watch John feed the baby."

"You can feed the baby yourself when you get back," Alice said. "It will take you ten seconds to get my sweatshirt. Please?"

Wren rolled her eyes but pushed back her chair and stood up. The minute the door closed behind her, Alice was back on her feet, one hand on Duncan's arm.

"This is *not* what it looks like," she said.

"Alice," he said, "I don't care." His indifference frightened her more than his anger would have.

John now held the baby in his arms and was giving him a bottle. He looked up at Duncan. "We ran into each other by accident here," he said. "I drove all night the other night to come up here and try to convince Georgia to come home with me, and the baby—without much success, as you can see. As soon as I finish feeding the baby, I'll get out of here. And, for what it's worth, I'm sorry, really sorry, for everything."

Duncan drew his lips together, and Alice felt the muscles in his arm stiffen under his hand, felt the anger rise in him. "Screw you," Duncan said.

"Duncan, please. Wren's here," Alice said. "We can't make

a scene. She doesn't know anything about any of this, and this isn't the time or place to fill her in."

And because Duncan was a gentleman and a kind man who loved his daughter, he sat down. He edged his chair back, as far away from John as possible.

"What time are you picking up Liza?" Alice said. She wanted Wren to return to a normal conversation.

"I'm not," Duncan said. "Georgia called me last night. She's getting Liza this morning. It seems Georgia's sister is getting married today, and they want Liza at the wedding. And because today is Liza's only official Visiting Day, it's Wren's only chance to see her. So Georgia invited us to the wedding."

"She's getting married today? Here?" Alice said.

"On the beach at Lake Con," Duncan said. "Georgia's sisters are here and the fiancé and Liza. And some friend of the groom's."

At this news John looked around the small restaurant, as though he expected them all to walk in and wanted to be sure of his escape route.

"I didn't know Chessy was getting married," Alice said.

"Neither did Georgia," Duncan said. "I think the idea to get married here was somewhat spontaneous."

"Chessy herself is 'somewhat spontaneous,'" John said. "To put it politely."

Duncan shot him a look that made it clear he expected John to shut up for the duration of their enforced time together.

"What time is the wedding?" Alice said.

"Six o'clock. But we're meeting Georgia and Liza at the cabin at nine so the girls can spend the day together. I didn't expect to be up this early, but we didn't sleep very well."

Alice glanced at her watch. She felt as though she had lived through an entire day since getting out of her moldy bed this morning, but it was only seven thirty.

Wren came in with Alice's sweatshirt and slid into the remaining empty seat at the table. "Did you order my waffles?"

"No," Alice said. "I forgot." She looked around for the waitress. And then, because her life now was not a normal life but something out of a movie, something unbelievable, the door to the restaurant opened again and Polly walked in with Liza.

27

Georgia
June 26, 2012

"Why aren't they back yet?" Georgia said. She stood in the kitchen doorway with one arm wrapped around a mixing bowl, beating together butter and sugar for the cake she was making for the wedding. Chessy had eschewed a traditional wedding cake—she had been serious about getting a Carvel ice cream cake—but Ez had finally admitted he loved the chocolate velvet groom's cake Georgia had made for a wedding in April, so she was making that. Baking at least gave her something to do, something else to think about.

Polly had left at six thirty to pick up Liza at camp. It was almost nine now, and given that Camp Pokomac was twenty-two miles away, Georgia couldn't imagine where they were.

"Maybe they ran into traffic," Chessy said. She sat at the table on the porch, cutting out large squares of bright-colored cloth for something for the wedding.

Georgia shot her a look. "On the Adirondack Northway? Oh, please."

Ez, who was sitting nearby in a rocker with Lily in his lap, said, "Maybe Liza wasn't ready at seven A.M."

"True. She's not much of a morning person," Georgia said. Then she immediately felt guilty because until last night she had temporarily forgotten she even *had* Liza—more evidence that she was indeed beyond the all-encompassing need to nurture that had characterized her entire life until now.

Georgia had called Duncan last night with the last-minute change of plans. She felt terrible that he and Wren had planned this week around Liza's Visiting Day, only to have Chessy's wedding mess it all up. She couldn't think of a way to make it up to them other than to invite them to the wedding, which Chessy said was fine with her as long as Duncan and Georgia weren't going to be in terrible, cynical moods because their own marriages were such a mess. So Duncan and Wren were to meet Liza here at Lake Con at nine. The girls would spend the day together, and Duncan could stay for the wedding or go back to Lake Placid if he wanted.

Georgia felt a little awkward with Duncan at the same time that she felt a deep kinship with him. Until that fateful day in her kitchen, Georgia and Duncan had had the kind of relationship most people had with the spouse of a best friend or the best friend of a spouse. They shared a love of their shared person. They had vacationed together, seen each other in their pajamas, laughed over family jokes, commiserated over raising kids, and occasionally talked about something significant, like the death of Georgia's mother. But they didn't *know* each other. Now they were sharp reminders of the pain they both carried, as though they each had the word BETRAYED tattooed across their foreheads in special ink, visible only to each other. Still, Duncan had held her hair while she retched in the kitchen, and punched John in the face. He held a special place in Georgia's heart.

No, seeing Duncan was not an issue. The bigger problem, the one that had kept Georgia awake most of the night, was the fact that Liza was now on her way to Lake Con, where she expected to see her new baby brother. And since said baby brother was God knows where with John, Liza's imminent presence raised all kinds of complications.

Georgia had tried calling and texting John for the past twelve hours, asking him to *please* come back with the baby just for the day, but his phone went directly to voice mail and he didn't respond to her texts. At some dark hour of the morning she wondered if he had been in an accident, fallen asleep at the wheel and veered into the guardrail, a pole, an oncoming truck. Her heart raced at the thought of shattering glass, crumpled metal, the baby in his car seat, so small and vulnerable.

Haven's absence dominated her thoughts, even her body. She couldn't get over the constant sense that she had lost something. It was as though she had written down some vital phone number—one she could never get again—and then misplaced it. Every time she sat down she'd think: *I should be searching.* But then she'd remember that the thing she was missing was the baby, and he was gone, not lost. It didn't help that her breasts were producing so much milk she had to express at least a little every three or four hours, or that every time she heard Lily cry her milk let down.

Her sisters said the same things over and over: *We support you no matter what. We know you would be a great mother to Haven, but if it's going to wreck your life, don't do it. Don't listen to John; what happened in your marriage is not your fault.*

But some of it was, if not her *fault*, then her responsibility. She couldn't stop thinking about what John had said, about how he felt useless, superfluous, lonely. She *had* cut him out of much of the care for Liza. It was so much easier to do things herself than to suffer through his fumbling attempts to bathe

the baby, or diaper the baby, or hold her in the right position to soothe her colicky stomach. Then it became ordinary, natural, that Georgia was the one to deal with whatever came up with Liza at every stage, right up until now. It was true, too, that she had been preoccupied—or, to be honest, *consumed*—with the effort to have another baby, for years and years and years. And why?

Chessy looked up from her fabrics. "You're good at sewing, right, Georgie?"

Georgia stopped her hypnotic stirring of the butter and sugar. Her arms were exhausted. The lack of an electric mixer here was a problem. "Oh, please, Chess. You're getting married in seven or however many hours. You can't expect me to sew something today."

"Fine," Chessy said. "I'll use pins."

Georgia decided not to ask if Chessy's wedding dress was going to be held together by safety pins, so be it—and went back to her stirring.

"I can sew," Ez said.

Chessy flashed him a look, a look that said, *Of course you can, you incredible man, and I love you like crazy.* Georgia felt a jolt of recognition, remembering a moment when she had walked into Truscello's during those heady early days with John, and he had looked up and caught sight of her across the restaurant and smiled and clasped both hands to his chest and spun around as though he'd been shot through the heart. It was theatrical and silly, and it had made her feel desirable and powerful and beloved all at once.

"Can we get a story straight on what we're going to tell Liza about why the baby isn't here?" Georgia said.

"John took him down to Glens Falls because he was colicky," Chessy said.

"*No,*" Georgia said. "John took him on a *long drive* because he was colicky. Then they ran into Jimmy A., John's old chef, in Glens Falls and stopped to visit."

"But what if you can't reach John and he doesn't come back today?" Ez said.

"He *has* to come back today," Georgia said.

They all turned at the sound of car tires on the gravel road. Georgia put the bowl down on the table. "Liza's here!" she said. She hadn't realized how she had missed her, how eager she was for Liza's smile, her voice, all of her. She flew down the step from the kitchen to the porch, flung open the screen door, and stepped onto the wooden stoop.

But the car that pulled up next to the house wasn't Polly's red station wagon. It was a big blue SUV, with flashing red lights and the yellow logo of the New York State Police on the side.

Two troopers got out of the car.

"Is it my daughter?" Georgia said. "Did something happen to my daughter?"

"No," the first trooper said, the older one. "Your daughter's fine. Your—"

"Oh, Jesus." Georgia's heart hammered against her rib cage. "It's my husband. I knew something must have happened and that's why I couldn't reach him. Is he dead?"

"No," the trooper said. "It's—"

"The baby." Haven's loss, which until this moment had been deep but abstract, suddenly exploded into something large and black and so all encompassing it threatened to devour Georgia, a black hole. Who cared if he looked like Alice? He wasn't part of Alice the way he was part of Georgia. Georgia was the one who had felt his heartbeats in her own body, as he had felt hers in his; the one who had dreamed about him, known him, loved him. *This is what happens when you throw away what you should treasure most.*

"Ma'am," the trooper said. "*No one* is dead."

"There was an altercation at a restaurant in town," the second trooper said. He was taller than the first and looked, to Georgia's middle-aged eyes, like he was barely old enough to shave. "Your sister was involved. She claims she is staying here. The other party declined to press charges, but we impounded your sister's vehicle."

"My sister?"

By now Ez and Chessy were on the stoop with Georgia, Ez with Lily in his arms and Chessy with a pair of scissors and a half-cut piece of bright red fabric. Georgia had to look at Chessy twice to make sure it *was* Chessy standing there. God knows Georgia would have voted Polly the *least* likely of the three of them to get in trouble with the police.

"Yeah. And we're nice guys so we gave her a ride back here," the first one said.

Georgia tried to peer into the back of the police car. "But where's my daughter? My sister went to pick up my daughter."

"Your daughter is with the other party," the second trooper said. Georgia wished he would stop demonstrating just how recently he had graduated from the Police Academy and speak regular English.

"*Who is* the other party?" Georgia said.

"Actually, the altercation involved multiple parties," he said.

"Oh, my God," Chessy said. "Can you just tell us what the hell happened?"

The first trooper, the older one, went over to the car and helped Polly out of the backseat. She wore the jeans and T-shirt and fleece jacket she had left in early that morning, and had a stain of what looked like blood down the front of her pink shirt.

"Are you all right?" Georgia said.

Polly's lips were pursed, her face tight. She nodded.

"That's ketchup, not blood," the older officer said.

"Where's Liza?" Georgia said.

"She's with John," Polly said. "And the baby."

"Oh, thank God."

"*What happened?*" Chessy said.

The older officer turned to Polly. "I'll leave you here to handle the explanations." He dug in his front pocket for a card and a pen, and wrote a number on the back of the card. "This is my card. Call the number on the back about getting your car back. I'd suggest you stay out of the Sugar Bowl restaurant for the next few weeks, or maybe the entire summer. I'd also make sure you stay out of trouble of any kind. Next time, you won't get off with just a warning."

Polly pressed her lips together and nodded. "Thank you, officer," she said.

"Thank you," Georgia said. She wanted to say, *I'll be sure she behaves from now on*, but since Polly was almost forty, it seemed ridiculous. They all watched the troopers get into their car and back slowly down the gravel drive, lights still flashing.

Ez, Chessy, and Georgia turned expectant faces to Polly. "Well?" Georgia said.

"Well, it's been a rough morning," Polly said. "Can we sit down?"

She walked over to one of the Adirondack chairs on the lawn in front of the porch, overlooking the wild iris and the lake beyond. She kicked off her sandals and rolled her jeans up to just below her knees, then looked down at her stained shirt. "I should change," she said. "I'm a mess."

"*Polly.*" Georgia felt desperate for information. She came over and sat down in the chair next to Polly's. Ez and Chessy followed her. Lily was squirming and crying in Ez's arms so he set her down on the grass, holding on to one of her chubby arms with one hand. Georgia looked around for something to keep Lily occupied and realized she was still carrying the wooden spoon she'd been using to beat the butter and sugar. She handed it to Lily, who sat down on the grass and began to lick the spoon.

"I picked up Liza," Polly said. "She wasn't ready at seven, but that was fine. I waited, and I told her on the way back that John had taken the baby for a drive because he was colicky, so she wouldn't expect to see him right away. She was pretty disappointed, so I said I'd take her out to breakfast, and we went to the Sugar Bowl, in town."

"Okay," Georgia said.

"And when we walked in, who should be there but John, with the baby. And"—Polly paused for dramatic effect—"Duncan, Wren, and *Alice*."

"Holy crap," Chessy said. She sat on the arm of Georgia's chair, cutting out the rest of her red fabric square.

"Alice is here?" Georgia's heart would not slow down.

"Yes."

"Why?"

"I don't know. Anyway, I'm a little sleep-deprived"—Polly shot a look at Georgia—"because I was up with somebody's baby all night the other night. Liza was all excited to see the baby, although she was kind of upset that Wren saw him first. It was tense in there. First the waitress came over and went on and on about how much the baby looked like Alice, so Liza got even more upset, and Alice looked like she was going to be sick, and Duncan started to turn really red."

"Oh, God," Georgia said. "You know we never told Liza or Wren about the egg donation. We were going to wait."

"For what?" Chessy said. "That was dumb."

"And Alice was so jittery her leg kept shaking the whole table," Polly said. "And Duncan looked like he was going to smack John. I couldn't believe the girls didn't feel all that tension, too, so I told them to take the baby for a walk, to get them out of there. They went off with the baby in his stroller."

"And then you spilled ketchup all over yourself?" Chessy said.

Ez smiled, then caught himself and put his hand over his mouth, so Polly didn't see him smiling.

"Very funny," Polly said. "Then I told John he needed to bring the baby back to Lake Con for the day. And John said something along the lines of he wished we'd decide what the hell we wanted because he'd taken the baby and then given the baby to us and then taken the baby back and he was tired of all the back and forth and just wanted to get some sleep. And I told him to grow up, and he told me to stop meddling and that he and you"—Polly nodded at Georgia—"would probably still be together if it weren't for me and Chessy always interfering. Then I said you guys would probably still be together if he had kept his dick in his pants. Then Alice blushed like crazy and Duncan said, 'Wait just a minute,' and John called me a bitch, and I picked up a glass of water on the table and threw it in John's face and then he dumped ketchup on me."

"Oh, my God." Georgia closed her eyes. "But how did the police get involved? And why did they impound your car?"

Polly gave an exasperated sigh. "Well, it was just bad luck. Dudley Do-Right and the other trooper were eating breakfast at the counter. After John threw the ketchup, Duncan tried to intervene—he is a real gentleman—and John told him to back off. Then Duncan got mad and looked like he was going to punch him again, so I jumped on Duncan to keep him from punching John, and then Alice stood up and I told her if I ever saw her anywhere again I'd run her over for what she had done to you, and then the officers came over and insisted on giving me a Breathalyzer—at eight fifteen in the morning!—and they impounded my car."

Ez and Chessy and Georgia sat in silence for a few minutes, absorbing the weight of Polly's story. The sun had cleared the treetops on the point at the edge of the bay, and the air was warmer now. A light breeze rustled the leaves on the trees in the woods. Georgia felt a sudden clarity. She stood up.

"I'll see you in a little while," she said. "I'm going to town."

28

Alice
June 26, 2012

Alice would not have thought it possible, but she longed for Dun Roamin'. Her musty bed and knotty pine room seemed cozy and appealing, a safe cocoon, after the public humiliation in the restaurant. It was bad enough that John had thrown ketchup like some thirteen-year-old and Polly had ranted like a crazy person, but the most painful part of the whole ordeal for Alice was the fact that as soon as it was over and Polly and John had left with the police, Duncan had turned to Alice and said, "Well. That's that," and then stood up and left.

She had fumbled to find her credit card to pay for John's uneaten eggs and her uneaten oatmeal, only to discover that the restaurant accepted nothing but cash. Then she'd had to scrounge through her pockets and purse for every bit of loose change to come up with enough money to cover the bill. By the time she got outside, Duncan was gone.

She walked down the sidewalk, toward the little park at the other end of town. Someone had to find Wren and Liza and Haven. She passed the old movie theater, with its dun-colored brick facade, and the realtors' office with the photos of log cabins nestled under tall firs, blue lakes gleaming in the background. She was almost at the coffee shop, the place with the lattes named after local mountains, when she saw Duncan.

He stood at the end of the block in the little town park, his back to her, hands on his hips. She increased her stride down the block, moving faster until she was running, her eyes fixed on her husband's back.

"Duncan." She stopped just behind him and bent forward, her hands on her knees, to catch her breath. She had sprinted the last thirty yards.

He turned, and she stood up straight. Her throat was dry and the cold breeze from the lake stung her eyes and made her nose run.

"Goodness, Alice," he said. "Are you all right?"

"Duncan, please. Can I talk to you?"

"I'm looking for the kids. I think they're there, down on the tennis courts."

He pointed to the asphalt court down the hill on the other side of the park. Alice could just make out two figures wheeling a stroller up and down the court. She recognized Wren's pink jacket. "Yes, that's them."

"I should get them to Georgia's. This wedding is today and I'm sure Georgia is wondering where they are."

She put her hand on his arm and he turned to face her. The lines around his eyes looked deeper, the skin over the sharp planes of his nose and cheekbones looked tighter. His face was so familiar—how could something and someone so familiar feel so strange?

"I came here to find you," she said. "I mean, I came to the Adirondacks. After you and Wren left—"

"You know what I remember?" Duncan interrupted her. "I

remember that time we went kayaking, on our second or third date. I brought you coffee. And you were *so happy* I remembered you liked it with cream. You couldn't stop talking about it. And I thought, 'God, is this woman easy to please.' You smiled at me like I'd handed you your heart's desire. I remember thinking I could be very happy with someone who smiled at me like that."

It was *my heart's desire,* Alice thought. *To be noticed.* She patted the pockets of her hoodie for a tissue, but couldn't find one. She wiped her nose on her sleeve. "You did," she said. "You did give me my heart's desire."

Duncan went on, as if he hadn't heard her. "As I got to know you, you were so clear-cut about what was right and wrong, so capable and efficient. I admired that; I admired you. And I admit: it was pretty clear no one had really taken care of you before, and I wanted to be that person. I wanted to give you the things you'd never had before—not just things like a house or a car, but the feeling that your life was secure and stable."

Alice stood very still. A flock of seagulls cried down on the beach, and a logging truck rumbled by on the road.

"But I couldn't please you after all," Duncan said. "And maybe you didn't want to be taken care of. Maybe 'secure' was boring. I don't know. I just know that I married one person, and you're not that person now."

Alice took a deep breath. "I love you and I want you. Please give me another chance." She waited.

He turned those blue eyes on her. "You know, Alice," he said. "You went right from your mother's apartment to a college dorm and then to living with me. You've never lived alone, ever. Maybe that's what you need. Obviously we have Wren, and I'm not going to suggest she live only with me and not you. But maybe you need to be an adult on your own for a while."

"I need my family," Alice said.

Duncan turned, raised his hand to shield his eyes from the sun, looked down toward where Wren and Liza wheeled Haven from the tennis court across the grass. He turned back to her.

"Let's give it six months," he said. "I'm going to move into the apartment above my office. It's only one bedroom but I can get a sleeper couch, so Wren can stay over. We'll figure out how to talk to her about it. It's something we need to try."

"It's not something I need to try," Alice said. "I know what I want. I want you, and Wren. I want us."

"Maybe," Duncan said. "But you didn't a few months ago when you slept with John Bing."

The truth of his words hit her like a slap. The icy ball inside her radiated cold fingers up into her chest, her shoulders, her back. Duncan was going to leave her, and she had made it happen. And that was the truth.

She looked up at the cloudless blue sky. She could almost see the great dome of the universe, stretching around and over the sparkling lake, the craggy undulations of the mountains, the highways and rivers that poured their way back home. She would have to work more hours, so she could support herself if Duncan decided not to come back. She would have to hurt Wren—she squeezed her eyes shut at the thought—by telling her about the separation. She would have to figure out how to make friends, other friends, since she had lost Georgia, too. It was being left home alone at age six, all night long, with only a record player for company. It was everything she feared most.

She looked at Duncan. "You're right," she said.

THE LAST TIME Alice had seen Georgia was at the baby shower in April. Alice had offered to throw a shower as soon as Georgia's pregnancy was confirmed, but Polly insisted on hosting because, as she said, there would be no reason for a baby shower if it weren't for Alice and her generosity in donating her eggs. Georgia wanted to wait until she was far along in her pregnancy, confident nothing would go wrong. She chose a date in April, six weeks before her due date and, as it turned out, at the peak of Alice's affair with John.

Polly went all-out and held a daisy-themed shower in the big sunny living room of her house in McLean, complete with white chocolate daisies sprouting from chocolate flowerpots and jars of pale yellow lemonade and little bowls filled with lemon drops and yellow jellybeans. Alice tried several times to bow out, pleading the end-of-semester crunch, but Polly said she would reschedule to suit her because she was a guest of honor, too. So Alice had put on her new navy blue pants and a yellow silk blouse, even though she looked terrible in yellow, because Polly had requested they all wear "daisy colors."

Alice had perched on the edge of Polly's big beige sofa, feeling as self-conscious and miserable as she had ever felt in her life. Polly had them play a game called Mommy's Secrets, in which Georgia had to write down the answers to questions such as "How did you tell your husband you were pregnant?" "Do you want a girl or boy?" and "If you could have your way, what would you want your child to be when he or she grows up?" It was a silly game—guests had to guess which were Georgia's "real" answers vs. a bunch of answers Polly had made up—and Alice had won the game by correctly guessing all of Georgia's real responses, right down to knowing she had told John she was pregnant by baking cupcakes with trinkets hidden inside—a baby shoe, a baby, a tiny rattle. John had almost broken a molar on the rattle because he wasn't expecting a trinket in his cupcake, but he'd gotten over it. Georgia had smiled a conspiratorial smile at Alice when she won the game, a smile that said, *Of course; you know me better than anyone.* And Alice had wished a meteorite would crash through the glass of Polly's elegant French doors and smack straight into her, obliterating her for all time because she was the worst person who had ever lived.

Then Polly turned the tables and had each guest write down a secret of their own. She read the secrets aloud and everyone had to guess which person went with which secret. Alice felt her skin flush when Polly explained the game. She remembered feeling that her secret must be visible to the entire party, a scarlet A of shame burned into her forehead. Georgia, who thought Alice was blushing because she was shy, had leaned over and whispered that Alice should make up an outrageous secret to show Polly how silly the game was. *I once danced naked in the moonlight on the school football field*, Alice wrote, because it was the most outrageous thing she could think of. If she had written the truth—*I'm having sex with my pregnant best friend's husband*—no one would have believed it in a million years. No one was that crazy.

ALICE HELPED DUNCAN strap Haven's car seat into his car, made sure Liza texted John to let him know they were going to Lake Con with the baby, and explained to Wren that she wasn't coming to Chessy's wedding because Ez was very shy and it was only Chessy's immediate family. The lie coated her tongue, thick and viscous. But Wren was distracted by the baby, and the excitement of the day, and paid little attention.

Alice hugged Duncan before he got into the car, wrapped both arms around the reassuring solidness of him, pressed her head against his chest. He patted her back. "I'll see you at home in three days," he said. "We'll talk more then."

Then she had to let go.

After they drove off she crossed the street to where her car was parked in front of the Laundromat. She didn't know where to go. She sat down on a white wooden bench by the door, listening to the rhythmic swoosh of water churning in the washers, the whir of the big fan inside. She had never in her life cried in public—she could count on one hand the number of times she'd cried in front of Duncan—but she cried now. She pressed her lips together so she didn't make a sound. The tears ran down her face and then her nose got so stuffed up she had to open her mouth to breathe. She wiped her nose on her sleeve.

"Hey," a voice said.

Alice looked up. Georgia stood on the sidewalk in front of her, in black capri leggings and a man's red flannel button-down shirt. A baseball cap covered her hair.

Alice wiped the tears from her cheeks with both hands. *Of course.* She felt as if she had known for years that she was scheduled for execution and now that the day was here, so be it.

"I suppose I should ask what you're doing here, in the Adirondacks, but I'm not sure I want to know," Georgia said.

"I came after Duncan and Wren," Alice said. "I had no idea you were here, or John, or your entire family. I'm sorry."

"Sorry you're here, or sorry in a bigger sense?" Georgia's voice was tart.

"Sorry for everything," Alice said. "For every single damn thing that's happened since November." It was true.

Georgia held up a hand. "I don't want to know what happened when."

Alice thought of Georgia holding out her arms to ten-month-old Wren and cajoling her to take tentative steps across the floor. She thought of herself cheering wildly at the sidelines of Liza's soccer game the day Liza scored her first goal, at age six. She thought of the countless sleepovers, from age three or four onward, with Liza and Wren wrapped around each other like puppies, forgetting where one ended and the other began. She thought of the joy she had taken in knowing that she had given Wren not just one but *two* families, two mothers, two fathers, a sister—all those people to love her. She remembered something she had not thought of in years—that she and Duncan had named John and Georgia as Wren's legal guardians in their wills.

This is my fault, Alice thought. *All of this. I have to make it right.*

"I made a huge mistake," Alice said. "Everything about it was wrong, and I'm sorry. I can't really explain how or why it happened. I was upset about Wren." She stopped. "John loves you."

"I don't need you to tell me what my husband feels."

Alice closed her eyes. "You're right; I'm sorry."

Silence filled the space between them. Alice heard the wind rustle the trees down by the lake, heard the *thump-thump-thump* of something heavy in one of the dryers inside the Laundromat.

"I hate you for doing this to my family," Georgia said. "And I hate you for doing this to *us*. I trusted you; I loved you. I thought you were like one of my sisters."

"I love you," Alice said. "You are the best friend I've ever had." Alice felt tears rise in her throat again. She missed Georgia with all her heart. "Duncan and I are separating. We haven't told Wren yet."

"I'm sorry," Georgia said. "For Duncan."

The pain Alice had caused was like a hurricane, something that grew and grew and grew and destroyed everything. But at the center was a still, small hope: Haven.

"Do you really not want the baby?" Alice said.

For the first time in their conversation, Georgia looked flustered.

"He looks just like you," Georgia said. "Polly said even the waitress at the restaurant noticed."

"But how could you give him up?" Alice said. "What would you tell Liza? She's so excited about having a brother—"

"I know!" Georgia said. "And it would have been nice if you or John had thought about that before you screwed each other, wouldn't it?"

Alice felt the dishonesty drain from her body, felt the burden of all those months of cheating and lying leave her. She could have floated right up into the clear blue sky. "If you really don't want to keep the baby, we'll tell Wren and Liza the truth," she said.

Georgia stared at her. "What truth?"

"*All* the truth," Alice said.

For the first time in a long time she felt certain, as though she had finally reached solid ground after making her way from tussock to tussock through a bog.

"We'll tell them I donated my eggs to you because you are my closest friend and I wanted to help you. Then we can tell them I made a mistake, that I spent too much time with John in a way that was bad for my marriage and hurt you."

Georgia stared at her. "You think we should tell the girls about you and John?"

"If that's what we need to do, yes."

Georgia rolled her eyes. "Dear God, it's all or nothing with you, isn't it?"

"What do you mean?"

Georgia pulled off her baseball cap and looked up at the sky in exasperation. "I mean you are *so* black-and-white about everything; you always have been. It's ridiculous to 'confess' about your affair to Wren, or to Liza for that matter, who's already upset that her father moved out, let alone trying to deal with the knowledge that he's a *cheater*. I understand you feel you need to do some kind of penance, but I don't want you to involve *my* daughter in that, and frankly, I don't think you should involve Wren in that, either."

"I'm tired of lying." It was the truest thing Alice had ever said.

"Oh, poor you," Georgia said. "For Christ's sake. There are lies you tell that are hurtful"—Georgia glared at her—"which you should know *plenty* about, and there are lies you tell to prevent hurt. And lying about your affair to Liza and Wren falls into the second category."

Georgia sat down on the wooden bench next to Alice. "It's getting warm," she said, her voice cross. "I hope it's not insanely hot for this wedding."

Alice sat still, feeling like someone who has returned to her most beloved and familiar place, only to find it strange. She didn't know the language of this new country.

"So we'll tell them about the egg donation," Alice said.

"Yes," Georgia said. "As long as you don't make yourself out to be Saint Alice for donating the damned egg."

"God, no."

"And not today—Chessy's getting married today. We'll figure out a way to discuss it with them once Liza gets home from camp."

"Will John raise him?" Alice's heart beat faster thinking about what might happen if John didn't want the baby, either. He certainly hadn't sounded as though he felt capable of raising Haven as a single parent.

Georgia sighed. "I don't know."

"So you'd put him up for adoption." Alice said it as a statement, not a question. She saw Haven's gray eyes, his solemn gaze. She saw the photo of baby Wren's dimpled fist, clutching Duncan's shirt.

"I don't know! I just gave birth a week ago. I never imagined I'd have to deal with something like this, feel something like this. How can I tell Liza she's not going to have a baby brother after all, especially now that she's seen him?"

"You can't." Alice's certainty returned. "You need to take more time, figure out what you really want."

They sat in silence for a few minutes. Alice wished she could put her arm around Georgia, hug her to her. She wished they could laugh away this trauma, as they had commiserated and laughed over so many things.

"Are you moving?" Georgia said. "I mean, when you and Duncan separate?"

"I don't think so. He said something about moving into the apartment over his office, so I could stay in the house with Wren." Alice tried to push down the terror that rose in her at the thought.

"You know, the girls will still be friends," Georgia said. "They'll be back and forth at our houses. We're still going to have to see each other."

Alice nodded. "It's your call. You decide how you want it handled, and I'll do whatever you say."

"What I want is not to have to see you again, at least for now. It hurts too much." Georgia stared out at the street, at the fountain in the park across the road splashing brilliant drops of water into the sunlit air.

"If I keep the baby, people will notice that he looks like you," she continued. "They'll notice that we're not close friends any-more. I don't want to put Liza—and myself—through that, being gossiped about that way."

Alice shifted on the bench. "I don't think people will notice. Anyone who knows you will expect the baby to look like you or John or Liza; they won't be looking for a resemblance to me."

"You don't have to look for it to see it," Georgia said.

Alice felt her practical self take over; it was like the old days. "*When* and *if* it becomes an issue you can talk to people on a case-by-case basis. Tell them I donated an egg and that then we'd both felt a little funny about it and pulled back on our friendship."

"And we both got separated or divorced at the same time?" Georgia said.

"People might think the egg donation was the issue. They'll take their lead from you, Georgia." Alice bit her lip, uncertain how far to go. "If you love him, if you feel like Haven is really yours, what everyone else thinks won't matter."

"That's the million-dollar question, isn't it?" Georgia said.

They sat side by side in silence for a long time, and then Georgia got up and walked away.

29

Georgia
June 26, 2012

*I*t could have been worse," Georgia said.

She and Polly stood in the upstairs bedroom of the cabin, in the dresses Chessy had given them to wear for the wedding. Both dresses were white. Polly's was strapless and made of satiny cotton, with a gauzy lace overskirt that fell from her waist to the ground. Georgia's knee-length dress was all lace, with a scoop neck and three-quarter-length sleeves. Chessy had given them each ribbons to wear in their hair, but neither Polly nor Georgia could figure out what to do with them, so Polly had tied hers around her head like a headband, and Liza had braided the others into a friendship bracelet and tied it around Georgia's wrist.

"I guess," Polly said. "With four kids and a station wagon, it's hard for me to feel like a Boho hippie."

"But you *look* like a Boho hippie," Georgia said. And Polly did look lovely, with her glossy blond hair and the dress high-lighting her lean figure.

"I guess we should be glad she didn't expect us to get tat-toos," Polly said.

Georgia heard a loud clumping on the stairs. The door opened and Chessy came in. She wore a sleeveless dress, with tiers of white crochet cascading to the floor and rows of gold and turquoise beading along the V-neck. Stacks of gold bangle bracelets covered her wrists, and her chestnut hair fell in loose curls around her shoulders. She had no veil, just a circlet of pink roses on her head.

"What is that God-awful noise?" Polly said. "What are you wearing on your feet?" She caught herself. "You look beautiful, by the way. Really, Chess."

Chessy lifted the hem of her dress to show off her shoes, wooden platform sandals with gold straps.

"You're going to break your neck—or at least an ankle—walking around the beach in those," Polly said.

"I'll take them off on the beach," Chessy said. "I just really, really like them so I wanted them for my wedding. Here."

She held a stack of the fabric squares she had been cutting out earlier, and she handed them to Georgia, along with two fabric markers.

"What's this?"

"Wishes. I want everyone to write down two or three wishes for our marriage. Then the girls will string them on that twine I brought and we'll stretch it across the beach." Chessy looked very pleased with herself.

"Really?" Georgia said.

"Yes. How hard can it be? I like the idea of having all those wishes at our wedding. I got the idea from a coffee shop I was in once, that had customers write down their wishes on wooden rectangles and then hung them all on strings from the ceiling."

Georgia and Polly looked at each other.

"Nothing snarky," Chessy said. "Especially since Chef Boyardee is going to be here."

John had returned with the baby that afternoon. Georgia had called him after she went to town to retrieve Polly's car and asked if he would please come back for the wedding and bring the baby, to keep things as sane and ordinary as possible for Liza. She had offered to keep the baby overnight, so John could go to a motel and get some sleep.

"Is Polly going to throw anything at me?" he had said.

"No," Georgia said. "And Chessy's getting married so she won't be throwing things at you, either."

John had paused for a long time then, contemplating, Georgia was sure, all the possible things that could blow up were he were to attend the wedding.

"Will Duncan be there?

"No," Georgia said. "And neither will Alice."

"I had no idea Alice was here," John said. "In the Adirondacks. I want you to know that. I was stunned to run into her in that restaurant."

Georgia sighed. "Okay."

"It would be nice to be a family again for one night," John said. Another long silence, then: "I could help with the food. I'd feel less awkward being there if I could just be off doing the cooking."

Georgia had asked Chessy, who hadn't really had a plan for the dinner beyond grilling something on the beach, and who had admitted that well, yes, it might be nice to have Chef Boyardee handle the wedding dinner.

"I already gave squares to Liza and Wren for their wishes," Chessy said. "And Ez"—Chessy smiled—"Ez took a bunch with him to town and told everyone in the Grand Union about it, and the cashiers and the manager and everyone who was shopping there wrote down wishes for us. I think this is going to be my favorite part of the wedding."

"You're my favorite part of the wedding," Georgia said. She leaned forward to kiss Chessy on the cheek.

Georgia felt as strange as she had ever felt in her life, caught in a whirlpool of emotion about John, Liza, Alice, Chessy, and, to her surprise, Haven. She could not stop thinking about that moment when she had seen the police car in the driveway; the bottomless sense of loss when she thought Haven might be dead. It was exactly the same gut-wrenching pain she had had when she thought Liza might be hurt, the awareness that the words "I'm sorry to inform you" from the trooper's mouth were a machete that could slice her in two, cut her life into before and after. At that moment, she hadn't cared at all if the baby looked like Alice or John or an orangutan—he was part of her.

Now Chessy, who was in a sense another of Georgia's babies, was getting married. Georgia missed her mother, the mother Chessy had never known. But Evy had known Chessy, Georgia thought, had carried Chessy all those months, talked to her, sung to her, imagined what she might look like, dreamed about her, soothed her, *loved* her—just as Georgia had done with Haven.

"I wish Mom was here," Georgia said, stating the obvious. Polly looked at her, and their eyes filled at the same moment. "And Dad."

"*You're* here," Chessy said. "Oh, God, don't cry. I do not want a wedding where everyone cries. The only people allowed to cry at this wedding are Lily and Haven." But she wrapped one arm around Georgia and one arm around Polly and hugged them both. Then she pulled away. "And if Ez cries, you have my permission to push him in the lake."

And before Georgia could wipe the tears from her cheeks, her sister the bride had clomped off down the stairs.

THE WEDDING, OF course, was beautiful. A light breeze rippled across the tops of the trees when they gathered on the beach at six. There were eight "guests," as Chessy said, with Georgia and Polly, John, Wren, Liza, Ez's friend Harris, and Lily and Haven. Polly said it was ridiculous to call them "guests" when they were all family, but Chessy said she could call them whatever she wanted on her wedding day, and Polly had agreed.

Ez had set two poles on either end of the beach, close to the water's edge, stretched a long rope between them, and pinned up all Chessy's fabric squares with the wishes written on them. The wishes fluttered in the breeze like prayer flags, bright red and yellow and green and white and orange against the backdrop of the silvery blue water, the green mountains, the cloudless sky.

Ez and Chessy stood underneath the banner of wishes with Reverend Finster and recited their vows, with everyone gathered around them in a tight circle. Georgia and Polly cried even though Chessy glared at them. Georgia thought she saw tears in John's eyes, too, at one point, but since she spent most of the ceremony trying *not* to look at John she decided it was probably just a trick of the light.

Ez had brought a giant cooler filled with flowers from home; Chessy carried a simple bouquet of pink roses, and Liza and Wren made little nosegays they placed in jelly jars on the arms of the Adirondack chairs along the beach, wound more flowers along the front of Lily's stroller, and pinned roses in their own hair. The girls were barefoot, in gauzy white dresses, their feet caked with sand and their hair tangled from running in the wind. Liza's loud laugh sounded more spontaneous to Georgia; she looked even prettier without her usual makeup or too-tight jeans. Liza held Haven throughout the ceremony, but had turned him over to John as soon as he started to cry—the limits of sisterly love.

After the ceremony Liza and Wren ran under the banner of little flags, trying to read the wishes before the wind swirled the fabric up, twisted the squares, and hid the words. Georgia and Polly sat in Adirondack chairs nearby, sipping the champagne Ez had brought and watching the clouds turn pink over the lake.

"This one says 'Peace,'" Liza said. She ran under the rope. "And on the other side it says"—she squinted and held a hand up over her eyes to block the late sun—"on the other side it says, 'May you learn to fight well.' That's dumb."

"This one says 'Money,'" Wren said. "That's not very creative."

"Money certainly makes marriage easier," Polly said.

"This one says 'Yo mama,'" Liza said.

"It does not," Wren said.

"Look."

Wren came around and stood next to Liza and squinted at the turquoise square. "It's not even English," she said. "It says 'U-M-A-M-I.'"

Georgia blushed.

"What?" Polly looked at her. "What is that?"

"I don't know," Georgia said. "Maybe one of those people at the Grand Union wrote it, someone who's visiting from Japan or somewhere."

"Uh-huh," Polly said.

John grilled fresh trout on the kettle grill Ez and Harris had brought down to the beach earlier, and roasted fresh ears of corn on the grill, too. Ez made a bonfire inside a circle of stones on the sand, and they pulled up the Adirondack chairs and ate dinner there in a circle. Wren and Liza watched the babies while John cooked, and then Georgia walked with Lily so the girls could eat. Haven slept in his stroller. Then they had the chocolate velvet groom's cake Georgia had somehow managed to get done. At one point Liza tripped and landed with a splash in the lake. Lily crowed with delight and Wren ran down and jumped in, too.

The first stars had appeared over the white pine on the eastern edge of the lake when they started to pick up everything to go home. Georgia untied the line of wish flags from the pole at one end of the beach, and then walked along unpinning and collecting the flags in a pile. Chessy would want to save them. She was curious, too, about what the others had written, whether John had written anything else. She began to flip through the pile of fabric squares, reading.

"What are you doing?"

John stood at her elbow, with Haven strapped to his chest in a baby carrier. He wore the carrier uneasily, as if he felt it wasn't something a real man would do, but he also kept one hand pressed protectively against the baby's back.

"I was curious," Georgia said. "I wanted to read all the wishes."

She didn't want to read them with John watching her. She sat down in one of the white Adirondack chairs, and put the pile of wish flags on the arm.

"Well?" he said. "Any good wishes? Or is it the usual—health, wealth, fertility?"

"None of those are bad things to have," Georgia said. "Neither is fidelity. Or trust. Or honesty."

"You're right," he said. "Okay. I deserved that." He paused. "It was a nice wedding. I'm actually glad I could be here."

Georgia was tired of being mad at John, mad at Alice, hurt and disappointed and confused. She wished she could just sit here forever with her toes in the warm stand and stare at the clear, still water.

"What did you wish for them?" he said.

Georgia shook her head. "I'm not going to tell you."

The baby began to fuss, and John started to rock from side to side, trying to soothe him.

"I saw you wrote 'umami,'" she said. "No one is going to know what that means."

"No one else has to," he said. "I wrote it for you. I wrote another one, too."

"What?" She looked up at him, curious.

His dark eyes bored into hers. "Joy."

"Joy?" Georgia wished he'd stop staring at her like that.

"Yeah," John said. "I had a lot of joy with you, and Liza. A lot of moments when I felt perfectly happy, like I didn't want anything more." He paused. "I wish that for Chessy. She's a pain, but she deserves it."

Georgia looked out at the lake, the surface still as glass in the twilight, reflecting the fading blue of the evening sky.

"You are the only one, Georgia," he said, leaning forward. "The only one I have ever in my life felt that kind of joy with. *Ever.*"

She had felt it too, but she wasn't quite ready to tell John that.

The lake lapped at the beach, swirled around the pilings of the dock, rippled with the faint breeze.

"Could we work on it?" he said. "I don't have to move back in; I know it will take time. But we could get counseling. I could get someone to do dinners at the restaurant three or four nights a week so I could be home to help with the baby, and I could take him in the mornings, so you could work."

The baby began to cry. John swayed some more and patted his back.

"Think about it, Georgia." His voice was low. "We can work on being partners, for Liza, and for this little guy. And maybe, maybe, we could be a family."

Haven's cries grew louder. John stopped swaying and extricated the baby from his carrier and held him against his shoulder. The baby continued to whimper. Georgia watched them for a few moments, watched John's dark head against the baby's, their hair the exact same shade of brown.

"Here," she said. John looked up.

"I'll take him," she said.

And she reached out her arms for her son.

About the author

About the book

Insights,
Interviews
& More...

Read on

The Author
Behind the Book

Matt Mendelsohn

KATHLEEN MCCLEARY is a journalist
and author who has also worked as a
bookseller, bartender, and barista (all
great jobs for gathering material for
fiction). Her first novel, *House & Home*,
was published by Hyperion in 2008.
She has written articles for the *New
York Times*, the *Washington Post, Good
Housekeeping, Ladies' Home Journal*, and
USA Weekend, as well as HGTV.com,
where she was a regular columnist. She

has taught writing as an adjunct professor at American University in Washington, D.C., and with Writopia Labs, a nonprofit creative writing group. She lives in northern Virginia with her husband and two daughters. ⌥

Little-Known Facts About Kathleen McCleary That May Surprise Her Friends

- At age twelve she was briefly considered for the lead role in *The Exorcist*, until her mother found out what the movie was about. (Her mom had a friend who was a casting agent.)
- She majored in comparative religion in college.
- She attended law school for a semester at Union University in Albany, which was very helpful in focusing her awareness on how much she did not want to be a lawyer.
- She enjoys crafting things and has, over the years, learned how to knit, hook rugs, sew, carve wood, make dovetail joints with hand tools, blow glass, and make butterscotch pudding from scratch (which is very, very good).
- She is fascinated by remote places and has visited Scotland's Outer Hebrides, Alaska, the San Juan Islands, the Appalachians, and the Adirondacks, among other wild places. ∾

The Story
Behind the Book
A Conversation with
Kathleen McCleary

Where did you get the idea for Leaving Haven?

I was in New York having coffee with my agent when she said, "I always thought that if I wrote a novel, I'd open it with a scene in which a woman gives birth and then walks out of the hospital and leaves her baby behind."

"Wow," I said. "What made you think of that?"

"Because I had identical twins two years after I had my first baby, and the thought of walking away did cross my mind, just for a second," she said.

My agent, Ann Rittenberg, in addition to being a brilliant agent, is a devoted mother to her three daughters, who are now out in the great wide world of college and beyond. And I will admit there was a moment early in my own parenting career when I got so frustrated with my kids that I ran outside and locked myself in the car for a few minutes. But *I did not drive away.* Still, it's one thing to get frustrated with toddlers or teenagers; it's another to leave a newborn. What would make someone do that?

We finished having coffee and ►

I didn't see Ann again for six months, and I didn't think at all about the woman who gives birth and leaves her baby behind, either. Until one day my husband and I were driving along a road somewhere in Virginia. Out of the blue I sat up very straight and said, "I know why. I know why she walks out of the hospital and leaves her baby behind."

"I have no idea what you're talking about," my husband said.

I told him the story of the woman whose best friend donates an egg so she can get pregnant, and who then finds out, eight months into her pregnancy [SPOILER ALERT], that that same best friend is having an affair with her husband.

As soon as we got home I called Ann and said, "Remember that idea you had? About the woman who leaves her baby in the hospital? Could I steal that?"

"I wanted you to steal it," she said. "That's why I told you."

Did you have to do research for a book like this, a book that's mostly centered on characters and what happens to them?

As a former journalist, I research *everything*. For this book I did a lot of reading on secondary infertility, and I read countless articles and books about infidelity and recovering from infidelity. I spent an hour with an attorney, David Roop, who specializes in family law in Virginia, to discuss various scenarios with him—what if Alice wanted to keep the baby? Could John prosecute Georgia or her sisters for kidnapping? What if Georgia wanted the baby after abandoning him, but John didn't want her to have the baby? Talking to David helped me focus on what had to happen in the book.

What's your writing process like?

I'm not a plotter; I don't outline. I start with a character and something they want very badly—in this case a woman who wants a baby—and then I go forward from there. As more characters come into the book, I try to figure out that one thing about each of them—what they want that they can't have, or don't have. And while I don't outline, this book was so complex that I did have to keep a detailed *time line* as I wrote, so I knew what events happened when. I had the time line written out in a notebook on my desk, all color coded for different characters and different months and different years. I lived in fear that my husband or kids would pick up that notebook to jot down a grocery list or something and I'd never see it again, so there were warnings written ▶

all over it: DO NOT TAKE THIS
NOTEBOOK.

I write in the mornings, as soon as
I drop my daughter off at school, and
try to write a thousand words a day.
I usually write at least six days a week;
often seven. There's a lot of "fermenting"
time, too, when I'm walking or
showering or lying in bed staring
at the ceiling, but it's all moving
the novel forward. I have an old
gray cashmere sweater with several
holes in it that I wear when I'm
writing—my equivalent of Jo March's
"thinking cap," for any *Little Women*
fans out there.

What role does your editor play?

My editor, Tessa Woodward, has played
a key role in shaping my last two books.
With this one, I wrote the prologue and
first three chapters very quickly. I had
written four chapters, all from Georgia's
point of view, when I realized that the
book would be much more intriguing
with two points of view. I also liked the
challenge of trying to make Alice—who
does something really awful in betraying
her own husband and her best friend—
sympathetic, or at least someone
whose motives and behavior you can
understand even if you don't agree with
her choices.

I wrote the first third of the book and

sent it to my agent and editor. They both had the same response: Georgia's and Alice's stories seemed too similar, maybe because they were both at similar life stages—working mothers living in the same suburb, struggling with their midlife marriages. Then my editor, Tessa, had a suggestion: What if I told one point of view *backward* in time, so it unspooled from the end to the beginning, and the other point of view the usual way, from beginning to end?

It was scary (I'd never attempted anything like that before); it was crazy (I'd never read a novel like that before, although I'm sure one has been written); and it was daunting (I'd have to rewrite a lot of what I'd already written). But it also was exciting. So I did it.

That makes it sound as though I went home and wrote and wrote and wrote and then was done. And of course it was nothing like that. I wrote and wrote and wrote and rewrote and rewrote and rewrote and was interrupted by major life events (daughter graduating high school! daughter starting college! mother moving to town!) and minor life events (What's for dinner tonight? Did you pay the Visa bill? Where are my socks?). But it came together, and I wrote the final third of the book as seamlessly and quickly as I have ever written anything in my life. ▶

The Story Behind the Book *(continued)*

You've written three novels now. Do you have a favorite?

The one I've just finished is always my favorite. I become a better writer with every book, my writing is tighter and sharper, and I get more deeply involved with my characters with every book. *Leaving Haven* is the first book I've written that left me with the feeling that maybe I wasn't quite done with the characters, or they weren't quite done with me—I want more. So I may write another novel involving Georgia or Alice one day. ❧

More from Kathleen McCleary

For more books by Kathleen McCleary check out:

A SIMPLE THING

When Susannah Delaney discovers her young son is being bullied and her adolescent daughter is spinning out of control, she moves them to remote, rustic Sounder Island to live for a year. A simple island existence—with no computers or electricity and only a one-room schoolhouse—is just what her overscheduled East Coast kids need to learn what's really important in life. But the move threatens her marriage to the man she's loved since childhood, and her very sense of self.

For Betty Pavalak, who moved to Sounder to save her own troubled marriage, the island has been a haven for fifty years. But Betty also knows the guilt of living with choices made long ago and actions that cannot be undone. The unlikely friendship between Susannah and Betty ignites a journey of self-discovery for both women and brings them both home to what they love most. *A Simple Thing* moves beyond friendship, children, and marriages to look deeply into what it means to love and forgive . . . yourself.

Don't miss the next book by your favorite author. Sign up now for AuthorTracker by visiting www.AuthorTracker.com.